ONONDAGA COUNTY PUBLIC LIBRARY
THE GALLERIES OF SYRACUSE
447 S. SALINA STREET
SYRACUSE, NY 13202-2494
WWW.ONLIB.ORG

|-|l 8x

# THE
# SLEEPING DRAGON

# THE SLEEPING DRAGON

## MIYUKI MIYABE

TRANSLATED BY
Deborah Stuhr Iwabuchi

KODANSHA INTERNATIONAL
Tokyo · New York · London

First published in Japanese in 1991 by Shuppan Geijutsusha as *Ryu wa nemuru*.

Distributed in the United States by Kodansha America, LLC, and in the United Kingdom and continental Europe by Kodansha Europe Ltd. • Published by Kodansha International Ltd., 17–14 Otowa 1-chome, Bunkyo-ku, Tokyo 112-8652.

ISBN 978–4–7700–3104-4

First edition, 2009
18  17  16  15  14  13  12  11  10  09      10  9  8  7  6  5  4  3  2  1

*LIBRARY OF CONGRESS CATALOGING-IN-PUBLICATION DATA*
Miyabe, Miyuki
  [Ryu wa nemuru. English]
  The sleeping dragon / Miyuki Miyabe ; translated by Deborah Stuhr Iwabuchi. -- 1st ed.
      p. cm.
  "First published in Japanese in 1991 by Shuppan Geijutsusha as Ryu wa nemuru"--T.p. verso.
  ISBN 978-4-7700-3104-4
  1. Journalists--Fiction. 2. Psychics--Fiction. 3. Missing persons--Fiction. 4. Tokyo (Japan)--Fiction. I. Iwabuchi, Deborah Stuhr. II. Title.
  PL856.I856R9813 2010
  895.6'35--dc22                     2009043241

**www.kodansha-intl.com**

# CONTENTS

The talent is well hidden indeed; how else could it have remained submerged for centuries with only the tip of the iceberg showing above a sea of quackery?

—Stephen King, *Carrie*

## CAST OF CHARACTERS

| | |
|---|---|
| Shogo Kosaka | Investigative reporter at *Arrow* magazine |
| Shinji Inamura | High school student and psychic |
| Naoya Oda | Young psychic |
| Daisuke Mochizuki | Boy with the umbrella |
| Goro Ikoma | Kosaka's colleague at *Arrow* |
| Satoshi Miyanaga | Budding artist and friend of Shunpei Kakita |
| Shunpei Kakita | Budding artist |
| Asako Moriguchi | Friend of Naoya: worked together at gas station |
| Saeko Kawasaki | Kosaka's former fiancée; wife to Akio Kawasaki |
| Akio Kawasaki | Saeko's husband |
| Reiko Miyake | Akio Kawasaki's secretary |
| Kaoru Murata | Retired policeman with experience working with psychics |
| Nanae Mimura | Mute friend of Naoya |
| Norio Inamura | Shinji's father and coffee shop owner |
| Captain Ito | Police officer and Sergeant Nakagiri's superior |
| Sergeant Nakagiri | Police officer |

# PROLOGUE

*This is the record of a battle.*

*Right off the bat, though, I need to make it clear that I was never on the front line. The heroes were two young men just past adolescence.*

*One I knew well, and the other I came to know well enough to be sure that he wouldn't mind me telling you what happened. If I had met him sooner, I might have been able to do something to actually stop the chain of events that occurred. But hindsight is always twenty-twenty.*

*One reason I've decided to speak out now is because leaving a written record of the difficulties the young men faced and everything they did for me is the only way I can think of to express my thanks.*

*This story is for them, first and foremost. It's also for that rare reader who may recognize, sleeping within, the same power they had.*

# PART 1
# A Chance Encounter

We first met on September 23, at about ten-thirty at night. He was crouched next to his bicycle somewhere near Sakura Industrial Park in Chiba. The reason I remember it with all the detail of a criminal's alibi was because a huge typhoon was making its way to the Kanto area. I had my car radio on and was listening to the storm updates every few minutes.

For once the typhoon arrived exactly as predicted. The weatherman said that westerly winds would pick up at about seven, and they had, followed by driving rain. I couldn't see more than a yard in front of me, even with my headlights on. The rain poured down and the road was full of puddles that sprayed higher than park fountains each time I went through one. Every few minutes one would splash over the windshield, blinding me.

I had started to think about parking somewhere and taking shelter until the worst had passed. That was when I found him.

If I hadn't been going so slowly, our meeting could have been a tragedy. You don't expect someone to be out on a bicycle in the middle of a typhoon. When the human outline first appeared in my headlights, I thought maybe it was one of those cutouts of cops they place along the road to scare people into driving carefully.

But I knew it was a real person when he turned in my direction and began to wave. He was wearing a thin plastic raincoat. The hood had blown off his head, leaving his hair dripping wet and his features pinched against the rain and wind. The only things I could glimpse that first moment was that he wasn't old and he seemed to be male.

He was on the left-hand side of the road, and when I stopped he quickly came around to the driver's side. I opened the window, only to have the rain and wind come blasting in until I had to screw up my face like his.

"What are you doing out here?" I didn't mean to sound disapproving, but I did have to shout to be heard.

"Flat tire!" he hollered back, pointing in the general direction of his bicycle. "I can't move it. Can you give me a lift to a repair shop?"

"All right, get in!" I yelled, and he hunched over and made his way back over to his bike, doing his best to pull it up and drag it through the puddles over to the car.

"Let me put my bike in the trunk!"

"Leave it here!"

"But I'll lose it."

"You can come back for it later!"

"But it might get blown away!"

I raised my voice as loudly as I could. "Leave it on the ground, on its side. Hurry up or I'll leave you here too!" The water was beginning to rise, and if I didn't move it, my old car could easily get stuck. It had a bad habit of stalling out at the least convenient moments. We had no love lost for each other, the car and I, but we were staying together for convenience's sake till something better came along.

"Hurry!" I urged him. He finally found a spot for the bike, laid it down, and ran back to the car. He struggled to get the passenger door open, with the wind blowing against it. Once inside, he gave a loud sigh, and I hit the accelerator. The tires spun a few times, and then it was my turn to exhale in relief when the car finally began to inch forward through the water.

"What a storm!" my hitchhiker said, dripping copiously onto the seat. He wiped his face with one hand and turned to look at me. "Hey, thanks for giving me a ride."

It was only then that I realized I'd picked up a teenager.

"What are you doing out on a bicycle on a night like this? You must live around here, right?" I asked.

"Yeah, Tokyo."

This kid's nonchalance was starting to irritate me. "You rode your bike here from Tokyo?"

"Uh-huh."

"Did you skip school?"

"We had the day off . . . tomorrow too. It's a holiday."

He was right. My work didn't afford me the luxury of following the usual calendar. I had forgotten about the holiday.

"Chiba's not that far," the boy explained. "I've been farther lots of times. I just sleep outside or find somewhere cheap to spend the night. If I hadn't gotten a flat tire, I would have found someplace to stay."

He was calm enough, almost as if the storm wasn't bothering him.

"You must have known the typhoon was coming," I insisted.

"Speak for yourself, uncle," he said.

Most Japanese over the age of twenty-five are liable to be called "uncle" or "auntie" by kids. It's a fact of life, but you're allowed to look unhappy about it until you're about thirty-five.

"I'm sorry," the boy said laughing. "I didn't mean to be rude. What should I call you?" He took another swipe at his dripping face and said, "Wait a second, it'd be better manners to introduce myself first. My name is . . ." He turned around to look out the back window, almost as if he had left his name back there with his bike.

"Don't worry," I said. "You're not under arrest or anything. You don't need to identify yourself."

"I'm Shinji Inamura."

"You in high school?"

"That's right. I just started. Which way are we going?"

"Unless I'm lost, we're going toward the Higashi Kanto Expressway." As long as I followed the Sakura Highway, the on-ramp shouldn't be far off. The windshield wipers whipped back and forth, but they weren't doing any good. I kept going on blind faith, figuring that as long as I couldn't see a pair of lights ahead of me there were no other cars.

"So you're going to Tokyo?" he asked.

"That's right."

"You must be in a hurry, to be out on a night like this."

"Yeah, you could say that." To tell the truth, though, I didn't have an excuse. I could have stayed at my parents' house until the typhoon passed, particularly since I couldn't really count on my car. I had just wanted to leave. I had said that I had work to do and driven off.

Shinji Inamura looked uneasy. After a few minutes I realized it wasn't just because of the way the car was shaking. I felt sorry for him out in that weather, and now having to depend on a complete stranger. I knew I should ease his fear.

I smiled as I continued to focus on the road. "There are no corpses in the trunk; no stash of heroin either. I promise you I'm not dangerous. Check the glove compartment. My driver's license and my business card are in there."

Shinji managed to find my card in the near-dark. "Shogo Kosaka," he read out. "Wow, you're a magazine reporter." I could sense the relief in his voice. "Are you going back to Tokyo for work? Or have you been out here reporting on something?"

"I came here on personal business, and there was really no need for me to go back tonight. I just thought I'd see if I could make it." It was the truth.

Shinji was still peering at my name card. "*Arrow*. I know that magazine."

"You mean you see it on newsstands or in bookshops?" *Arrow* was a weekly magazine that sold a decent number of copies. Including freelance reporters, it had a staff of about forty. *Arrow* claimed to be an independent operation, but the truth was that a major newspaper corporation owned it. In fact, it was staffed by former newspaper reporters, most of whom had offended someone important or proved themselves failures and been removed from an elite career track in daily news to the backwaters of the weekly magazine.

I was no exception. Transferred from the newspaper to the magazine three years earlier, I was painfully aware that my "assignment" to *Arrow* was essentially a demotion.

"No, I've read it. Really. Not often, but they've got it at the shop."

"The shop?"

"My parents run a coffee shop. My dad buys *Arrow* every week."

"Your father has my deepest appreciation."

We were on the move. I made a few turns, and stopped once to check the map. We needed to go further south.

"It's not like we're out in the middle of the rice fields," Shinji commented, "but it does get dark around here at night."

"Probably has something to do with this storm."

"Where are you from, Mr. Kosaka?"

"Funato City."

"Isn't that near Kasumigaura?"

"You sure know your geography."

"I've been there. If I were you, I would have taken the Narita Highway back to Tokyo."

"I would have too, but it's closed because of an accident. Some truck spilled its cargo all over the road, and several of the cars behind him apparently weren't able to stop."

Shingo gave a high-pitched yelp and then began laughing. "Now it makes sense. That's why you were lost on the road where you picked me up."

I had to laugh, too. "You got it!"

At just that instant, the car hit something, and we were jolted out of our seats.

"Are you all right?" I asked.

"Did you run over something?" Shinji responded.

"I don't think so. It was probably a tree branch." I tried to sound positive, but I was disturbed. I braked slowly and the car almost floated to a halt.

To be perfectly honest, I would have kept on going if I had been alone. But with Shinji sitting next to me, I felt obligated to act like an adult. I flung open the door and, as sheets of rain poured onto my face, tried to see behind me without getting out of the car. Everything was pitch black except for the blurry lights of some houses or streetlights off in the distance.

"Can you see anything?" asked Shinji.

"Nothing." I didn't have any other choice. I swung one leg out and was surprised to find I'd stepped into a rapid current of rainwater flowing down the middle of the road.

I looked around. There was a narrow road off at an angle, and I could see the unrelenting rain pounding the surface in the headlights. There wasn't as much water there.

"There's something odd," I said and leaned back into the car. "Open the door on your side and look at the road. Don't get out, just look at it."

He did as I asked, and looked back at me, blinking the water out of his eyes. "You're right! There's a river out here. Look!" Shinji pointed at something I couldn't see. "There's a roaring sound coming from over there."

I leaned out again, and then heard a new sound.

"There's a flashlight over on your side. Hand it to me, will you?" I took off my coat and shoes.

With the flashlight in one hand and latching onto the car door with the other, I gingerly stepped out onto the road. The water was colder and deeper than I had imagined. I rolled up my pant legs.

"Be careful," Shinji said. He moved over to the driver's seat and grabbed onto my belt until he was sure I had secure footing.

"You can let go now," I said. I moved forward, keeping one hand on the car. I had never realized how dangerous it was to walk along the road in a flood. Then I saw it, in the light of my flashlight. Something large, made of metal.

"You see anything?" Shinji called.

I was still trying to figure out what it was. I moved the flashlight around. As I headed toward the rear of the car, the roaring sound grew louder. Still holding onto the trunk, I yelled back, "I've got it!"

"What is it?"

"A manhole. The lid is off!" I felt queasy as I looked at the half-moon–shaped hole that the lid only partially covered. The sound we were hearing was rain gushing into the sewer. I had run over the cover, and that's what made the car jump.

It was too dangerous to get any closer, so, now sopping wet, I took a moment to look up at the sky. The clouds were speeding overhead—the typhoon wouldn't pass for hours yet.

On the other hand, the manhole couldn't be left uncovered. I used my flashlight to look around and instinctively closed my eyes at a strong blast of wind, but just before I did, I saw something white flit across the edge of my peripheral vision.

I whipped around to see what it was, and I saw it fly by again. It was an umbrella. Not white, but a yellow nylon umbrella—the kind they give out to first graders. It was blowing along the roadside among the weeds.

My heart began to pound. A child's umbrella and an open manhole. This didn't look good.

I walked around my car, searching the area with my flashlight and calling out, "Is anybody there?" There was no response; just the taunting movement of the umbrella caught in a bush.

"Mr. Kosaka!" Shinji had opened the door and leaned out to call me. "Someone is coming from over that way."

It was an adult, bent over against the rain. He was wearing a raincoat.

Unlike Shinji, his hood was tied around his head and he was wearing boots. He carried a large flashlight.

It only took a minute or two for him to come within hearing range, but it seemed longer. His head still bent over, he called out.

"Have you seen a child around here? A boy about this tall." The man held his hand up to waist level. "He's wearing a yellow raincoat and carrying a yellow umbrella. Have you seen him?"

For a moment, I was unable to speak. The sound of the rain and the groaning winds disappeared, and all I could hear was the pounding of my heart. Shinji gave me a doubtful look, and the man looked back and forth at us. I was dripping wet, but I felt my lips and throat go dry.

"Your son?" I finally forced myself to ask.

The man nodded, "Yes, and . . ." He stopped mid-sentence, and I automatically turned around to follow his gaze. He'd seen the umbrella, now blowing across the road. His mouth opened, and the hand holding his flashlight fell limply to his side. He turned to run toward it, but I managed to stop him just in time. "Wait! It's dangerous!"

"What do you mean?"

"There's a manhole, and the cover is off."

It took a few seconds for the man to figure out what I meant, but when he understood, he shook off my arm and ran toward the umbrella. I grabbed the back of his raincoat, and pulled him back, yelling, "Is that your son's umbrella?"

He couldn't respond. He stood there and called out, "Daisuke? Daisuke?" I shook his arm and repeated my question.

"Is that your son's umbrella?" He turned and looked over at me and nodded several times.

"I think so."

I left him there and went over to the umbrella, managing to grab it and bring it over to him. Like the umbrellas of all schoolchildren, the name of the owner had been inked onto the handle: Daisuke Mochizuki.

The two of us hurried over to the manhole. I held onto his raincoat as he gripped the edge of the manhole cover and, with the stream of water washing over him, shone his flashlight into the gaping hole. Then we carefully got back on our feet and began calling the boy's name. There were no replies, no tiny shadows, no small figures in yellow raincoats.

"Do you live far from here?" I yelled.

"Over . . . that way." The man pointed shakily in the direction he had come. I saw a clump of lights in the distance.

I pulled the man back over to the car, where I shoved the yellow umbrella and my flashlight into Shinji's hands.

"Stay here," I instructed. "If anybody comes by, shine the light to warn them to stay away from the manhole. Do you understand?"

Shinji suddenly looked lost. He held the tiny umbrella in his hand and appeared to be gazing far beyond me.

I spoke a little louder. "Look, I'm counting on you. Can you hear me?" Shinji came to attention and looked into my face. He held the umbrella tight.

"Don't you go near it either!" I ordered.

I left Shinji by the side of the road, shoved the man into my car, and stepped on the gas. The man slumped in the seat.

"Pull yourself together," I urged. "We don't know what's happened yet. Let's find a telephone and call your house. Any kid could lose his umbrella in a storm and make his way home. It happens all the time. Are you listening to me?"

It was the first time in my life I had lied so loudly, but the man didn't answer.

# 2

The boy hadn't returned home. Within half an hour, the manhole was surrounded by cars, lights, and people. There were three patrol cars and one emergency truck from the water company, all with their red and yellow lights flashing. The effect was almost festive—completely unsuited to the occasion.

The police had also set up a floodlight that produced a harsh white glare, and they aimed it down into the manhole. The man from the water company had a lifeline tied around his waist and was peering into the hole that dropped straight down to the sewers below.

Shinji and I were sitting in my car answering a patrolman's questions as best we could. Shinji handed the yellow umbrella over to the patrolman and looked down glumly while I explained how I had found it.

The wind was as strong as ever, and the raindrops looked like millions of sewing needles in the white light. Every new gust of wind would drive a huge sheet of needles sideways into the faces of the men at work.

"How does it look?" I asked. One raincoat-clad policeman shook his head. He was probably old enough to be the missing boy's grandfather.

"There's not much that we can do at this point. We'll send someone down to search the main sewer, but I doubt we'll find him. Our best bet is probably to wait at the net of the sluice gate at the water processing plant." He maintained a perfunctory tone, although I wondered if he really felt as matter-of-fact as he sounded.

The boy who we now assumed had been swept into the manhole was Daisuke Mochizuki, age seven. His parents were Yusuke and Akiko, and the three of them lived in a housing development just a few blocks from the site.

"What was the boy doing out in weather like this?" I asked.

"His father isn't saying much, so we don't really know yet. He mentioned that the boy was looking for a pet."

Shinji lifted his head and said in a small voice. "Her name is Monica."

"Monica?"

"A cat. He loved it. Monica went out in the storm and didn't come back. He went out looking for it." When he saw the policeman and me exchange glances, he quickly added, "I heard the other officers talking about it over there."

"I see," the policeman said. He shook his head, and water dripped from his silver hair. "Kids are so unpredictable; you never know what they're going to do."

"Will you be able to catch whoever did it?" Shinji asked, lifting his head to look into the policeman's eyes.

"Did it?"

"You know, whoever took the lid off that manhole. There's no way anybody from the water company would do something like that."

"We'll check into it," the policeman said. "We need to find out why it was open."

"If somebody did it on purpose," I added, "I'm sure the police will catch him."

Shinji looked down again. Over his head, the policeman and I looked at each other, and I wondered if we were suspects. Chances were small that anyone would have seen anything, or that any clues had been left behind. If someone had been stabbed or a woman molested, you could start by looking for felons who had committed similar crimes in the past, or by studying the history of similar cases in the area to determine any trends, but there couldn't be many criminals who specialized in "lifting manhole covers."

I suddenly remembered when I was working for *Nikkan News* in a Tokyo branch office. A flowerpot that had been dropped from a balcony had killed someone in a nearby housing development.

There hadn't been any intent to kill. Some guy living on the fifth floor of an apartment building had gone out on the balcony and, while looking at the plant his wife had bought that day, all of a sudden began to think about how much fun it would be to push it over the edge. Nothing more. The only problem was that he hadn't stopped to think about whether anyone might be passing by on the street below.

I interviewed the guy later. He was normal, a hard-working husband and father.

Thinking of that incident, I mumbled, "I sure hope whoever did it didn't have any malicious intent."

"Huh?" Shinji lifted his head.

"Nothing."

The policeman quietly scratched his nose, coughed, tried to move his knees in the cramped space, then closed his notebook.

"You're free to leave, both of you. Why don't you give this young man's parents a call? They must be worried about him."

Of course. I should have thought of that.

"This storm isn't going to let up anytime soon. The two of you need to check into a hotel somewhere close by and dry off."

I myself planned to stay right here and see how this investigation played out.

"Is there anyplace around here where we could stay?"

The policeman pointed a stubby finger toward the lights I'd seen when I first ran into Yusuke Mochizuki.

"There's an all-night restaurant and a business hotel that way. It's kind of a dump, but there's sure to be a room available."

We thanked the policeman as he got out of the car, and then backed away and headed in the direction indicated. We found the hotel right away. It was called "Pit"—no, make that "Pit Inn," although the neon lights reading "Inn" had given out. It wasn't much, but as long as it had a roof and a phone, it would do for our needs.

A sleepy-looking young man ran the front desk. With one eye on the TV to his right, he told us we could have any room we liked. We chose a room with two twin beds, and I paid. As Shinji and I stood there filling out our paperwork, I saw that Shinji's hands were shaking, so I stopped and asked if he was all right.

He just nodded, and seemed to be preoccupied with something else entirely.

"Is something the matter?" The clerk turned away from the TV for a few moments to ask. He seemed to wonder what our relationship was. "I heard police sirens going by a while ago . . ."

"They think a kid may have fallen into a manhole near here."

The young man stood up straight. "Really? Someone from around here?"

"Probably."

"That's awful." He frowned. "Is it someone you know?"

"No, that's not it," I said and pulled a damp name card from my pocket.

"You're a reporter?" the clerk said, oddly impressed.

"That's right. And this boy is a hitchhiker I picked up. We're going to stay here, but I've got to get back to the scene. Do you have any clothes I could change into—any kind of rain gear?"

"Sure, I'll find something. You're both sopping wet. Bring your clothes down to the desk and I'll get them washed and dried in the coin laundry behind us."

I looked at my gray jacket, now black with water. "Even my suit?"

"Sure."

"I don't know . . ."

The young man reached out, took my jacket, and looked at the label. "No problem. This is sturdy enough to mop up the floor with, if you needed to."

Even Shinji cracked a smile. Relieved, I smiled too as the clerk went to work.

Before changing my clothes, I called Shinji's parents from the telephone in our room. He spoke to them and explained what happened. Then I got on the phone and told them who I was and promised to bring Shinji home the next day. I spoke to his father, who sounded polite and grateful, but not as worried as I had expected.

"Your dad doesn't rattle easily, does he?"

Shinji smiled weakly. "He likes cycling, too, so he's had lots of unusual experiences."

With his shirt off and a towel draped over his head, Shinji looked smaller than before. "I never get treated this well, though," he added. "Thanks for everything."

If nothing else, the kid had good manners. I waved my hand vaguely and said, "You're welcome. Now take a bath and get into bed. I'll probably be out for the rest of the night, so don't wait up."

The man at the front desk lent me a pair of clean slacks and a sweatshirt, along with the oilcloth jacket he'd worn to work that day. He also came out of the back room with a pair of rubber boots that he said the cleaning staff sometimes used. Thus prepared, I headed back to the scene.

I considered contacting *Arrow* and asking them to send out a photographer, but a glance at the TV news showed that the typhoon was causing widespread damage. Chances were that no one was available. I finally decided to go alone and just see how it all played out. Weekly tabloids were not as desperate for pictures or up-to-the-minute reports as newspapers. I'd get details off the wires later when I was putting the article together.

Back at the site, there was still a large number of workmen standing around trying to figure out what to do. There was always at least one person talking on a two-way radio. Then I saw a patrol car parked off by itself, away from the floodlight. I went over to it and saw a couple huddled in the back. I tapped on the window.

It was the missing boy's parents. Akiko clung to her husband, burying her face in his chest. Yusuke turned in my direction and lowered the window. His eyes were vacant.

"They haven't found him yet," he said.

I nodded, and his wife lifted her head to look at me.

"It's possible he might not have fallen in there, right?" she asked, gripping her husband's arm so tightly that her fingertips were white. She was wearing a sweat suit that looked like pajamas and had thrown a raincoat over it. Her face was covered with tears and her eyes were bloodshot. "Nobody actually saw it happen," she ventured almost hopefully. "He might not have fallen in at all. Am I wrong?"

I looked into her face and then at her husband, who had averted his gaze. "Of course, ma'am. There's always that possibility."

"Of course," she said and then went almost limp. "I . . . I only took my eyes off him for a minute, and he was gone."

"It's not your fault," her husband mumbled, rubbing her back.

I spoke again, as softly as I could. "I understand he was looking for his cat."

Yusuke nodded vaguely. "Daisuke loves that creature. I told him animals know how to take care of themselves in bad weather, but he's a kid, and he was worried, so he went outside to look for it."

"Children can become really attached to pets." I remembered what Shinji had said. "Was Daisuke the one who named it Monica?"

Yusuke tensed up. "Monica?" he asked.

"Isn't that the name of his cat?"

"No," he said, shaking his head. "The cat's name is Shiro, you know, 'white,' it's a white cat."

Now Akiko spoke. "Daisuke wanted to call it Monica, but we told him no. We told him it should have a name that would be easier to say." Then she put her hands over her face, and the tears welled up again. "We should never have gotten a cat."

I started to say how sorry I was, but I stopped. It would have sounded as if I thought the boy was dead. As long as they still had some hope, they would surely not want to be consoled.

"I'm sure they'll find him," I said instead. "It'll be okay." I turned away from the car, feeling as if I'd been telling one lie after another all evening, when what should pull up in a blast of headlights and muddy water but a broadcasting truck from the local TV station.

They would be of no help in finding the boy, and nobody was happy to see them. Yet the crew piled out of the truck looking as if they considered themselves indispensable.

I sought the policeman I'd talked to earlier. He was standing by the roped-off roadway. There were none of the usual curious spectators, but there were a few other local reporters milling around, sopping wet.

The policeman was soaked too, and he looked even older than before. I said hello, and he seemed surprised to see me.

"What are you doing back here—oh, that's right, you're a newspaper reporter, too."

"Magazine."

"Same difference. Where's that boy who was with you?"

"He should be asleep at the hotel."

"That's good. I was afraid he'd gone into shock," the policeman said. "It's hard for me, too. I've got a five-year-old grandson." Then he sighed and added, "Don't know why something like this has to happen."

Policemen never talk to the press unless they're trying to put up a smoke-screen, they've reached a dead end in an investigation, or they're too tired to care.

"He was just in the wrong place at the wrong time," I offered. In my mind I could see a boy, both hands gripping the yellow umbrella as he walked in the rain, calling his cat. He may have been on the verge of tears—afraid and frightened by the storm.

He would have been completely unaware of the hole in the road. Probably fell into the darkness without ever realizing what had happened.

"They ought to teach kids in school to be careful about this sort of thing," I muttered. "Never have faith in a green traffic light. Never have faith in the fact that you're in a crosswalk. Never have faith in the idea that a manhole is going to be covered. You just never know."

"I'll tell that to my grandson," the policeman said.

Work was at a standstill. The floodlight was on, but the wind and rain continued unabated. We were all hoping for a miracle, but there were no signs of one yet.

3

The rain finally let up at about seven the next morning. The typhoon swept past the Kanto Plain, at the edge of its storm zone. There was no lull during the night to indicate that the eye of the typhoon was passing over. There may have been a few moments when the wind from the west felt like it was slowing, but it was replaced by an easterly wind before the storm gradually began to let up.

Without the rain, the search for the boy became easier, but there were no breaks. The level of the water rushing through the sewers had risen. Someone from the water company said that the road had either been designed or constructed poorly—the sides of the road were higher than the middle, and if a manhole cover were removed, rainwater would funnel right in.

At 7:30, a few patrolmen remained on the scene while the rest went back to the precinct to rethink their strategy. They wanted to widen the search. Hearing that, I went back to the hotel, wet enough to start my own flood. The soles of my boots squished noisily with every step I took.

The same man was still at the front desk, but he was now engrossed in a conversation with a middle-aged woman. When I walked in, though, he stood quickly.

"Did you find the boy?" he asked.

I shook my head. The man's shoulders drooped, and the woman walked back into the employee office, muttering angrily under her breath.

"She cleans for us," the man said by way of explanation as he helped me out of my wet clothes, "and she used to live in the same housing development as the missing boy and his family. She said that some of the neighbors had joined in the search, but all they found was the family cat."

I looked at him. "A cat?"

"That's right. The cleaning woman said it was named Shiro."

"Was it still alive?"

"Sure, animals can take care of themselves."

I was sure that hearing the cat was okay would be little comfort to Daisuke's mother and father.

"They're not allowed to have pets in that building, but apparently nobody pays any attention to that. The kid is pretty attached to the cat, I guess." So saying, he handed me the clothes he'd dried for me. As I was riding up in the elevator I noticed how tired I was. Shinji was awake too—actually, he hadn't slept a wink all night.

"I guess you didn't find him."

"No," I said, heading for the bathroom to take a shower. I had been so cold that when the hot water hit my skin I broke out in goosebumps and started to tremble. I was thinking about how cold little Daisuke must be wherever he was and almost didn't hear Shinji calling me from outside the bathroom door.

"What?"

"The guy at the front desk says that checkout is at ten, but we can stay into the afternoon as long as the owner doesn't find out. Shouldn't you try to get some sleep, Mr. Kosaka?"

"I'll be fine once I've had a shower. I've got to get you home, and I need to get back to Tokyo, too." I'd found a reporter who worked for the newspaper that owned *Arrow* and had asked him to let me know if there were any breakthroughs in the investigation. "And don't start telling me you'll ride your bike. I promised your dad I'd take you home." Then I remembered and added, "And we've got to go back for your bike."

"I'm on my way out to get it now," Shinji said.

"Do you know where it is?"

"Yeah, I had the guy downstairs draw me a map last night."

"You're not going to walk, are you?"

"It's not that far. I can walk there and wheel it back. It shouldn't take more than twenty minutes." It was no big deal, so I let him go. Little did I know where the exchange would lead.

I got out of the shower and changed. By the time Shinji got back, I was feeling almost like myself again. It had taken him forty minutes, twice as long as he'd promised. And he looked very pale.

"Couldn't you find your bike?" I asked and received no response. I stood there for a few moments watching him, trying to decide if I should try to shake him and bring him around.

Suddenly, though, his eyes focused on me. "No, I found it," he said softly.

"Are you all right?" He had me worried.

"Is what all right?" he asked.

"You. Are you all right?"

"Me? What's wrong with me?" He was acting stranger all the time, but his eyes were clear and he was standing up straight.

"You feeling okay?"

He shook his head as if to clear it, then nodded. "Yeah. The guy at the front desk says we can get breakfast downstairs."

"All right," I said as I stood up. "Let's go, then."

But Shinji didn't follow. He stood there lost in thought.

I waited for a few seconds, and, still facing in the opposite direction, he suddenly called my name. "Mr. Kosaka!"

"Yes?"

His mouth closed again. I had one hand on the doorknob and one on my hip, and I had begun to wonder if he was about to explode.

"Mr. Kosaka!"

"I'm listening."

Shinji finally turned around to look at me but was finding it difficult to speak.

"What is it?"

He swallowed hard, as if forcing down the words back down his throat, and finally said, "Your tie's crooked."

"What?"

"Your tie. It's not straight."

He was right. The receptionist had apparently ironed it with a crease in it, and it was lopsided. "Is that what you wanted to say?"

"Yes."

I knew he was lying. Any fool could see it. There was something else on his mind.

"Anything else? If my pants are on backwards, I hope you'll mention it before I go out into the hall."

"That's all," he said and turned toward the door. His expression had softened, but I felt that I'd failed to grasp something important.

The restaurant the hotel used was next door. We went outside and crossed an alley. If anything, the restaurant was in worse shape than the hotel. There were four booths, a few counter seats, and a fourteen-inch TV. Two of the booths faced the tiny TV, which was tuned to the news. One booth was occupied by a man and a woman sitting side by side, and the other by two men, one on each side of the table.

Shinji and I took a seat in a booth next to the window and were greeted by a waitress, surprisingly young and pretty, who notified us that there was only one menu item, and that was what we would be getting for breakfast. I could see that the other guests were all poking at identical-looking plates of food.

"You can get coffee refills, though," she said by way of consolation, before adding, "Your necktie is crooked."

I decided that was enough, and I took off my tie and put it in my pocket. Shinji, sitting across from me, didn't laugh or even change his expression.

The waitress left and quickly returned with two cups of coffee. I was grateful for the hot liquid. Then she leaned over and said in a low voice, "You're from *Arrow*, aren't you?"

I was surprised. "How did you know?"

"I heard from Hiba. Those two men at that other table are reporters, too. They must be your rivals. Should I try to get information out of them for you?"

I peered over at the other two men. "What do you think they know that I don't?"

"You know, the manhole business. A scoop!"

For a few moments I took her seriously. "Have they found the boy?"

"Nope," she replied blithely and then leaned in further. "But don't reporters want to know what other reporters are up to?"

Maybe newspaper reporters—which I wasn't anymore.

"Sure." It seemed a shame to waste her enthusiasm.

"Leave it to me!" Just then, someone called out to her from the kitchen, and our adventurous waitress hurried off. Shinji watched her go.

"She watches too much TV," I said. Shinji's eyes lost their focus again.

"She wants to impress you so that you'll get her some work as a pinup girl."

"I doubt that!"

"It's true. I know it." He was serious as he spoke and then began rubbing his temple with his fingers. "I think I'm slipping."

This last sounded as though he was talking to himself, so I didn't answer. Then suddenly, almost as if he had just got the green light to go on, he began to speak rapidly, almost as if he was reading from a manuscript.

"Hiba is the nickname of the guy at the front desk. They call him that because he looks like Hibagon, a mythical beast. That waitress goes out with him from time to time, and they use Room 102 of the hotel when they're low on entertainment funds."

I had to laugh. "So you and that Hiba had a long chat last night, did you?"

Shinji shook his head. "All he did was show me the map. But I know all of this."

Now it was my turn to look disoriented. Shinji's eyes opened wide, and he stopped me from speaking just as I was about to open my mouth. "Let me tell you what I have to say. I need your help because I don't know what to do."

His rubbed his hands and then his knees. I put my own hands on top of the table and looked over at him.

"Okay, I understand. I'm not sure what you mean, but it's all right. Try to relax."

Shinji nodded and then continued on in short spurts. "I—I feel like something inside me just—opened."

I was confused. The night before he had seemed like a mature young man, and now he was showing signs of emotional trouble.

The waitress brought over our plates. She looked as pleased with herself as if she were about to share some secrets with her best friend. She set down the plates, leaned closer to me, and said, almost in a whisper, "They're from *Tokyo Nippo*."

I could almost catch the scent of the gum she was chewing. I decided to play along. "What do they say they've found out?"

"The boy who fell in the manhole was looking for his pet cat."

"Really? Anything else?"

"The boy's father works at city hall."

"You don't say?"

"His poor mother is so upset, they've taken her to a hospital."

There was nothing there I didn't know, but I tried to sound impressed. "You did a good job!"

"Can you use it?"

"Of course, but you know you'd be better off helping them out. *Nippo* is much bigger than *Arrow*."

She looked down and blushed.

"I always go for the good-looking guys."

"I'm honored," I said with a laugh, "but just so you know, we don't hire amateur models."

The waitress slowly straightened up. "Hmph!"

"Sorry."

"How did you know? Busybody!" She turned right around and left the table. I noticed her finger hooked on her apron pocket.

I called after her. "As long as I'm being rude, I've got another question for you. Do you know if they know the name of the cat the boy was looking for?"

She turned around and gave me an irritated look. "How would I know?"

"Would you ask them for me?"

She said bluntly, "Is there a tip in it for me?" There was obviously no longer any benefit in being a good-looking guy.

I nodded. Her shoulders settled and she moseyed off at a much lighter pace, water pitcher in hand, toward the table of the *Nippo* reporters. I could see them exchange a few words as she filled their glasses, and she succeeded in making them laugh. Then she walked back over to the counter and set down the pitcher. But instead of coming back over to our table, she merely turned to us and mouthed the word, "Shi-ro." I lifted my hand in response.

"The cat's name is Shiro."

Shinji wrapped his arms around himself and looked at me.

"You said it was called Monica, didn't you?"

"That's what he called it."

The night before Shinji had told me he heard one of the policemen mention that name. I leaned forward. "Listen . . ."

Shinji tried to stand up, but he did it clumsily.

"I don't feel very well," he said. His complexion had gone ashen. He held his stomach with one hand and tried to maneuver around the chair with the other. The waitress hurried over to him and put a hand on his back. I stood up, too.

"You're not feeling well?" She looked at his face and then stared over at me as if it were entirely my fault.

"Which way is the restroom?" asked Shinji, now obviously in pain and sweating profusely.

"Over there," the waitress pointed over to the left of the counter. I offered him a hand, but Shinji pulled back.

"Don't touch me! I'll be all right in a few minutes. Could you wait here for me?"

His voice had such a strong air of determination that both the waitress and I pulled our hands back and let him go.

"Nobody's ever told me not to touch them before," she said.

"Really?"

"I've told a few lechers to keep their hands off *me*."

"That's a little different. Dirty old men on the street?"

"No, nightclubs."

"So you didn't like working there?"

"That's why I switched to waitressing." This was obviously not a topic she wanted to discuss, and she walked off. I went back to my seat and sat down. The *Nippo* reporters had taken an interest in the three of us, but now that the fun was over, they went back to their food.

My eggs and toast were getting cold, and the salad was limp. I was feeling too upset to eat anyway. What I really wanted was a cigarette, but I made do with the coffee.

Shinji did not reappear.

The man and woman in the other booth got up and left. Another news program was just getting started on the tiny TV. I suddenly realized the grave error I had made, and I put down my cup and stood up so fast it startled the waitress.

"Is there something wrong?" she asked, apparently fearing that I had suddenly gone nuts on her. She took a few steps toward me, but I couldn't say a word.

*Him? Did he do it?*

I looked over at the door of the restroom, still closed. The waitress came over to me, her arms folded across her chest.

"It's nothing," I said. "Thanks."

She shook her head and walked back into the kitchen, obviously determined not to have anything more to do with us. I figured it was just as well.

Shinji must have been the one to open the manhole. I didn't know why—maybe it was just to be mischievous—or how, but he had opened it and then gone on his way. By and by, the little boy had come down the road carrying the yellow umbrella and calling, "Monica!" Shinji probably realized from his tone of voice that the boy was looking for a pet and didn't think anything of it at the time.

Shinji had been lost when I found him. After he got in my car, the two of us had accidentally ended back by the open manhole. After I was forced to stop the car and we had seen the umbrella, Shinji must have realized what had happened. I remembered how stricken he'd looked when I gave him the umbrella to hold. He was almost in tears when he asked the policeman if they would find the person who had done it.

Nor had he slept all night. He'd been white as a sheet when he came back after insisting on going back to get his bike, and he hadn't been right since then. He must have gone back to the scene; he had been unable to stay away. And now he was ill from the guilt.

At that moment, the restroom door opened, and Shinji came out. His complexion was still poor, but his step was steady. I watched him walk back over to the table and sit down. His eyes were clear.

For an instant I felt as though he had been probing inside my head. I felt like an examinee who'd peeked at the answers of the guy in the next seat only to find the proctor staring down at me. I wanted to say, *I know what you're thinking, I know what you're doing. Stop it!*

But what I said was, "You did it, didn't you?"

Shinji was silent, but I could see the tension leave his face.

Bingo!

"I just realized that that was what must have happened. I guess I'm just slow. So I'm right?" I did my best to sound much nicer and more understanding than I was, but Shinji shook his head.

"No."

"What do you mean, no?"

Not only that, but now he was laughing at my surprise. His shoulders dropped and he breathed a sigh of relief.

"No, I didn't do it!"

"What's so funny?"

Shinji continued to smile, and finally spoke. "Let's go somewhere quiet. I'll tell you the whole story."

I looked around at the empty restaurant.

"This is pretty quiet."

"I'm 'open' right now, and all sorts of other stuff is flying in. It's too tiring. Let's go somewhere where there isn't anyone else around."

Still confused, I agreed to leave. I completely forgot about the tip for the waitress, and she watched us leave with a scowl on her face.

# 4

After we left the restaurant, we walked for a while until we came to a large piece of land apparently designated for development. There were no people in the vicinity, just an earth remover with a half-raised shovel. The air was filled with the smell of rain and mud.

Shinji walked ahead of me, picked out a spot on a plastic sheet covering a pile of construction materials, and sat down.

"This'll do," he said. "Give me a hand."

"Of course," I said. "I'll do whatever I'm capable of." I put both of my hands in my pockets and stood looking down at him.

He smiled. "That's not exactly what I mean. I want your help, that's for sure, but I literally need you to 'give me a hand.' Maybe 'put out your hand' is a better way of saying it."

I didn't understand what he was trying to say, and after a moment's pause, Shinji went on.

"Let me put it this way: Let me hold your hand."

Now I was really confused. Shinji was smiling, but it didn't sound like he was trying to joke with me.

"Hold my hand?"

"Yes."

I took my hand out of my pocket, took a quick look at it, then stretched it out toward the boy. "If you're ever interested in a girl," I added, "you'd better come up with a better line than that."

Shinji slowly gripped my hand, just as if he were shaking it in greeting. His own hand was small, like a girl's, warm and smooth.

He shifted his gaze from me to the large piece of land and looked out over it. His shoulders went up and down as he breathed, and then it was as if—he was no longer there.

He was still sitting right there in front of me, but it was if his presence, his temperature, his breath had all vanished.

At the same time, I began to feel smaller. I could no longer distinctly feel the hardness of the ground beneath my feet or the post-typhoon breeze on my cheeks. It all seemed to be far away and receding further. It was as if the only thing left was the nerve endings beneath my skin, and the rest of me was getting sucked inside.

"When I was younger," Shinji began in a singsong voice. "A child . . . ten years old . . . maybe eleven . . . with a white schoolbag over one shoulder . . . he was probably in an accident about then . . ."

My eyes flew open, and I could feel the dirt under my feet. Shinji's voice, the sound of traffic—everything returned to normal.

Shinji, though, was still sitting there, half sunk in some dream world, still gripping my hand. His bangs had blown across his forehead, making him look even younger.

"A truck, dark green. Two-ton, full of lumber. Logs . . . logs cut into quarters, the bark is still on them. Resin dripping from the cut parts. There's a narrow road . . . a road with three forks. With a friend, red T-shirt. Never thought we'd get hit. Standing off the road . . . just standing and watching. But . . ."

I could feel goosebumps on my neck. Shinji had the expression of a junkie who had just entered that stage of soft, silver hallucinations. I tried to pull my hand from his, but he simply gripped it harder. His voice rose in pitch and sounded as if he was cautioning someone.

"What did I tell you? Stay away from big trucks! You can get hit. The back tire cut the corner a lot closer than the front one. How many times have I told you?"

I was startled to realize that he sounded like a memory I had of my mother, something I hadn't recalled in years.

"You're lucky you weren't hurt worse." Shinji had gone back to his regular voice. "You'll be out of the hospital in no time. They told us children's bones are soft. Soft, almost like cheese." Then he clucked. Someone I knew talked just like that. It was as if Shinji was mimicking an acquaintance we had in common and trying to make me laugh. He didn't even have to work at it.

"But I still don't like trucks. I avoid roads where I see them lined up. The one that hit me, that broke my left shin, was green. I still want to run away when I see a green truck . . . I remember telling somebody that. Who was that . . . Saeko . . ." Shinji dropped my hand. It was almost as if he flung it away. He almost tumbled from his perch.

Both of us were out of breath even though neither of us had moved an inch.

"What the heck was that? Some kind of magic trick?" I demanded.

Shinji stood up next to the pile of construction materials, swallowed, and coughed a few times in evident distress.

"It surprised me, too," he said, gripping his right hand, the one that had held mine. "My hand feels like it's been burned."

"Burned?"

"Some kind of overload, maybe. I went too far."

I took a step forward. If it had been anyone but this earnest boy, I'd have grabbed him by the collar. "What were you talking about?"

Shinji, much calmer now, looked up at me without a hint of mischievousness. "Wasn't it all true?"

His question left no room for a vague response. It was all true. "I was hit by a truck as a child, struck by the back tires as they swung around a corner. I was on my way home, at a road with three forks in it. I didn't remember myself, but afterward someone told me it had been loaded with lumber."

"You must have seen the lumber when it happened. It was in there."

"In where?"

"In your memory."

I was speechless. "Mine?"

"Yeah, I read it. Like reading something off a computer disc."

"Impossible!"

"I can do that." Shinji stood up, and I unconsciously took a step back. He put both hands behind his back.

"I won't do it again. Don't worry."

"Do what?"

"I call it 'scanning.' Like a CT scan." He let out a sigh. "I almost never do it because it's too tiring, and it's rude. But I had to do it to make you believe me."

"Believe you about what?"

Shinji took a few unsteady steps back. "Mr. Kosaka, you've heard the word 'psychic,' haven't you?"

I just stood there dumbly as he continued.

"Well, I am one."

The thing that was most startling was hearing the name Saeko. It was a name I had tried hard to forget, and now I was hearing it from the mouth of a boy who couldn't possibly have known her or who she was. The shock of hearing him say that he was psychic paled in comparison to hearing her name in a context where it had no business being.

"You want to sit down?" Shinji asked.

"No," I said, shaking my head. "I'm fine."

"Well then, I'll sit down," he said and eased himself down on the plastic sheet covering the building materials.

He sat there looking up at me. Neither of us was sure what to say next. I was an adult trying to figure out how to act like one, and Shinji sat there and watched me do it.

After a while, he began to look distressed. "I'm sorry," he said putting his hands over his eyes. "I must have hit a nerve—it must have hurt you."

"What?"

"The name Saeko. Isn't that what got you so upset?"

I sighed. "You probably don't have to be a psychic to understand that. All you have to do is look at my face." I tried to smile. I needed to look calm. He was just a boy.

"It's the name of a girl I knew a long time ago," I explained. "It was a shock to hear it after so many years."

"A girl you knew?" Shinji repeated my words as if knowing there was more to it, but he considerately decided to stop there.

If I didn't tip my hand, I wasn't going to be able to prove he was a fraud. That was what I thought at the time. I decided I'd have to let my guard down and be honest with him. The result, however, was the opposite of what I had intended.

"Saeko was the name of a girl I was engaged to. But we eventually broke up. She married someone else and probably has children by now. I don't even know where she is."

"I see," Shinji said, his head in his hands. "I'm sorry. I won't ask about her again, I promise."

I was taken aback by how seriously he was taking this whole business. Had I really been so deeply affected by the loss of my old lover? Hadn't I been able to forget her? What inside me had evoked such great regret in this boy who had so innocently come out with her name?

I felt bad, but my words must have sounded harsh. "How did you know her name? If she's some relation to you, you'd better come out with it now."

Shinji looked up at me with bloodshot eyes. "How could you think that?"

"It's not so hard to imagine. If you knew her it wouldn't be impossible for you to come up with something that had happened to me as a child. I talked to her about lots of things."

A single bad memory came back to me. It was so clear that I almost came out with it. The first time I slept with her, she had asked me about the scar on my left shin and I had told her about the accident.

"Tell me how you know!" I growled in a low voice. I was starting to get angry. "What are you trying to pull? Why are you still hanging around?"

For an instant, Shinji's face went blank. "What am I trying to pull?"

"That's right."

"Why would I do such a thing?"

"That's what I'm asking you!" I let him know I was angry, but he didn't come back at me. He just sat there and spoke in a flat tone.

"I'm not some kind of scam artist. I never asked to be like this, just like you never asked to be such a hardheaded idiot."

"What?" The blood rose to my head, and I almost grabbed him by the front of his shirt. The only reason I was able to exert some self-control was because of the grin I saw working its way across his face.

"You're better off not touching me," he said, "unless you want me to scan you again."

I still remember the look on his face. He was doing his best, but he knew he had the upper hand, and it showed in his face.

"I don't believe a word," I said and turned my back on him.

"Well, listen to me first," he said. "After that you can decide whether or not you believe me. You're a journalist. You shouldn't dismiss me as a crackpot without hearing me out."

"You're a real brat."

"I may be a brat, but I'm not a liar!" It was the first time I'd heard him raise his voice. I clenched my teeth and looked back at him. "Listen to me!" he begged.

He seemed to grow small again and looked even younger than his sixteen years. "I don't know why I was born with this power. I first realized I could read people's minds when I was about eleven. I always knew who the teacher was going to call on next."

I laughed. "All kids know that. It's because they're nervous; kind of a sixth sense. Everyone has that."

"While she was teaching us math, she was actually thinking about how, if her salary was just a little higher, she might be able to buy the house she had seen a few days before. If only she had three million yen, she'd have enough for a down payment. Do you think anybody else knew that?"

We fell into a silence. From far away, I could hear an impatient car horn blasting.

"It's true," Shinji said. "I knew that. I saw it, and other things, too. Then I learned that not everybody knows these things. That's when I got scared. When I was younger, I often peed in my pants. I always had to leave to go to the bathroom, and my friends thought it was hilarious. It was because I was so scared. It's scary to feel like people are constantly telling you what they are thinking."

I said, "And then?"

"Then," Shinji said, licking his lips and closing his eyes as if trying to concentrate, "it got so scary that I finally told my father about it. I was sure he'd scold me. It just wasn't normal. Anything that wasn't normal was bound to be bad. But my dad didn't get angry. He listened to everything I told him, and then the next day he let me stay home from school. He took me to see a relative I'd never met before."

They went to the home of an aunt of his father's. At the time, she was seventy-two and lived alone. "I'll never forget what my father said to her the moment we arrived. Without even saying hello, he said, 'Aunt Akiko, it looks like our Shinji is just like you.'"

Shinji looked up at me. "My aunt let me into the house and looked me over for a while. That's when I learned I wasn't the only one. I knew it because she began talking without having to ask me any questions. 'You poor thing,' she said. 'When did it start?' She felt sorry for me. I can't tell you how relieved I was. I'd never have made it this far without her sympathy."

"Have made it?"

"That's right," he said. "There have got to be more kids like me around. We just don't know about each other. The problem is we don't live very long—I think it's too easy to be overwhelmed with the power."

"Now there's a theory I've never heard before." I laughed, but Shinji remained completely serious.

"It's not quite accurate to say I was born with a special power. Everyone has it, or at least some degree of potential for it. And it turns out that the power starts revving up at age eleven or twelve, just like it did with me. It's kind of like a secondary sexual characteristic. It's the same with any sort of talent, artistic, athletic, anything. When a child reaches puberty he can understand it himself. 'Yeah, I'm just good at drawing,' or 'I can run faster than anyone—without practicing.' That's talent, right? Even parents recognize it and tell people their child is a born artist or a born athlete—he takes after this or that relative who can do the same thing. I guess it's all genetic."

"Hold on a second!"

Shinji cut me off. "Psychic power is the same as any other talent. Some people have more of it, and some less. Even if you have it, you've got to use it. If you practice, you become very good at it. Usually.

"If your power is limited, or if people around you react badly, the power will just go back to sleep, and then it won't be any trouble at all. Someone might have the talent to paint beautiful pictures but still live a happy life without ever painting one. You know? The problem is when your psychic power is so great that you can't ignore it, and it won't just go back to sleep. Unless you work to control that power, it'll finish you off."

"How do you control it?" I thought I'd try to get this conversation going in a narrower direction. "Some kind of switch on your back?"

"Do you always make jokes about things you find it difficult to believe?"

"Sorry . . ."

"Aunt Akiko took me to the headquarters of the phone company once.

She wanted to show me the huge satellite dish on its roof. 'Shinji,' she told me, 'you've got one of these inside your head.'" He tapped his temple. "It's like I'm a signal receiver. So, actually, learning to control it means learning to make a kind of switch that I can turn on and off when I need to. Do you understand what I'm saying?"

"So is it like you just did with me? You don't hear anything unless you touch the other person?"

Shinji shook his head. "Not necessarily. It works better that way, but sometimes I can read someone's mind just standing next to them."

"Sounds like fun."

"Once in a while it can be." Shinji laughed. "Like that waitress in the restaurant just now. I was starting to open up, so I went ahead and caught her thoughts: *I wish they'd use me as a pin-up girl.*"

"What do you mean, 'open up'?" I remembered what had just happened at the restaurant. "It affects you physically?"

"Yeah. Especially my heart."

"So, even if you're not 'open,' if you turn on your switch too often—"

Shinji laughed. "I suppose that's what I would do if I were suicidal."

I couldn't say his tone of voice was completely unpretentious, but I couldn't get rid of a nagging feeling that he was just putting me on. But why would he do that?

"Let me ask you a question. You told me that you could read people like they were a computer disc, right?"

"That's right," Shinji said, sitting down again.

"Do you read people's memories rather than their emotions or thoughts?"

"Yes."

"So, then it's more like telepathy."

"Mr. Kosaka, what are you thinking about right now?"

"Eh?"

"What are you thinking about?"

"What do you mean? I was thinking about the question I just asked you. Otherwise why would I ask it?"

Shinji shook his head. "That's not what I mean. A brain is not that limited in its capacity. You were thinking about the question you asked me, but you were thinking about lots of other things, too. You may have wondered whether or not the chills you were feeling were a cold coming on, noticed the sky clearing up, wondered whether or not Daisuke Mochizuki had been found. And you were probably wishing you'd never picked up this Shinji Inamura. You weren't even aware of it, but there is quite a bit of traffic in your head. And at the same time, you were pulling out all sorts of memories from your past. You wouldn't be able to 'think' about something unless you had something to compare it to. There's really no such thing as the present in your brain."

"Where did you learn all that?"

"I didn't *learn* it anywhere. Nobody has made a real study of any of this. It's what I've got from my experiences. Reading someone's mind means reading his or her memories. When I was scanning you, I found out that it has been two months since the fourth time you quit smoking, about that accident you had as a child, a big fight you had last night at someone's house and how angry it made you. It was all mashed up together. I just grabbed onto the parts that were easiest to pull out. That's why your memory of the accident and your memory of showing the scars to your girlfriend came out together. It's like you've got them both on the same shelf in your brain. Even though they happened more than twenty years apart."

I was speechless. I was getting a lecture on cerebral physiology right here on the side of the road. And from a kid who was half my age.

"That's what I mean when I say what I do is different from telepathy. Although I probably have some of that too. I'm sure I could do mental communication if I tried." Then he was quiet for a few moments. It was as if he was trying to remember someone's face. His attention was somewhere else.

"Do you know any other people like you?" I asked.

"No," he said a little too hurriedly. "There's no one." Then he continued. "That's why I call it scanning. There are some researchers who call it psychometrics." He shrugged his shoulders. "I can scan things, too. Not just people, but inanimate objects—and substances."

"Do things have memories?"

"Sure. The emotions and memories of the person who owned it or touched it. Memories are visual; they're very clear."

Memories are visual—that much made sense.

"When I touch an object, it's like—sort of like being able to feel the warmth of the person who sat in a seat right before you. I can see the memories it holds. It's hard to make distinctions, though."

"What do you mean?"

"There are memories of the person who made the thing, the person who owned it, and the person who just touched it for a minute. It's hard to sort them out. But the memory that's the strongest jumps out."

Shinji looked up at me as if asking if I had any more questions for him. Like a teacher might ask a slow student.

"I see." I folded my arms across my chest and looked down at him. "So does that complete the case for the defense? Or are you the prosecutor? Whatever. What is it you want me to do? Why are you showing me your tricks and lecturing me?"

"So you still don't believe me?"

"Why should I? I'm not some TV producer."

Shinji's expression changed to one of determination.

"A red Porsche," he said with confidence.

"What?"

"A red Porsche 911. With a Kawasaki license plate. I can't see it all, but the driver is wearing sneakers with a blue line down the side. A young man. There were two of them. One is wearing a red sweatshirt with a hood, and they're both in a hurry."

I looked at him in astonishment, but he didn't blink or wince.

"They're the ones who took the manhole cover off. The ones who killed that boy. You're a reporter, so you know how to find people. I want you to help me."

# 5

As a child, I read a story about a vampire. It wasn't *Dracula*, but the Sherlock Holmes mystery "The Adventure of the Sussex Vampire." I forget the details, but it was about a woman who was supposedly drinking the blood of her baby night after night. At any rate, Holmes solved the puzzle in a logical manner and said something to Watson about not being taken in by Bram Stoker.

When I read it, though, I thought that perhaps the woman could have been a vampire after all, and I was disappointed that none of the characters in the book voiced a doubt over Holmes's sleuthing.

Reality and unreality, logic and illogic live side by side in similar forms— two parallel rails that never cross. We mentally drive with a wheel on each. A politician who is supposedly as solid as a rock relies on the revelations of a spiritualistic medium. A religious figure who tells us he has transcended this world spends his evenings figuring out ways to avoid taxes. A construction company wouldn't think of beginning to build a building with the latest in high-tech features without conducting a Shinto groundbreaking ceremony to purify the site. Completely avoid the illogical rail, and you'll end up with a cold heart, but lean too far toward it and people will think you're crazy. Either way you're likely to crash.

On that particular day, I was trying to choose between believing everything Shinji Inamura told me and not believing any of it. In the end I chose to make an escape.

"You're overestimating me," I said. "Or maybe you're overestimating *Arrow*. Even if everything you say is true and I believe it, how are we supposed to find the red Porsche you're talking about? It's impossible."

Shinji wasn't convinced. "It's not like we're looking for a Toyota Corolla. Only a few places import those things. If we check out the dealers, we should be able to get a list of people who've bought them. I know it was a Kawasaki license. That narrows it down even more. Don't try to talk me out of this."

He was stubborn—and smart to boot.

"But even if we did . . ." I was desperately trying to think of another way out. "Even if we did find the car, and the creep with the sneakers with the blue line—then what would we do? We don't have any physical evidence. Do you think all you have to do is give him a demonstration like the one you just gave me, say, 'And you're the one who did it,' and wait for him and his friend to confess?"

"Well," Shinji said, at a loss now, "I guess we can work out the details after we find them. He might understand if we just explain it."

"Not likely. Real life doesn't work that way."

"So you're saying we should just let them get away?" Shinji stood up. "Doesn't it make you angry that a seven-year-old boy is dead?"

"Of course it does, and of course I don't want to let whoever did this get away with it. But it's a job for the police. It's not something either of us is prepared to do. Pay attention here! Listen, no one single person can take responsibility for everything that happens in society. We all have our own role to play, and we don't want to get in the way of other people playing theirs. I'm sure you can understand that."

"So you're going to pretend none of this happened?"

It was like a slap in the face.

Shinji continued to prod. "How are the police going to find anyone without evidence? This is even worse than random attacks on the street. You know they'll never make an arrest."

Yeah, I knew that.

"I may be a pain in the neck, but face it, Mr. Kosaka, you found me, and you know that little boy is dead. I've got the clues to find the culprits. And you're still trying to avoid doing anything. You should be ashamed of yourself!"

"Yeah, yeah, I'm full of shame and deeply apologetic," I said. "And on top of that, I'm leaving you here. Find your own way home. You don't need me. You've got your big, bad psychic power, so you might as well just take it on over to the police and let them in on it. Give them your clues.

They might take you more seriously than I can."

The instant I was ready to turn right around and walk away, or rather run away, the perfect parting shot occurred to me. Here I was with a sixteen-year-old boy, dealing with him on his level and still determined to win.

"Don't forget," I began, "we don't know that the child is dead. He might just be lost and without an umbrella. There is still that possibility. I'll be praying that when you are at the police station giving them this ridiculous story of yours, they don't get a report that the boy has been found, safe and sound. See you, kid."

I walked away, taking large strides, and had got as far as the street before Shinji yelled after me.

"I touched the umbrella! Don't you remember?"

I stopped in my tracks. I did remember. I had put Yusuke Mochizuki in my car and left Shinji near the manhole. I remembered Shinji's expression when I handed him the umbrella.

*"When I touch an object, it's like—sort of like being able to feel the warmth of the person who sat in a seat right before you. I can see the memories it holds. It's hard to make distinctions, though."*

I looked over my shoulder to see Shinji standing there, his arms dangling, as if he had used up every last ounce of energy he had.

"I saw it when I held his yellow umbrella. I saw him fall in the manhole. He slipped . . . and then everything went black. I experience the whole thing over again when I see memories. When he fell in, he hit his head on the edge of the manhole—right about here." Shinji touched the spot just behind his left ear.

"He didn't suffer much, but he felt the cold. It was cold and scary, and then it was over. Mr. Kosaka, he's dead!"

Shinji went on. "That's why I wanted to go get my bicycle this morning. I went back to the scene. I slipped through the police guard and touched the manhole cover. It was terrifying. I saw the red Porsche and the two guys laughing as they pulled off the manhole cover. They were laughing! And that's why I've got to find them.

"Please." Shinji was begging me. "You don't have to believe me. And you know the police won' do anything. One or two may listen out of curiosity, but then they'll either kick me out or send me to a doctor. I'm asking you because I thought you might believe me."

I felt something move inside me, but I ignored it. I refused to pay attention.

Shinji put one hand on his forehead, stooped slightly and dragged the words out. "They laughed. They said they would . . . just let the water flow in so they could clear it all up. The engine of their brand-new car got wet because the water was so high, and they were in a hurry. They were going to 'jai alai,' that's what it sounded like. They had promised someone, and they had taken that road as a shortcut."

"Jai alai? Did you say jai alai?" I asked.

Shinji nodded. "Do you know what it is?" he asked.

"Are you sure that's what it was? Not something else?"

"Yeah, that's what I heard. That's what the one in the red coat said." Shini looked at me questioningly. "Do you know what it is? What is jai alai?"

I had to take several deep breaths before I could answer, but Shinji waited for me to speak.

"There's a pub by that name near my parents' house—Jai Alai. The owner lives in the area, but he doesn't own just the one place, he's got a chain. There might be another one around here somewhere."

I relented. "Look, I'll just do this one thing. And that'll be the end of it. I'll go look for this Jai Alai place. We can check out all of them. If we don't find a red Porsche in the parking lot of any of them, or if we can't find anyone who remembers seeing one, that'll be the end. Do you understand?"

"Thank you," said Shinji with relief. "That's all I can ask."

**6**

There were three pubs in the Jai Alai chain, we were told by a man with a gravelly voice when we called the number for the main shop. He said that one of them was on the northern side of the Narita Highway.

"Is it close by?" Shinji asked as soon as I hung up.

"What, you need me to tell you everything? Why don't you just read my mind again?"

"Come on, don't get mad."

"I'm not. Let's go." For once, my car started as soon as I turned the key.

The site of the accident had been cleaned up, and cars were being let through. The flow of traffic was smooth. The only leftovers from the typhoon were bits of trash scattered about.

A deep blue sky spread out from the west. Clouds rolled across it. All signs of the flood of the night before had disappeared. I wondered how things would have turned out if we'd had this weather yesterday.

"If only the cat had run away on a day like today," mumbled Shinji. I was confused now. Had he just happened to be thinking that, or was he responding to what I had been thinking?

What a mass of contradictions! I didn't think he could really see inside my head, yet I felt like I was standing naked in front of him. If he really had the power he claimed to, I'd appreciate some visible sign when he was using it.

"I've got a question," I began.

"What is it?"

"When you touch someone, do you wind up reading their minds even if you don't mean to?"

He thought a moment and seemed to be searching for the right words. "That's a hard one. Sometimes I do, but usually I don't. Maybe I unconsciously put a lock on my power, so I don't get exhausted. I'm all right unless I'm overcome by an emotion strong enough to break the lock." He laughed. "So if your car goes over a rough spot and we bump into each other, don't worry. You'll be safe."

"Thank God for small blessings." As we drove along, looking for the pub, we frequently stopped to take a look at the addresses. My heart pounded every time we rounded a corner or checked an address. I wasn't sure we'd ever find it, but we did.

It was on the second floor of a building, above a coffee shop. The signs for both were dilapidated, and the two establishments seemed to be in competition to see which could lower the value of the building faster.

"What a dump!" said Shinji as he got out of the car. "Do customers actually come here to drink?"

We drove around the building, but there didn't seem to be any parking. Nearby was a large restaurant that looked like a truck stop, so I pulled in and parked there.

"I'll take a look inside. You wait here," I ordered Shinji.

"Why? I'm going in too."

"You'll just make things worse."

"Try and stop me." Shinji took off ahead of me and began to climb the steep staircase. I caught up with him and grabbed his arm.

"Promise you'll let me do the talking. Don't say a thing, all right?"

Shinji didn't look pleased, but he nodded.

We climbed the stairs to a narrow landing. On our left was a door with an inlaid wooden design and the words "Jai Alai" written in a script that was almost illegible. Another sign said "Closed," but I turned the doorknob and found it unlocked.

The place was small inside, with a counter made out of a single board that ended right at the door. It was lined with several oddly shaped stools that looked like a row of space aliens. As I leaned in for a closer look, I saw a booth that could seat six; both the table and the lamp standing next to it were as odd as the stools.

"This looks like the sort of place you'd like," I said to Shinji.

"Why's that?"

"It looks more like an occult meetinghouse than a watering hole."

Shinji was unfazed. "So you've seen lots of occult meetinghouses?"

The curtains were open, and the inside was sunny. To the far left was a gaudy beaded curtain, beyond which there appeared to be a tiny kitchen of sorts. A speaker was playing a schmaltzy, old-style song I didn't recognize, but there was no one in sight.

"Hello!" Shinji called out in a loud voice. "Is anybody here?"

We heard footsteps, the beads parted, and a man with a beard stuck his head out.

"Yes?" he said pleasantly. "We're not open for business yet."

"We're not customers," Shinji said almost apologetically.

The man blinked his round eyes and looked at the two of us. I looked at a small placard hung on the wall; it announced the name of the person in charge of fire prevention on the premises.

"Are you Mr. Imaichi?" I asked.

"That's me," the man said.

"Are you the owner?"

"Yes, is there something I can do for you?" Imaichi finally came through the screen and toward us. He was enormous, a head taller than me, and probably weighed more than Shinji and me put together. The T-shirt he wore was pulled tight across his chest.

"We'd like to ask you about last night. Did you have two customers, young men, come in during the typhoon? We think they may have been driving a red Porsche."

Imaichi pulled at his beard and cocked his head to one side. "And who are you?"

I really didn't want to give him my name card, and I had a story prepared just in case I had to come up with something, but Shinji piped up from behind me.

"He's a reporter from the magazine *Arrow*."

I wanted to give him a swift kick, but instead I addressed him out of the side of my mouth. "You were supposed to stay quiet."

"I know that."

Imaichi was suitably impressed. "*Arrow*, huh? So what are you looking for?"

"I'm not at liberty . . ."

"Are you checking my place out? What do you think? Not bad, huh?" he said, indicating the interior with his substantial arm.

"What is all this?"

The man smiled with pleasure. "It's art! Each piece of furniture is also a piece of art."

"Did you make it?"

"Of course not. I don't have that kind of talent."

Lucky for him.

"I love this stuff. So when the owner of the building told me I could change the interior, it was the first thing I thought of. A friend of mine made all the furniture. He'll be famous someday!"

"Did you have any customers last night?" Shinji was obviously trying to get the conversation back on track. "Two young men. One was wearing sneakers. The other wore a red jacket with a hood."

Imaichi appeared startled by what Shinji had said. "Are you two really reporters?"

I patted Shinji's head. "This one's still in training," I said. "Actually, he's just a part-timer."

"I thought he seemed awfully young." Imaichi was finally satisfied. "Sure, I had customers last night. Not just two, there were quite a number. It was a hurricane party."

"Were they all just ordinary customers? Did any of them make an appointment to see you?"

"Actually, yeah. Funny you should ask. A couple of them called ahead of time to say they were bringing in some pictures."

He looked at the yellowing walls. "I let artists hang pictures here, as long as they fits in with the overall atmosphere. These were friends of a friend of a friend, something like that—they said they had just what I was looking for. They were thrilled to have a place to display their work. Especially a place like this, where artists hang out."

"Two young men?"

"Yeah, that's right. They said they'd bring one picture each. What with the storm, I told them they shouldn't risk ruining their paintings. But they wanted to get here while the party was still going on. A famous pop art critic was supposed to come. You probably know him."

He mentioned a name I'd never heard before, adding, "He's a personal friend of mine."

"So? What were the two guys wearing?" Shinji piped up again.

"What do you mean?"

"Did one of them have on sneakers?"

"They were barefoot by the time they got here. They were wearing sweat-shirts. The pictures were all wrapped up, and their heads were even covered with a plastic sheet. I can't remember if one of them had a hood."

They must have got soaking wet and taken off their shoes and jackets.

"Did you see their car?"

"No, not in that weather. I didn't go out at all." Then Imaichi laughed. "I'm expecting them back any time now. You can talk to them yourselves."

"They're coming back here?" Shinji's voice went up about an octave.

"Yeah, the hooks they brought with them to hang the pictures were too small, so they've gone out to look for something larger. They should be back any minute."

"Do you mind if we wait?"

"Of course not. How about a cup of coffee? I'm sure they'll be delighted to know you're thinking of writing them up."

I felt a pain in my left arm. Shinji was pinching me. His eyes were wide open, and he didn't let go until I jabbed him with my elbow.

"Sorry," he hastily apologized. "I wasn't trying to do anything."

Imaichi went into the back and in a minute or two we heard the sound of a coffee mill grinding beans. Shinji and I waited in the shop as nervously as if we were in court waiting for a verdict to come down. Shinji stood against the wall, a balled-up fist pressed against his mouth. I went over to the window, looked out, and waited for the sound of an engine.

"Like to take a look at their work?" A smiling Imaichi poked his head out of the kitchen. "I'm sure you'll like them." He brought out two frames, each the size of a windowpane, one under each arm. As if he'd already considered the way the light would hit them, he put them up against the wall and then adjusted their positions. Twisting his beard, he turned to ask us, "So, what do you think?"

The one to my left looked like nothing more than a checkered pattern. Maybe a fancy raceway flag.

"The one on the left looks like a Mondrian," said Shinji.

"Oh no, you've got it wrong," Imaichi started in. "This is a symbol of the city. People are being crushed between the lines. Everything has been forced into straight lines."

The painting on the right had a monotone blue background with a traffic signal drawn on it. The light was red. When Imaichi saw me looking at it, he enthusiastically began to explain it.

"Isn't this great? The title is *Warning*."

There was no way of ignoring the enormous red light. Where did the painter pick up this image? Could there possibly been a traffic accident that inspired it? Was there a residue of emotions scattered over the site that evoked the piece?

It reminded me of the way Shinji had explained his power to me.

*Psychic power is the same as any other talent. If you practice, you become very good at it.*

A warning, a red light.

I shook my head; what was the matter with me? I turned to the window and gasped. There on the road below us was a bright red Porsche.

The two young men who walked in could have been brothers. They had different body types, and after a good look, it was clear that their noses were different, but they gave off a similar impression. It figured, since their paintings were similarly incomprehensible.

Even their clothes were the same: blue jeans, polo shirts, white sneakers. There was no red jacket anywhere to be seen. As Imaichi came forward to introduce us, I leaned up against the window frame and put my hands in my pockets and balled up my fists. I needed to stay in control and prevent myself from saying something I'd regret later. Shinji stayed rooted to the same spot, one hand resting on an oddly shaped stool.

Imaichi told the men that we'd come because of our interest in their work. The two looked doubtfully at me, and then Imaichi, and then at each other. They didn't look convinced.

"Where did you hear about us?" the taller one asked.

"From a contact I have," I responded. "The thing is, we're not just here about the pictures."

"Figured as much. Sounded too good to be true!" he said, and they both laughed.

"What was your name again?" asked the shorter of the two—although he wasn't much shorter than me.

I gave him my name, and the taller man said, "I'm Shunpei Kakita, and this is Satoshi Miyanaga."

"Which one of you painted the picture of the traffic signal?"

"I did," said Miyanaga. "Do you like it?"

"Yeah."

"That's great. It's one of my favorites, too."

"You like all your own pieces," teased Kakita.

"Otherwise painting wouldn't be any fun, now would it?" Miyanaga responded.

I could see Shinji off to the side staring at me. I pretended not to notice.

"Are you two in college?" I asked.

"That's right."

"Art school?"

"No," they laughed, obviously embarrassed.

"No way we'd ever get in."

"We tried, but it was too hard."

"Never even got a nibble."

"We're both in general studies at a school you've probably never heard of."

"Have you been friends for a long time?"

"Yes, we met when we started painting . . .", Kakita's voice trailed off as he began to get suspicious. "Do you mind telling us why you're here? I get this feeling we're being interrogated."

"Come on, cut it out," said Miyanaga.

"No, he's right," I said. "I do have some questions to ask you."

The two glanced at each other.

I pointed toward the window. "Is that Porsche down there yours?"

After a pause, Miyanaga responded. "Yes, it's mine . . ."

"Wow, it must have cost a bundle."

"Actually, it's my brother's. He doesn't know we have it. We needed it to bring our paintings here."

"We couldn't get a taxi," added Kakita.

"I see. What time would you say you arrived here last night?"

Imaichi, who had been standing there watching the exchange, spoke up first. "It was late. Past twelve." He seemed uneasy. "Is there some problem?"

Shinji leaned forward and I glared at him, hoping he'd stay still.

"You came by way of the Narita Highway, didn't you? It's the most direct route."

"No, we came on the Higashi Kanto Expressway. It's faster that way from home."

"You got off at the Yotsukaido Exit, and went straight north?"

If they said yes, that would mean they hadn't gone through the intersection where the manhole was, and we were barking up the wrong tree.

"No," Miyanaga said, "we went to Sakura and got off there. We thought it would be a shorter trip north that way, but we got lost. We didn't know our way around."

"I should have given them better instructions," Imaichi said.

My throat went tight. I reached up as if to loosen the tie I wasn't even wearing.

"You got lost?"

"Yes," they both nodded.

"Do you remember if you were anywhere near Sakura Industrial Park?"

"Not really," Kakita shook his head and looked over at his friend.

"I was driving," said Miyanaga. "We couldn't see anything in the storm—that's how we got lost in the first place."

They began to look uncomfortable and confused. I had to think fast. If they'd removed the manhole cover and done it with malicious intent, they would never have been forthcoming about the route they'd taken. If they were guilty, they would have been suspicious the minute Imaichi let them know we were interested in them. They might even have said, "Sakura Industrial Park? Sure, we passed right by it. Wasn't there a bad accident there last night?" I was sure that they had no idea a child had gone missing.

Things were getting sticky. I had to choose my words carefully. I needed to get them to volunteer the information about the manhole. After they admitted it, then I could deliver the shocking news. Their crime was obviously one of stupidity, not criminal intent.

Just then, Shinji spoke up and cut me off.

"Last night, right around there, a little boy fell into an open manhole. He's dead."

In one fell swoop, Shinji had destroyed the house of cards I'd been carefully trying to assemble. I was speechless.

As were the two aspiring artists. They looked at Shinji with their mouths open.

"Is that true?" Imaichi was stunned, too. "I didn't know. Was it on the news? I haven't seen any TV since last night." He shut up when he realized the surprise on Kakita and Miyanaga's faces was of a completely different variety.

There was no mistaking their guilty astonishment. At the same time, we had lost any chance of getting them to confess.

"You were the ones who took the cover off the manhole, weren't you?" Shinji glared at them. "You *were* the ones!"

The air in the shop grew heavy with silence. Miyanaga moved his hand as if he was about to say something, but Kakita spoke first. "We don't know what you're talking about."

His words were toneless and his face devoid of expression.

"Liar! You two did it! You opened it up to let the water in and protect the engine in your car! Then you left it open. Last night," Shinji pointed to one, "you were wearing a red jacket, and you," he pointed to the other, "were wearing sneakers with a blue line in them. You laughed as you took off the cover!"

Shinji was passionate in his accusations, but Kakita responded just as I imagined he would. "What makes you think we did it?"

Shinji looked over at me, and so did the other three. This impetuous boy had rushed headlong into the situation and I was the adult in charge of him. I was silent as I stared at Kakita. It was all I could do, and it was the most effective tool I had.

"We . . . ," muttered Miyanaga.

"Shut up!" Kakita didn't even look at his friend, nor did he take his eyes off me.

We were in a precarious position, and I knew that we had to give these two young men a path of retreat. Now that they knew there'd been an accident, we had to convince them somehow things weren't as bad as they seemed.

"We don't know for sure that the boy fell in," I began slowly, "but he's been missing since last night, and he was last seen near there."

"Mr. Kosaka?" Shinji said in a squeaky voice. "Stop talking like a zombie."

"Be quiet."

"How can I? You—!"

"Did you hear me? I told you to keep quiet!" I knew I shouldn't have brought him along. I tried once again, but I was growing desperate.

"The boy might still be alive. We don't know where he is. He might not have fallen in at all."

Kakita's expression was unchanged. He continued to stare at me, while

Miyanaga's face drained of color. He was going to be the easier of the two to break. I decided to address him.

"Did you open the manhole? If you did, you ought to speak up now. We know what time the boy left home. If we know what time you opened the manhole, we can compare the two and rule you out without even involving the police. Or maybe you saw something, and we can let them know they can stop poking around in the sewers and start dragging riverbeds or look for a pervert who likes little boys. You might even help us find him." I knew that the young men knew nothing, but I thought it was worth a try.

Miyanaga shifted uneasily. His Adam's apple went up and down as he swallowed. You could see he felt he was drowning, and I had just thrown him a lifeline. I almost had him.

"Come on, tell us. The police are stuck at the manhole, and that boy might be close to death somewhere else." I concentrated so hard on Miyanaga that I completely forgot about Kakita until he grabbed his friend's shoulder.

Kakita was no longer looking at me. His eyes were on Shinji, whose eyes were telling a completely different story. Kakita's hand on Miyanaga's shoulder was warning him not to believe me.

"Come on, talk to me," I tried again. But it was too late. Miyanaga shook his head.

"We didn't do anything."

"Nothing," Kakita added for emphasis.

His patience gone, Shinji came flying out at Kakita, knocking him over and taking a couple of the bar stools with him. Kakita was bigger, and while he'd been taken by surprise, he quickly managed to get on top of Shinji and pin him down. Imaichi and I leaped forward and managed to pull them apart. Shinji, though, grabbed onto Kakita's arm and stubbornly refused to let go.

Shinji sat on the floor, with Imaichi holding him from behind, still clinging onto Kakita with every ounce of strength he possessed. His eyes were fixed, and I could see veins popping out on his temples. One of his lips had been cut in the scrape, and his clenched teeth were already covered in blood.

"What the—!" Kakita muttered. He couldn't take his eyes off Shinji, nor could he shake him loose. It looked as if some kind of electricity were running through his body and had rendered him motionless.

I must have looked like that when Shinji did the same thing to me earlier in the day, I thought. I had felt robbed of my free will and had been nailed to the spot. Even now, I could tell him to stop, but I was too frightened to try to pull him away from Kakita.

I didn't want to touch Shinji. He was chanting something. "Engine, engine . . ." He began to mumble. "I'm worried about the engine. If it gets wet, I'll need a new one. Come on, we can do it . . . If we take the lid off and let the water run down into it, the street will empty. Think about the other people in the neighborhood. With all this water building up, they'll thank us for it."

I felt the strength going out of my knees. For a few moments, Shinji's voice even sounded like Kakita's.

"We didn't do it!" screamed Kakita, pulling himself back with a burst of energy that finally shook off Shinji's hand.

"We didn't do it! We didn't do anything like that! It's all a lie!" He was furious. He ran into me now, and we both fell against the wall under the counter. I hit my head on it and saw stars. Before I knew it, I was sitting on the floor holding Kakita down.

Shinji's arms dangled at his sides, and he seemed to be having trouble breathing. Imaichi had let go of him and was backing away cautiously.

"Are you all right?" I asked, but Kakita was too stunned to speak.

"Who, who is he?" he finally managed to get out, and crawled away from me and over toward Miyanaga, where he finally pulled himself up. They stood huddled together like children who had been scolded. Their faces were dark as they stood there panting. The sun poured in from the window behind them.

"There's something wrong with that boy," said Imaichi. I stood up too, and, although I felt nauseous, managed to grab Shinji's arm and pull him to his feet. He was shaky, but he was able to stand.

"Please leave!" We didn't need Imaichi's urging. I was already heading for the door. I pushed Shinji on ahead of me and apologized to the three of them as we left. None of them said a word.

As we made our way down the steep stairway, I could hear someone giving the door an extra shove to make sure it was shut tightly.

Neither of us spoke for a while after we got into the car. There was stop-and-go traffic all the way back to Tokyo. As the weather cleared, the temperature rose. I took off my coat and tossed it in the back seat. Even then, I was careful not to look Shinji in the eye.

As we entered the city, he finally spoke, leaning his head against the window. "I'm sorry."

His voice was soft, and I didn't reply. At the next traffic signal, he tried again. "I know I messed up."

I sighed. "Why couldn't you just keep your mouth shut?"

"I couldn't stand it anymore."

"We were okay until you piped up." I banged both hands against the steering wheel and looked over at him. The light turned green, and the car behind me honked impatiently. "They didn't know about the accident with the boy. If you hadn't opened your mouth, they might have admitted to opening the manhole cover. They might have told us how they didn't want the car engine to get wet, and then bragged to us about how they'd kept the streets from flooding, and what a good deed it was for the whole neighborhood. How they didn't mean any harm."

"Didn't mean any harm?" Shinji said, looking over in my direction. "How can that be? Any idiot knows it's dangerous to take off a manhole lid in the middle of a storm and just leave it that way. What sort of adult—let alone a college student—doesn't know that?"

"Believe me, there are lots," I said. I was certain that anyone was capable of acting stupidly on the spur of the moment.

"I just don't understand. I thought they were pretending not to know anything. That's why I got so angry."

I was upset. Shinji had frightened me so many times that day, and I was embarrassed at my own reaction. I was no longer able to choose my words with any care.

"Don't you realize what you've done? They didn't know about the chain of events. They're not bad people. If they had heard on the news that a child had drowned after falling into an open manhole, they might have gone to the police themselves. They were careless and dangerously foolish, but that doesn't make them vicious criminals."

Shinji's head dropped, and I went on. "You backed them into a corner until they felt they had no choice but to lie. We *made* them lie. I'd do the same thing in their place. They were scared, but I'm sure they regret what they did. They'll probably go to the police. But if they don't, I can't say I blame them. And I certainly wouldn't go to the police to inform on them either."

"Why?" Shinji looked up. "You saw their expressions when I told them a child was missing. You don't need to be a psychic to be able to read what was on their minds. They did it."

"Have you been listening at all?" I said. "All we needed to do was get them to admit that they took the cover off the manhole. The rest would have come naturally."

The next light turned red when I wasn't expecting it, and I jammed on the brakes. I continued my lecture.

"You saw how scared they were. Now they know exactly what happened, and they're afraid no one will believe that they didn't mean any harm. Now they might not go to the police. It's not like adults can just say 'I'm sorry' when they realize they've done something wrong. It's not that simple. First of all, they have to protect themselves. It would be cruel to turn them in just because they were looking out for their own interests."

Shinji began to shake, and I have to admit, it felt good, giving him a piece of my mind. Thinking back on it now, it was a gutless thing to do. But I wasn't finished.

"I don't care if you're psychic or not, it takes years to understand the way people work. You've got to stop acting like you're superior to everyone. You need to learn to keep your mouth shut and your eyes open. You think you can read people's thoughts, but you don't have any idea!"

Shinji was silent. I looked over periodically at his limp body, and gradually my head began to cool. He was still a boy, after all.

"Sorry," I finally managed. "I might have said too much."

"It's all right," said Shinji. "It's all true."

I realized that I didn't know where he lived, but when I asked him, he was hesitant to reply.

"Don't worry, I won't start yelling at your parents. I just want to see you safely home."

"I know, but if I don't calm down a little, it'll only worry my mother and father."

He asked me to let him out at a small park on the border of Arakawa Ward.

He said he lived a short walk from there. There was a long bridge nearby and several high-rise apartment buildings that poked up high into the blue sky.

"This is where I come when I need to think," he said. He remained quiet as he pulled his bicycle out of my trunk and reassembled it. He wouldn't even look at me. It bothered me. Looking back, I'm embarrassed to say that he may have been the more mature of the two of us.

"Those two guys were budding artists," I said, and Shinji finally looked up at me. "I'll keep an eye on them. I wrote down the license number of their Porsche, and that should be enough to get their addresses."

"Thanks," Shinji said shortly.

We were having trouble saying goodbye—it seemed like one of us should say something. But I was unable to come up with anything to provide closure.

"Well, then," I finally said as I closed the car door.

"Mr. Kosaka," Shinji suddenly said. "I'm sorry for acting like an idiot."

"Don't worry about it."

"I've got to be more careful about how I use my power. I won't make the same mistake again. But . . ."

"But, what?"

"I didn't ask to be born like this." His voice was low. "I can't always control it. I feel like I've got to make things right because I can see and hear so much. You don't have to believe that I'm psychic, but would you think about how someone might behave if they were?"

I thought a second, and then nodded.

Shinji went on. "Just imagine that you were an ignorant kid who had the power to know things you really didn't want to see or hear. Wouldn't you want to do the right thing? If you were like me, could you honestly say you would have done things differently?"

All I needed to say was *I might have done things the way you did*. It was the answer he was looking for, and it would have comforted him to hear it. If he had had that comfort, the chances are things would not have unfolded the way they did.

But what I said was, "I don't know."

Shinji looked down. Then he said goodbye and walked away. I regretted that I hadn't given him more assurance, but by then it was too late; he couldn't have heard me even if I had called out to him.

PART 2
# Ripples

A week passed, and Daisuke Mochizuki was still missing. No one came forward to admit to removing the manhole cover, and there was no rumor of any leads.

There were many who noted that anybody could pry the lid off a manhole if they wanted to, and that it was dangerous to leave them so vulnerable to vicious pranks. The local water company promised to take quick action, but meanwhile a spokesman had been quoted as saying, "We just assumed nobody would ever try a stunt like that," and had become an object of ridicule in the press.

During the course of the week, though, there had been two cases in Saitama, and one in Tokyo, of manhole covers being slid open. None of them resulted in injury, and they were all thought to be copycats. If anything, it clarified that there were plenty of people with little ability to recognize danger, and just as many who recognized it but were still willing to meddle with it.

In the next issue of *Arrow*, the original incident was mentioned in the summary page of news headlines. I wrote the article, and a photographer went to the scene and took a picture of the manhole cover, securely in place, on a day blessed with clear, blue skies.

On a personal level, I used the license number of the Porsche to look into the elder brother of Satoshi Miyanaga, the car's registered owner. He was a sales rep for a top-ranked securities company, still just twenty-four years old. I was startled that such a young man could afford such an expensive car, but the salesman at the dealership told me it was a used car, sold at a substantial discount because it had previously been in an accident.

"He still wanted it," the salesman said, "so I sold it to him." So the big brother had shown it off to his little brother, telling him it was new. And then Little Brother took the precious ride out during a storm without asking.

I imagined the fight the next day. Either that, or maybe Miyanaga hadn't been up to it. At any rate, neither Satoshi Miyanaga nor Shunpei Kakita had come forward, and I was not inclined to turn them in. I went so far as to look up the Miyanaga family's phone number, but when I picked up the receiver to dial, I thought better of it and put it back down.

When I wrote the article for *Arrow*, I gave it a spin that was ever so slightly sympathetic to the perpetrators. "It appeared that the act was more thoughtless than malicious." I was restless the day the issue came out, wondering if either of the youths would try to contact me, but nothing out of the ordinary happened.

One evening when I had gone out for a drink with a colleague, I asked, after a few beers, what he would do if a UFO came out of the sky and landed and its crew told him that they knew who had committed a major crime that the police were investigating. The answer I got was, "I'd go home and go to bed," followed by, "And if I woke up the next morning and was still pretty sure I'd really seen it, then I'd have myself committed. I'd probably see goldfish swimming in the IV drip, too."

I had to laugh. Not at him, but at myself. I realized that if I was comparing Shinji Inamura to a UFO, it just went to show that I didn't really believe him. Come to think of it, I hadn't heard from Shinji either.

I quickly settled back into my routine work. It was boring, but there was nothing alarming to deal with.

Although *Arrow* was not technically a tabloid, it was not exactly the sort of magazine you'd set out in a bank lobby either. Even if we ran a feature on the Gulf War, we never actually bothered to get opinions from foreign policy specialists. Most of what we wrote had to do with the effects of the war on the domestic cost of living and currency exchange rates. If there was any sign of life from the Self-Defense Forces, our headlines would immediately worded to press the reader's buttons: *Is the Military Draft Back?* It all boiled down to the old theme of "how will current events affect you personally?"

None of us reporters had a beat per se. But we all had subjects we were good at, and as we went about our work we developed information networks that we learned to call on regularly. In this way, we had what we called "specialties, more or less."

I myself had come up from the domestic news desk and had spent a number of years on the police beat. The editor at *Arrow* who had given me the job was good at domestic issues, so I ended up being sent out to work on one incident after another. It sounds flashy, but my articles were the first ones to go when something more interesting came up.

Unfortunately, the magazine was understaffed, and I was occasionally called upon to pick up the slack for a columnist or someone writing a piece in installments. That was what took me and a young photographer to a tidy little coffee shop in Ginza ten days after the manhole incident. We were there to interview the leader of a group of women united against beauty contests for the way they objectified women. In other words, even though we were there to interview a woman, it wasn't the sort of assignment your average guy would rush off to with great expectations.

"Wouldn't this be something a woman would do better at?" I protested. Out of the corner of my eye I saw Kanako Mizuno glaring at me as she stood at the copy machine with a sheaf of papers in her arms.

"It's a good chance for you to learn something," she shot back.

"Learn something . . ."

"That's right. Kosaka, you're one of the most hardheaded reporters we've got."

"Me?"

"That's right. Don't pretend you don't think of me as a tea server-cum-copy machine. Typical male chauvinist. You'll never find a wife at this rate."

"Is that so? Well, I tell you what. If you're still single by the time you hit thirty, Kanako, I'll make you an honorable woman."

"Honorable woman? Who said I was dishonorable? That's exactly what I mean, you moron!"

What was her problem, I wondered as I watched her go off in a snit. The magazine hired her to work part time, but she was as good as any of us who qualified for full-time pay—despite her tone of voice.

I stayed at the office as long as I could, and when it was time to go, Kanako came back around. The photographer and I were sharing notes, and he elbowed me and pointed in her direction. There she was with an armful of mail and a look on her face that declared she still had something to say.

"What's the problem?" I asked. "I'm on my way to be educated."

"That's not it," she said with an uneasy glance at the photographer.

"What?" he smiled mischievously. "Am I in the way here?"

"Dummy. It's nothing like that." She looked down at her bundle and ceremoniously pulled a letter out and handed it to me.

"Another one," she said.

A glance told me what she meant. It was the sixth one I'd got. My name was printed over the address of the *Arrow* editing division on a common white envelope. There was no return address. The first five letters had contained nothing but a sheet of blank stationery. This one was no different.

The photographer came around behind me to peek at it. "What's this?"

"A blank love letter. Or maybe my sight is bad," I said. "Can you see anything written here?"

"It might be invisible ink," he said, taking the sheet out of my hand and walking over to the window. "There might be something to read if you hold it up to the light."

"Shut up, I've tried everything," I sighed.

"Even invisible ink?"

"That too. There's nothing there. That's all there is to it."

The editor in chief, who'd been shouting at someone on the other end of the phone, caught my eye and called out, "Same thing again?"

"Completely blank."

"Pay your bills, I tell you!" the editor continued. "You've been running up a big tab somewhere!"

"There aren't any places willing to take a risk with my credit," I replied.

"I've got it!" The photographer was obviously enjoying himself. "Someone is trying to tell you to write to them—in code!"

Now the colleague across from me joined in. "A code! Unlikely and out of date!"

Kanako furrowed her brow. "Isn't it creepy?"

"Why?" I asked. "It's not like someone's threatening me."

"But..."

The photographer calmed down and gave the matter some serious attention. "When did you get the first one?"

"Hmmm," Kanako replied before I had a chance. "I think it was in June."

"Gee, Kanako," the photographer was teasing her again. "I didn't know you cared so much about him!" Then he stopped and added, "Kosaka, do you have any idea where these might come from?"

"Any idea?"

"Right. You'd better find out what they mean while they're still blank. You never know when someone will come in here and slap a subpoena on you."

That got to me. Unbeknownst to him, he had come uncomfortably close to a dark secret in my past.

"Hey! Why did you flinch? You must have something to hide."

Someone hollered out, "Better get it off your chest now!" as he left the room.

"This is a riddle," the photographer said as he carefully folded up the paper and put it back in the envelope. "Which side is this one going to fall on?" he smiled.

"It's not going to fall on any side," I blustered. "The mass media is constantly harassed by people with too much time on their hands."

The only thing bothering me was that it was clearly addressed to me. As far as I knew, I hadn't done anything as a reporter to distinguish myself from anyone else. And as far as I could remember, I certainly hadn't been involved in a story that would have set me up for revenge. Maybe if I searched far back in the file, maybe I'd find something that fit the bill. The letters had begun arriving a few months ago.

Could it be a woman? Saeko and I had broken up three years before, and if this was about a relationship gone bad, it would definitely be that one—but no, Saeko didn't have the passion or the patience to send a series of blank letters, at least to me. Come to think of it, if I had ever been involved with anyone to whom I'd meant that much, I'd like to know about it.

I wasn't in the habit of telling women I dated once or twice about where I worked or what I did. I let most of them think I was a schoolteacher.

"You're all idiots!" Kanako was clearly irritated. "Doesn't this scare you at all?" She looked at the envelope. "It scares me. It's a lot worse than if something was actually written on it. The postmarks are from different places. Whoever sent it obviously doesn't want us to find out where they are."

"Stop worrying," I reached over and gave her a tap on the head. "Nuts who send letters aren't capable of much else."

"I tell you, you must owe somebody some money!" the editor in chief stuck to his original line—it must have happened to him before.

"You can't tell me you're not worried." Kanako was just as stubborn. "You've saved all the letters."

She was right. They did bother me, and I had saved them. But how did she know that?

"I don't have all of them," I started. "I lost one."

"Liar."

"Yeah, Akiyoshi was sure it was invisible ink and took it off to the men's room and poured ammonia on one of them. Come on, it's time to go." I got the photographer out of his chair, and we left the building. Loaded down with equipment, he was still grinning at me.

"What?" This was getting annoying.

"Nothing, nothing. I was just thinking that Kanako was kinda cute." His teeth were white in his deeply tanned face. "And naïve. You ought to ask her out sometime."

"Ask her yourself!"

"I've tried . . . I have, but she's not interested in me. All she does is ask me about you. Does Kosaka have a girlfriend? Wasn't he engaged once? Why did they break up? What was she like? Was she prettier than me? I finally gave up."

"Really?" I said, taken aback. Kanako looked as if she hadn't been out of high school more than a year or two. I found it difficult to believe she'd find an older man like me attractive. That was why I enjoyed teasing her; she seemed safe.

"How old is she anyhow? Nineteen?"

"She's twenty. An adult, or so she says. I think she's ready to settle down."

"If I were her, I'd look somewhere else for a husband. What could anyone in this business have to offer her?"

"It's all part of her plan. She's looking for someone with job security. She won't give any of us contract workers a second look; it doesn't matter whether or not we've got money. But a lifetime employee like you—one of these days, the newspaper is going to call you back. That's what she's counting on."

"Why would I be interested in her?"

"Come on, now she's going to hate me. She's a good kid. Aren't you even a little bit intrigued?"

I thought a moment and decided not to answer. The photographer scratched his head. "I shouldn't have said anything—stirring up the past."

"What's that supposed to mean?"

Now the photographer was really confused. "It's just that—oh, nothing. I mean, I heard . . . it must have been a rumor."

Saeko Soma happened before I was transferred to *Arrow*. In fact, it was because of her that I had been reassigned.

Gossip. It got around faster than the flu and stuck around a lot longer.

The photographer was desperately trying to get himself out of the hole he had dug. "It was all third-hand. You can't believe any of it."

*I won't ask about her again. I promise.*

All of a sudden, Shinji Inamura popped back into my head, and I wondered why.

The woman we had been dispatched to interview, the head of a group with an absurdly long name, gave the impression that she had come to a batting center to hit a few balls. Every question I tossed out was slammed back at me.

"I know you bastards in the mass media just think of us as a group of jealous ugly women and refuse to take us seriously. But we are merely standing up for our rights. You can print whatever you like!"

If she really didn't care what we printed, she never would have used that line.

And she went on and on. "Appearance is something we're born with. There's not much you can do about it by way of effort. That's why it's improper to rank women based on what they look like. By holding these beauty contests, men in a male-oriented society give preferential treatment to women who conveniently meet their standards. They want all of us to fit into their molds."

The photographer and I, as representatives of "men in a male-oriented society," listened obediently to what she had to say. Every once in a while, she'd ask for our opinion: "What do you think about that?" But as soon as one of us opened our mouth, she'd come out with the response she expected of us. Finally we chose respectful silence.

"It's wrong! It's wrong for human beings to be ranked with what they were born with and to ignore the efforts they make!"

"Yes, I agree. It's a mistake." The photographer finally spoke, after giving up on any sort of wrap-up on my part. "But it's not like you can just tear into everything that's wrong and fix it the way you want it to be, now is it? Why don't you just let beauty contests be? Why don't you just loosen up a little?"

It's what you call adding fuel to the fire. The photographer lowered his head and shut up again as the tirade continued. Eventually the words *you can't change what you were born with* began drilling their way into my head.

*I never asked to be like this.*

I let our interview subject rant on as I began to think. What if—just what if you were born with the power to "scan" someone, what would happen if you used it now? What if you could look deep into the heart of this woman and see what even she didn't know? Or maybe she did. Maybe she was aware of her own desires and feelings of inferiority and was doing her best to keep them hidden where they wouldn't be found . . .

*I almost never do it because it's too tiring, and it's rude.*

I believed in what the woman was saying, and I knew it was worth my while to pay attention. But I still felt that the motivation for all of this lay deep inside her heart. Her motivations—which I felt sure included anger and jealousy—were a personal matter. I could only imagine how much I might learn about her if I had the power to read her mind.

*It's scary to feel like people are constantly telling you what they are thinking.*

Seeing and hearing everything. It would indeed be an insult to human dignity. I felt gooseflesh break out on my arms as new questions formed themselves in my brain.

If Shinji was a psychic, as he claimed to be, then he had ahead of him a life of torment. How would he manage? What sort of job would he do? Where would he live? What sort of woman would he fall in love with? Would he ever have a family of his own?

And all the while being flooded by the true feelings of other people bottled up inside of them. Shinji would have to control his powers as well as his emotions in order to protect himself.

He'd know the sort of thoughts people usually had no idea of unless they were spoken aloud or expressed in an attitude. It was how we managed to get on with our lives—we didn't always have to listen to the way people really felt.

But what if you couldn't avoid it because you had the power to hear it? Even if you knew that you'd lead a more peaceful life without it, would you be able to control your curiosity? And then once you knew the truth, would you be able to act as though you didn't?

Would you be able to trust anyone?

*I'm asking you because I thought you might believe me.*

I realized that those must have been words Shinji would never say lightly. I should have gone easier on him. I should have, whether or not I believed he was really a psychic.

I went straight back to the office after the interview, planning to give Shinji a call. I opened the door, and Kanako Mizuno came right over to me.

"You have a guest. He's been waiting since about three." She pointed in the direction of our tiny reception room. It was already four-thirty.

"Who is it?"

"It's a boy. He refused to give me his name."

"By young, do you mean younger or older than you?"

"I'd say younger."

I knew it was Shinji, and I was overwhelmed with relief. Seeing it in my expression, Kanako smiled up at me.

"Someone you want to see?"

"Yeah."

But when I opened the door, I saw that it was a different young man. The words of welcome died on my lips.

The boy stood up. He looked pale and nervous. Before he spoke, his right hand went up to his earlobe.

"Are you Mr. Kosaka?"

He told me his name was Naoya Oda. This was how I met the young man who was to die a regrettable death in the events yet to come.

**2**

"We *were* friends—good friends." That's what Shinji said when I asked him about it. "But we had a difference of opinion. That's why Naoya came to see you."

"So it was all a lie?"

"That's right. He put one over on you." Naoya Oda had come to see me to tell me that Shinji Inamura had only tricked me into believing he was psychic.

He was obviously agitated, the way he quickly introduced himself— "between jobs at the moment, but trustworthy"—and then got right down to business.

"Now wait a second," I put my hand up to interrupt him. Just then, Kanako came in with some coffee for our guest, which gave me a few moments to regroup.

She looked at the two of us, trying to figure out our relationship, and finally left the room. As soon as the door shut, Naoya and I both began talking at once.

"If you'd just let me explain . . ."

"There's no need to rush . . ."

Then we both fell silent. We both started talking again at the same moment, then we both stopped. Naoya laughed out loud, shrugged, and said, "Okay, you first."

"I don't quite understand what's going on here," I began slowly. "What's your relationship to Shinji?"

"I'm his cousin. Our mothers are sisters."

"I see. And you're older than him?"

"Yes, I just turned twenty." His responses were prompt, and he delivered them with a smile. It wasn't an unpleasant smile, but it seemed somehow forced.

He was pretty skinny. About my height, but his belt was buckled one or maybe two notches tighter than mine. His complexion lacked the glow of health; sort of like Shinji's right before he ran into the restaurant bathroom to throw up.

"Listen, I hope you don't mind me asking," I said, changing the subject, "but have you been sick recently?"

Naoya shook his head. "No. Why do you ask?"

"You look a little pale."

"You think so?" he asked as he absently rubbed his jaw. "Must be a hangover. I drank too much last night, and I can still feel the drink."

I'd seen plenty of hangovers in my day; I knew he was lying.

"All right, whatever. So are you close to Shinji?"

"Yeah, I'd say so. We've gone on bike trips together. I like to travel, too."

"I see. So you like to do some of the same things?"

"Yeah, and we're kind of like brothers. Both of us are only children, but lots of people say we look enough alike to be brothers."

I might have been wrong, since Shinji wasn't there, but I didn't think Naoya looked anything like him. The only feature they shared was their eyes—the type of eyes that girls love.

"Just like brothers. Now isn't that bucolic?"

"Warms your heart, doesn't it?" That smile again. The whole time we'd been chatting, Naoya had been compulsively jiggling his left knee. I realized that it only stopped when he had to concentrate on smiling.

The jiggling abruptly stopped. "It's a bad habit. My mom always told me guys who can't sit still don't make much of themselves."

He certainly was sensitive, I thought. It didn't seem strange to me that he'd be nervous about visiting a stranger on behalf of his cousin. "I don't like it myself," he continued.

"You mean, jiggling your knee? Lots of people do it."

"No, I mean, coming here to tell on Shinji." His smile was gone and he looked down. "But if I just let it go, who knows what will happen? He'll get hurt, and you'll be stuck."

"Why would I be stuck?"

"Aren't you going to write an article?"

"About what?"

"Shinji. He told you who left the manhole open, didn't he?"

Now I was surprised. "Is that what he said?"

"No, but . . ." The left knee was moving again. "I'm sure he was hoping you would—that's why he tried to trick you."

I leaned back in my chair. "I'm not sure about being tricked or not, but I don't plan to write about Shinji." I hadn't even considered the possibility.

Naoya looked almost shocked. "So, ESP isn't all the rage anymore?"

"Yeah, you could say that. And I really don't think Shinji was looking for a write-up. Has he told you everything that happened?"

Naoya nodded. "He's a fool."

"Why do you say that?"

"Trying to trick an adult like you." He looked up at me as if expecting me to see that as the complete and entire truth. "He's so immature."

"Well, he's pretty young . . ."

"He just wants to be noticed; he loves to be dramatic. You know how teenagers are. He tells everyone he's psychic. He's got a pile of books on the subject, full of stories that sound almost plausible."

"It makes sense. He explained it all to me."

"I knew it," Naoya shook his head. "I wish he'd knock it off."

I looked at him for a few moments. His temples were throbbing; he really was angry.

"If Shinji was trying to fool me," I leaned forward, "I've got to say that I really didn't believe him at first. I mean it's not the sort of thing you just nod and accept right off the bat. To tell the truth, I thought *he* might be the one who had left the manhole cover open."

Naoya was nodding in full agreement, obviously anxious to keep the conversation going in this direction. "That's right. It makes sense to come to that conclusion."

"But it turns out that if what he's saying isn't true, then some things just don't make any sense." I went on to tell Naoya everything that had happened the night of the typhoon and the next day. He hung on my every word.

"Well, it's the same story he told me. He's clever, I'll say that much for him." Naoya shrugged again and I smiled wryly.

"If it were all made up, and everything he said conveniently matched perfectly with what happened or if he was clever enough to set it all up to work just right—that's the sort of thing I'd write about," I concluded.

"Let me tell you how he did it." Naoya was ready to fight a little harder. "All of it has a logical explanation."

I left him for a few minutes to get a pen and a note pad. I planned to get it all down. Things were sure going differently than I had expected.

"Let's start with the manhole cover," Naoya said. "That was something he just happened to see. He saw the two guys in the red Porsche remove the lid. He took note of what they were wearing and memorized their license plate number. When he told you about it, he just mentioned that it was a Kawasaki number—that would sound spookier. And, of course, he heard them talking about going to that Jai Alai place."

"If he saw them, why didn't he do something about it?"

"He had no idea what would happen. And it was the two of them against him, right? Any kid would pretend not to have seen. There was no way he could put the lid back on after they left. A manhole cover is too heavy for one person."

I nodded. "And then?"

"After the two guys left, Shinji was there alone in the rain. Who should come by but the kid looking for his cat. How was Shinji to know he'd get washed into the sewer?"

And that would be why he knew that the cat's name was Monica. I had thought that far myself.

"And then you picked him up," Naoya continued. "You just happened to drive past the open manhole, and that's when he got the idea to try a little ESP."

"*Try* ESP?"

"Sure. You have to admit it's more dramatic than just saying he saw something. I told you he's interested in psychics, right? Why let all that study go to waste? And it turns out you're a reporter. He couldn't pass up a chance like that!"

"Can I ask you a question?"

"Shoot."

"Is this what Shinji told you? Or is it what you assume happened?"

Naoya blinked. "Um, I'm just telling you what he told me."

"He told you all about it?"

"Right."

"He told you he'd tricked me?"

"Yes."

"Okay, go on." I leaned back again. "I'm interested."

Naoya cleared his throat, took a good look at me, and continued. "When you found the yellow umbrella, he was just as shocked as he looked. He realized the boy must have fallen in the sewer. There's nothing remarkable about that, is there? Nobody would have to be 'scanned' to figure that out. He felt even worse because he had actually seen the boy."

I nodded. "Of course. But the thing is, Shinji told me the boy hit his head on the edge of the open manhole. What about that?"

Naoya was not impressed. "He's got to have hit something somewhere. After a tumble like that, the corpse is bound to be bruised from head to toe. He was pretty safe with that line."

"You're right. I couldn't make any judgments based on that. If he saw the two guys opening the manhole, I could eliminate everything that had to do with it. But you know . . ."

"Now you're thinking about the man at the hotel front desk and the waitress in the restaurant," Naoya plodded on. "Simple. While you were out all night at the scene of the accident, the waitress visited the front desk, and Shinji heard the two of them chatting."

"That's how he knew that the man's nickname was Hiba, and that the two of them occasionally used 102 to 'take breaks' in."

"And that the waitress wanted to go into show business," Naoya concluded with a laugh. "I can imagine the entire scene. The man telling her, 'Guess who's here? A reporter from *Arrow*. I'll send him over to your place for breakfast. Be nice to him and get them to agree to take pictures of you for their magazine.' "

It all made sense, and it wouldn't be the first time something like that had happened. But I still wasn't convinced. As a matter of fact, I felt as strongly unconvinced by what Naoya had to say as I had when Shinji had told me he was a psychic. I found it hard to believe that Shinji was that clever a con artist, maybe because I remembered how crushed he had looked when we parted.

"The night I picked Shinji up," I began, "I had just had an unpleasant experience and was on my way back to my apartment from my parents' home." Naoya nodded, listening carefully. "Shinji knew that, too. He knew I was irritated after having an argument. He also knew I had just quit smoking for the fourth time. What about that?"

"He could tell you were irritated from the way you were acting. That was an educated guess. But about the smoking . . ."

"How about it?"

"The ashtray in the car was clean, you didn't smoke at all while you were with him, but there were two lighters in the glove compartment—both of them empty. And there was a single piece of nicotine candy. That's what he told me."

He had me. "It makes him sound like Sherlock Holmes. What about the number of times I'd tried to quit?"

"Are you sure it's your fourth try?" Naoya snickered. "Even people trying to quit don't always remember how many times they've done it. If someone in your office had said, 'This is your third attempt!' you'd probably have believed that, too. Once Shinji had figured out you were trying to quit, it was just a matter of making a guess and being pretty sure you'd go along with it."

Was this what they called manipulative psychology? How to convince people of things that are not true?

"Shall I go on?" Naoya looked at me. "Let's talk about the accident when you were young."

"Yeah," I sputtered, "that was what really got me."

"It surprised me, too. Shinji's got an incredible memory. Look at the April 5 issue of this year's *Arrow*. After he told me about it, I went to the library to find the back number . . ."

I stood up and left the room before he could finish. I went to our bookshelf and pulled the issue off the shelf. I came back in, flipping through the pages. So that was it.

We had done a four-part feature entitled "Traffic Accidents: The New Social Menace." I hadn't done any work on it, and that's why I had forgotten. But the writer in charge of the project had talked to me about my own experience, and included it in the piece.

"The April 5 issue was about accidents involving trucks, wasn't it?" said Naoya.

He was right. Nowadays drivers of large trucks tended to park on the road at night, and passenger cars would misjudge the distance and run right into them, getting caught in the undercarriage.

That wasn't all. The feature also explained that because the driver's seats of trucks were so high up, their mirrors covering the lower reaches of their vehicles had numerous blind spots, and there was an increasing danger of pedestrians getting hit by trucks on the move.

The reporter included a series of photographs that showed the different sizes of arcs described by the front and back tires of trucks as they turned, and accompanied it with this text:

> It is a simple matter for small children to get caught in the tires of a truck. One of our reporters, who we'll call K, was involved in such an accident as a child. He and a truck loaded with lumber were both waiting at a three-way traffic signal. When the light changed, the back wheels of the truck hit him as he stood there waiting for the truck to turn the corner, and he still has the scars on his shin to show for it. According to the victim, the truck started out slowly, but by the time K realized what was going to happen it was too late. To this day, says K, the sight of a large truck is enough to send him running.

*A road with three forks. Full of lumber. Logs . . . logs cut into quarters. I still want to run away when I see a green truck . . .*

I looked up, and Naoya was standing there nodding.

"It just used my initial—" I mumbled.

"He saw the scar on your leg."

"When?"

"When you went out to inspect the open manhole. He said you took off your jacket and shoes and rolled up your pant legs."

He was right.

"Not everyone has a scar on their left shin, and after that it was a matter of piecing the accident together. Even if he didn't get it all right, your memory can't be very clear, can it?"

I tossed the open magazine on the table and looked up at the ceiling.

"How could I have believed him?"

"And then he told you about a girl."

He was talking about Saeko.

"Don't go and tell me she's your cousin, too. But at this point I'd probably believe that too."

Naoya asked me a startling question. "Are you wearing the same jacket you wore the night this all happened?"

"Huh?"

"Is it the same jacket?"

"No, it's not. Why?"

"Well then, when you get home, take a look at the lining in that jacket. The edge of the left sleeve has been mended."

"What are you saying?"

Naoya replied calmly. "You can see the stitches. Because she used white thread. Someone sewed it up for you and even stitched in the name 'Saeko' next to it. You took your jacket off when you got out of the car. That's when he saw it. That's what he told me."

I was at a loss. "Are you sure?"

"I'm sure! Go home and take a look." Once again, Naoya shrugged and looked down. "I'm sorry. I didn't mean to pry into your private life."

"I've never noticed that jacket had been mended." If I had, I never would have left the stitches in.

"You'd never notice it unless someone pointed it out. Shinji told me about it. No one but a wife or a lover would do something as mischievous as that. Your mother sure wouldn't!"

She had been a domestically inclined girl. We didn't have a lot of time together because of my job, but she'd stop by occasionally and clean up my place. I'd always known when she'd been there. She'd even said that she had a special talent for housework and enjoyed being left to take care of it. She had wanted an ideal household. She had wanted to have children.

"Excuse me?" Naoya broke in on my reverie. "If you had had a girlfriend who did such intimate things for you, then you certainly would have told her about the accident. He knew that if he mentioned her name, he could tell by your reaction whether or not you were still seeing her."

"Enough!" I signed. "I give up."

Naoya nodded.

"What else do you have to tell me?" I asked after a few moments.

"Nothing. But I do have a request." He sat up straight and spoke. "What Shinji did was horrible, but I'm asking you to forgive him this once. Don't get angry—just leave him alone, and don't try to contact him. I've already read him the riot act, so I'm sure he won't bother you again. I'll make sure of it."

"I wasn't planning to scold him," I said. "But do you really think I shouldn't see him?"

"He's sick," Naoya said almost lightly. "If he has anything more to do with you, he's bound to tell more lies. Do you remember when there was all that hype about bending spoons using supernatural powers?"

That was in 1974. All of a sudden there were kids who could bend metal spoons just by touching them. There was a huge fuss about it until *Asahi Weekly* did a special issue debunking it all.

"Yeah, I remember. But you're not old enough to remember it."

"Shinji has looked it all up. Now they say it was a form of mass hysteria. I figure kids always want to be a little bit different from their friends. They get excited just thinking about it."

"You think they enjoy fooling adults, too?"

"Sure. And Shinji's no different. He goes into a lot more detail, that's all. I've got to do something about him." He stopped and thought for a moment, then laughed. "If there were psychics . . ." he said, stopping in midsentence.

"Yeah?" I prodded.

"They wouldn't be bending spoons and forks for the media. They wouldn't be talking about themselves. They'd be scared—and they'd stay hidden away, out of view." Then he asked me once more to avoid contact with Shinji, and stood up to leave. "I guess the two guys who removed the manhole cover haven't come forward yet."

"Right."

"And all because Shinji couldn't control himself. So what are you planning to do? Report them to the police?"

"I'd have to tell them about Shinji."

Naoya looked troubled. I could tell that this was what he most wanted to avoid.

"But I won't," I said quietly. "I told Shinji I couldn't bring myself to do that. The two of them are bound to give themselves away at some point."

"That would be best."

Naoya seemed satisfied and left. As I watched him go, there was something about the way he slumped that made him seem old beyond his years. But then again, I just might have read too much into it.

The situation was starting to get old, but I decided to ring the clerk at Pit Inn. You could label it a bad habit, or you could say I had an inner calling for research.

Another staff member picked up, and I waited for a while until Hiba got on the line.

"Aren't you the reporter from the other night? This is a surprise!"

"Sorry to interrupt you, but I've got a few questions to ask."

"What about?"

He laughed when I asked him if he'd had a chat with his girlfriend the waitress late that night.

"Is this some kind of important matter?"

"Extremely."

"Okay, then. Yes, I did see her. She's supposed to work until nine, but the storm was so bad that night, she couldn't get home. She was in the restaurant all night, so she came by to see me and bring me something to eat."

"Did you chat in Room 102?"

"Huh? How'd you know about that? Don't tell the owner. I mean, we always change the sheets."

"What does she call you?"

"Me?"

"Yeah, does she call you Hiba?"

Now he was truly astonished. "I didn't realize how slick *Arrow* was. How did you know that?"

"No big deal. Thanks." I made ready to say goodbye and then thought of something else. "Listen, tell her she doesn't have what it takes to be a model. Ask her to marry you and settle down."

He laughed again. "We're going to get married after she gets her career going and starts earning big money."

"You think that when that happens, she's going to be satisfied with you?"

"I don't know. I've always thought I had it in me to be the most successful gigolo in Japan."

And on that note, out conversation ended.

I sat at my desk, thinking. After a while, I lifted my head and asked a colleague on the other side of a huge pile of documents for a cigarette.

"I thought you had quit for the fourth time."

"And I'll quit again," I said. "Later."

This was all so ridiculous, I thought. I went home and checked the sleeve of my other jacket. Sure enough, the name "Saeko" was stitched into it.

I could neither laugh nor feel anger. I picked up a pair of scissors to rip out the stitching, but then thought what the hell and just threw the jacket in the trash. That made me feel a little better.

There was another typhoon the following weekend. First there was a lot of waiting and watching the weather reports as the storm came nearer. Then it started raining, and the wind rose. Houses were washed away, and there were landslides. It was a repetition of the week before, except this time no children went missing. Instead, one was found.

"They've found the body of Daisuke Mochizuki." I got the news from a reporter I'd worked with before at another branch. "I guess the flood this week pushed his body up out of the mud in the sewers. Poor kid."

"Has there been an autopsy?"

"Not yet. Was there some problem?"

"No, nothing."

*The corpse is bound to be bruised from head to toe.*

# 3

The phone woke me up early the morning after we'd worked late into the night to put our next issue to bed. I searched under my pillow for the receiver and put it to my ear, only to hear Kanako's voice wipe away every last vestige of sleep.

"Kosaka? I'm sorry, I really am."

"Listen," I moaned, my eyes still closed. "I don't care. Whatever you've done, I forgive you. Good night."

"Wait! Don't hang up! There's an emergency."

"Leave me alone. It's my day off."

"Shut up and listen! Someone's here to see you. A boy. He was here waiting when I got in. He says he's got to talk to you. He's pale as a sheet. Are you awake?"

This time it really was Shinji Inamura.

I'd promised not to see him. It ran through my mind over and over as I got dressed. I thought about contacting Naoya Oda.

But then I realized that after getting such a complete explanation of everything that had happened, I should be able to talk to Shinji without falling for any of his tricks. I decided not to scold him or tell him I knew everything.

Nine a.m. in the editorial department was a completely different scene, depending on whether we'd been up all night working or not. One difference was certainly the amount of cigarette smoke in the air. When I arrived, Kanako was wiping the dust off the top of desks, but she flew over as soon as she saw me.

"It's almost clean in here!" I said to her.

"It's good to see your brain is functioning," Kanako responded dryly. "He's waiting for you in the reception room. You'll be wanting some coffee, I assume?"

"The largest cup you have, please."

I walked into the tiny reception room to find Shinji in the same seat Naoya had occupied, and stooped over just the same way. All the young men I'd met lately seemed listless and out of sorts.

"I'm so sorry!" Shinji said, scrambling to his feet as soon as he saw me.

"Let's not come out with the apologies so early in the morning, it makes me feel like a priest. What's the matter?"

"I can't sleep," he said, slumping back down into his seat. "I'm so worried." He had circles under his eyes, and his cheeks were sunken in. It was painful to see.

"Have you been eating?" I asked.

Shinji shook his head.

"Going to school?"

"Not today."

"Good idea. Go home, eat something and spend the rest of the day in bed. You'll feel better."

He looked up at me with bloodshot eyes. "They found his body, right?"

I nodded.

"But those two still refuse to come forward."

I nodded again.

"Is it my fault?"

"Of course not."

"No, I know it's my fault."

I sighed and plopped down on the sofa. It wheezed out a sigh, too.

"So, what if it's your fault? What do you propose to do?"

Shinji was silent.

"There's nothing you can do. Which means it's not your responsibility." It wasn't his fault little Daisuke had died.

"I don't know what to do."

"Forget the whole thing."

"I can't."

"Then try harder. Don't they teach you that in school? Genius is one percent inspiration and ninety-nine percent perspiration and all that."

"Cut it out! Why can't you be serious?"

"I was up all night. When humans reach their limits, the brain anesthetizes itself and you start acting silly."

Shinji looked even angrier. I looked away. Well, I was angry, too, because he didn't seem like the kind of kid who would try to fool you. I hadn't taken him for a liar.

Finally he spoke. "Okay, I see now."

"What?"

"Naoya's been here, hasn't he?"

I felt like a pitcher who sees the first batter up hit a home run. There was no time to even act like I didn't know what he meant. Just then there was a knock at the door, and Kanako came in with a tray. She caught me with my mouth open. "Wh-who?" I sputtered at Shinji.

Kanako flinched and looked at me sideways. Now Shinji was truly upset. "You know who I mean! I know Naoya was here! What did he say?"

I spread open my hands. "I-I asked you who you were talking about!"

Shinji looked at me and yelled out, "Miss!"

Kanako jumped again, and responded, "Yes?"

"Has there been a college student here to see Mr. Kosaka?"

Kanako looked down at me. I looked up at her. I tried to use one side of my face to say, *Don't answer that!* I was pretty sure she had understood.

Now Shinji was on his feet. "Miss, there was someone here, wasn't there?"

Kanako backed up in my direction. I put my hand on her elbow and pushed her toward the door.

"Would you give us a few minutes?" I asked.

"Miss!"

"Just go," I begged.

Bewildered, Kanako nodded and almost ran out. Shinji whipped around to look at me and cried out, "What did Naoya say?"

I was less angry than I was unhappy. How had I gotten myself into this mess?

"Sit!" I commanded.

Shinji refused to move.

"Have a seat. Please."

Although obviously still upset, he finally sat down. I waited for him to calm down before I said anything more.

"Listen, I'm twice as old as you. More than twice." I wasn't sure where I was going with this. "And . . . and, to someone older than me I might seem young, but still, I don't have nearly as much energy as you or Naoya Oda. My brain isn't nearly as pliant, and I'm having a hard time keeping up with what you two are thinking."

The only thing Shinji reacted to was the name Naoya Oda.

"So he really was here."

"Yes, he came, and yes, I listened to what he had to say."

"He told you that I lied to you."

"That's right. Everything he said made sense, and he was able to back it up."

Amazingly, this made Shinji chuckle, which irritated me even more.

"You find that funny? I wish I could laugh about it, but I can't. I don't have time to sit around listening to the two of you. I have work to do. And if I don't work, I don't eat. Surely you can understand that."

Shinji nodded.

"So let's be honest here. I'm the one who is having the hard time. I really did believe you."

Shinji finally looked up at me.

"That's right, I believed you. I hate to admit it, but it made sense at the time. Not everything in life can be explained logically. You hear about things like this all the time. Some guy dies, and then he goes to visit a friend who lives far away to say goodbye. Or someone else has a dream, and every detail in it comes true. I even felt sorry for you, for how difficult it must be for you to go through life as a psychic."

Shinji blinked a few times and then looked down again.

"And then your cousin shows up and tells me you're just a well-read liar. He explained it all to me and told me not to have anything more to do with you. And now you're back asking me why I don't believe you. What do you guys expect of me?"

A long silence followed.

"I just want you to believe me," Shinji finally said, rubbing his face with both hands. "That's all. I'm the one who's telling the truth."

"So why would Naoya show up just to tell me lies?"

"Because he's a psychic, too."

I just sat there looking at Shinji. Things were making less and less sense.

Shinji began to talk. His voice was a monotone, almost as if he was chanting.

"He's not my cousin. I'm sure he just told you that to make his version sound convincing. He's the only other person besides my aunt I've found who has the same power as me, but his is a lot stronger."

He went on to say they had met two years ago. "It was at the Kinokuniya bookstore in Shinjuku. You know how it's always so crowded? I can't even remember what I went to buy. Anyway, I was just walking around when I heard his voice."

He said he heard Naoya's voice in his head, and he almost smiled at the memory. "It's exciting to go out in crowds, but it can be really tiring, too. If I don't keep my power under control, I pick up every thought that goes by. If I'm not careful, I can get caught in someone's frequency, and then I have to listen to it all. It's like . . . I know—have you ever done synchronized singing?"

"You mean like a kids' song?"

"Right. In turns. Something like 'Are you sleeping, are you sleeping, Brother John?'"

"Sure, in school. I was never very good at it."

"Me neither. I would get distracted by the other person's part. That's what it's like."

"Being in a crowd?"

"Yes. You try to sing your own part and mind your own business, but you end up adjusting to the guy standing next to you. Then you have to work to get out of it. And you hold your own for a while until you get pulled back in by someone else. Sometimes I feel like I'm losing myself. There have been times when I walk up to the cash register with something someone else planned to buy. Naoya calls that 'getting drunk on someone else's thoughts.'"

He sighed a moment and went on. "I met Naoya right about the time I had finally learned to control my power. That's why I enjoyed going places where there were a lot of people. It's like when you first learn to ride a bike and you want to go everywhere. I would go out, use my power a little, and then rein it back in. It was a lot of fun. I latched onto Naoya while I was doing that."

"How? You said you could hear his voice."

"Yeah, I heard him, but not through my ears."

"What was he saying?"

"He was low on money and feeling desperate."

"Money . . . but two years ago, he was a student, right? What about his family?"

"He left home as soon as he was old enough to quit school, at fifteen. He's been alone ever since. He's looked after himself."

I nodded. I remembered he'd said he didn't have a job right now. He looked badly off. His jeans had holes in them, and his shirt was too light for the season.

"Did he ever tell you why he left home?"

Shinji was suddenly excited and raised his voice. "That's an easy question! Because he was psychic!" He sounded as though he couldn't believe I'd ask such a stupid question. "And his power is so much stronger than mine. He has a lot more trouble keeping it under control. He's got bad luck. At least I've got a relative with the same power. If he had had someone, things would have been easier for him. He's had to deal with everything on his own. His family was a mess, too. His parents got a divorce and fought over everything they owned. It would be hard enough for a regular kid to deal with. It'd be even worse if you were psychic, and you knew what they were thinking. You couldn't put up with it!" Then Shinji seemed to realize how excited he was getting and lowered his voice.

"I get worried, too. What if I ever have problems with my parents?" He looked terribly sad. "I worry about whether I'll be able to get along with anybody."

"You're afraid that you'll be all alone?"

"Yeah. I have a hard time making friends."

I remembered my interview with the female head of the association with the long name and said, "You mean you have to listen to people's true feelings even if you don't want to?"

"That's right."

"But can't you avoid that by controlling your power?"

"Yes, but . . . ," he looked down again. "Think back to when you were my age. What if there were a cute girl, and she kept a diary. If you could read it without anyone knowing, what would you do? Would you refuse to even consider the matter because it would be invading her privacy?"

I laughed. "I'm not that serious-minded."

Shinji laughed, too. "Me neither! If I like someone, it's even harder—I want to know what she's thinking. So I scan her, and then what? Do you think it makes me happier than I was? Or do I just get disappointed?"

"I don't know. I'd imagine, hmmm, I'd think you'd be disappointed more often than not."

Shinji narrowed his eyes. "Sometimes I'm really lucky. Last Christmas, I wanted to give my girlfriend a present. I tried to think of something good, but finally gave up. All I had to do was read what was in her heart, right?"

"So you scanned her?"

"Yeah. I asked her to go skating with me. Not bad, huh? She was cute, but not athletic. So she had to hang onto my arm just to stay on her feet."

"So what did you find out?" Now I was interested.

"She was knitting me a sweater, and she wanted a makeup set just like the one her sister had. I didn't have enough money for the whole set, so I just bought her the lotion and face cream."

"She must have been thrilled."

"She was at first," Shinji lowered his voice. "Yeah, she was for a while, but then her attitude began to change . . . now that I think about it, I was always doing something like that. We'd go to the movies, and we'd have to decide what we were going to see. I'd try to figure out which one she wanted to see; I'd ask her questions. We always went to see the one she wanted to go to."

"That sounds good. I hear girls nowadays like boys who are more considerate." I said it almost without thinking, but Shinji didn't even smile.

"She told me it was creepy."

I tried to keep a straight face.

"She said it made her nervous that it always seemed like I knew what she was thinking." Shinji let out a sigh. "So that was the end of that, and I've avoided girls ever since. I don't want to go through that again, and I know I'd do it all the same way because I'd want to know all about the girl I liked. And she'd leave me, just like the last one did.

"And it's the same with guys. Even some of my teachers avoid me like the plague. I don't mean to do it. I must look like I feel superior to them. Like I've got them all figured out."

I didn't say a word, but I had to agree. I'd seen that expression on his face, too. I saw it when we were at the construction site and he was reading my thoughts.

*You'd be better off not touching me, unless you want me to scan you again.*

No matter who I sided with—whether I believed Naoya or Shinji—I had to admit that if there were such a thing as psychic ability, it would be a terrible burden to bear.

Shinji was a smart kid. He was imaginative. He was definitely convinced he was a psychic. It didn't look like an act. But what if he was just pretending? I'd come full circle, and now I was becoming hopelessly confused. It was almost funny.

"What are you smiling at?" Shinji asked.

I didn't have time to come up with an excuse. "I don't know who to believe."

"That makes sense, I guess." Shinji's head drooped. "But it isn't surprising. Even the experts are so confused by the scam artists that they don't know a real psychic when they see one. Do you remember Yuri Geller?"

"Yes, and he was a scam artist."

"A model scam artist." Shinji almost spat out the words. Then he changed the subject. "So what proof did Naoya give you that I was lying? I told him everything about how I met you and what happened that night. How did he serve it up?"

While I explained, Shinji sat and listened. He kept his eyes down and didn't move a muscle. Not, that is, until I mentioned the April 5 edition of *Arrow*.

"I don't know anything about that. And I never saw any scars on your leg."

"But don't you think that what was in the article and what you guessed were pretty much the same? Almost word for word."

Shinji seemed to be thinking hard. "All it means is that Naoya did everything in his power to come up with some kind of proof."

"But what was in the article and what you said were too close to be accidental. You can't prove you didn't know."

Shinji was agitated now, and rubbed his hands up and down along his thighs. "The only thing I can come up with—"

"Go ahead," I urged him.

"The accident you were in was more than twenty years ago, wasn't it? You must have forgotten the details yourself. But you thought about it this spring, when you spoke to the reporter about it for the April 5 issue, and some of it came back to you."

He was right.

"You spoke with someone about the accident. If you talk about something, you can rebuild your memories. And then you remember them in that new way. The next time you think about what happened, that's what you'll come up with. So when I scanned you, I got the information you gave the reporter. It's not surprising."

I frowned, and Shinji began to look worried.

"Can't you understand?"

"Yeah, I think so." But I still had my suspicions.

"I can't explain it any better," he said, discouraged.

"What about the other details? Like the name sewn into my jacket."

If he hadn't seen it, there would be no other way for Naoya to have known about it.

Shinji looked wounded. "I did see that," he mumbled.

"Hm."

"But that has nothing to do with scanning you and having that name come out!"

So he hadn't been honest, yet he wanted me to believe him.

"I can explain about the hotel clerk and the waitress who came to see him that night. I'm sure they did stand there and chat, but I didn't see them. It's the truth! I only came down when the man was at the front desk alone. I asked him to dry my clothes. I 'read' their conversation when I touched the counter. That's why—"

"I see."

"No, you don't! Listen to me!"

"Enough. You're just confusing me. Tell me one thing."

"What's that?" Shinji's face was red with frustration.

"Why would Naoya go to all the trouble of coming here just to lie to me?"

"Because he's afraid!" Shinji replied without hesitation.

"Of what?"

"He doesn't want anyone to know he's psychic."

I started as I remembered what Naoya had said to me.

*If there were psychics, they'd be scared—and they'd stay hidden away.*

"But why would he bother about you?"

"Same reason. We're friends, but we can't agree on this one point." Shinji curled his hands into fists and placed them on his knees.

"I want to use the power I was born with. I want to use it to help people. Otherwise, what would be the use? I'd always be exhausted for nothing. In other countries, psychics help the police with investigations. Everyone knows it. Japan won't get that far soon, but I want to use any opportunity I can to come forward. But I blew it this time and ended up causing more trouble.

"But Naoya's different. All he can think about is escaping. I can under-stand that. He's had so many terrible things happen to him, all because of his powers. He doesn't have a place to call home, and he can't keep a job, so he never has enough money. When I first met him, he only had change in his pockets. He was trying to figure out what to do with himself. I heard him thinking—about suicide, actually. He was leaning against a shelf in the book-store, and he looked half-dead already."

An image of Naoya, his pale complexion and thin, frail body, passed through my mind.

"He can't keep a job because he scans people too often. Imagine him with a job at a convenience store. One night the receipts don't match the cash in the register. While it's being recounted, everyone stands around nervously, wondering whose fault it was. Naoya doesn't dress well, and he doesn't look healthy either. Nor does he act like he's had much education. He's the first one they all suspect. But nobody actually says anything. They don't say any-thing, but Naoya can hear them anyway. Once that sort of thing happens a few times, he can't take working there anymore. He never gets fired—he just can't deal with the place and quits. It happens over and over."

"So why doesn't he just stop scanning?"

"You'd think he would, but it's harder than you'd think. It's harder for him than it is for me. His power is a lot stronger than mine, and, like I said before, he doesn't have anyone to support him the way I do. And he's never had any-one to teach him how to control his power, so his power has control over him."

I remembered the way Shinji had used the word "open."

"I can't imagine what he goes through," Shinji continued. "Every single day must be hell for him. I want to help him any way I can, but there's not really much I can do."

He paused and thought a few moments before he went on. "He told me that he 'bought' a woman once."

I grimaced. Not because prostitution shocked me, but because I figured out what came next.

"See?" Shinji said, noticing my expression. "It's horrifying to even think about. He laughed when he told me about it, but his eyes were dark. The whole time they were doing it, the woman was thinking about how awful it was."

He was quiet again for a little bit. "He had to give up partway through. He told me he'd die of sexual frustration if nothing else."

I tried to think of something positive to say, but nothing came to mind.

"He told me I'd better prepare myself. Intimate moments were when people were most honest. He said it wasn't all fun and games."

"I guess not." I wondered if either of them would ever get married and settle down. They say ignorance is bliss, and it's true that we're able to muddle through life because we don't try to understand everything.

"He'll never have a love life. I won't either. But Naoya's not strong enough for some things—he can't bring himself to use his power to commit crimes. He's really very gentle, but I'm worried about him!" Shinji raised his voice. "He won't be able to last much longer at this rate. He's 'open' too often. It weakens him, and that makes it even harder to control his power. He needs help, but he's too scared and exhausted to come forward. He can't show his power to anyone. I want to help him—but he ruins every opportunity."

Shinji's hands shook. He put one hand up to his head and closed his eyes. "It's all so hard. I don't know what to do anymore." He was quiet, but his breath was ragged.

"Are you all right?" I ventured, but he didn't say anything for a while.

"Yeah," he finally managed, "I'm okay."

"Have you tried a public agency of some sort?"

Shinji nodded. "But where? I've heard rumors that the Self-Defense Agency is doing experiments. But I wouldn't want the two of us to be treated like secret weapons."

"You know the mass media won't do right by you."

"No, of course not. That's why I'm at a dead end."

I'd heard the whole story now. The only thing left was to decide whether I believed the stooped, worn-out boy in front of me.

"Let me think some," I said. Shinji looked up at me with his bloodshot eyes, blinking a few times. "I'll see what I can do. Just . . . just do me a favor, and calm down."

"All right." Shinji slowly stood up. He seemed strong enough to leave under his own steam.

"And stop worrying about Daisuke Mochizuki and that manhole. You've done what you can. Promise?"

"I promise." He moved to the door and mumbled, "Probably seventy-thirty, huh?"

"What?"

"You're leaning about seventy percent toward not believing me."

He was pretty close, but I was too tired to keep talking about it. "Listen," I said, putting a hand on his shoulder and trying to sound as nice as possible. "Let's just leave it at that for now. Okay?"

The sad little head nodded. He left the room and walked over to Kanako at her reception desk. "I'm sorry about the other day . . ."

Kanako looked surprised, but automatically responded with, "Don't worry, it's all right."

I put Shinji into a taxi and made him promise to call to let me know he'd made it home safely. When I got back to the office, the editor in chief was there to greet me.

"You're early today," I said.

"It's hard to sleep when my wife and daughter are discussing how much life insurance they should take out on me. They're not sure how long I'll last, since I never get any sleep."

"Not too conducive to relaxation, eh?"

"Laugh all you like, you're still single." He nodded in Kanako's direction. "She told me you've been counseling young men."

"Sorry about that."

"Don't worry. But you've got to tell me about anything that comes of it. Has something happened?"

I didn't respond immediately, so he clapped me on the back. "Forget about it until you've got something. Whatever it's about, it seems to be taking a toll on you."

"You can tell?"

"Your hair's going gray."

I went to the men's room to check, but it wasn't true. The old man had a droll sense of humor.

He laughed when I came out.

Shinji called about forty minutes later. When I asked if I should talk to his parents, he said, "Don't worry about that. They understand. Thanks for the taxi voucher. It made me feel like I was moving up in the world!"

"I didn't pay for it, so don't worry about that."

"That nice lady said something about taking the day off for something. Does that mean you can rest?"

"That's right."

"If all goes according to plan, you might hear some Bach tonight."

"Bach? As in classical music?"

"That's right. She'll say it was swollen molars and she doesn't want to go alone, but it will be a lie. She bought two tickets to start out with. Suntory Hall." Then he hung up.

I went around to a few bookstores during the morning and bought all the books I could find on extrasensory perception. I was surprised by how many there were. Even while I was having meetings and getting ready to start on our next feature story, half of my brain was still preoccupied with Shinji. I was done with work about four, so I took all the books into the conference room and started reading.

One was written by Colin Wilson, author of *The Outsider*. It turns out he was also an authority on the subject of ESP, and he made scientific inquiries into the matter.

On the other hand, there were books that explained in detail how all so-called psychic activity was done using tricks. These books were convincing, too. There were even illustrations to show how it all worked.

I went to get two teaspoons from the break room and tried to concentrate on making them bend. How could this have been so appealing to young people? There was a knock on the door, and Kanako poked her head in.

"Mind if I come in?"

"Be my guest," I replied.

"What are you up to?"

"I'm just . . ." I had to admit it was too embarrassing to talk about. "I'm just doing a little research."

Kanako came over to the table and started reading the titles of the books. "ESP? What's your interest in all this?"

"Well, excuse me!"

"Bending spoons? If you fling it over your shoulder, it'll bend. It was popular a long time ago."

There was no way Kanako could remember anything that was popular in 1979. She must have heard about it somewhere.

"Does it really work that way?"

"Sure. Give me a spoon." Kanako pulled a spoon out of my hand, gave a cry, and pitched it. It fell on the floor with a loud clang. She hurried over to pick it up. "See? It's bent!"

Sure enough, it was just a little more warped than the other one.

"If you threw anything with that much power, it's bound to bend," I frowned.

"Of course!" Kanako laughed. "But I wonder why people always think of bending spoons when they think of ESP. A bent spoon doesn't prove anything."

She was right. If you read the instructions, you could learn how to do sleight-of-hand tricks. That wasn't the problem.

"It's easy, it makes an impression, and it's easy for people to understand, I guess."

"That's all? You might as well use a bicycle spoke. If I really had ESP, I'd bend something that meant something."

"Go right ahead. Bend anything you like. How about the new city hall buildings in Shinjuku? Now that would make an impression!"

"That would be a good trick for King Kong," Kanako laughed. "If I were going to twist something, it would be your bad mood. One little bend might get it back in shape."

"Bend the chief's ulcer out of his stomach, then."

"Yuck!"

She was awfully cheery. I tossed the spoon back on the table and looked up at her.

"What?" I asked.

"What do you mean, what?" she replied.

"Why did you come in here?"

"Oh yes, well, uh . . ." All of a sudden she turned serious, and I got a bad feeling.

"Another one of those letters?"

"Hmmm? No, that's not it." She put her hands behind her back, shrugged, and began to walk about as if she was totally unconcerned about anything.

"So, do you have anything to do tonight?" she began. "I've got tickets to a concert. Two of them."

My heart stopped. *If all goes according to plan, you might hear some Bach tonight.*

"I was going to go with a friend, but she cancelled on me at the last minute, and I don't want to go alone. You're the only one in the office who seems like he might like classical music."

She sounded casual, but she was talking twice as fast as usual. The photographer had been right. She really was sweet.

"So what do you think? They're good seats. It's a nice hall."

"Where?"

"Suntory Hall."

My heart leaped into my throat.

"Is something the matter?" She looked worried. "You've got a scary look on your face."

"Sorry," I answered. I avoided looking at her directly and answered hurriedly, "I can't go tonight. I've got plans."

"All right, then," she answered quietly. "I'll see if anyone else is free."

*She bought two tickets to start out with.*

"Kanako," I called her name and she stopped and turned around.

"Hmm?"

"Why couldn't your friend go tonight?"

I had caught her off guard. She *was* awfully young. I could almost see her lining up several excuses and trying to pick one.

I couldn't help myself. "Was it swollen molars?"

Kanako's eyes opened wide and she stood straight up. "That's right. How'd you know?" Without waiting, she opened the door, said, "You're just mean!"

and then slammed it behind her. I could hear her quick footsteps heading in the opposite direction.

So you could just hurt people's feelings anytime you liked.

*She said it made her nervous that it always seemed like I knew what she was thinking.*

# 4

I needed to talk to an expert, but where could I find one? It wasn't the same as looking for a scholar on nuclear energy, sales taxes, or the Constitution. If I needed information on nuclear energy, I could count on getting the same basic information from experts, whether they were for or against it.

ESP, though, was something that people could not agree on. Experts and scholars and researchers were all divided. I didn't know how far I should believe those who said it existed, or how much data against it I should take seriously. The more I read, the more confused I got.

At any rate, I decided to make a list of the authors and translators of the books I had and put check marks against the ones I thought I might be able to meet and talk to. By now the books were full of post-its and folded pages. I put them all in a cardboard box, went back to my desk, and sat down at my desk.

"All done studying?" asked Goro Ikoma, the editor whose desk was next to mine. He was the only one left in the office. Some of the overhead lights had already been turned off. "You sure are interested in whatever it is," he continued, working out the kinks in his back as he spoke.

He looked like a bear, a huge man unable to buy clothes off the rack. He was in the habit of saying that he was worth his weight in gold, but he was well known as a chain smoker, and his wife would usually respond that he was worth his weight in tar and nicotine. He sat with a cigarette between his yellowed fingers. An ashtray that was dangerously full was balanced on a pile of files at the edge of his desk.

I could see that the whole thing might fall into my lap as soon as I took my chair, so I picked up the ashtray and tossed its contents into the wastebasket before sitting down.

Ikoma grinned. "It's good to have a neatnik nearby."

"You must have a death wish," I retorted.

"Not at all. My father was a good man who never touched cigarettes or alcohol, and he died young of liver cancer. I always imagine how he must have regretted never having any fun. I consider every cigarette I smoke a stick of incense burned in honor of his memory."

"I see you've got your arguments all thought out!" I laughed as I reached for my own pack.

"You try marrying a woman who used to be on her college debate team. You've got to wear a suit of verbal armor just to eat a meal in peace. So, you giving up on your effort to quit?"

"Let's just call it a temporary ceasefire."

"You might as well surrender. You can't quit as long as you're sitting next to me." He gave a full-throated laugh, stubbed out the cigarette in his hand, and reached for a new one.

I heard that Ikoma had finally managed to buy a house for his family, and rumor had it that his wife refused to sacrifice the wallpaper to his filthy habit, sending him outside to smoke. Either he spent all his time outside or his wife had given up by now.

"What are you up to?" I asked.

Ikoma had a weekly magazine spread out on his desk. He flipped it shut to show me the cover. It was one of the more conservative rags.

"They're doing a feature on cosmetic surgery. There are a lot of scary stories, but all of them are thrilling. I'm going to take it home to show Yumiko."

Yumiko was his eldest daughter. She must be about sixteen at this point.

"She wants to get a nose job. I keep saying her nose will take care of itself by the time she's a little older, but she refuses to listen."

I'd been over to his house a few times, and I recalled his daughter as taking after her pretty mother. She'd grow up to be a beautiful woman.

"Tell her she doesn't need it."

"Kids that age never listen to their parents."

"Then tell her it won't last because her bones are still developing."

"I've tried. She just says that it means she'll be miserable her entire youth.

She tells me that since I don't have any fun, it means she'll never have fun when she grows up either. I ask her who she thinks is going to take care of her when I'm not around, and she says, 'Hey, we'll have your life insurance.'"

"It's just a phase."

"Well, I got back at her by telling her I get fun, all right—by sneaking peeks of her in the bath. Now she locks the door and I hear her scream whenever I start down the hall to the toilet. What's wrong with girls anyway?"

I had to laugh just thinking about it.

"It's no laughing matter!" Ikoma frowned, but his eyes were laughing. I knew he was a family man at heart who doted on both his wife and daughter. "Well, it was good to get a smile out of you," he said, leaning back and sticking his big feet out in front of him. "These last few days, you look like a guy who's been seeing his dentist regularly—like you've just had all your back teeth pulled. Or is it kidney stones?"

"Not likely," I said, leaning back and folding my hands behind my head. "But to tell the truth, I've been having problems."

"It's finally coming out! What's the matter?" Ikoma's face went serious. He was forty-seven and a veteran of all sorts of book and magazine publishers. He probably couldn't even remember some of them—but he had been around and knew the trade. I quickly decided that if I could confide in anyone, it would be him.

I had no intention of working the situation into an article, and that was why I'd avoided talking to my colleagues about it. I knew they'd be quick to tell me I should use the story somehow. I decided I could count on Ikoma to keep quiet. I took another look around to make sure no one was left in the office.

Ikoma was already intrigued. "So it's something you don't want anyone else to know about?"

"If possible," I replied. "Some of the others would jump on it if word got out." I started at the beginning and told him everything. I even described what had happened with Kanako that evening.

Ikoma went through ten cigarettes in the course of the story. As I wrapped up, he stubbed out the last one and grabbed another, but refrained from lighting it. He put his big hands flat out on the table, exhaling as he spoke. "That's heavy stuff."

"So you see what I'm up against. I don't know what to do."

"Kids are always so serious. Even when they're playing around—it's impossible to figure it out."

"But I don't think he's playing with me. Why go to the trouble?"

"On the contrary, he's enjoying the effect of all the tricks and turns he's put into it. He's having a great time."

I raised my eyebrows. "So you don't think he's for real?"

"I don't think so," Ikoma nodded. "I'd be more inclined to believe what Naoya Oda said. His story makes more sense."

"How do you explain the concert ticket?"

Ikoma shrugged. "Weren't the two of them here alone when she called to wake you up? He must have seen her tickets. Maybe he even heard her practicing what she was going to say to you. She's not very good at hiding her feelings. It's like she's wearing a sign that says she's got her sights on you. You must have figured that out."

I nodded. "I knew something strange was going on."

Ikoma sat up and leaned back in his chair. "How should I put it? She's not actually in love with you. She's in love with an illusion in her head. She's probably got a friend who just married a man a lot older than her. She'll snap out of it before too long."

He snorted out a laugh as he thought of the possibilities. "Now if it were some of the younger guys, they wouldn't let the opportunity pass, and I'd take her aside and warn her about the evils of men. I'd make sure she knew that she'd be the one to suffer any consequences. But I know you wouldn't take advantage of her. Despite the fact that you've had some unfortunate experiences with women . . ."

"I haven't got the energy," I said.

Ikoma bellowed with laughter. "I wouldn't know about that! But I know you're too nice—even my wife says so. She says it's because you've had your heart broken."

Ikoma was one of the few people who knew what had gone on between Saeko Soma and me. He and I often worked on projects together, and one night when we'd gone out for a few drinks after work—at the third or fourth bar we visited that night—he asked me.

*I've been hearing rumors, but I don't put stock in hearsay. And I don't really care why you got transferred to* Arrow. *But I just thought I'd ask you out-right . . . Are the rumors true, or was it all just a coincidence?*

I told him the truth, and he'd listened in silence. When I was done, he had merely said, *All right. I won't mention it again.* This was the first time he'd brought it up since then.

"Just so you know," he said, "I'm not talking about the past, I'm talking about this boy. Let's look at the facts again. The details wouldn't be difficult for him to work out. Kids can put a lot of energy into things once they put their minds to it."

"So Shinji is a scam artist." I looked up at the ceiling. I could see the shapes of insects that had got trapped and died in the fluorescent lights. "He's a problem child."

"But you don't want to believe that, right?"

It was my turn to laugh. "I don't."

"I understand that. But if you don't put a stop to it, he's the one who'll suffer for it all. I have to tell myself the same thing. I've had a similar experience."

When I looked surprised, he nodded. "It's not something I like to talk about. It's a blot on my record." Then he began to tell me about an incident that happened in 1974, right in the middle of the ESP boom.

"The magazine I was working for was in direct competition with *Asahi Weekly*. We operated under the policy that we would go ahead and assume the validity of the youth busily bending spoons. But it all turned out to have been an act. A good one—we all bought into it and didn't work too hard trying to pin down the facts. Meanwhile, *Asahi* was hard at work on discrediting the whole story, and the bottom began to fall through.

"Then one day, the editor in chief called us in. He told us we couldn't just let the kids get away with what they'd done to us. He suggested we let them tell their own stories."

"Tell their own stories?"

"Right, have them tell the world how they'd been fooling us all along."

"So you made them admit their lies?"

"That's right." Ikoma's face clouded over. "We should have just left them alone. We should have told them the game was up, and they weren't selling issues for us anymore—just waved goodbye. *Asahi* didn't have any problems because they had denied the whole business from the start. But not us; we'd taken the kids' side. Then one day, we flipped on them and put them on the chopping block. There were the headlines: *The Perfect Scam! Even Our Editors Fell For It!* It makes me want to puke when I think of it now." He reached out for another cigarette.

"What happened next?" I asked.

Ikoma blew out a stream of smoke before he responded. "There was a death."

"One of the kids?"

"Yup. He jumped off the roof of his school. It was the same as if we'd put a ladder up against the wall and cleared the way for him to climb to the top, then pulled it out from under him. He was only ten. I don't want anything like that to happen again. For a while I even thought about suicide. What kind of job is that when you drive a child to kill himself?"

The fluorescent light on the ceiling blinked. It was on the verge of going out.

"And here I am now, still at the same job." He laughed sadly. "But we can't let the same thing happen again. There's no such thing as psychics or ESP. It's something adults would like to believe in. When adults have a dream, children can help us achieve it with a little bit of mischief. They know what they're doing. What they don't understand is what will happen when the dream wears off."

Ikoma raised his eyes and looked straight at me.

"Save Shinji from himself. Get him out of this—this nightmare of a dream. It won't be easy, but you've got to do it. Fate has brought you together, and he's depending on you."

I looked away, over at the overflowing ashtray with a thread of blue smoke rising still.

"I'm an atheist," Ikoma went on, "but there are times when it feels like there's a reason for everything. So, what I want you to know is that, no matter how difficult it is, the burdens we have to bear are usually no greater than our ability to bear them. Right now Shinji's future is your burden to bear."

"But what should I do?" I asked. "I've been sucked into the whole thing and can't even figure out which way to move."

"It's like I said. Don't get bogged down by what you can see right in front of your nose. Start digging. A sixteen-year-old boy has a history of sixteen years. If he's a psychic, he'll have a history to prove it. You can't change history by scamming. Investigate—talk to people who know him. His family and friends, his teachers. Go back to Naoya and ask questions. He might be the one with the key to all this."

Ikoma jabbed his own chest with his thumb. "And you can count on me if you need help. I've been through this before, and I know a few people." He added a few more words about the need to pull myself together and then said, "If you look into his background, and you still think he might be a psychic—or rather, you're convinced he is one—and you've got the evidence to back you up, I'll quit smoking on the spot!" He smiled "What do you say?"

I folded my arms and nodded. "It's a deal!"

PART 3
# The Past

Naoya had told me he worked at a gas station. It was tucked away in a corner of an area on the eastern edge of Tokyo that was occupied largely by high-rise condominiums and public housing developments.

By the time I found the place, though, Naoya wasn't there anymore. He'd quit.

A small, middle-aged man was in charge. He wore a uniform with a matching billed cap, and I chatted with him as he hosed down cars as they came out of the carwash machine.

"He was a good worker," he said as soon as I asked for Naoya. "I wonder what went wrong."

"When did he quit?"

The man frowned as he tried to remember. "About a week ago."

That was when he had come to see me. Was he trying to keep me off his trail? "Did he say why?" I asked.

"I wish I knew. He said it was 'circumstances beyond his control.' You ever hear a kid that age use a phrase like that?"

"Did he say where he'd be working next?"

"Not a word."

Of course. "How long was he here?"

"Not very long. Maybe three months."

"Do you have an address or a phone number for him?"

"Yeah, but," he looked at me sideways, "what brings you here anyway?"

"Circumstances beyond my control."

The man had the courtesy to laugh. He lifted the cap off his head and readjusted it. "I know what you mean, seems like everything's beyond my control these days. I'll give you what I have on him. It's in the office."

I used a corner of a cluttered desk to copy the information from Naoya's job application. The man stood next to me with his hands on his hips and his foot tapping impatiently. It was a single page long and Naoya had filled it in in small, almost illegible characters. He hadn't even attempted to fix his spelling errors.

He had left the "hobbies" column blank and listed his health as "good." There were no names of "other family members."

"Have you ever tried to reach him at this address?" I asked.

The man shook his head. "He was never late or absent. He was a good worker—I never needed to. Why?"

I tapped the paper with my finger. "The telephone area code doesn't match the address."

"You don't say." The man picked up the paper and gave it a good look. He squinted and then held it out at a distance. "I'm getting farsighted," he offered as an excuse. "I don't ask for guarantors anymore. I couldn't get anyone to work for me if I did."

"But isn't it unusual for an employee to hide his identity?" I followed up. "What sort of young man was he?"

"It's hard to say . . ."

"But you said he was a good worker."

"That's right. He wasn't lazy or anything, but he wasn't real pleasant either."

"Was there anyone who worked here that he was close to?"

The man thought a few moments. "I suppose he got on all right with Asako."

"A girl?"

"Yeah, she brightens the place up. She works part time, too."

"Could I talk to her?"

"She has the late shift; won't be in until evening. Come back about six. I'll tell her to expect you."

I thanked the man and turned to leave, when he quickly added, "Is Naoya in trouble?"

"No, it's nothing like that."

"Well, all right then . . ." The man frowned as if he was thinking. I waited for him to say something, and watched his face go almost comically serious.

"He was a strange guy. There were times when I wondered if he was up to something dangerous."

"Such as?"

He put his hand to his cap again. "I've got a son in high school. He doesn't have a brain in his head, and he spends more of his time out on the street than at school. Sometimes he comes around here to extort a little money—at his own father's workplace. I don't know how he got that way."

He got that way because he knows he can walk all over his dad, I thought.

"He came by one time when Naoya was here," the man continued. "As soon as he left, all of a sudden Naoya says to me, 'You should get him off the paint thinner.' That was a shock!"

"Your son's on thinner?"

The man looked down. "It's the kids he hangs out with. I suspected it."

"You *should* make him stop."

"I know, I know. But it's not that easy. He's bigger than me now, and . . . well, it doesn't really matter." He was starting to sound angry. "Most people wouldn't be able to tell if someone was on thinner just by looking at him. It made me think Naoya had done something like it himself. Takes one to know one, you know? He might be even worse off than my son; he always looked kind of sickly. My son looks a lot better than that. How could he tell?"

*You can't change history by scamming.* That's what Ikoma had said.

"Maybe he could smell it. Maybe your son looked high," I suggested.

The man looked at me as if I'd hurt his feelings and shook his head.

"No way. If there was anything wrong with him, I'd be the first to know. I just would."

It was already eleven by the time I got to work. The editors were in a meeting in the conference room, so I had the office to myself.

Kanako wasn't there, and there was a mountain of unsorted mail on her desk. Her lap blanket was neatly folded and hung on the back of her chair. Maybe she was taking a break.

I picked up the mail and carried it over to my desk. Just as I was about to start going through it, Ikoma called me. Startled, I looked around and saw that he was seated at the one computer we had; it was set up over by a window. He had a cigarette dangling from his mouth as he waved me over.

"What did you learn?" he asked.

"He's gone."

"Who?"

"Naoya. He quit his job. Vanished completely."

"What's it mean?"

"I'd like to know the answer to that. What are you doing?"

"A little high-tech work. Putting all those computer seminars to use." He jabbed at the screen with his big finger. "I'm checking out all the newspaper articles on ESP since 1974. I'll print them out for you. Then you can look through the magazines and find out who the frequent contributors are. Look up a few of them and ask them some questions."

"Thanks. But didn't you say you knew of an expert or two?"

"Yeah, but then I remembered something." He scratched his chin and cigarette ashes flew over the keyboard.

"There was one guy from the ESP boom. He helped the cops solve a case. I never met him myself, but I read about him—I'm pretty sure it was in the newspaper. But I can't remember when or where I saw it. I thought about it last night while my wife was gabbing about something, but I can't remember. I don't keep scrapbooks, but I'm sure it was a Tokyo newspaper. It's got to be here somewhere. You interested?"

"Very." I stood next to Ikoma and watched the green light on the modem blink. I realized I had no idea how it actually worked. Yet I never doubted its reality. Perhaps, like computers, ESP was simply beyond the reach of my understanding.

"And there we have it!" Ikoma pressed a button to put the noisy printer into action. I went over to a phone on the other side of the office and made a call to the ward where Naoya's résumé claimed he lived, and asked about the address. The block he gave didn't exist. I hung up and then called the phone number on the résumé.

The number began to ring. So it belonged to someone. It continued to ring, ten, fifteen times. I hung up after twenty.

The phone company refused to give out addresses connected to phone numbers, so I'd just have to keep calling every once in a while till someone picked up. It might be faster to talk to Shinji.

I decided it was time to go see Shinji's parents. At this time of day, all good high-school students were bound to be in class taking notes. I called his number, and a woman picked up after just two rings. I gave her my name, and there was a pause.

"I know this is sudden," I said, "but I'm sure Shinji told you about me."

"Yes, yes, we've heard," she said hastily. "I'm Shinji's mother. Thank you for helping him out—"

I told her I had something I wanted to talk to her about, and she quickly turned the phone over to Shinji's father. I recognized his voice as the one I heard in the hotel the night of the typhoon. According to Shinji, his father knew he was psychic.

"Your son told me an amazing story," I began, "and after that—"

Shinji's father cut me off. "Do you mean that he told you that he wasn't, er, normal?"

"Not normal?" I heard a little buzz come on the line. I looked up and saw that Ikoma had picked up an extension and was listening in.

"What exactly did Shinji tell you?" his father asked.

"He can, uh . . ."

"Read other people's thoughts?"

The receiver still to my ear, I looked over at Ikoma, who nodded.

"Yes, that's what he said. Shinji told me that he knows what people are thinking—and can pick up on thoughts left behind on inanimate items. A table or a chair that someone touched . . ."

"I see."

"He seemed terribly upset by it all."

"And that's why you're calling us?"

"Yes. If possible, I'd like to talk with you in person."

After a few moments, Shinji's father responded. "I understand. We'll do what we can. We knew this sort of thing would happen someday."

We set up a time and date, but before we hung up, Shinji's father said, "There was some noise on the line before. What was that?"

I could hardly tell him it was the heavy breathing of my colleague, so I said, "A printer in the background."

"That's the way it usually happens," Ikoma said after he had hung up. "Even the parents get taken in. Just because they live together doesn't mean they understand their son's pranks."

"You seem awfully excited about it all," I noted.

"It's just like the last time with all the spoon bending."

Just then there was another voice. "Who's snuck off with my work?" Kanako was back. She stood next to the pile of mail on my desk, her hands on her hips.

"Kanako!" said Ikoma, laughing. "Don't get angry, now. I thought you had taken a day off, and I just thought I'd help." He started to divide up the mail, and Kanako looked even more put out.

"Hmph!" she sniffed and reached for the bundle, effectively pushing Ikoma out of the way.

As she bustled off to her desk, Ikoma came back over to me, his face suddenly serious. "Good thing for you I found this before she did. Don't let her see it."

He put an envelope on my desk. The handwriting was the same as on the other envelopes.

"How many does this make?" he asked.

"Seven." Just as before, there was no return address, and there was a single piece of paper inside. "But . . ."

"What?"

I handed the sheet to Ikoma. This time it wasn't blank. On it was a single word.

*Revenge.*

# 2

The Inamuras' coffee shop was on the first floor of a white-walled building facing the main road. Next to the partially opened door was a blackboard bearing a Coca-Cola logo. It listed the three menu items available for lunch as well as the coffee of the day—Kilimanjaro.

It was already two p.m., well after the usual lunch hour, but the shop was still full. The instant I opened the door, all heads turned around to look at me. It was faintly alarming.

"Mr. Kosaka?" The greeting came from a middle-aged man on the other side of the counter. He wore a red apron that also bore the Coca-Cola logo. "I'm Shinji's father, and this is my wife," he indicated a small, worried-looking woman on the other side of a bank of coffee siphons for making individual cups of coffee.

"Nice to meet you both," I said in a low tone. "If you're busy right now, I'll come back later."

"Oh no, now is fine," said Shinji's father, moving over to me. The customers must have noticed his slumped shoulders and the way he kept bowing to me. I probably looked like a small-time extortionist.

"Something wrong over there?" a man called out from one of the tables.

"No no, it's fine," Mr. Inamura reassured them.

"Something about Shinji?" the man continued, although in a softer voice.

"It's fine, really," Inamura put on a smile. He lightly took my elbow and whispered. "Why don't we go outside?" He asked his wife to take over for a few minutes and guided me out the door.

"Sorry about all of that," he said as he patted his broad forehead with a towel. I could see customers sitting at window tables staring at me.

"Stop apologizing," I begged. "They'll all think I'm coming to shake you down."

"What? Oh. Right." I finally got a real smile out of him, and he stretched his back and straightened up. "I knew you were coming, and I was ready, but I guess I'm still a little nervous."

Ikoma had warned me that parents were taken in by their own kids. That was probably true in this case. There was nothing insincere or calculated about Shinji's father.

"My name is Norio Inamura. Nice to meet you."

The weather was fine, so we decided to walk and strolled down the main street. Just beyond it was the tall, sloping bank of the Arakawa River drenched in the warm autumn sun. We climbed up the bank and then walked along with the river on our right and the town on our left.

"This was where I taught Shinji how to ride a bicycle."

"It's a nice area. Have you always lived here?"

"No, we moved here when we set up shop."

I thought I'd seen the place on TV, and Inamura told me that it was the actual location used for a TV series.

"Shinji came to watch them tape it. He had a crush on one of the actresses."

"He told me he used to have a girlfriend," I suddenly remembered.

"I think it was one of his classmates. My wife and I never met her. I probably took a couple of calls from her. Imagine, a girl calling a boy! I'm not sure what that says about Shinji either."

"You've got a well-mannered, thoughtful young man for a son."

Inamura scratched the top of his head and looked down at his shoes.

"What did you want to talk about?"

"Did Shinji tell you anything that happened the night of the storm?"

"He told me that you helped him out, that's all. My wife and I wanted to visit you and personally thank you, but Shinji was dead set against it. He never said why."

It made sense, I thought.

"Well then, let's talk about it. But first you've got to promise me that you won't mention that we've spoken unless Shinji says something first. Please don't scold him for anything I'm about to tell you."

Inamura nodded in agreement. "Of course. There's not much you could tell us about Shinji that would shock either one of us."

As we walked along the long riverbank, he listened in silence while I told him about the night of the typhoon.

When I began speaking I could see a bridge off in the distance. By the time I was finished, we had arrived at its approach. Vehicle traffic interrupted the bucolic pedestrian path, and we stopped and waited for the light to change, watching the cars zip by. After we crossed the road and were back on the path, Inamura spoke.

"I see. It explains why he's been so down these days."

"He looked exhausted when he came to see me yesterday. I was sure you must be concerned, too."

"I appreciate your coming." He bowed again and wiped his forehead.

"Shinji told me that you know about his, uh, powers. He mentioned an aunt with similar capabilities."

"Yes, that's right. My father's youngest sister. She's Shinji's great-aunt. She passed away a few years ago."

"He said that you took him to meet her when he told you that he was a psychic."

"Yes, I did. I believed in her, and I knew how much she had suffered." Inamura stopped, felt the cool autumn breeze come off the water, and looked over at the river.

"Mr. Inamura," I began, "I have to admit that I don't believe in Shinji's powers. Not yet, at least. It's not the sort of thing you can take at face value."

"I know that."

"Naoya was convincing when he explained to me how Shinji fooled me. You do know about Naoya Oda, don't you?"

"We've never met him." Inamura shook his head sadly. "Shinji told me how glad he had been to find someone like him. It was quite a surprise."

"Did you ever ask him to bring Naoya home to meet you?"

"Lots of times, but he never came. Shinji told me Naoya didn't like that sort of thing. It made sense, actually. It's not easy to meet new people. Especially when you're going to understand what they're thinking. Even if my wife and I had no intention of hurting Naoya, we can't stop ourselves from thinking all sorts of things. We'd be worried, for instance, about the influence he'd have on Shinji and whether it wouldn't be better to keep them apart. It wouldn't be pleasant for Naoya to hear."

I looked up at the sky and into the brilliant sun and said, "So you believe both of them?"

"It's not a matter of believing or not believing," Inamura said slowly. "For us it's just the way things are." I looked over at him, and he had a faint smile on his face. "Shinji's our son. His problems are our problems. I've watched him do things that didn't make any sense—I don't know how many times. The days are long past where it was a matter of believing or not. Plus I knew about my aunt even before Shinji was born."

"What sort of person was she?"

Inamura thought for a few moments. "I felt sorry for her. Her life couldn't have been happy. But she was strong—tough as steel. That's how she managed to survive so long."

I thought about how he used that word—*survive*.

"She was a beautiful woman," he went on. "She had more marriage offers than my grandparents could count. My grandfather owned a large lumber wholesale business. According to my father, the family had an old storehouse on the property that was opened once a year to air it out. There were old swords and suits of armor. He told me there were even some old kimono packed away in heavy trunks. He said he got in trouble dragging some of the things out and playing with them in the yard.

"They lost everything during the war. When it was finally over, my father was put in charge of the family business, and he wasn't much of a business-man. I doubt whether things would have been different even if the world had stayed at peace—wait a minute, we were talking about my aunt, right?"

"You said she was beautiful."

"That's right. She got married long before the war started, and her family evacuated the area to escape the air raids. Word has it that she predicted that the relatives left behind in Tokyo would be killed on the night of the Allied blitz. Her mother-in-law refused to believe her at first, but when they all moved back to Tokyo, she was able to locate the remains of loved ones buried in the ruins. After that, the groom's family was unable to handle having her around, and they sent her back to her parents in 1946, the spring after the war ended.

She had three children, but the family didn't even give her a chance. I think she was in her late thirties by then. I was six or seven, just about the age when children begin to get curious about what the adults are talking about."

"So the family sent her back because she was psychic?"

"I guess so. They couldn't have a bride who had creepy powers like that. Her grandfather was outraged. In those days, it was a grave dishonor to have a daughter sent back from her marriage home." Inamura tugged at the edge of the apron he was wearing when he left the coffee shop. "My grandfather was a scary guy, but my aunt was just as tough. She let him know that she hadn't asked to be born like that.

*I didn't ask to be born like this!* Shinji had said pretty much the same thing.

"She was a beautiful woman, and I'm sure that couldn't have sat well with her mother-in-law. I imagine the ESP was just a good excuse to get rid of her. Years later, my aunt told us the whole story. She said she first became aware that she was different when she was fourteen or fifteen. But it wasn't easy for women back then. They depended on men for the food they ate and the bed they slept on. She kept everything to herself. It was only after the city was bombed—when it was a matter of life and death—that she spoke up.

"I remember it all. After her husband's family asked her to leave, she went into a back room and sobbed for hours. She was gone soon after. I didn't see her again for years. Not until she was almost sixty and I had a family of my own. My wife was pregnant with Shinji, so this must have been about sixteen years ago."

They had run into each other at Tokyo Station.

"I was heading for the bus stop when I heard someone calling me by my childhood nickname. I turned around and there she was. I recognized her right away. But she had aged.

"Then she smiled. She said she hadn't been sure whether she should say anything. We went to a nearby coffee shop, and even before I had a chance to open my mouth, she said, 'You're married now, and you're going into business! You're much better at that sort of thing than your father, so you'll do well.'" Inamura smiled. "Of course that wouldn't tell you anything, but I had just quit working for a coffee bean wholesaler and was trying to decide whether or not to open a shop of my own."

"The shop you've got now?"

"Right. I was astonished. But then I remembered the old days, and I asked her if she still had the same powers. She laughed and said, 'Of course! It's my calling in life.' Then she told me my wife's name and that she was pregnant. She even knew that the baby was in the breech position. My wife worried about it all the time, and Shinji ended up being delivered by cesarean section." Inamura sighed.

"I'm sure you're confused. But she also said something else. She told me not to borrow money from a man named Ishimori. She said there'd be strings attached, and I'd regret it later. 'Borrow from a bank even if you don't think you'll be able to make the payments now.' She said it was why she'd finally decided to call out to me at the station. She wanted me to know that. Ishimori was a man I knew. He had told me he'd finance me if I wanted to start my own business. I'd been thinking about that as I walked to the bus stop that day."

"So, what did you do?" I had to ask.

"I turned Ishimori down, and it was the right decision." Inamura told me that after their chance meeting he began to meet his aunt for coffee from time to time, but she refused all his invitations to his home. But she did come to the hospital to see Shinji after he was born. He also mentioned that he never knew how she made her living, but she had stayed single.

"As soon as Shinji told us about his power, I contacted my aunt. I didn't even tell my wife at first. My aunt said, 'It's too bad, but there's nothing you can do. The Inamura family gets one of these every few generations. I'm sure your father knew something about it. He's the eldest son. He's got to have heard about it from other relatives. I remember he was angry when my husband divorced me, but he didn't seem too surprised.'"

So it was inherited, I thought to myself. It was like hemophilia, a latent characteristic that is always present in a bloodline. It manifests itself in the right combination of genes. I remembered reading an article about this sort of thing.

"My aunt was an uneducated woman, but she taught Shinji how to live and take care of himself. She did a good job." Inamura rubbed the top of his thinning head and shrugged his rounded shoulders.

"She died late one night, somewhere around three a.m., in February. It was sudden. Her heart stopped, and she died in her sleep."

"Who found her?"

"Shinji. He knew."

"He felt it?"

"Probably. She lived in Koenji, and so did we. Shinji woke me up in the middle of the night. I asked him what was the matter, and he said, 'I saw it, I saw it,' and started crying. We went to check up on her, and it was—just like he said."

I remembered how Ikoma told me it was impossible to dress up the past. What was I supposed to think about this then?

"After the funeral, he told me she hadn't suffered. You can laugh if you like, but it was a great comfort to me."

I was quiet. I had to be careful of what I said.

"So that ends my long story," Inamura went on. "I believed Shinji because of my aunt. She had a talk with my wife and me once. She told me, 'I know it's not easy for you two, but you're the only parents Shinji has. Listen to what he says and be patient with him. It's different from when I was young; it's even harder now. You'll never understand what he has to go through. Watch out for him, and listen to him whenever he needs a sounding board. That's all you can do. He's smart and he has a gentle heart. I'll do everything I can for him, and I'm sure he'll grow up right. Just stay there behind him and let him know you'll be there for him.' That's what she told us, and that's what we've tried to live by."

Inamura looked up at me. "It's so sad that that's all we, as parents, can do. Once my wife and I were watching a car race on TV; it was some race in a foreign country, and one of the racers was from Japan. He was in a crash, and we just sat there watching the car go up in flames. My wife turned to me and said, 'It must be awful for parents to watch a child who decides to do something like this, knowing that an accident could happen at any time. But they're just like us. All they can do is stand back and watch.' I was proud of her, for both of us, for getting that far—to be able accept our fate. It took a while.

"Look, I know Shinji was wrong; he was way out of line in this manhole business. He tried to help, but he just made everything worse. He was rash, and now he's suffering because of it. It's my job to suffer through it with him."

Inamura finally smiled and gave the first inkling that he was the older and wiser of the two of us. "Shinji makes mistakes, but I believe that he basically makes the right decisions. He made the right choice when he decided to ask you for help."

"That's hard to believe," I said.

"Oh no, I agree with him. If you had wanted to write about it and make it all public in a comical sort of way, you would have done it already. But you didn't. You stopped and thought about it first. And that's why you showed up to talk to me about it."

"I'm confused. I don't know what to do or who to believe. And I don't want to make any mistakes."

"But if you want to write about it, you certainly can."

"You can't read a scale before the needle stops swaying back and forth."

Inamura smiled and said, "I see. Well, all I can say is that Shinji saw something in you that he felt he could believe. I think so, too." Then his face went serious. "But you can't make all your decisions on your own. Circumstances will come up that you have no control over. I understand that better than Shinji does. Don't worry about us. No matter what you decide to do, no matter what you feel you have to do, Shinji's mother and I will be right there with him. We can take care of ourselves."

I didn't have anything to say in return. I looked down at the street alongside the riverbank. A group of first-graders in yellow caps ran down it, all of them holding hands.

"Things were great until Shinji was about that age," Inamura said wistfully. We watched the yellow caps as they bobbed out of sight. "Kids that age still do what they're told. You can protect them. Sometimes I wish Shinji had never grown up."

# 3

I was pretty sure school hadn't yet let out for the day, so I didn't expect to get a chance to talk to Shinji, but I found him in the schoolyard dressed in gym clothes and doing exercises with about thirty other boys.

I stood just outside the fence and watched. When the teacher blew his whistle, they all began to do handstands. Most of them were unable to accomplish the feat on their own. Shinji, though, who was smaller than most, threw his legs right up into place. Then the teacher counted to thirty, and Shinji maintained his position until he received the signal to quit.

As soon as the teacher blew the final whistle at the end of the class, Shinji came running over to me, waving his hand. He was pointing toward a tiny gate in the fence, and we both headed in that direction.

"I didn't expect to see you!" he said. He put his elbows on top of the fence and leaned toward me. "How long have you been here?"

"About ten minutes. Not long."

"What's up?"

"You're good at handstands."

"Yeah, I'm in the gymnastics club," he smiled. He still had sweat on his forehead and his cheeks were flushed. There were dark circles under his eyes, but his expression was cheery. "I mean it's not really a club; we just get together to practice."

"Don't you have to change clothes?"

"No, the club is meeting right after school."

The concrete along the walk was covered with yellow ginkgo leaves.

"Naoya is gone," I said.

Shinji's eyes opened slightly, but there was not much alarm in his expression. "Does this happen often?"

"He moves around. He never works or lives in the same place very long. He probably doesn't want you to find him."

"How do *you* get in touch with him?"

Shinji shoved his bangs out of his face. "He usually calls me. We don't see each other very often."

"So you don't know where he lives?"

"That's right."

"How about his phone number?"

"No, I don't really need it."

"How do you contact him then?"

Shinji looked down, and then turned his face up and looked into my eyes. "I call him."

"And he hears you?"

Shinji nodded. "Don't you remember asking me if I could communicate with others? I didn't answer you then because I wasn't sure if I really could."

"Why?"

"Well, it's just that . . . when I feel like I'd like to see him, he calls me. Or I get the feeling that he'll be at the park on a certain day, so I go, and there he is. It's nothing as clear as a command."

"But he gets the message."

"Yeah. I think his power is probably stronger than mine. He can do things I can't."

"Like what?"

Shinji thought for a moment. "Are you sure you want to know? It'll just confuse you even more."

"More? I doubt it. So tell me. What else can he do?"

Shinji was hesitant, but he finally spoke up. "He can move."

"What?"

"Teleportation. I'm sure you think I'm lying, but it's true. He even showed me once."

"You mean he can move from point A to point B?"

"That's right. But it's hard on him, so he doesn't just do it for fun. All it takes is a second. He showed me once at the park; he moved from the bench at one end of the park to the swings at the other end. I tried to do it, but I couldn't. My power is a little different from his."

"Too bad," I said. I meant it as a serious reflection, but he didn't hear it that way.

"Please don't get sarcastic and say something like, wow, wouldn't that be convenient if you didn't have to pay for train fare."

I coughed and tried to change the subject. It was the only move left at my disposal. "By 'park,' do you mean the one you sometimes go to to cool off?"

"Uh-huh. There are lots of trees. It's shady, and there aren't many houses nearby. It's actually kind of gloomy; not the sort of place you'd take kids to play, so I usually have it mostly to myself. Naoya and I can relax there."

"I see," I said, putting one hand in my pocket and looking upward. "I'd like you to do that, then. Call him and tell him you want to see him at the park. He looked sick when he came to see me. I've got some more questions to ask, and I'm worried about him."

Shinji rested his chin on the fence and mumbled, "You've been to see my dad." He was looking at the paper bag I had in one hand. Inside were the albums from his elementary school and junior high. On my walk with his father, we'd stopped off at their house so he could lend them to me.

*Shinji doesn't seem to like his teachers, but he has a few good friends. Why don't you contact them and ask them about him?*

I had been carrying the bag so that he couldn't see inside, but he wasn't fooled.

"Did you read my mind or see into the bag?"

"I read your mind. Sorry, I know it's not polite." He gave me a smile and asked, "You doing research on me?"

"I'm doing research on both you and Naoya."

"Thanks."

"I don't know if you'll be thankful for anything I come up with."

"But I know, you see, I know." He didn't sound worried. "So, did you go hear Bach?"

I shook my head. "I didn't want to start dozing right in the middle of it."

"Hmmm. I don't think she would have minded. She likes you—but you probably know that already."

"You shouldn't be doing things like that."

"I didn't do it on purpose," Shinji said hastily. "The other day when I visited your office, I could tell the minute I saw her face. It was the only thing on her mind." He waited a couple of seconds, then added, "It's true! But I shouldn't have told you. I'm sorry about that." He kicked at the leaves on the ground. "I felt sorry for her because you don't feel the same way about her."

"So, do you have your antenna up all the time these days? I thought you could keep from hearing things if you tried."

Shinji shrugged. "My antenna is always up, especially when I go somewhere for the first time. It's like a space probe that leaves the rocket before the astronauts do—to make sure it's safe."

I took a name card out of my jacket pocket, wrote my home telephone number on the back, and handed it to Shinji. "Let me know if you manage to get hold of Naoya. I don't care if it's in the middle of the night, just remember to use the phone, will you? I won't hear if you try any other method."

"Gotcha," said Shinji laughing.

"You look a little more cheerful these days."

"Really? Yeah, I guess so. And the weather has been good, too." Shinji spread his arms toward the sky. "God's in His Heaven, all's right with the world."

I looked at him in surprise.

"What's the matter?" he smiled. "I'm a student; I can give you a quote or two. See you!" He waved as he ran off. I watched him disappear into the school building, and then I turned and walked off.

Back at the office, the editor in chief gestured me over as soon as I walked in. We walked together through the morning bustle of the office, toward the copy machine.

"I'm glad I ran into you," I started. "I'd like to take some time off."

He stopped in his tracks. It was the first time I realized that he and Shinji were about the same height; the editor in chief had always seemed a lot larger.

"What?"

"I need a few days off."

"I'm asking you why."

"I want to check some facts out, but I don't know whether I can turn them into an article."

He snorted at me. "Is this part of your new job as youth counselor?"

"I guess so."

"I told you to let me know when you had something ready."

"That's what I plan to do, but I might not be able to write anything about it."

"There's always something to write about." He jutted out his already stubbly chin. "Anyway, I'm the one who decides what is worth writing about, not you."

"I know that, but I won't be much help here until I can get a few matters settled."

"I didn't see you at the morning meeting."

I cringed.

"Don't you want to know what we're planning?"

"I guess it will be about that infanticide case." Obviously surprised, the editor was quiet.

"I saw Kuwahara getting the photos together over there."

"That job won't take more than two to put together."

"Which is why . . ."

"But I won't let you use your days off; just show up at the office and then go off and do what you need to do. Let me know when you've got a story."

"That's incredibly big of you."

"Paid vacation is what you take when you've got a girl you want to sneak off with for a few days. Got it?"

"I'm sure that's not the sort of behavior that got you where you are today."

"And what would be the point of making it to this position if I didn't enjoy the work?"

I had to laugh. "Yeah, you always look like you're having fun."

"It's not fun; it's an addiction!" He spat out the words and then looked around to make sure there was no one else around.

He continued. "Ikoma told me you got a seventh letter. He's worried about you. I don't feel like I can let this go any further. This last one had something written on it, did it?"

"That's right."

"'Revenge'?"

"Yeah."

"You sure you don't know who's sending them? Come on, it's just the two of us."

"I'd be happy to tell you if I had any idea."

"It might be something you did at the newspaper."

"But wouldn't it have begun before this?"

The editor folded his arms across his chest. "You never know when someone's going to fly into a fury. It could happen long after you've forgotten something that happened."

"I'm not really worried about it," I said. "It's just a little harassment."

"I hope so, but there's still got to be a reason for it! The letters are addressed to you."

"I swear," I said. "I don't have any idea who is sending them."

The editor sighed. "Well, be careful for now. Avoid dark roads at night. Don't forget to lock up before you go to bed." He turned back toward the office, but suddenly laughed and turned back to me. "You're *sure* you don't owe money at some bar?"

"I'm sure. I always put my drinks on your tab. Is that all?"

My desk was piled high with articles Ikoma had printed out for me. It was going to take hours to go through them all. He was on the phone but hung up after I sat down.

"I found out who that police officer was. I haven't talked to him yet, but I found out that he's retired and lives with his daughter's family in Odawara. I'll try to go see him tomorrow."

"It'll take all day to get to Odawara and back. Are you sure you don't mind?" I knew that Ikoma and his group were working on a series about the Imperial family. The readers loved it.

"Not at all. There are plenty of people at work here. So, how did it go?"

I gave him a quick summary of my morning, and he listened carefully, a cigarette in his hand as usual.

"Sounds bad," he frowned. "Are you sure about that aunt?"

"Do you think we need to doubt her story?"

"Of course. But since she's dead, there's not much we can do."

Before I started in on the pile of papers, I tried again the telephone number that Naoya had given his former employer. There was no answer. I called every half hour, and on the fourth call, someone finally picked up after the tenth ring. "Got an answer," I said.

Ikoma, who had been looking through Shinji's albums, quickly picked up another extension.

"Hello?"

All I could hear on the other end was a kind of noise, and a faint clinking sound of metal on metal. I kept calling out, but whoever was on the other end had nothing to say.

"Naoya? Is that you? Answer if you can hear me. Hello?" I didn't give up until I heard the sound of the receiver being replaced.

Ikoma and I looked at each other.

"Well, someone picked up. But why wouldn't they say anything?"

"It could have been a child."

"It's one of the first things kids learn how to say—'hello?'"

I tried calling again, but there was no answer.

"Forget it for now," Ikoma advised. "You're meeting his girlfriend at six, right? Let's see what we can learn from her." He stood up.

"You going too?" I asked.

"Of course!" he said, hiking up his belt. "Why miss a chance to sit down with a sweet young thing? We can buy her dinner!"

# 4

Despite his enthusiasm, Ikoma proved surprisingly low-key when we finally met Asako, the gas station employee who the boss claimed knew Naoya best. She was tall and as pretty as he had said, and she had a forthright air about her.

"I'm dying for a good steak," she said, and even named the restaurant she had in mind, a high-class establishment where wealthier corporations took decidedly classier clients.

"What about your job?" I asked her.

"The boss lets me do what I like. There's nothing to worry about." She turned around and called out to him cheerily, "I'll be back later!" She walked off ahead of us, quickly flagging down the first taxi to pass by.

It was obviously more than Ikoma had prepared himself for, and it was all I could do to keep from laughing out loud. "So what do you think of her?" I asked.

"Don't you dare laugh!" he warned. "We've got to eat too, don't we?"

"This is going on your expense account, old man!" I warned.

Her full name was Asako Moriguchi. She was twenty, a student at a local junior college.

"I'm in the domestic science department," she said breezily. "I'll make someone an excellent wife."

Ikoma leaned over the table in her direction. "Whatever. But tell me, do you always dress like this to work at the gas station?" She wore a flower-print blouse with a skirt and jacket and three-inch heels. Her makeup was applied perfectly.

"This? No way! I showed up in jeans, and the boss told me a reporter would be coming by, so I ran out and bought this outfit. I had to look good to come here, right?"

She ate heartily and drank a lot of wine. And she talked. Unfortunately, she was her own favorite subject, and no matter how hard we tried to steer her in another direction, she always came back around. By the time she had finished the saga of how she and her latest boyfriend had broken up during a romantic evening in Yokohama, I decided to cut her off.

"And about that boyfriend," I said, "was it Naoya Oda?"

She blushed and made a noncommittal sound.

"Well, which is it, yes or no?" Ikoma was there to back me up.

"No, his name was Cody! We went to the same elementary school, and he was famous for breaking in and running around the school grounds at night. Not that I ever saw him—but I know it's true!"

"Okay, fine. So what kind of young man was he?"

"Who?"

"Naoya. You went out with him, didn't you?"

Asako held up her wine glass and stared at the deep red liquid. "I don't know!"

"But you did go on a date with him?"

"Yes."

"Was he a bore?"

"Not really." Next she stared up at the ceiling. "He was kind, but he didn't have much money to spend on me, and I can't have that." She sounded as though she truly regretted the matter.

"What do you mean 'kind'? Do you mean he understood you well?"

Asako clapped her hands. "Yeah, that's it! He's the type of guy you can talk to about anything. He listened to me complain. I had a boyfriend who was fooling around on me, and I was upset about that. Naoya was so sweet."

Ikoma looked around and asked in a low tone, "Did you ever sleep with him?"

Asako sat up straight, and I braced myself for an indignant outburst. But instead she leaned toward us and said quietly, "Yes, I did. But he couldn't—you know."

"He couldn't what?" asked Ikoma, his expression serious. Asako's hand fluttered up and waved him off.

"Stop it! He couldn't do it, you know what I mean! It was about two months ago. I like to work at night because it pays better. And I like to go out for a drink after we close. Besides, there are fewer customers, and I might meet a good-looking guy. During the day, all you get is truck drivers and salesmen. That night, there was a guy in a blue BMW who asked me out for a drive."

"He seemed okay, and he was playing jazz on a classy audio system. I was about to say 'yes,' when Naoya came over and told me to refuse. I thought he was just meddling, but he insisted. 'Just don't go with that guy tonight!' I was surprised at how serious he was."

The mention of the blue BMW reminded me of something, but I couldn't remember just what.

"I thought he was jealous, which was kind of nice, so I said I didn't want to go home alone and he invited me out. We went to see a movie, ate in a restaurant near the theater, and had a few drinks. I was a little drunk, so he took me home in a taxi."

"And then you just kind of fell into bed?" prodded Ikoma.

"I guess so. He's skinny, but handsome when you get a good look at him. I knew he was a nice, quiet guy, so I thought, why not, just this once. My latest relationship was on the rocks, and I was lonely."

But it didn't work out. "A total failure. I told him it was probably the alcohol, and he shouldn't worry about it, but I've never seen anything like it."

"Did it seem to bother him?"

She shook her head. "It was hard to tell. I'm sure he wished it had all gone differently, but now that I think about it, he seemed preoccupied with something else. He kept looking out the window; it was if someone was after him."

Ikoma looked over at me.

"And then he said, 'I got in trouble, and there's a private eye following me around.'"

"What private eye?"

"I don't know. He didn't say. I fell asleep, and he was gone when I woke up. That was it. I didn't try to get together with him again, and he couldn't have been proud of what happened. He never asked me either."

Ikoma and I asked a few more questions, but she didn't have anything further to add. All she said was that Naoya was mysterious; a guy she couldn't really understand. She did say something that was almost poetic.

"He was like a novel you pick up and start reading in the middle. None of us knew anything about his life before he came to work at the gas station. Kind of thrilling."

Asako finished her wine, then rested her chin on her hands and looked up flirtatiously. She grinned. "If you take me to one more place, I just might remember a little more!"

We carefully refused her offer, tucked her into the back of a taxi, and sent her back to work. Then Ikoma and I walked to the subway.

"Well, that cost us big," moaned Ikoma. "Do you think she's really in school?"

I was trying to remember something about a blue BMW. And jazz. What was it?

"She didn't give us a thing worth writing down. Total lack of manners. Of course we were the ones who let her lead us on, but . . . ," Ikoma mumbled to himself. He didn't notice I'd stopped until he was a good five yards ahead.

"What's the matter?"

"I've got it!"

"What?"

"The blue BMW! And the jazz!" I ran toward the subway station, with Ikoma trying to keep up. "I've got to check on something!"

There were still some people in the office when we got there, and the phone was ringing, as always. I went straight for a stack of *Arrow* back issues and began flipping through them. Ikoma peered over my shoulder.

"What're you looking for?"

I finally found the page, and shoved it into his face.

The headline of a brief article read, "Serial rapist uses jazz and a BMW to lure victims."

"Don't you remember? Last month this guy was caught in Kawagoe. He drove a blue BMW. There aren't any murder charges against him, but he has twenty known victims. They say he was obsessive. Once he set his eyes on a mark, he'd follow her around, drag her into his car, and attack her. In some cases he even forced his way into the victims' homes."

And he loved jazz. He apparently always made his assaults with Art Blakey's "Moanin'" playing in the background.

Ikoma read the article, looked up at me, and said in a small voice, "You think this is the guy Asako told us about?"

"Of course. It happened two months ago, right? Right about that time he was picking up girls all over the city. There's every chance he could have stopped at that gas station."

Ikoma shook his head and put the magazine back on the shelf. "You're reaching," he said.

"How can you say that? It's a match!"

"The only thing that matches is that blue BMW. Do you know how many of those there are on the road? It's just a coincidence."

"What about the jazz?"

"That girl wouldn't know jazz from a Sousa march."

"Then why would Naoya have asked her out on that particular night? He told her not to go with that guy."

"He wanted to talk her into going out with him. He made it all up. You've never done anything like that?"

By now the two of us had raised our voices, and the staff in the office had turned around to see what the fight was about. Ikoma clapped me on the shoulder and dropped his voice.

"You're reading too much into this. You've got to be careful or you'll start falling for anything. Before you know it, your clean laundry'll start to look like ghosts."

I looked up at his big face. "What do you mean?"

"The exact same thing happened to me years ago."

Just then, someone yelled for me to come to the phone. Still full of pent-up anger, I grabbed the receiver.

"Yes?" I almost yelled at the caller. No one responded. "Hello?" Silence. I remembered the call I'd made that evening. I pulled the receiver from my ear and looked at it. It couldn't have been from the same number. "Who is this?"

Then I heard a voice. It was hoarse—I could barely hear it. "Kosaka?"

"Yes, speaking."

I couldn't tell if the caller was male or female, it was so raspy. "Shogo Kosaka who used to be at the Hachioji office?"

"Yes, may I ask why you're calling?"

There was a laugh, or maybe the caller was clearing his throat.

"Did you read that seventh letter?"

My expression must have frozen, because Ikoma, sitting across from me with a cigarette in his hand, stubbed it out and sat up.

"You read it?" The caller spoke again, and chuckled.

"I read it," I said slowly. At that, Ikoma almost leaped to my side, and silently picked up the extension.

"Who are you?" I demanded.

"Heh, heh. Who could I be?"

"Did you send those letters?"

"Who knows?"

"Why are you doing this?" Standing next to me, Ikoma made a sign to keep the caller talking. I exhaled and tried to sound calm. "I just want you to know that I can't figure out what you're trying to say. Why don't you explain?"

There was a pause before the breathy voice went on. "We're long past that point, sorry to say."

I felt a chill run down my spine. "What's that supposed to mean?"

"Don't you remember? Or has it been so long that you forgot?"

I'd moved to *Arrow* from the newspaper office in Hachioji three years ago. "Was it something that happened in Hachioji? You'll have to explain more." I waited for him to start, but he just laughed in a mocking tone.

"Hello?"

"Be seeing you . . ."

"Wait a minute!"

"Not just you, but that other one—that Saeko. She ought to watch her step, too." The line went dead. Ikoma and I stared at each other as we held the beeping receivers in our hands.

"Did you recognize the voice?"

I shook my head.

"I couldn't even tell what sex the caller was. Maybe he or she was using one of those voice scramblers."

When I finally hung up the phone and sat down, I wasn't so much scared as angry and irritated. Ikoma disappeared for a few minutes and came back bearing cups of instant coffee.

"So, have you thought of anything that happened while you were in Hachioji?"

"I'm thinking."

"Were you ever involved with the police or the courts there?"

"Just once, but it wasn't a big case."

"So you covered the local news?"

"Yeah."

Ikoma frowned. "Organized crime?"

"No, they showed up about the time I left." I lifted my head. "And besides, this isn't how they operate."

"You never can tell. I got caught up in a bad deal once, and they called me every night."

"Threats?"

"No, they played tapes of funeral chants. For an entire month. I even memorized a few. Thanks to them, I'll go straight to heaven."

His joke relaxed me. "I think he'll call again," Ikoma said. "And when he does, try harder to get him to talk. We need more information."

"I'll do what I can."

"Let's record it. I've got a recorder that will work with these old phones."

Ikoma stood up, put his hands on the desk and looked at me. "But there *is* one thing we can do right now."

I knew what he was about to say.

"Contact Saeko. He mentioned her name. You'd better find out where she is now."

I sighed.

# 5

I didn't get another strange phone call that night. I finally left the office at about eleven, taking a bunch of unread articles with me. My apartment is a fifteen-minute walk from Ichikawa Station. It was late, but lots of shops and bars were still open, and the streets were well lit.

The last few yards to my apartment, though, were dark, and I looked carefully before stepping into those shadows. Up the street, I saw what looked like a teenaged couple on bicycles leisurely crossing the street. Over my head somewhere, I could hear the faint sound of splashing—somebody taking a bath. It all seemed peaceful enough.

"Stop acting like a fool!" I said it out loud and felt better somehow. I lived in a four-story building. Most buildings of its size, shape, and age were called "mansions," which had an airy, new-construction ring to it, but my landlord, Mr. Tanaka, who lived on the first floor, had dared to use the more old-fashioned sounding "apartments," conjuring up an image of lonely rooms in a drafty wooden building, perhaps with a roll of toilet paper hanging beside each door for visits to the shared toilet down the hall. Nor did the landlord go for the usual French-style appellation. My home bore the unimaginative name "Tanaka Apartments."

The landlord was the sort who couldn't let things pass without a word or two of caution, but he did keep the grounds in order. He had even cooperated with the police in a crackdown on burglaries in the area and proudly displayed the certificate of thanks he had received for it.

I had been living in the Tanaka Apartments for two years. When the realtor had brought me there to see the place, the landlord had been reading an article in the newspaper about the attack at the *Asahi* newspaper offices, where reporters had been shot and killed. He noted that I was in a dangerous business.

I was sure he'd turn me down as a tenant, but no, he insisted that he, too, was a "champion of justice" who would defend the right to free speech to his dying day. He invited me to move in under his protective wing.

The realtor later told me that the landlord was a retired teacher who also taught the traditional art of kendo sword fighting. I assumed he didn't visit the dojo much anymore, but every once in a while I would see him beating the dust out of his futon in the yard, and noted that he hadn't lost his power or technique.

It could be his "protective wing" would soon be put to the test. For the time being, I only received letters and phone calls at work, but there was always a chance I might be harassed at home as well. I had no idea how thoroughly I had been checked out or what might come next.

Ikoma had once evaluated my taste in interior decoration when he crashed on my couch after a night on the town, and dubbed it "spare." I sat on the floor with a can of beer, drinking and thinking by the light of a small bedside lamp. I tried to go back over cases I had covered—those that had made a strong impression or involved special problems. I brought the faces of the different people I had been involved with to mind, but none of them fit my present situation.

*You never know when someone's going to fly into a fury*, my editor in chief had told me. I also realized that you never know what might trigger that fury. But what did Saeko have to do with anything? That was the part I found the most troubling. It wouldn't be too hard to find her. We had friends in common. A phone call or two and a word of explanation should do it.

It wouldn't have been so bad if it had been no more than lost love or a bad breakup. A few years would have healed the wounds. But what had happened between Saeko and me had left scars that hadn't even started to fade.

I had told Ikoma the whole story and described Saeko to him as a "selfish bitch." I had said that because I wanted to believe it myself. I felt differently now. She had had her own "convictions," and I had not fit into them. I was pretty sure that was all there was to it.

Our relationship had not been a romance based on love at first sight. A friend from college had introduced her to me—or should I say forced us together. It was an arranged match of the informal kind. Saeko had just graduated from college and was engaged in the profession euphemistically known as "helping with housework." In other words, instead of spending a few years in the workforce, she lived at home and was in the market for a husband.

Her father taught at an elite high school, and he had graduated from the same college as me. He had a reputation as intelligent and proud, but as far as I could see, he was a father who doted on his only daughter. She was sweet-looking and so petite that a good wind would practically blow her away, all of which must have contributed to her father's protectiveness.

I myself had decided it was about time to settle down, and my friend had led me on by saying, "You don't have a girlfriend right now, and this isn't a bad match. Why not go out with her for a while and see how you get along?"

I had taken him at his word. Saeko and I got along fine. We weren't fiercely in love, unwilling to spend any time apart, but she did make me feel safe and secure. I loved the warmth she exuded. Still, every once in a while she would suddenly complain so sharply about something I'd done that it would astonish me.

She was definitely from a "good" family—not wealthy, but well cared-for. Her parents protected her and kept her on the straight and narrow. Her allure drew me in; it was like magic for someone like me who had had a patchy childhood and now worked in an even more patchy profession.

I had the illusion that I was protecting this innocent young woman from the rest of society. It felt good—the sort of thing that once you get a taste of, you never want to give up. Marrying her would mean holding her and protecting her for the rest of my life. I was drunk with myself.

After seeing each other for six months, we decided to get married. I proposed, Saeko immediately assented, and our parents were all delighted. There wasn't a problem with any of it. We set the date for a formal engagement ceremony and reserved a hall for the wedding itself. Our official "go-between" was the city desk editor in chief—a man who, coincidentally, came from the same area as Saeko's father. The two had known each other for years, and, coincidentally, I had been tapped for a future position under him.

Saeko had considered the link providential, and I was pleased, too. How were we to know the harm it would lead to?

I had been transferred to the Hachioji office, a bit of a backwater, two years before Saeko and I got engaged, but one of my superiors at headquarters, now promoted to the city desk, had promised to reel me back in after a couple of years. The two of us had worked the police beat together, and he had taken a shine to me. I trusted that he had enough influence to keep his word.

In fact, a spot on the city desk was a position that every reporter dreamed of. I was secure in the notion that the way had been paved for me.

I didn't have a worry in the world. Not a single one.

It all fell apart a month before the wedding. The reason was simple. A routine physical exam showed that I was incapable of fathering children.

"Why did that matter?" Ikoma demanded angrily when I told him about it. "There are lots of childless couples who get along pretty well. I can't believe they refused you just because of that!"

Ikoma's words sounded sensible, but it was easy enough for him to say because he already had two daughters of his own.

Bearing children—it was a major issue for most women. I can see that now. When she told me it was all over, Saeko had said, "You've got your work, but what about me? I won't have anything without children to raise."

Saeko had wanted a family. And children were an essential part of that picture. She had a beautiful album of images in her head: a perfect childhood, a perfect youth, a perfect romance, and the perfect marriage. It all had to be perfect. And I was an inadequate partner for her on her path to perfection.

Her top priority in life was this photo album. Anything that got in the way had to be removed, no matter what emotions were involved. Even love.

There's an old saying: you'll never be a man until you've fathered a child. It made no sense to me, but Saeko believed she had to have children as a part of her perfect life.

So we broke up. That was all there was to it.

Saeko didn't go into hysterics, she just cried and kept repeating, "I just don't have the confidence to go through life with you." All the parties involved got together for discussions a number of times, but Saeko soon stopped showing up.

We talked once on the phone, and I asked her to see me for one last try. But she refused. I wanted to protect her; I was sure I was in love with her; I needed her—I tried every line at my disposal. I refused to give up. Just thinking about it still filled me with chagrin.

"You don't have the right to force me into an unfulfilling life," she had insisted. "Stop saying everything that pops into your head. If you really loved me, you'd let me go, so I could be happy."

That was when my eyes finally opened.

Force her into an unfulfilling life? It had all been nothing but an illusion. There had never been love or trust between us. I had loved her and protected her, and I had believed we'd spend our lives together. But it was all on my side. I'd never been a priority for Saeko. Nothing was more important to her than that album; there was no room for touching up the photos in it.

And she hadn't required protection. She was capable of taking care of herself. I felt like a used car she'd taken for a test drive before deciding to buy a newer model instead.

"Just tell me one thing," I had pleaded. "Before you decided to dump me, did you think it over at all? Did you have any doubts?" Saeko didn't answer. She just cried.

It took a while and a lot of work to get matters straightened up. The invitations had been sent out, and most of the arrangements had been made. The strangest thing of all was Saeko's father's demand for compensation.

"She's damaged goods now," he had claimed. I suppose he meant that he had let her stay out late with me because we were engaged.

The first time we had slept together, Saeko had been a virgin. I'm sure she had a spot in her album reserved for losing her virginity to the man she would marry. That made me the man who had ruined that picture.

When my parents asked for official arbitration, the matter of compensation was dropped, but her father let me know in no uncertain terms that I was never to speak of her honor—it would be a disadvantage the next time around.

My future boss, who had acted as go-between, had tried to maintain a neutral stance, but it was obvious that his pride was wounded.

Then Saeko cut her wrists on the day that we had originally planned to be married. It hadn't been much of a suicide attempt; just a scrape with a razor. She had been fully conscious when the ambulance arrived. She was wounded, to be sure, but it wasn't over our relationship. It had to do with the new image of herself she now had to carry: someone whose carefully laid plans for marriage had fallen apart at the last minute.

I found out she had told a friend that she was so disappointed at the fuss because it drew attention that was sure to hurt her future prospects for a "happy" marriage.

So that's what I was to her: too much "fuss."

And matters got even worse as the affair devolved into a scandal of sorts. I was a humble reporter, just starting out on his career, but Saeko's father had social status to protect. There he was, a respected teacher in an elite private school. Not only had his daughter backed out of an engagement, but now she had attempted suicide.

That was how it all played out. My prospects for a position at the city desk disappeared. When my erstwhile go-between was forced to placate either an angry old friend or a rookie subordinate, he chose the longstanding friendship. I knew that personnel assignments frequently balanced on this sort of business, and I didn't have the childlike sense of justice I would have needed to fight back.

My old pal, the one at the city desk, was my only ally. He was angry at his boss, at himself, and even at me. In the end, he was the one who got me out of Hachioji, where things had gotten uncomfortable among my colleagues who didn't know how to deal with me.

"A friend of mine, Miyamoto, is the editor in chief at *Arrow*. Some people see it as a burial ground for journalists, but Miyamoto is different. He's got plans for that rag. Why not spend a few years under him until this blows over?"

Miyamoto was my current editor in chief, the one who worried over my bar tabs. And I had to admit that *Arrow* was improving, although the road ahead was still rocky. Being assigned here was still the same as being demoted, but at least it had gotten Saeko's father off my back. Otherwise, he would have been the first one I suspected of sending those threatening letters.

Even after I got the transfer to *Arrow*, rumors over why it had happened refused to die.

The city desk editor in chief from the newspaper kept the real reason a secret, and that just fueled the fire. Eventually the entire story was replaced with a series of alternate scenarios that bore little resemblance to the truth.

It wouldn't have bothered me if the only version was of me backing out of a marriage that a respected superior had arranged, but some said that I had discovered I was more interested in men than women, and others said I had fooled around with the mistress of one of my superiors.

At any rate, it was common knowledge that Kosaka had jilted his fiancée. The only way to put a true end to the rumors once and for all was for me to find another girl and get married.

It was easy to say, but much too difficult to contemplate. First of all, I now knew for a fact that I was unable to father children, and that would seriously narrow the field. I talked about it once to a female reporter. She was a veteran on the job and the mother of three.

"Society is at fault here. Women are never allowed to feel complete until they've produced children," she told me without hesitation. "Why do you think women go to such great lengths to have in vitro babies or hire surrogate mothers? They all want to be accepted as normal human beings. In Japan, adoption is still rare—you've got to have a baby that shares your DNA, one you went through labor with."

"It makes sense," I replied. "And it makes me miserable to know I won't have anyone to carry on after me."

Then she clapped me on the back and raised her voice. "Look at you! Don't you see value in the life you're leading now? Don't tell me you just think of yourself as a generational link. Do you have to have someone with your last name left behind to prove you had a right to be here? If everyone thought like that, we'd still be drawing pictures on cave walls!"

Whatever, I thought. It was fine for her to talk this way, but what if she was in the same position?

And there was another thing. I had completely lost the courage to try again. There was no guarantee I'd ever succeed. These days I made sure to keep a lid on my heart.

*You don't have the right to force me into an unfulfilling life.*

And now—why did Saeko's name have to come up again? I thought about it for so long that it was long past the hour when it would have been polite to call.

I stretched my legs and recrossed them and noticed a dust ball stuck to one sock. I realized I hadn't cleaned the place at all recently. I only came here to sleep anyway. I rested my head against the wall and considered the possibility of sleeping in my clothes. Then I heard a soft swishing sound. I opened my eyes.

Not again! Somewhere a pipe was leaking. There wasn't much my landlord could do—the building was just getting old. I was the one who usually heard the leaks. Either me or the young wannabe-playwright downstairs. We were the only ones up and about at night while the rest of the residents were fast asleep.

I decided to go up to the roof, close the valve on the water tank as usual, and leave a note for the landlord. He always woke up at the crack of dawn, so he could go up and open the valve for everyone's morning needs. Then, I knew, he'd close it again and call a plumber. If I left it alone, someone was bound to wake up to water dripping down the wall.

The routine was so familiar I didn't even need a flashlight. I left my apartment and started up the stairs to the roof. Someone with a flashlight was already up there. It was the wannabe-playwright.

"I thought I might see you here!" he laughed.

"No rest for the weary," I returned.

"It's like we're in charge of watching over the plumbing, isn't it? I'll take care of it this time," he said.

"Okay, I'll leave the note," I rejoined.

"Use this," he said, holding out a note that had been written and neatly printed on a computer. I took it and went back downstairs, past the sign in our landlord's bold handwriting: *Be quiet on the stairs; keep the halls clean!*

I obediently tiptoed on—until I saw it. Someone had written a message at the foot of the stairs in thick red paint. It hadn't been there when I came home that evening. I bent down to touch it; it wasn't even dry.

I stepped over it and ran out to the alley. Whoever had done it couldn't have gone far. But there wasn't even a stray cat to be seen. By the time I got back, the playwright was standing in front of the writing, looking down at it.

"I saw you run off," he said. "What do you think this is all about?"

"What do you think it is?" I asked.

"It looks like the character for 'death,' doesn't it?"

So "death" followed "revenge."

*God's in His Heaven, all's right with the world.*

What a lie.

# 6

"Police won't give us the time of day for anonymous letters," was Ikoma's first comment. "You'd have to be stabbed, run over, shot, or poisoned before they'd get involved."

"Shut up, will you?" Kanako came in with a tray of coffee cups. "Don't even joke about that. Once you say something, it's more likely to happen."

"Ha!" laughed Ikoma in an unnaturally loud voice. "So that's how you plan to find a boyfriend? Just ask out loud for one each night?"

"And that," said Kanako icily, "is why I hate old geezers!"

After she left, I spoke. "I'm not counting on the police to help me."

"What happened to that graffiti?"

I had to laugh. "My landlord was so mad he had veins popping out of his forehead! But he helped me scrub it off. He thinks it was just a prank."

"Did you tell him the whole story?"

"No, I just asked him to make sure that he locked up at night. I can't tell him too much—he's the type that would probably go off and get a license for a machine gun to protect our right of free speech."

"It's people like him who keep the country from falling apart altogether. And what about that Saeko? Did you talk to her?"

I showed him a Post-it with her name and number on it. I'd made a call that morning to the friend who'd introduced us in the first place. He had been on his way out and hadn't had time to ask me any sticky questions. "He sure seemed suspicious. He asked me over and over if it really was an emergency. I guess he thought I was planning to take revenge for the agony I've suffered since she dumped me."

"That's good, sounds like he's got a guilty conscience." Ikoma commented as he looked at the Post-it. "So she's married?"

Her name was now Saeko Kawasaki. I had been surprised to learn that she lived very close to the *Arrow* office.

"What about her husband?"

"He's a teacher. Probably at the same school as her father."

"Let's go," Ikoma said as he gulped down his coffee. "I'll be there to make sure she doesn't call the police on you."

"You're too kind." I cringed.

"The sooner the better. How about tomorrow? I'll set it up. This is not your problem—*Arrow* needs to be dealing with it."

"Aren't you going to Odawara today?"

"Yeah, but I can make a call from anywhere. You too. Call Naoya again. He picked up once; keep on trying—he'll catch your vibes eventually."

Well, my vibes didn't work very well that day. I spent all morning glued to my seat, calling the same number every ten minutes. The phone just kept on ringing. I even tried a call to the phone company.

"We can't give you the name of the party."

"What about the prefix then? Is this an Edogawa Ward number?"

"Yes, it is."

"What section?"

"I can't tell you that."

I love the phone company. Next, I grabbed a copy of the Edogawa phone book and started at the beginning, looking through the phone numbers one by one. Finally, I called the number on the Post-it, hooked the receiver under my chin, and let it ring as I read the endless rows of tiny numbers. I thought my eyes might cross.

"You might try a magnifying glass." Kanako walked over to my desk. "Can I help? If there's another phone book, we can cut the work in half."

I took her up on her offer, and we worked on it a while before she piped up, "Do you mind if I make a suggestion?"

"What?"

"Isn't there a chance the number is unlisted?"

"Pessimism will turn your hair gray."

"You're the one with the gray hair!"

"Shut up and keep looking."

We looked through the entire book without finding the number.

"Are there any phone books that are older than this?" Kanako wondered.

"Probably, but do you want to keep looking? If it's not in this one, it probably won't be in an older one."

"But it might be," she prodded. "And you've got to keep busy, to keep your mind off it all." She walked off and came back in a few minutes with another phone book.

"Thanks," I said. "But you've done enough." I tried to think of a way to show my appreciation in a way that wouldn't lead to any misunderstandings about my intentions, but as it turned out, she had ideas of her own.

"You know, you should take me to lunch," she said.

"Well, okay."

"Terrific! I've got the place all picked out!"

She dragged me all the way to Ginza; there was a new Italian restaurant she was dying to visit. It was after the usual lunch hour, but the place was full. We chatted about nothing in particular at first, but once we got settled in, Kanako suddenly fell quiet and began playing with the rose in the tiny vase on the table.

Finally she said, "How did you know? That concert the other day. I wasn't exactly telling the truth about it. I had bought two tickets and thought of all kinds of excuses to get you to go with me. But you knew that. Did you hear something?"

I couldn't bring myself to tell her it had been a boy with ESP. Then she'd really feel like she was being teased.

"The wisdom of age," I said, and she finally laughed.

"You're not that old. I lied about the gray hair."

"I'm glad to hear that. I've been feeling older recently."

"It's the topic you're working on. ESP doesn't suit you!" She propped her elbows on the table and cupped her chin in her hands. "Do you want to hear something even more surprising?"

"Sure."

"I was there that night."

"Where?"

"Your apartment!" She looked up at the ceiling and laughed. "Are you mad?"

"No, but . . ."

"I wanted to see for myself. You had a date, didn't you? You said you had something else you'd promised to do, so I wanted to see what kind of girl you came home with. I was sitting at the concert hall listening to the music and I couldn't stand it anymore, so I just . . . went."

I remembered that I had gone out drinking with Ikoma that night. He had told me all about his experience with the 1974 ESP boom, and we talked for hours as we went from one bar to the next. I didn't get home until after three.

"How long were you there?" I asked.

"Till a little after two. I spread out a newspaper and sat there like someone in the unemployment line."

That was why she'd been late the next morning.

"You didn't come home," she said, pressing on both her cheeks. "I figured you'd spent the night with your girlfriend, so I finally left. And just so you know, I was in tears!"

The waiter brought our lunch, and Kanako leaned back from the table. After he left, she apologized. "I know this isn't the sort of thing you want to talk about while you're eating, but this is the only chance I've had to be alone with you. It might be my only chance ever. You won't want to take me out drinking again, I suppose."

We had never been out anywhere alone together. There was always someone else with us. I hadn't really invited her anywhere since I'd become suspicious of her behavior toward me.

"I sowed the seeds myself, so I can't complain," she said softly. "When I got home that night, my sister chided me. You're a fool, she said. She told me that if I really liked you I shouldn't go blasting in like that. I should be more . . . subtle. She said love always involves bargaining. I guess she knows what she's talking about; she's a veteran of the subtle approach."

I was pretty sure Kanako didn't really understand what her sister had told her. I could see a tear on her cheek.

"So, tell me," she said, looking up. "What's your girlfriend like? I'll give up if she sounds better than me. Is she pretty? How old is she? Can she cook?"

I opened my mouth, but she quickly went on. "I know there are old rumors. They tell me that's the reason you're so careful. One of the guys told me you had had experiences I'd never be able to deal with. Is that true? What happened that hurt you so badly?"

From the corner of my eye, I could see the people at the next table looking at us. I gave them a quick glance so that Kanako would see what was going on, and she closed her mouth and sat up straight.

"Everything is coming at me at once," I said.

"You mean me?"

"No, I mean that business behind those rumors."

Her eyes opened wide. "Are you still seeing her?"

"No, it's not that. It's just—well, I've just been handed the opportunity to relive it all."

"Was it hard for you?"

She looked so concerned that something inside me twitched. I had to give her credit for choosing to bring it up in a crowded restaurant in the middle of the day.

"Listen, you've got things that you don't like to talk to anyone about, right?"

"Well, sure."

"So do I. I don't want people to know the truth about what happened. It would only hurt the others involved, so I put up with the rumors. It's over, and there's nothing anyone can do to change things."

"I see."

I continued to talk as if I were teaching her a lesson. "You got some good advice—you can't deal with what I've been through."

Kanako went pale.

"There are better guys out there for you. You'll find someone who can share your feelings."

She muttered, "I don't like men my own age."

"That's just the way you feel now."

"One of my friends married a man fifteen years older than her. They're so happy together. It happens, you know."

I thought about Ikoma and what he'd said about raising daughters. He was right about how complicated it could get.

"That's your friend, and I'm happy for her. But that doesn't mean it's right for everybody."

"Do you dislike me?" Kanako finally hit the core of the matter. "If you do, then I'll give up. But if you like me—"

"Is that all there is to it? Whether you like someone or not? Don't you ever think about the future? Don't you care what happens next?"

"Of course. I don't just throw myself at anyone." That did it. She'd been valiantly trying to bat her eyelashes to keep the tears back, but one defiantly slid down her cheek and around her mouth.

"When your sister said love was bargaining, she was telling you not to rush into anything. If you don't have a plan of defense, how are you going to back out of a relationship when you run into a rotten apple?"

"I don't care, be a rotten apple for me."

I knew she didn't mean what she was saying, but I had gotten as far as I could. "You go home and have another talk with your sister."

Kanako was apparently up for the challenge. "I'd rather go back to your apartment. What would you do?"

I was about to tell her I couldn't take responsibility for my actions when I remembered the writing on the stairway.

"That's not funny. You stay away from there!"

"Why should I?"

"It has nothing to do with you. Just stay away. It might be dangerous." Then I quickly added, "My neighborhood isn't safe. A young woman shouldn't be wandering around there at night. You understand?"

She finally agreed, although halfheartedly.

"Look," I said, relieved, "I understand how you feel, and I'm flattered. I'm flattered, but I just can't say, 'thank you very much' and move on. We're not children. I'm sure you understand . . . but knowing someone likes you feels good, so—so just be careful."

Kanako was silent and she kept her gaze down.

"Ask your sister about it." It was the only thing I had left to say. "She can probably explain things better than me."

"My sister told me that if I had anything to say to you, I should do it in a public place in broad daylight."

She was right; her sister was definitely a veteran.

7

I couldn't stay on the phone all day. I dialed the number yet again, vowing to give up if no one answered. It was just after two.

"Pick up, you son of a bitch!" I muttered to myself, right before somebody actually picked up the phone.

"Hello?" I ventured. I could hear that metallic sound in the background. "Naoya? It's me, Kosaka from *Arrow*. I've been trying to get a hold of you. We need to talk again. Where are you?"

Silence.

"This isn't Naoya? Naoya Oda?" There was a tapping sound. The person on the other end was tapping on the receiver.

"Hello?" The tapping continued. Irritated, I took a deep breath to start talking again, but the tapping got louder. It was if the person wanted me to listen to it.

Someone had answered the phone, but he or she tapped instead of talking. I finally had it.

"You can't understand me?"

The tapping speeded up, and then stopped.

"No? So you *can* understand?"

The tapping started up again, and then paused as if waiting for my next question.

"So . . .?" What else could it be? "Pardon me, but are you unable to speak? You can't use your voice?"

The tapping started up again at an urgent pace. That was it!

"All right then, this is how we'll do it. I'll ask you questions, and you tap twice for yes, and once for no. Can you do that?"

There were two taps.

I gave the person my name and occupation again, and said that I had got the number from the gas station where Naoya Oda used to work. "Are you a relative of Naoya?"

*No.*

"A friend?"

*Yes.*

"Does he live there with you?"

*No.*

"Did he live there before?"

*Yes.*

"Tell me where you are? Edogawa, right?"

*Yes.*

"I'm going to read off a list of neighborhoods. Tell me when I get to the right one." It was Higashi-Komatsugawa.

"Would you tap out the numbers of the address?"

*4.*

4-chome.

The next one was longer.

"Sixty? The block number is 60?"

*Yes.*

Then two taps. 4-60-2.

"So the building is 2. Is it a house?"

*No.*

"An apartment building?"

A pause. *Yes.*

"Did Naoya live there until recently?"

*Yes.*

"Do you know where he is now?"

*No.*

"Are you worried about him, too?"

*Yes, yes!*

"Would it be all right if I came to talk with you? I need to find Naoya, and I don't have many clues."

*Yes.*

"What is the number of your apartment? Does it have three digits?"

*No.*

"One digit."

*Yes.* Followed by two more taps.

"Apartment 2. Thank you. I'll be there soon."

I took the subway to Funabori Station and walked for about twenty minutes. I finally found it; an old rickety apartment building built against the Arakawa River. Someone had painted the name of the place directly on the wall of the building: No. 2 Hinode-so.

I didn't have to search for apartment 2. A young woman in cotton slacks and a white jacket was waiting for me at the entrance. She held her elbows with both hands to keep herself warm.

As soon as she saw me, she started waving and making gestures as if to ask me if I was the one who had called.

"That's me," I said. "Are you the one I talked to?"

She nodded, and her ponytail bobbed, too.

I wondered if I had found Naoya's girlfriend.

# PART 4
# An Omen

At her foot was a small whiteboard. She quickly picked it up and started writing.

*My name is Nanae Mimura. I work at a day care center nearby.*

I nodded to indicate that I understood and said, "Have you known Naoya for a long time?" She erased the board and began writing again.

*He moved here about six months ago. We've been friends for three.*

"Were you close?"

She thought a moment and wrote, *I guess you could say that.*

Nanae was obviously used to conversation in this form. She wrote quickly and her penmanship was neat and easy to read even when the sentences were long. The hard part was standing next to her and reading it all. I was trying to speak quickly in response to her rapid responses, and she in turn was doing her best to keep up the tempo.

"I'm sorry to have to make you work so hard," I said when I realized what was happening, but she seemed puzzled at the question. "What I mean is, um, is this how you talk to everyone?"

She nodded.

"What about sign language?"

She nodded again.

"I wish I knew it. It would make things easier for you."

She looked me up and down and then began to write again.

*Don't worry. I'm used to it.* Then she smiled, and I could see fine lines at the corners of her eyes. Her eyes were large and expressive. She didn't wear makeup to hide the freckles on her nose. I guessed her to be in her mid-twenties.

I wasn't used to making such close inspections of people I was meeting for the first time, but I had to stand close to chat with her while reading what she wrote. She came up to about my ear, which meant she was tall for a woman. The fingers that held the pen were long, and she wore an engraved gold ring on her right ring finger.

"When did he leave?" What she wrote on the board matched the story from the gas station manager. He quit his job and moved out.

*He left in the middle of the night. When I woke up the next morning, he had left a note for me under my door.*

There was one more thing I needed to ask her before I asked to see the note. "I hate to be so blunt, but were you and Naoya lovers?"

She was a few years older than he was, I was pretty sure, but it might not have mattered. She giggled and shook her head.

"So you were just friends?"

She wrote, *That's right. He was like a younger brother to me.*

"Did he feel the same way?"

She laughed again. *I don't know what anyone else thinks, but that was the impression I got.* I must have looked confused. She added, *He was a polite young man.*

She was obviously advising me not to get the wrong idea. Her expression turned serious, and she stepped away from me so she could write in private. She wrote for quite a while, and she looked even more serious when she finally turned back to me.

*Does the fact that you're looking for Naoya have anything to do with why he left? Do you know why he left? I assume you're looking for information, but I don't know yet whether I should help you. Even with something small and insignificant.*

I felt her eyes on me the whole time I was reading. She had made it very clear that whoever might be on what business, she was on Naoya's side. Of all the people I'd met in relation to this case, she was the first one to present this attitude.

I gave her back the whiteboard and said, "It's probably my fault that he disappeared." Nanae furrowed her brows. "But I'm looking for him because I'm worried. Doesn't he give you the impression that he's ill? He seems very weak and run-down."

Nanae looked away and then nodded. She erased the paragraph on the board and wrote, *I'm worried too.*

"Did it look to you like he was seeing a doctor?" She shook her head. "I imagined as much. Then I thought for a few moments about what I wanted to say next. "Did you ever meet his friend, a high-school student named Shinji Inamura?"

She seemed surprised. She wrote over her previous sentence: *Why are you asking about him?*

I'd first met Naoya through Shinji. I'd only met Naoya once, but if Nanae knew about Shinji, then Naoya must have actually trusted her. She was the first person I'd met with whom that seemed possible.

"The two of them seem to have special powers. Did you know about that?" Nanae looked at me for a while.

"I think it was the power that was ruining his health. It was hard on him in all sorts of ways, tangible and intangible. That's what I heard from Shinji. Shinji's worried about Naoya, too. I've asked him to contact Naoya so I can talk to him again."

Nanae looked away and seemed to be thinking. She picked up the whiteboard and nodded in the direction of the apartment house entrance. She held out one arm as if to show me in, and then led the way.

I followed her inside. This was the place—the old run-down apartment that had been Naoya's home until just a few days before.

There were four wooden doors along the hallway. Nanae passed the first one, then passed the second one with its nameplate bearing her handwritten name, and pushed a red tricycle in front of the third door aside before stopping in front of the fourth.

"Is this where Naoya lived?" I asked.

Nanae nodded, and then stood on her tiptoes, stretching a hand up to the top of the doorframe and pulling down a key.

"Will the landlord be angry if you go in without getting permission first?"

She laughed and shook her head. She turned the key in the lock, opened the door, and nudged the doorstopper into place with her foot to hold it open. She walked in, and I waited at the entrance. I heard her open a window, and then she came back and indicated that I could come in.

There was a tiny space for removing shoes—otherwise, the door opened directly onto the kitchen. It was about four and a half mats in size. Beyond that there was a room of about six mats that was shut off with a glass door. There was no furniture, not even any odor to indicate that someone had recently lived there.

A curtainless window opened out onto the wall of another apartment building. There was a tiny balcony, but absolutely nothing to see from it. If my bearings were correct, the window faced south, yet not much sun came in.

What was interesting, though, was that the inside of the building was much nicer and more solid than the outside would lead one to believe. The door was heavy, and fitted with a lock and a chain. The window had an aluminum sash with a double lock and a storm door. When I took a peek, I saw that it was designed to be soundproof.

There was a water-heating device on the balcony that provided both the kitchen sink and the tiny bathtub with hot water. All you had to do was add an air conditioner, and it would be just as comfortable as a much more modern dwelling. Anyone who makes frequent moves is bound to run into this sort of lucky find once in a while.

On the other hand, there were people who were good at finding places like this. It occurred to me that, if what Shinji said about him was right, Naoya might be that type of person.

Anyway, it was a relief. A relief? Why would it even worry me? I wondered. Then I realized I was thinking about Nanae. The whole time I'd been standing there, I'd been unconsciously worried about the safety of a young woman in such a dump.

I reminded myself what I was doing there. "There's no phone," I said, looking back at Nanae, who nodded. She was standing next to the kitchen sink, with one hand resting on the edge.

"Was the number I called yours? Or is there some kind of public phone here?"

Nanae began writing on the whiteboard. I felt bad. I should just try to stick to yes/no questions.

*It was the phone in my room.*

"So the two of you shared a phone?"

She cocked her head.

"You didn't share it?"

She shook her head.

"So he asked you to let him write your number on his résumé?"

She nodded twice in a way that dared me to question the propriety of the situation.

"But it would have been a problem for you if he got phone calls, wouldn't it?"

She wrote again. *He promised me there wouldn't be any.*

"But even still—"

Nanae giggled. Then she stopped and wrote quickly. When she flipped it around to show me, there was just a hint of irritation.

*You want me to say that we were lovers. But if we were, we would have moved in together.*

As soon as I was finished reading it, she flipped it back and continued to write. *We were friends. Please try to understand.*

"I see," I finally conceded, although I don't think I sounded convincing. She erased the board. "I don't see any marks from furniture," I noted next, looking at the tatami mats.

*He didn't have many things.*

"He must have found it inconvenient. Did he ever say anything about it to you?"

*No. There's a coin laundry in the neighborhood, and he ate out or bought prepared food.* Then she thought for a second and hurriedly wrote, *I cooked for him once in a while, too.*

"As a friend?" I asked. She nodded emphatically. I laughed out loud at the unlikeliness of that, and she laughed too. *I don't lie.*

"I'm sure you don't!" I opened the closet. It was empty and dust had gathered in the corners. "Has he been back since he left?"

Nanae shook her head.

"Has he contacted you at all?"

She looked down. She was right; she was a bad liar.

"So you have heard from him?"

She hesitated and then wrote, *He called me once.*

"When? What did he say?"

*The night before last. He said he was wondering how I was doing.*

"Did he ask if anyone had come around asking about him?"

*Yes.*

"Did he ask if it was someone like me?"

*Yes.*

"And did he tell you to be sure to say you didn't know him?"

Nanae nodded tiredly. Then she turned her back to me, put the white-board on the drainboard and wrote. *Naoya told me there would be a reporter from* Arrow *magazine. He told me that if I talked about him, I'd get myself mixed up in the matter, so it would be better not to say anything. But he didn't say what it was about.*

"You mean he didn't want you to talk about his powers."

She looked up at me with the same expression as when I'd first brought up the topic.

"Would you please answer the question?"

Nanae nodded and wrote, *I can't.*

"But you didn't just turn me away—you answered my phone call. Why?"

She wrote, *I was worried about Naoya. He's running away from something, but I don't know if he really needs to. I want to know. I want to know if there's anything I can do for him.*

"I feel the same way," I said.

**2**

I wasn't much good at surveillance. But I had to do it. I had to keep an eye on Nanae, because I believed that she was the key to finding Naoya.

I left the apartment building and walked around for a while, looking for a good spot. As luck would have it, there was a large parking lot nearby. If I had a car, I could park there. I'd be able to see the entrance to the apartment. I called the office, got permission to borrow a part-time gopher, and asked him to find a company car that wasn't in use. After about an hour he showed up in a banged-up white Corolla.

I had him stop under a No Unauthorized Parking sign. He was used to this sort of job.

"I filled it up before I came. Here are your binoculars and something for dinner." He handed over a bag from a fast-food restaurant.

"Thanks. When you get back to the office, let Ikoma know where I am. If he insists on coming, tell him to take off his shoes and walk in his stocking feet—he's got to be quiet!"

"Got it. And good luck. Oh, and don't forget to turn down the sound of your beeper. There's nothing worse than a beeper going off during surveillance."

"Has it happened before?"

"Our beloved editor in chief."

I stretched out in the front seat, did as I was told, and then waited. There was no way of knowing if anything would come of it.

But Naoya had called Nanae the night before. Nanae was worried about him, so he'd most likely try again. He was obviously concerned about her. Either that, or she would figure out a way to find him to let him know I had been there. Or she might have been lying. She might know where he was.

Or—she might do it the same way as Shinji. Just look up into the sky and "call" him.

Whatever. I believed it was worth betting that Naoya would show up or call Nanae and ask her to meet him somewhere. He would have to see her in person if he wanted more than "yes" or "no" answers from her.

Nanae stayed in until six p.m. Once I saw her walk past the hallway window, but she just came downstairs to check the mail and went straight back to her apartment. Later, she came back to the entrance and, carrying an old-fashioned shopping basket and wearing the same thin jacket, set out. I got out of the car and followed from a safe distance.

It turned out to be nothing but shopping. A few hundred feet from the apartment building she turned onto an endlessly winding lane of shops. Not long ago, the place would have been the exclusive domain of housewives with small children in tow, but nowadays the crowd included businessmen shopping on their way home from work, so I didn't stand out too badly. I did my best to keep up the act, stopping at some of the shops to inspect the goods or pretending to make a call in a phone booth. There was a large supermarket in the midst of it all, and Nanae did most of her shopp ing there. She stopped at a vegetable shop and bought a bag of persimmons from the pile displayed in front. She used gestures to communicate with the shop owner, who called her by name. She seemed to get along just fine despite her handicap. I got the impression that she had made a comfortable life for herself here.

From the vegetable shop, she headed straight back to her apartment. Her basket was full to brimming and looked heavy as she shifted it from one arm to the other, the green onion stalks bobbing every time she did. I had to suppress an urge to run up and offer to carry it for her. Maybe Naoya had done the same thing.

She was expecting company, I thought. Why would a girl living alone stock up on groceries when all she had to do was step out to go shopping? I remembered her mentioning that she had cooked for Naoya.

My expectations ratcheted up a notch.

I watched from a distance as she went inside, then I went back to the car. Just after eight it began to rain. It was more like a mist. Eventually, though, I could no longer see through the windshield, and I had to lower the window to maintain my view.

If I'd had someone with me, we could chat to pass the time, but all by myself, it was a fight against boredom and sleepiness. I couldn't listen to the radio, and reading was out of the question. But the time passed relatively quickly, since my mind was occupied with thoughts about Nanae.

What was it like to be unable to speak?

Where was the rest of her family? Did she have any? She said she worked at a day care center. How did she get her work done? Her hearing was unimpaired, so she could play the piano and dance in time to music with the children. Maybe she took care of children with similar handicaps.

There was nothing sad about Nanae. She lived a normal life as far as I could see. She didn't give the impression of being uneasy or fearful. I couldn't imagine exactly what her life was like, but she seemed to be happy and somehow fortunate.

Fortunate? No, that wasn't the right word. She was simply living her life fully, as was her right. There was no excuse for a developed country not to provide more help for people with disabilities.

Why couldn't a country that had the technology to build an electric appliance for the sole purpose of beating eggs use that same inventiveness to make life a little bit easier for those who really needed it? Society offered one invention after another to save time and trouble for the able-bodied. But it seemed as though we cruelly urged those with fewer abilities to work a little harder to get ordinary things done, rather than create a machine or two to help them out. Just think what a video telephone would do for someone like Nanae.

The matter had never occurred to me before. I realized that if I had never met Nanae and taken a liking to her, I might never have even thought about it.

Beyond the drizzle, I could see the light on in Nanae's apartment. I wondered what Naoya had meant to her. That is, if he could really read people's minds. They might have been able to hold a conversation without sign language or whiteboards, laughing and enjoying themselves. He could have helped her out with the smallest of chores—even opening a jar. All she'd have to do was hold it out, and he'd take it. If she had come home late at night, she wouldn't have to call him from the station, he would have just shown up to walk her home; she could have depended on him.

He could have done everything she needed—if he were psychic, that is.

But he didn't want people to know about his ability, so he had left, despite his concern about Nanae. I wondered if Shinji knew about her. He might have been less concerned for his friend if he had.

Just then, a red rose of an umbrella opened up in front of the apartment building. When it tipped to the side I could see Nanae's face beneath it. She looked around and began to walk. I sat up to watch, and I could feel the tension building inside me. She was heading straight for the parking lot.

The red umbrella came closer. She had changed into something warmer than the jacket she had worn earlier in the evening. She carried the whiteboard under her arm.

I'd done surveillance and tailed people lots of times, but I don't remember ever being such a complete failure at it. I leaned against the window and waited, nodding in greeting when she came up to the car and looked in through the passenger door window. I reached over to open the door for her.

"What can I do for you?" I asked quietly. She showed me the whiteboard.

*Let me in, and then start driving around.* Next she wrote something that astounded me. *You know how to get rid of a tail, don't you?* She slipped inside and looked at me, nodding quickly. I turned on the ignition.

I pulled out of the parking lot and onto the street, my eye on the rearview mirror. There were two headlights right behind me. I tried pulling off on the shoulder and letting the car go by, but at the next intersection, there it was again, right behind me. When it had passed by, I saw that it was a domestic car, the same size as the old Corolla I was driving; it was gray and there was just one person in it. Unfortunately, the license plate was covered in mud and I couldn't read it at all.

"That must be it," I said, and Nanae nodded without looking over at the car.

"Has that car been watching you, just like I was?"

Nanae wrote quickly on the board, *I'll give you the details later.*

It didn't take much longer to get rid of it. I waited to cross an intersection until just before the light changed, made a quick right, and drove halfway down the block, then pulled in under an overpass and waited.

We waited for fifteen minutes, but the car never showed up. The only sound we could hear was the windshield wipers. Whoever it was was quick to give up, I thought. Nanae sighed in apparent relief. Then she took up her pen and began writing again.

*Come back to my place, someone wants to talk to you.*

I read it over twice.

"Who wants to talk to me?"

*Naoya.*

"Is he there?"

She shook her head. *He was in the neighborhood, but realized you were there and left. He's living somewhere else now, and he'll call from there.*

Now I sighed. "So I didn't fool anyone; maybe I should get another job."

Nanae hesitated, and then wrote, *Naoya didn't see you with his eyes.*

She seemed to regret having written it, and quickly erased it and wrote, *That car wasn't watching me. It was following you.*

The next day, Ikoma and I decided to walk to the home of Akio and Saeko Kawashima, where we had agreed to meet them at two p.m. It was a good distance on foot, but we had a lot of things to talk over, so we decided not to call a cab.

"Then what?" asked Ikoma as he strode along. "Did Naoya call?" We passed a group of three women wearing company uniforms.

"Yes, he did."

"What did he say?"

"He said he didn't have any more business with me and that I should just leave him alone."

"Is that all?"

"He didn't ask me any questions. Apparently he already knew the answers."

The rain had let up and the sun was out. Although it was almost November, there was barely a hint of autumn in the air. Both of us had removed our jackets and walked with them hung over one shoulder. The trees along the road also seemed confused—they still had their summer greenery.

There was a strong wind, but it was lukewarm, like spurts of air from an old heater that had trouble getting going. It didn't suit the posh Ginza area, which we were walking through, at all. Every time there was a new breeze, Ikoma put his hand up to his face. He was clearly becoming annoyed for other reasons as well.

"What can that boy be thinking?" he said. "And what about that car following you?"

"I asked him about it."

Naoya's only response had been to wonder if another company might be trying to scoop me. He said he didn't have any idea what it was all about. "I just noticed that you were being followed," he said. "Or would you rather that I hadn't said anything?"

The call had been short. Naoya had spoken in a monotone. He sounded more cross than anything else, or at least that was the impression he wanted to give.

"Stay away from Nanae. If you give her any more trouble, you'll be hearing from me."

*I'd be delighted to hear from you,* I had thought. *I've got lots of questions. Everything would be a lot easier if I could just hear from you.* I didn't say it, though, because Nanae was watching me the whole time with a concerned look on her face.

The floor plan of her apartment was the same as Naoya's. The difference was that she had made hers into a home. She kept it clean, and the faint scent of cleaning liquid wafted from the kitchen.

On top of the counter was a large colander full of vegetables that had been cut up, ready to be cooked. I was sure that she was ready to fix dinner for Naoya, something warm on that chilly night, if he decided to show up.

She had a bowl of tangerines on the table and was killing time juggling one between her hands the whole time I was on the phone.

When she had let me in the room, she had left the door open and motioned me in with a wave of her hand, indicating a chair. She had then gone out into the hallway with her whiteboard; I imagined that she had let whoever lived next door know that she was having a guest. I had to give her credit for knowing how to take care of herself as a woman living alone, and I was sure that it made her feel safe to know that she could count on her neighbor. On the other hand, though, I felt just a little jealous knowing that she probably hadn't done the same when Naoya was visiting her.

"So, was she pretty?" asked Ikoma. Still in a reverie, I nodded without even thinking about it.

He sneered. "Who do you mean?" he asked.

"Who are *you* talking about?" I retorted.

"Nanae Mimura."

"Yeah, she's pretty. Not astoundingly, but still . . ."

"Ha!" Ikoma said in a loud voice. "You get lucky every once in a while."

We crossed Showa Avenue and headed toward East Ginza, and the atmosphere began to change. There were more and more buildings and fashionable boutiques. The area was home to the striking Kabuki Theater, but once you turn off onto a side street, it's not that much different from a typical Tokyo residential area.

It became more residential as we neared Saeko's neighborhood. The buildings were lower, and crowded in between them were older homes, not the generic cookie-cutter buildings you find in newer housing developments. I saw a ramen shop with its window air conditioner jutting out onto the street, and signboards for a doctor's office.

Some referred to this area as the "Ginza Tibet," but it felt nostalgic and comfortable to me. The much newer area in front of Tokyo Station, for instance, full of shiny new office buildings, seemed like a migrant to the big city, with family that lived in the quieter old neighborhoods like the one we were passing through.

"I contacted that police officer," said Ikoma as he checked the names of the apartment buildings we passed. "He's retired—and quite a character."

"When I told him about Shinji and the two guys and the manhole cover, he was anxious to hear more. He said he has nothing but time on his hands, so he'd be glad to come into Tokyo if we gave him a call."

"Is it true he once solved a case with the help of a psychic?"

"He said it was, but he's no longer in touch with her. She got married and moved to Kyushu."

"So this cop believes that psychic powers are real?"

"I was surprised," said Ikoma, scratching his neck. "He said the same thing as Shinji and his dad—that it wasn't a matter of believing or not believing, it was just the way things were.

"The cop was a detective in Kanagawa. He never moved up very high in the ranks, but they say he was good. He's sixty-two and sharp as ever as far as I can tell. His name is Kaoru Murata." Ikoma explained the characters that made up the name by quoting an archaic poem. When I gave him a questioning look, he added, "Read the classics! It's from *The Tale of Genji*."

"Haven't had the pleasure since I was in school."

"My wife reads it in bed. That means that when I'm in the mood, I have to dress up like a courtier, burn a little incense, and ask formally for her permission. But then she'll quote from some other classic to turn me down: 'In the spring it is the dawn, and all the rest is pathetic,' or something like that."

"I don't think you've got that last quote right," I said.

Ikoma ignored me. "And on top of that, she gets all excited about the old days when women had control over family fortunes. It must have been tough on men back in those days."

"I've heard the story told differently. You could have had a harem if you liked."

"It tells a lot about you, if that's what you remember from *The Tale of Genji*." We stopped and looked up at a brand-new two-story house with clean white walls. "Here we are. Now the jacket. The least you can do is try to look handsome!"

4

We rang the doorbell, and a man spoke to us over the intercom before coming out to let us in.

He looked to be in his mid-thirties. He wore a starched white shirt with a tie, neatly creased trousers, and a thin sweater. When I heard he was a teacher, I had expected someone bespectacled and mousy, but I was wrong.

"We've been waiting for you," he said. "I'm Kawasaki."

So this was Saeko's husband.

The house was spic and span and the interior decoration impeccable. Ikoma and I were shown into a formal sitting room. It all made sense. This was a "nest" suitable for Saeko. Even if she and I had married she would have managed to create a home so clean and shiny that it would be ready for visitors at the drop of a hat.

Unfortunately, on my salary, we probably couldn't have afforded the leather sofa or the numbered lithograph by an artist I'd read about in an art magazine. She would have had to cut it out of a glossy coffee-table book and have it framed. There was a cupboard filled with cut glass that had been polished to within an inch of its life. If she had been with me, the cupboard might have been filled with cups given out at liquor stores and bars, with shop names and phone numbers featured prominently. I had to admit, she had made the choice that was right for her.

Kawasaki was now relaxing in an armchair, the way you'd expect the man of the house to behave. On his left wrist was a watch—I couldn't tell you the make, but I could guess at the price range. He was obviously not from new money, not a man who would make a casual attempt at showing off a Rolex.

"Thanks for seeing us in the middle of your work day," Ikoma began, but Kawasaki put up his hands magnanimously.

"It's no problem. I'm between classes right now." It turned out that he was the only son of the chairman of the board at the private high school where Saeko's father taught. He served as both vice-chairman and English teacher. Plans were in place for him to take over his father's position and become the youngest chairman in the history of the school. While most private schools were wading in red ink, his was practically turning a profit. Kawasaki was well known in academic circles for his business acumen, and he was largely given credit for the state of the institution as a whole—this much I had gotten out of Ikoma on our walk over. Apparently he hadn't had the time to check into the details of how Kawasaki and Saeko got together, but word had it that he was first attracted to her. They had been married about a year and a half.

He offered us an ashtray, even though he didn't seem to be a smoker. I noticed a hint of chalk on his right middle finger and a wedding band on his left hand.

The ashtray sat in the middle of the table on a lace tablecloth. The message I got was that there would be hell to pay if anything as filthy as ash fell outside of its confines. Ikoma, however, appeared to lack the slightest compunction, and he pulled out a cigarette.

"I'm terribly sorry," Kawasaki began, "but my wife can't be here to see you. You can tell me what you have to say." It might have been my imagination, but I saw a fleeting look of annoyance cross his otherwise decorous face. "She hasn't been well the past few days."

"That's too bad," Ikoma said. "I hope she's not ill."

Ikoma's question resulted in another moment of discomfort in Kawasaki. "She's pregnant, you see, and having trouble with morning sickness."

Ikoma stopped cold in mid-drag, but I automatically responded by congratulating Kawasaki, and the tension finally eased out of his shoulders. He smiled.

"Thank you."

They were just words, but they were obviously meant to be a sign of truce. I didn't know how he really felt, but I had no desire to explore the question, and evidently neither did he. The past was the past, and we would now act according to our respective positions and roles.

He was the one who had passed Saeko's test, and he had to face me—the one who had failed. He wasn't entirely comfortable, but there had to be a combination of smugness and superiority at work.

I knew he was aware of my previous relationship with his wife because Ikoma told me that Kawasaki had said that unless there was some grave emergency, it would be better if he and I didn't meet. I respected his gentlemanly attitude.

On the other hand, he could have glossed over Saeko's absence by saying she had a cold, but he had clearly chosen not to consider my feelings.

I didn't mind. Honesty was always the quicker path to take.

"I heard most of the story over the phone," he went on. "I understand the problem, and I appreciate your concern for my wife's safety." It might have been the result of his job, but his speech seemed somewhat old-fashioned for a man of his age. "Still, even if you've been the victim of some unpleasantness, I don't really see the need for us to meet just because my wife's name came up."

Ikoma glanced over at me, and then turned his attention back to Kawasaki. "Have you received anything?" he asked.

Kawasaki spoke in the same patient tone of voice that he might take with a student. "She received a blank letter."

Ikoma and I looked at each other.

"When was this?"

"About a week ago. Just the one. There haven't been any others."

"Do you still have it?"

"I'm sorry," Kawasaki said with a look of true regret, "but we threw it out."

Just then there was a knock on a door, perhaps one leading to the kitchen. At a glance, the woman who popped in looked like a clerical worker of sorts; probably about the same age as myself. She was dressed in a charcoal gray suit with a skirt that was about knee-length; she wore very little makeup, but she didn't need any. She was stunning even without it. Her hair was short, and she had on silver earrings.

She opened the door but did not come in, instead bowing deeply in the doorway. It was as if she had just completed a course on corporate manners.

"This is my secretary, Reiko Miyake." After Kawasaki's introduction, she bowed again, although not quite as deeply. Then she left, closing the door behind her. She returned in a few moments with a cart of the sort you see in luxury restaurants. A complete tea service had been laid out on top of it.

"Reiko helps us out at home, too," Kawasaki explained. "When we have a large number of guests, or when it's time to send out winter and summer gifts, it's more expedient to have her discuss matters directly with my wife. She was the one who found the letter in question."

His secretary finished serving us at exactly the same time Kawasaki finished this line. It was almost as if the entire scenario had been rehearsed. Right on cue she gave us a brief bow and pulled the cart out of the way before perching on an ottoman and placing her hands on her knees.

"That's right. I found it and showed it to Mr. Kawasaki." The tone of her voice gave the impression that, although she took orders from her boss, she was quite comfortable giving them out to others. I was suddenly curious about her relationship with Saeko. Which of the two was in charge?

"You didn't show Mrs. Kawasaki first?" asked Ikoma.

"That's correct," answered Kawasaki. "I get nasty letters every once in a while. It's inevitable for someone in my position. I try to make sure my wife is unaffected by them. That's why I ask Reiko to check the mail that comes to the house. When my wife receives mail without a return address, for example, Reiko is careful to run them by me first."

His tone bothered me. Was it right for a husband or wife to read a spouse's private letters without permission? Kawasaki smiled uncomfortably, and I supposed that was because Ikoma and I were wearing the same puzzled expression.

"You might think me highhanded; it's not the sort of thing I would usually do, but things are different right now."

"His wife is in a delicate condition," Reiko Miyake added.

"Yes, and she is somewhat excitable. My school is well known for its long history, but it is just as famous for in-house conflict. I'll be taking over as chairman of the board before too long, but there have been some problems."

"Anonymous letters crop up whenever people and money move," said Ikoma in a serious tone.

Kawasaki laughed out loud, and he looked suddenly younger. "You're exactly right. You'd expect a group of teachers to be dedicated to their students, but who knows what lies just under the skin."

"It's all for the best," Ikoma responded. "If children were taught by saintly old souls, they'd have a heck of a shock waiting for them when they went out into society. They need to have a tough skin if we want to keep the world in good running condition." Then he picked up the delicate gold-rimmed teacup and gulped the contents down in a single swallow.

I got back to the subject at hand. "That letter . . . did it come addressed to your wife? Did it bear her married name or her maiden name?"

Kawasaki looked over at his secretary, and she took over. "It was addressed to Saeko Kawasaki, and it had the correct address."

"But the letter was blank?"

"Yes."

"So you threw it away?"

Kawasaki responded this time. "That's right. It was strange that my wife received an anonymous letter, but I could never have imagined that it was connected to something larger. I just assumed that it was sent by someone looking to rattle me, by way of my wife."

"How about telephone calls? Has anyone called to tell your wife that she'd better be careful?"

Kawasaki looked into my face, and answered shortly. "No."

We glared at each other for no more than a few seconds, but it was a clear message that there was absolutely no room in Saeko's life—be it threatening letters or phone calls—for her name to be connected to mine. I was the first to blink, but I was not admitting defeat.

"Have there been any suspicious characters around your house or the school?" Ikoma asked quietly. I could tell that he was trying to stifle his laughter.

"Anyone wandering around in the neighborhood or following you or your wife?" I asked. "How about a gray sedan? I know it's not much to go on, but I was followed by a car like that last night."

Kawasaki and his secretary looked at each other. Her eyes maintained their look of intelligence and propriety even as they grew larger.

"No, nothing like that," answered Kawasaki.

Ikoma put a fist up to his mouth and nodded for a few seconds. He must have been thinking the same thing that I was.

After a minute I said, "Well, it sounds as if there's no immediate danger."

Kawasaki looked relieved. "I agree."

"But I would like to ask you to be careful. We don't know who we're dealing with, and we can't take any chances. Agreed?"

Kawasaki nodded briefly. *I don't need you to tell me how to take care of my own wife,* his expression read.

"Would you please talk to the police and ask them to patrol the area?" I asked.

"As Mr. Kawasaki is very well connected," Ikoma said with a smile, "I'm sure they'll agree without a fuss."

"All right, fine," Kawasaki answered, rubbing his nose as if thinking about something. "But just so you know, my wife doesn't even know you called."

I looked over at Reiko Miyake. She kept her eyes on her boss and seemed completely oblivious to me.

"And I have to admit that I was lying to you. She's not in bed upstairs. This was her day to see the obstetrician, and she'll be spending the night with her parents. That's why we were able to see you today."

"Mrs. Kawasaki is terribly concerned about any influence on her unborn child," Miyake spoke up, "and we can't subject her to unnecessary anxiety."

"How wise of you!" Ikoma almost laughed. "You are a first-class secretary!"

Miyake almost smiled.

We were informed that the pair had been particularly careful about leaving Saeko alone at home in the evenings, especially since she had gotten pregnant. During the day, she had a routine she followed, and they would know immediately if something unforeseen happened.

After a few minutes more of small talk, Ikoma and I rose to leave. As we crossed the sitting room, I noticed a framed picture of Saeko in her wedding dress. I didn't stop to examine it, but I could see at a glance that her face was wreathed in smiles.

It must have been a splendid wedding.

"It's love," said Ikoma.

We took off our jackets again as soon as we got back out on the street, and we began to walk at a refreshingly brisk pace. It was a relief to be out of the Kawasaki home.

"No, it's not!" I said.

"Oh yes it is!"

"How can you tell?"

"The eyes."

"Well, you're wrong," I said flipping my jacket over my shoulder.

Ikoma looked over at me. "I'm not talking about you being in love with Saeko. You're too quick off the mark."

"Then who?"

"That secretary."

"Reiko Miyake?" I stopped in my tracks.

"That's right."

"In love with Kawasaki?"

"Yes, who else would I be talking about? Unless you're in love with me?"

"I was afraid you'd catch on one day."

"Forget it. I'd never cheat on my wife."

Two girls in school uniforms passing us made a double take, and Ikoma and I exploded in laughter.

"I've got enough shame in my life as it is," I gasped after a few moments. "Please allow me my dignity while I'm walking down the street."

"I'll do my best. But let's get serious, Kosaka. It's a known fact that secretaries fall in love with their bosses." Now I'd done it. Ikoma only called me by name when he was teaching me a lesson. "I don't think they can do their jobs unless they're in love with their bosses. No matter how wretched he may be, there's always something. The way he works, or how masculine he is, or how he acts when he's in a good mood. That woman loves everything about Kawasaki. He's got it all and is handsome to boot."

"What does any of that have to do with what we came for?"

"Who knows? I'm just giving you my impression. When I see a beautiful woman, I'm naturally interested in the sort of man she's interested in."

As is almost always the case, the trip back to the office seemed shorter than the one out. It wasn't long before we were back in Ginza under the Wako store clock.

"There's no love left," Ikoma mumbled.

I refused to get caught this time. "Who are you talking about?"

"You!"

"That's right."

"I knew it all along, but I wasn't sure if you did."

"Sure I did. Did I act so broken up?"

"Not really, but Saeko did serious damage to your self-respect. Some people can't give up a lost love because they want to keep their pride intact. They're looking to make things right in a do-over."

"Don't worry," I assured him, "I'm not that persistent." We stopped at a corner where a crowd grew as it waited for the signal to change. Then I remembered. "You almost started laughing back there—when Kawasaki and I were glaring at each other."

"And?"

"What was so funny?"

"Men refuse to lose face no matter how minor the point."

Now I laughed. "You're right."

"But there was something he said that bothered me. There he was with his wife's old boyfriend sitting in front of him. And he's saying that there might be trouble for her, and it has to do with *his* job. If it was me, my first impression would be, 'what an impudent son of a bitch!'"

"Right."

"I'd think, 'She's done with you, get out of her life!'"

"Exactly."

"Even if you managed to hold your anger in, it would spill out in your attitude."

"That's what I thought, but Kawasaki didn't seem to have any of that."

"None! He was a picture of composure, except for that one nasty look."

The signal changed, and we walked across the street with the crowd.

"That Kawasaki . . ."

"Yeah, he's completely . . ."

Ikoma and I said the same thing as we made our way over the crosswalk: ". . . got himself together."

At the same time, it felt like we'd both left something unsaid.

# 5

Back at the office, there were two messages on my desk. One was a call from the woman who represented the group opposed to beauty contests. I talked to the reporter who had taken the call.

"She sounded pleased," he said. "She said that she appreciated the lack of negative spin. Said male reporters rarely seemed capable of that. She asked me to thank both the reporter and whoever wrote up the article. When I told her it was a column, so the same son of a bitch did both, she was surprised."

The editor in chief walked past and glared at him. "What's this 'son of a bitch' business when talking to readers?"

I wondered if the caller would have been as happy if she had known that I'd written the article with my mind still on the matter of psychics, and that I hadn't had the energy to do any more than write up what she'd told me.

It was then that I had a realization. "An interview!"

I spoke out loud, getting the attention of Ikoma, who was looking for an ashtray from among the mess on his desk.

"What? Did you just remember something?"

"If it was an interview, my name would have been on it!"

"That's right," agreed Ikoma. "It would have had a byline."

I hadn't thought about byline articles.

"Did you write any while you were at the Hachioji office?" he asked.

I nodded. Local reporters did a little bit of everything. Elections, sports, police beat, local educational matters—whatever needed to be covered. "I did some, but not a lot because I'm not good with interviews. I either just sit and listen or ask too many pointed questions and get the subject angry. The problem was that the interviews I did back then were usually meant to flatter the subject, and I couldn't do that either."

"But what are the chances that you got somebody's goat three years ago and they're just getting around to revenge now?" ventured Ikoma.

"It wouldn't hurt to take a look," I said. "I'll read through them all again to see if anything comes up." Not particularly motivated by the task, I went back to my messages. The second one was from the man who ran the gas station where Naoya used to work. He wanted me to call back.

I quickly dialed the number, and the man sounded like he was in a hurry. He had news of Naoya and might know where he was. I pulled up a chair.

"Did you see him?"

"No, it's not that—someone came to see him. It was the owner of the convenience store Naoya worked for about six months ago. He said he'd seen him working here once as he passed by, and he'd come back because he figured he'd still be here. 'He used to work for me, until one day he quit all of a sudden. It was a surprise to see him again,' he said. But I had to tell him he'd quit this place, too."

"Did you ask the man for any identification?"

"No, but I've got something even better!" He laughed at his own cleverness. "The man said that a couple of weeks after Naoya quit, a private investigator came around asking questions. He wasn't interested in answering any of them, so he sent the investigator on his way. But he'd heard since then that the mass media was looking for Naoya too, and now he was more interested."

Naoya had told Asako that he had been followed by a PI. So it wasn't a lie.

The man went on. "I got the investigator's name and address. He'd asked the convenience store guy to contact him if he got any information on Naoya, and he had left his card. It's not every day you get a card like that, so the store owner held onto it. Shall I give you the number? The guy said he didn't want to get involved, but I don't mind!"

I called the number, and a woman answered. She announced herself as the president of Tokyo Research, and said no, they weren't private investigators, but researchers who specialized in missing persons. If the president was answering the phones, I imagined the company couldn't be too large.

She was up to date on Naoya's case, but said their investigation had been suspended.

"Why suspended?" I asked.

"At the request of the client, why else?"

She and Ikoma would make great conversational partners, I thought.

"Does that mean you found him?"

"No, we didn't."

*Why then?* "You probably know that Naoya Oda ran away from home right at age fifteen," I began.

The woman was silent, so I took that as an affirmative.

"Your client must have been his family." It had to be. I wanted badly to speak with them. "I need to contact them."

The woman replied tersely, "I can't give out that information!"

"I know, but I'm asking you to bend the rules a little. I—I'm planning to do an article on him."

"I don't believe you."

"I've got information, too, you know. His parents divorced when he was young, and there was a matter of dividing up the estate."

The woman on the other end was silent for a long time. When she finally spoke, she kept her voice low. There must have been someone else in the room.

"All right, fine. I can't have you bothering me. I won't give you the client's name or address. I'm sure she wouldn't talk to you even if you showed up."

"She?"

"Yes, my client was Naoya's mother." She went on to give me two important pieces of information. Naoya's parents had divorced when he was eight for two main reasons. The first was that his mother didn't get along with her mother-in-law, Naoya's grandmother. "The Oda family ran a large liquor shop in Itabashi for generations. Naoya's father was the fourth generation; he was an only son. Unfortunately, he married a former bar hostess more than ten years younger than him, and his mother was dissatisfied with her from the start. The matter came to blows from what I heard."

The other reason was that the liquor shop went bankrupt.

"Naoya's father guaranteed a loan for another man who later disappeared. He had to make good on the loan, and his wife ran out of patience with him. There was trouble over money, but the main problem was who would get custody of the boy. His mother wanted him, but she lost her parental rights."

So now she was looking for him. "She said she'd been worried about him for years, and now she finally had a little money of her own."

"Why did she give up?"

"She remarried, and her husband wasn't interested in looking for Naoya. She was pregnant, and they were going to have a child of their own."

I guessed that it made sense, but still . . .

The woman went on to say that Naoya's mother had promised to get in touch again once things had settled down.

"What about his father?" I asked.

"Drank himself to death."

A bad aftertaste remained even after I hung up the phone. Naoya had grown up in tragic circumstances. Shinji had told me about the divorce and the money, and that it had been impossible for a psychic to remain in the house.

I badly wanted to meet Naoya's mother and ask her about it all. I tried to figure out a way to get around the roadblock put up by the president.

At a loss, I picked up a newspaper someone had tossed on the desk next to mine. I sucked in my breath at one of the headlines—the type was plain and the article so tiny that I was surprised I even saw it. And after I read it, I wished I hadn't.

*Fatal leap off Hijiri Bridge.* The tiny headline was followed by a brief description.

> A youth was seen jumping off Hijiri Bridge, a span across the Kanda River in Chiyoda Ward. Rescuers quickly recovered the body. A driver's license in the victim's pocket identified him as Satoshi Miyanaga (21), a student at Tokyo International University.

It was one of those two budding artists, one of the duo who had removed the manhole cover during the storm. I remembered the painting he had done. The eternally red traffic signal. The never-ending stop sign.

PART 5
# A Turn for the Worse

The day was warm but the sky was filled with clouds. Shinji and his father and I got off at Makuhari Station, which was filled with people who were casually dressed, ready for the weekend. We saw the occasional all-black outfit, and I assumed that most of those people were headed to the funeral being held at the Miyanaga home, a few minutes' walk from the station.

What with the autopsy and police investigation, not to mention the need to choose an "auspicious" date, the funeral didn't take place until four days after Satoshi's death. During those four days, the shock had worn off somewhat, but the pain was still raw; in fact, I felt worse as time went on. It was like a bruise that spread out and got darker.

I met the Inamuras at the station, and I could see that Shinji, too, was badly bruised. Among the crowds of youth, laughing and talking, the unsmiling Shinji and his equally somber father seemed to disappear. I regretted agreeing to go with them. Instead, I should have encouraged them to stay home.

Shinji was in his dark blue school uniform, neatly buttoned up to his chin. By contrast, his face looked very pale. I could tell he hadn't been sleeping, and his cheeks were covered with the resulting acne.

"I think you should go home," I said to Shinji's father as they approached. I leaned over and peered into Shinji's face. "It's not your fault, you know. I take responsibility for it all. I should have gone to the police with the information."

Shinji shook his head, and his father spoke. "Mr. Kosaka, hindsight is not helpful."

"But what else do I have to go on?"

"Shinji is responsible," he said quietly. "My opinion is not going to change, no matter what you say. And whether or not you go to the funeral, I'm taking my son. Let's be on our way."

Shinji walked ahead of us toward the taxi stand. His father made a move to follow, but I grabbed his elbow first. "He's only sixteen," I insisted. "He's still a child."

"But he's not a normal child," he said matter-of-factly.

I looked at him and said, "That's true. Let's go."

Although the Miyanagas lived in a good-sized house, the sheer number of mourners made it look small. It was much too small to accommodate them all.

There were mountains of flowers, a multitude of mourners, a photograph of the departed, and tears of lamentation—but it felt empty somehow.

Sitting before the altar was a middle-aged woman kneeling on the floor, her body bowed over, almost flat to the floor, following the position of prayer her religion required. Listening to the whispers of the people around me, I learned that she was Satoshi's mother.

This was the second time I had witnessed the sorrow of a mother involved in this particular case. The first had been the mother of Daisuke Mochizuke, the little boy who had drowned in the sewer. In neither case did the women have the answer as to why their sons had died.

Only a few of us knew what really happened. Daisuke had been swept into a manhole, never knowing why it was open or who had done it. Miyanaga had suddenly committed suicide. He had jumped off a bridge in broad daylight, surrounded by crowds of passersby. I heard the other mourners speculating about his motive. The deceased had left no will and no note hinting at his reasons for wanting to end his life. I had done my best over the last few days to dig up information, but it was clear that he had taken his secrets to his grave.

I hadn't had any luck contacting his pal, Shunpei Kakita, who had helped him take off the manhole cover. I couldn't pick him out at the funeral either. Despite the fact that almost everyone wore identical clothing, I was sure I'd be able to pick his face out of the crowd, but it proved impossible. A voice deep inside was telling me that I was responsible for the deaths of both the seven-year-old boy and the twenty-one-year-old budding artist.

Shinji and his father stood slightly apart from me. Near them was a young woman who was crying so hard she was hiccupping. Another woman had her arms around her and was crying, too. I decided that Shinji had chosen that spot on purpose so he could hear the sobs.

The Miyanaga home was not particularly modern, but it had an attached garage that looked like it might be new; it was outfitted with shutters that were closed. At some point during the ceremony, two men who looked to be employees of the funeral company opened the shutters just enough to bend over and get through. I got a glimpse of the tires. I bent a little lower and saw a glint of red from the Porsche 911.

Until the funeral employees came out of the garage and lowered the shutter again, all I could think of was that red car in the midst of that typhoon. And the yellow umbrella we'd found in the bushes.

Just then someone tapped me on the shoulder. I whipped around to see the wasted face of Shunpei Kakita, Satoshi's partner in misadventure.

"If I'd been there, I could have stopped him from jumping," were the first words out of Kakita's mouth. He looked as though he was speaking to his friend, far off in the sky, rather than me.

Then he pulled me out of the ring of mourners. Shinji saw us and made a move to follow. Before I could say anything, Kakita looked over at Shinji and shook his head, indicating that he wasn't to come. Shinji froze, and I saw his father put his arm around his shoulder.

"We have some time until they carry the coffin out," I said. "Let's take a walk." I wanted to get away from there. The closer we were to Shinji, the more likely he was to "listen in" on our conversation.

"That's the kid," Kakita said in a low voice. "He saw us do it. He saw it and then followed us to the Jai Alai coffee shop."

We were about two blocks away from the Miyanaga home, and we began to slow our strides. We passed a utility pole with a sign attached that pointed the way to the funeral.

"That's right," I replied truthfully—it was the best way to handle matters. "But what happened after that was my decision, not his."

Kakita remained silent, walking unsteadily.

"We know you did it. You pulled off the manhole cover to drain the rainwater off the street so the engine wouldn't stall."

Kakita nodded without saying a word. He finally looked up at me with his bloodshot eyes and asked, "Why didn't you call the police?"

I didn't have a reply. Anything I said would sound like an excuse. It would be better just to agree to whatever conclusion he came up with himself.

"You felt sorry for us, didn't you?" he said.

"Sorry?"

"That's right. We were stupid, but we didn't realize what could happen. I admit it. You could tell we didn't mean any harm, and that's why you didn't notify the police. You must have thought we'd give ourselves up on our own. That's what I planned to do anyway," he said. "We'd been warned, and I was sure we'd end up confessing."

"How about Miyanaga?"

Kakita didn't answer my question. "We read the article in *Arrow*," he said. "I told Miyanaga that we had to do the right thing. I told him there was still time to make good."

Even though we were several blocks away, the scent of funeral incense was still in the air. I felt as though Miyanaga was with us, listening in on the conversation.

Kakita blinked and rubbed his chin with the palm of his hand. I saw that his hand was shaking. "I was the one who drove him to suicide. I told him I wanted to come clean, but he said that would ruin his career as an artist."

Witnesses had said that moments before Miyanaga jumped he had been leaning against the handrail, looking over the Kanda River. Something must have snapped.

"He told me he was going out to buy some paint. He needed cadmium yellow to start his next piece." Kakita went silent as he gazed into space.

"It was Miyanaga who suggested taking off the manhole cover," he said faintly. "I told him I thought it was impossible for us to lift, and then we decided to try. We used a bar and car jack to make a lever. We laughed about how easy it was. We never imagined that somebody would fall in there. We thought that getting rid of the water would be a public service."

I remember Shinji telling me that the two had believed the neighbors would be pleased.

"But Miyanaga said nobody would believe us if we took that story to the police." Kakita spoke so quietly I could hardly hear him. "It all sounded like an excuse, he said. They'd arrest us, and we'd be criminals. He was terrified of the idea."

We stopped and he looked at me. "Miyanaga said you and that boy were the only evidence against us. He even talked about getting rid of the two of you so we wouldn't have to worry anymore."

"Do you think he meant it?" In my mind I saw again the gray sedan, the one that had been following me when I went to see Nanae.

Kakita continued lethargically. "He talked about it, but he'd never be able to pull it off. Maybe that's why he jumped." He dragged his feet as he walked. "We got along really well. I didn't know him for that long, but he used to say that our moms probably fed us the same brand of formula, used the same disposable diapers, and powdered our butts with the same talcum powder. We were great friends." Then he added, "That was the first time we'd argued—after that accident. I wanted to go to the police, but Miyanaga was dead set against it."

Where had I heard a similar story? It was Shinji and Naoya—great friends, but torn apart by a conflict of opinion.

"I'm going to the police after the funeral," Kakita said. "Nobody understands why Miyanaga killed himself. But his family said he'd been acting strange. That's what they told a detective who came to talk to them. If they investigate, they're sure to come up with something, and I want to come clean before that happens. Satoshi's dead, and I don't have any excuses for it, but I don't want people just guessing what happened. If I confess, the police are bound to treat me better than a criminal they have to hunt down."

"That's true," I answered.

"So I'm begging you to forget that you ever met us at that coffee shop. I want the police to believe I came in without any—encouragement."

It was a simple enough request. And it was the development I'd been hoping for anyway, although it seemed a shame coming so late.

Kakita turned to go back to the funeral.

"I'll tell the boy what I'm planning," he said. "So you don't have to worry about that."

Back at the Miyanaga home, I watched Kakita go over to Shinji and talk, exactly as he had promised. After he had finished, he grabbed Shinji's hand

and shook it with an air of great sincerity, but something wasn't quite right. Shinji's face was expressionless. After shaking Kakita's hand, he stood there like a clay figure.

It was then that it dawned on me that Kakita had not once mentioned regret for Daisuke's death; he was more worried about the consequences for himself. Was this the way young people these days thought about things?

When it came time for the coffin to be carried out of the house, Shinji was mistaken for a member of the family; maybe the school uniform made him look like a younger brother or cousin. One of the funeral company staff handed him a white carnation and asked him to put it inside the coffin. Shinji looked confused, but he did as he was told.

The coffin was carried out to the hearse, and the hearse left for the crematory. Shinji and his father and I left with the others.

"Shinji, did you read something from him?" his father asked quietly.

Shinji looked at us blankly, and said. "No, nothing." Then he took off ahead of us.

I talked to Shinji's father as we walked. I told him I knew a retired police officer who might be of more help than I could be. That is, if Shinji agreed to it.

"I'd be grateful," Inamura said. "He might do Shinji good."

"Try not to get your hopes up," I warned. "I've never met the man myself."

"We'll try anything at this point," he responded sadly.

Shinji walked on ahead of us. There was purpose in his step as walked down the plain, dusty road.

Kakita kept his word. Three days after the funeral, I found his name in the newspaper. I talked to a colleague who knew a lot about law. He told me the young man would probably not be punished too harshly.

"He moved the manhole cover without knowing the danger it presented. It was a foolish thing to do, but he'll probably get manslaughter and pay a fine of two hundred thousand yen at the most. Social opinion is bound to be harsher than the law, but with time the whole thing will be forgotten."

With one case cleared, it was only a matter of time before the next one came up. I got another letter that evening. The eighth.

This time, the text read "Anger."

My editor in chief had finally commanded me to get some work done, and I had put Shinji and Naoya on hold for the past three days. I figured if I worked twice as hard as usual, I might get a little more time to deal with the two of them. So I'd been busy. On top of that, we had to completely replace a lengthy feature article at the last minute. The entire office was involved, and none of us had the time to even consider the letter. I just wrapped it in the rubber band that held the other seven letters and shoved it to the back of the third drawer in my desk. Kanako came around with the mail with a dejected look on her face, but I didn't have time to chat.

There were no phone calls either. The recorder Ikoma had set up for me sat on my desk collecting dust. Ikoma called the Kawasakis to check on Saeko, and she was fine. There was no more graffiti on the stairs of my apartment building. For three days I was frequently out of the office, but I didn't get a sense of anyone following me.

On the evening of the third day, I called Nanae. That is, I talked and she tapped, so we didn't discuss anything very complicated.

"Has anything out of the ordinary happened?"

*No.*

"Has Naoya contacted you?"

*No.*

"Let me know if he does. I won't do anything to harm him."

There was no reply.

"Please?"

Silence.

"Nanae, are you afraid you're never going to hear from him again?"

*Yes.*

"But why? Is he really that determined to stay hidden?"

A pause, and then *yes.*

Nor did I hear from Shinji. I knew he must be "calling" Naoya as hard as he could. Maybe Naoya was deliberately ignoring him. Either that, or there was no such thing as the power to "call" someone. I no longer knew what was possible and what was impossible. Then I heard a tapping on the receiver. Nanae was waiting impatiently for my next question.

"I'm sorry, there's one more thing. Have you ever called Naoya to come to you? Have you ever called him in your head? Or tried to?"

Nanae didn't reply. As I held the phone to my ear, I heard again that metal-on-metal scraping again. It was low, but it was definitely the sound I'd heard when I had called before.

I couldn't really ask her what it was. It would take all night to figure it out. I felt impatient. Nanae must have spent her life feeling impatient and irritated. And she would continue to do so.

Finally, she tapped twice.

*Yes.*

I said, "Thank you!" and hung up the phone.

I spoke to the sneaker dangling in front of my face.

"You know that's dangerous. Come on down." The sneaker belonged to Shinji. He had climbed up into a sycamore tree and sat with one leg on either side of a large branch.

"Don't worry, I won't fall," he said, his voice calm.

We were in the park where Shinji came to cool off or, occasionally, meet Naoya. Just as he'd said, it was almost deserted, despite the warm fall afternoon weather. An expressway had been built overhead, and the park got almost no sunlight. The legs of the swingset were cold to the touch.

"I didn't know you were a tree climber."

"Didn't you climb trees when you were young?"

"There was nothing but persimmon trees where I grew up."

"Couldn't you climb those?"

"The branches aren't very sturdy."

"I never knew that. Guess that shows the difference in our ages."

Shinji looked relaxed. The color of the leaves reflected on his cheeks and made him look slightly green, but his voice was energetic.

"Did you hear about the man from your father?"

"You mean about the policeman? Yeah, I heard."

"Would you like to meet him?"

Shinji nodded, and a few yellow leaves fell off the tree. "Yeah, I guess."

"Great, I'll take care of the details."

"Are you going to report on it?" Shinji adjusted his position and looked down at me with a serious expression. "Are you going to write about me in *Arrow*?"

"Do you want me to?"

"I don't know."

"Well, then, I don't have anything to say on the matter."

"That's not fair, but it's sort of funny. If I said 'no,' would you say you wouldn't write it up? It's hard to believe."

"No comment."

I heard him laugh. "You sound like a politician!"

It had been a long time since I'd been to a park. Without a girlfriend on my arm, or a small child, I tended to frequent places without greenery. "Do you remember telling me that you'd like to use your power to help people?"

After a pause, he said yes.

"If this retired cop has an opportunity for you to do that, they'll want to keep your presence a secret."

"Really?"

"Sure. If people knew about you, they'd be after you night and day. You'd be a celebrity."

"The psychic detective," Shinji said to himself, and he swung his feet some more.

"Sounds good."

"Not really. It's not like I'd be Philip Marlowe or anything."

Shinji had asked me if I believed in him. He must have been tired. "Thanks for coming out to see me. But I wonder why my parents look so nervous every time you show up. You'd think a mobster had come to visit."

I knew that it was because it reminded them of what they were facing. If people found out about Shinji's power, there would be no end to the questions and notoriety.

"I promise I won't bother you anymore, Mr. Kosaka."

"It's not really a bother."

"It's stressful, I can tell." His feet stopped moving. "There's something else that's bothering you, isn't there?"

I reached up and grabbed his pant leg. "Come on down. I'm worried about you up there. I can hear that branch giving way."

Shinji stayed put. He was silent. Then he spoke in a quiet voice. "If I fell, I'd die, and that would solve everything." A gust of autumn breeze rustled the leaves on the tree. "Why do you think I go out in typhoons?"

I lifted my head. "What do you mean?"

"When I was out on my bike, I knew the typhoon was coming. It wasn't a mistake. I went out to see what the storm was like."

"Not a very healthy hobby."

The branch creaked again.

"It's a relief for me to see nature in full force. It makes me feel smaller and less powerful. Sometimes I'm full of pride—it's hard not to be when you know what other people are thinking. It makes me feel special and unusual, and that's not good." His voice was full of self-disdain. "Naoya won't come. I've tried calling him."

"I see."

"I might never see him again. We're taking different paths. He's always saying that there's no way we can help people with our power. That I can't ask other people to help me out—like the way I got you to help with that manhole business. He told me I shouldn't meddle in other people's affairs unless I intend to set everything right on my own."

I wondered what process of trial and error had led Naoya to that conclusion. He'd seen his mother fighting with his grandmother and seen his father turn into a drunk. All the while, he'd known the way each of them had suffered and what their dreams had been. When he decided he couldn't do anything for any of them, he left home and set off on his own.

"I don't know what to do any more," Shinji said softly. "I've started to believe what Naoya said is true and now I'm more confused than ever."

I was about to tell him that Naoya was more interested in others than he liked to let on when the branch suddenly made a loud crack.

Shinji slid precipitously down the tree. I leaped forward and was showered with sycamore leaves. The branch hadn't broken off completely, but I could see the white wood that had been exposed where the branch was still connected to the trunk.

I offered Shinji a hand, and he stood up, twisting around to brush debris from the seat of his pants. "Wow, that was scary," he said. "I wonder if I'll get in trouble for damaging public property?"

He smiled when he let go of my hand. "You're thinking about a girl!"

"What?"

"I got a peek when I grabbed your hand. Sorry about that." He put his hand behind his back, as if trying to keep it under control. "It's a bad habit. But look, the girl you're thinking about is a good person!"

"How do you know?"

"I felt warmth. The memory I saw was warm. She's not the same as that Saeko."

I had planned to tell him about Nanae, Naoya's girlfriend, but now I couldn't bring myself to do it.

"You're a pain in the neck!" I kidded him, and he smiled again.

"Yeah, even I know that! But I realized one thing. See, I can see all sorts of things that people keep hidden in their hearts. Some of them are things that are pushed way down, that will never see the light of day. When I 'scanned' you before and saw a woman named Saeko, I thought that you'd been in agony over her, but I was wrong. You stowed her away for good a long time ago. That was a memory you were never going to take out and try to relive."

I remembered how Shinji had apologized to me about her. I had been alarmed to think that it looked as though I was still obsessed with Saeko.

"So you see? You can end up making someone even more confused if you bring up the past and don't interpret it correctly."

It had been a long time since Shinji smiled in a way that actually made me feel better.

He went back to his original topic. "I only got a glimpse of what you were thinking about, but it felt good. I think that woman is just what you need."

That was it. I decided once and for all not to discuss anything about Nanae with him.

# 3

The offices for *Mirai*—a journal about education—occupied an entire floor of an office building. It was full of noise and confusion.

"Hey! Over here!" In order to get closer to Masaki Shimizu, who was waving his arms at me, I had to step over two mountains of magazines bound up with string. I managed, but Ikoma failed.

"The Berlin Wall is coming down," he said laughing to a woman busily checking a manuscript at a nearby desk. She turned to look and made a gesture as if to stab him with her red pen.

"I told you you didn't need to come out here!"

"What, and miss a scandal? No way!"

I had first met Shimizu after I was assigned to *Arrow*. He was an assistant chief editor at *Mirai*. He could sniff out a story almost before it even happened. Of course, he saw to it that all of the good parents in Japan got the information they needed to raise their children properly. On the other hand, he was also privy to the seamier side of the education industry.

"There's no room to get anything done here," he moaned, as he grabbed a couple of temporarily unoccupied chairs for us. "If you wanted to know about Yomei School, all you had to do was read our feature on it."

Yomei was the school where Saeko's husband, Akio Kawasaki, was vice-chairman of the board.

"We want to hear about the parts you can't print."

"For example?"

"Whether Kawasaki has woman problems."

Shimizu laughed and plucked what looked like a cigarette out from behind one of his enormous ears. It turned out to be an aid to quit smoking.

"So you're quitting?"

"Doing my best. I might just make it this time," he said with a proud smile.

Ikoma grumbled, "The end of the world is in sight when Shimizu decides to quit smoking!"

"If I were to die of lung cancer," Shimizu laughed, "just think of the effect on the future of all the good little girls and boys out there! The truth is, my wife just had a baby, so I decided it was time."

"Ah yes, the balance of power shifts away from the father once children are in the picture—consider that as a topic for your next issue." Ikoma did his best to sound stern, but even he was smiling.

"So what about Kawasaki and other women?"

"Exactly, we need to know about any scandals, under way or in the works."

Shimizu crossed his legs and stated matter-of-factly, "He's having an affair with his secretary."

Ikoma gave me a sidelong glance. "Reiko Miyake?"

"That's right. Have you met her? She's something else." Shimizu tapped his forehead. "And she's smart, too."

"Does Kawasaki's wife know about it?" Ikoma asked.

"Probably not. Everyone else does, but none of us would be stupid enough to let his wife in on it. It wouldn't do us any good to destroy their family, and besides, we don't make money publishing that sort of trash."

"How long has it been going on?"

Shimizu tilted his head to one side. "At least as long as I've been in this position."

Now that was a surprise; he'd been assistant chief editor for four years. Kawasaki had been involved with Reiko before he met Saeko.

"Kawasaki had wanted to marry her," continued Shimizu, "but his father was against it. Oh, the tears that flowed."

"Why did his father object?"

"Class distinctions, of course," Shimizu said with a laugh. "Can you believe it's still happening in this day and age? Life's different in the upper echelons."

Reiko had graduated first in her class in a public high school before getting a clerical job at Yomei School. She was the vice-chairman's secretary by the time she was twenty. She stayed in the position when Kawasaki got the job and had been with him ever since.

"She's a nice girl, but she never even attended college. And her family is small—her father runs a stationery shop, and he only got as far as ninth grade. She's got a brother who I've heard drives a truck. It wouldn't matter to me, but bluebloods can only deal with other bluebloods."

"Kawasaki's wife doesn't come from a particularly good family, does she? Her father teaches at the school, too," I offered.

"But her parents both graduated from college, and her father gets a lot of respect at the school. He's retired now, but he was famous for keeping the students in line—and he was a big supporter of Kawasaki's father, the current chairman of the board. It must have seemed like a decent match. Kawasaki's father got them together, from what I hear."

Ikoma blinked a few times. "My information said that Kawasaki was the one who made the first move."

Shimizu waved it off. "That's the official story."

"I thought I could tell the difference."

"What can I say? I'm sure you can in your own field." He grabbed an unfortunate female staff member who was passing by his desk and pressed her to bring us three cups of coffee. Then he leaned forward conspiratorially. "Look, I heard there was some sort of understanding."

"Understanding?"

"Between the chairman and his son. He couldn't marry his secretary. His father vowed he'd throw him out of the school if he tried. On the other hand, if he married the woman the chairman picked for him, he'd be assured of getting the chairmanship when he retired." Shimizu gave us a look that indicated there was more to the story. "If he kept the affair discreet, he could carry on with his secretary as long as he liked."

The three of us were silent for a few moments. Finally Ikoma spoke. "Some father! Son of a bitch."

"I agree," Shimizu said. "And what about the other father? I'd never send my daughter into a marriage like that!"

"It's the secretary I feel sorry for," I said. "You've got a school that is proud of the number of graduates it sends on to Tokyo University. But so what if the wife of the chairman of the board only graduated from high school? It's not as though it would contradict everything the school stands for. When will people learn that your academic record's not the only thing that counts? Personality and abilities are important, too. It's not all about the name of the school on your diploma."

Shimizu nodded. "That's right. Since he was young, Kawasaki had rebelled against his father's insistence that he go to Tokyo University. He rebelled plenty, but never enough to alienate his father. The position of chairman is an attractive one."

"And this position will be opening soon, we hear?"

"I'm about eighty-five to ninety percent certain. Maybe even by the end of the year," Shimizu said, glancing up at the calendar. "The chairman had a mild stroke this past spring. He's all but retired already. Kawasaki has taken over the work his father was doing. But dad's cronies come with the job. They'll have plenty to say about how the younger Kawasaki runs things."

"Does that mean father and son don't agree on everything? Do they fight?" Ikoma asked.

"Sure, all the time," Shimizu said. "You'd think a school would be different, but it's a company like any other. The man who runs the company relies more on his subordinates than on his leadership-deficient heir apparent."

The female staff member showed up with our coffee, and Shimizu thanked her for it sweetly. He grabbed her elbow and pointed a thumb in my direction. "He's a friend of mine—single!" Some people couldn't help themselves. "I'm right, aren't I?" he was polite enough to check. "Or do you already have someone picked out?"

Without waiting for my reply, the woman said, "Well, *I* do!" and stalked off.

"And that," Shimizu concluded, "is how the chairman fixed his son up. That's the way it worked. Except that his father didn't give his son a tap on the elbow; he came at him with a sledgehammer."

"But why did his wife agree to the match," asked Ikoma. "Her name's Saeko, right? She's still pretty young."

"I guess she was twenty-four or five. She's a looker, but not particularly worldly. She probably did what her father told her to. And there was something else, I'm not really sure . . ." He leaned in closer. "Saeko also had her own past. I hear she had marriage plans that were cancelled at the last minute, maybe three or four years ago. When the chairman asked her father about making the match, it was a big relief to all of them. I don't know the details; they don't talk about it."

I'm sure he would have fallen out of his chair if he knew I was the ex-fiancé. Ikoma was probably thinking the same thing when he said, "So there are things even you don't know about, eh?"

"An old scandal about Kawasaki's wife wouldn't be of any interest to me."

"So tell us something that would be of interest. You're saying that the reason Kawasaki is going to be promoted to chairman is because he stuck with the program and did everything the way his father wanted him to?"

"That's the story for now, and the school is doing well. But I'm guessing the school will change when Kawasaki junior takes over. Right now he's saving up money for the reforms he has in mind. He gets contributions by keeping it a breeding ground for the elite. You know, I'm kind of looking forward to any new plans he's got."


Shimizu finally decided it was time for a drink and dragged us off to a favorite pub. It turned out to be the watering hole of choice for the *Mirai* staff, and the place gradually got noisier and more crowded. By the time Ikoma and I got out, it was almost eleven.

"Who would have guessed editors at an educational magazine could drink so much," Ikoma said as he hiccupped loudly. "The Japanese future is bright. At least the owner of that pub won't have to worry about paying her taxes." We turned off of the deserted alley and onto Yasukuni Boulevard; it was definitely late.

"You're awfully sober," Ikoma commented.

"Yup."

"Thinking about something?"

"My estimates were off."

"Use a calculator. It's less work. I'm good with the abacus, so I don't need one. What kind of figures are you working with?"

"I'm thinking it's Reiko Miyake, Kawasaki's secretary."

Ikoma was as red as a barn. "You mean those letters?"

"It's not the work of a pro. There are better ways to scare the pants off me."

"Yes sir, got to get up pretty early in the morning to unhinge a good reporter." Ikoma laughed and then tried to look serious. "You're right, of course."

"That car that was following me gave up without a fight. The graffiti only happened once. And who drags buckets of paint around? It's almost too cute for someone with a real grudge."

"I see what you mean."

The subway entrance was right at hand, and the lights around it were bright.

"I think someone's pretending."

"Pretending?"

"Sure, pretending to want to intimidate me. There's some other objective behind it all."

"What do you mean?"

"Suppose someone pretends to be after me for an old grudge, and they bring Saeko's name into it. Sooner or later, I'm going to end up contacting her. It's the only thing that makes sense."

"You're right," Ikoma grunted.

"And maybe that's what this person is looking for."

Ikoma stopped. "But why?"

"It's like I said before. Even if her husband knows that she and I are finished, he's not going to be happy having me come around. He's the target—someone's looking for smoke where there's no fire."

My voice got louder as we descended the cavernous stairwell into the subway, and I turned down the volume. "Kawasaki's got to be wondering why his wife's name came up when he knows she and I are through. But would it convince him that he's the one they're really after?"

Ikoma clapped his hands. "Of course! It would be logical for him to wonder if you and she were still seeing each other!"

We stepped out onto the deserted platform. It smelled like oil and metal.

"And I tried to call her without her husband knowing for the same reason. I didn't want to cause any trouble. But Kawasaki has got the lid on his wife, and we ended up talking to him. And he was so cool about it."

"Yeah, that's it!"

"Even if I'd been able to talk to her alone, she wouldn't have been happy about it. It's creepy. Sooner or later she would have told her husband, and then we'd be in a mess."

Ikoma began speaking in the voices of the characters he was talking about. "Kawasaki would say, 'Why didn't you tell me about this before?' and Saeko would say, 'Oh, but I didn't want you to worry.' Then Kawasaki would get the wrong idea."

"The only person who would benefit from it would be Reiko. A man followed me, but she could have hired someone to do it. She could have changed her voice over the phone . . ."

"Only his mistress would enjoy making trouble between Kawasaki and his wife."

"Right! The only problem is that it turns out she's sharper than we thought, and she's got Kawasaki in the palm of her hand. Why bother?"

"Yeah, if he was a piece of real estate, she'd be the squatter you couldn't get off the property."

"The eighth letter came the other day. It said *anger*. In terms of warfare, though, it feels almost like a retreat. There've been no more phone calls, no cars following me, no paint. Maybe my reactions haven't been what the sender hoped for."

"A big disappointment."

"Right. There's some recalculation going on."

The subway rumbled noisily into the station.

If I'd gone straight home, it would have meant not showing my face at the office all day, so I went in to work. But there was nothing new on my desk, no memos or letters.

I started thinking about Shinji again. If I could get him together with the retired cop, I wouldn't have much to do until I'd found Naoya. I might be able to get Tokyo Research looking for him again. That would be the quickest way to do it. Once I'd found him, I could worry about what to do next.

I'd spent so much time on the two boys, I was half terrified and half looking forward to catching up with my work. I had to admit I loved it. While straightening up my desk, I noticed that one of my books—one on psychics that I'd bought myself—was out of place. No matter how cluttered I kept it, I could tell when someone had been there—like a stray dog defending its territory.

There were still a few other reporters left in the office. They were huddled around a TV, watching a video. I called out to them.

"Did someone pick up one of my books?"

"We haven't touched it," called out one. "It looked interesting, but I wouldn't be so bold."

The books I'd bought were all of the flashy, mass-market variety, like *One Hundred Psychics You Can Believe In*. They were full of unlikely information.

"Is something missing?" another one asked.

"No, that's not it." I pushed my chair in and turned around to find Kanako standing in front of me.

"Welcome back," she said. I hadn't even heard her come into the room.

"You're like a cat," I said. "Why are you still here?"

"I've got business with you. I've been waiting." She had a petulant look on her face.

"Sorry. What's up?"

A couple of the men turned around, smirking, to see what was going on.

"What is it?" I asked again.

Kanako was unhappy, and she wanted me to know it.

"You had a guest."

"Yeah?"

"Yes, about five-thirty. Waited forever and asked when you were expected back." Her emphasis on "forever" was unsettling.

"You should have called my beeper."

One of the men called over. "Kanako, tell him the truth and stop interfering."

"All right. It was a woman," she said. "She wouldn't answer my questions. She couldn't talk, anyway."

It must have been Nanae. Kanako was looking daggers at me. "So you know who I'm talking about, I see."

"Yes, yes. So what did she do? How long did she stay?"

"You seem awfully interested. Who is she?"

"Come on, don't be childish."

"She must be important to you!"

"Kanako!" scolded the other reporter. "Stop acting like a fool and give him what she brought for him. Don't forget what you're getting paid for!"

"What did she give you?" I asked.

"I won't give it to you until you tell me who she is!"

The other reporter had had as much as he could take, and he ran up behind her and took from her the brown envelope she was hiding behind her back.

"You're not in high school anymore!" he muttered, and then explained matters to me. "Since she couldn't speak, she wrote down what she wanted to say, and said you'd know what she meant. She left about seven."

"Thanks."

I opened the envelope to find a note written in Nanae's hand.

*I saw that gray car again. Last night. I think it's watching my building, so I took some pictures of it and had them printed up. I've left you the negatives, too. I've never seen this person before.—Nanae*

There were six photos in the envelope that she'd obviously taken in quick succession. It was definitely the same gray sedan. The face of the driver was blurry, but I could tell it was the same man as before. The first two were taken from an angle, but the third was perfectly clear. There was more blurring in the fourth, and in the last two the car was driving away.

Since the photos were taken at night, I figured Nanae must have used a flash to get them this clear. The driver must have seen the flash and rushed to get away. I wondered if she had considered the notion that he might come back to get the photos.

I arrived at Nanae's apartment, but there were no lights on. I knocked on the door, but there was no response. The next-door neighbor came out to check. It was an older woman.

"I don't think she's home," the woman said.

"Do you know where she has gone?"

"No," she said, giving a blissful yawn. "I wouldn't know."

"Would you mind looking over at her balcony? If she's out, that's fine. I just want to check to make sure."

The woman looked me over once or twice, then said, "Hold on a minute." She was back in a few moments, and looked completely awake now. "Her window is open—she'd never do anything that thoughtless."

I ran around to the back of the building, slipped through the narrow space between it and the next building, and got closer to the window. The other windows on the first floor were dark, but the one next door had the storm doors open, and some light came through. I saw that Nanae's window was halfway open. I could also see a round hole cut in the glass next to the lock. I peeked inside and saw that a table had been overturned and some bureau drawers tossed onto the floor. Clothing had been scattered all over.

I took off my shoes, wrapped my hand in a handkerchief, and climbed inside. I turned on the light and checked the other doors. Nanae was gone. There were two spots of blood on the tatami. The hairs stood up on the back of my neck.

"Call the police!" I called out to the next-door neighbor, who was waiting fretfully at the door, and she sprang off. I heard a crash; she must have run into something.

The spot of blood on the tatami was dry. I looked to see if there were any others, and found one on the floor of the bathroom. I couldn't think clearly.

"I called the police!" the neighbor ran back to announce.

"Do you know where Miss Mimura works? Is it close by?"

"Midori Day Care. But who would be there at this time of night?" She stopped in mid-sentence and closed her mouth. She was looking down the hall. "Oh my," she said. "She's back."

Nanae appeared out of the shadow of the door. She looked surprised.

# 4

"So you're saying nothing was stolen?" The police officer turned to look at Nanae. She nodded. "Your cash and bankbooks are accounted for," he said. "Good. It looks like the idiot who got in cut his hand on the glass."

The police had found blood on the round piece of glass lying on the floor.

"Do you mind if I ask, miss, where you keep your valuables?"

Nanae gestured the officer into the kitchen and pointed at a small bottle.

"Your pickle jar?"

She nodded, then pointed to the bucket where she kept her rice.

The officer beamed, "Excellent!"

I explained the matter of the photos to him, but Nanae was more surprised than he was at the whole business.

It turned out that both the policeman and I had gotten the same impression.

"Hmmm," he said, looking around. "I've seen a lot of break-ins, but there's something that looks staged about this one."

Exactly. The table was turned on end, but here was Nanae, safe and sound. There had been no violence of any form. If the culprit had been looking for photos while she was out, what use was there in flipping over a table without any drawers? It was also done quietly—not even the next-door neighbor had heard a thing.

Another case of pretending.

If the culprit had really wanted the photos, he could have snuck in, waited for Nanae to get home, and forced her to hand them over. It would have been faster. He wouldn't have made such a mess of the room and then just given up.

Which meant—whoever had done it had wanted us to believe that it was a bigger deal than it really was. But why?

"I can't figure it out," said the police officer in a languorous tone. "You say that someone has been watching the place. You're with the media, right? You must know it could be anything."

"But she doesn't have anything to do with anything. I'm more concerned that she was being watched last night than that someone broke in here today, making it look like they were searching for photos."

"You're in and out of here all the time, aren't you?" the officer asked. "Maybe someone's waiting for you to show up."

I tried to downplay the possibility, but he wasn't convinced.

"I'll make sure we have someone on patrol, and I'll check in again tomorrow." The officer left, and Nanae's neighbor spoke up.

"You stay in my room tonight, dear. I'll lay out a futon for you," and she left to prepare for her guest. I was left alone with Nanae. I sat down on the tiny sofa, the only piece of furniture left in place, and she spread out her skirt and sat on the floor. She looked upset.

"An unarmed assassin," I said, attempting a smile. She looked up at me with a tired expression on her face. "The next time you think you're being followed, don't try taking pictures."

She looked around; her whiteboard was missing. I took out my pocket calendar and gave her a pen.

*I was sure it was one of your rivals.*

"Reporters are not in the practice of following each other around."

Nanae gave me an exaggerated look of disbelief. *Then why is someone following you?*

"I don't have a clue."

*Can't you think of anyone?*

"No one."

*When Naoya called me to tell me you were being followed, he said that it was all part of your job and that you'd know what was going on.*

"Well, he was wrong."

*He doesn't make mistakes like that. He can read minds.*

She was finally being straight with me. I looked at her. She nodded and wrote, *That's what happened that night. The thoughts of the person following you came to him, and that's why he wanted me to tell you.*

"No kidding," I said in surprise, and she looked insulted. "Then tell me, what did he tell you about that person?"

*That they were bored.*

"I see. Well, that's a relief."

*It's true. He said you weren't in danger, but it wasn't pleasant, and that's why he wanted me to warn you.*

After she wrote that much, she gave me a look daring me to complain, and showed it to me.

"You really trust him," I said slowly.

She nodded defiantly.

I took the calendar from her and reread what she had written.

*The thoughts of the person following you came to him.*

Shinji had said that Naoya was "open" much more often than was safe. If he was open, he might be able to hear the thoughts of someone doing surveillance from a parking lot. They might be clear as a bell to him.

If he was really a psychic.

Nanae came over to me and wrote on my calendar balanced on my hand, *You know about Naoya's powers, don't you?*

"Yes, I do. But I don't believe they are real."

Nanae looked surprised. *Why?*

"He has never proven them to me. Not only that, but he has never told me himself that he has them. On the contrary, he denied that they even existed."

*It's because he's so scared.*

"Why?"

Nanae thought, and then wrote, *Do you know the story about the One-Eyed Kingdom?*

"Yes, I do." It was about a group of explorers who went looking for a race of one-eyed people so they could show them off. Instead, the one-eyed people caught the explorers and showed *them* off. Nanae looked up at me as if to say, *It's the same thing!*

*I met Naoya when I had appendicitis.*

"Appendicitis?"

*I woke up in the middle of the night with a stomachache, and he came knocking on my door. He asked if I was ill. That was a surprise! Later I asked him how he knew, and he told me.*

She continued to write, slowly and carefully. *When I was a child, there was an explosion at a chemical factory near my house. That's when I lost my voice. If you visit my hometown, you'll find a number of people with the same disorder. Our throats were burned by the chemicals in the smoke. We were lucky we survived.*

"Do you have family?"

*My father was a technician at the factory. He died in the explosion. My mother lost half of her liver from the effects of the accident, and she spends most of her time in bed. She lives with my brother and his wife.*

"Why did you come to Tokyo on your own?"

*There was nothing for me to do at home. There were no jobs. I found one here, and that's why I moved. I can't depend on my brother to take care of me.*

"You teach children?"

Nanae nodded. *I teach sign language to deaf children. Midori Day Care is an unusual place. Children with handicaps are mixed in with normal kids.*

The use of the word "normal" had an unpleasant ring to it, I thought.

*I was shocked to hear Naoya's story. He's different from me. I suffer from what I lack. He suffers from having something extra.* She thought for a little longer and continued. *He made me change the way I think about things.*

"Has he contacted you recently?"

She shook her head.

"Not at all?"

*Just that one night. He doesn't answer when I call for him. But he might be close by.*

"Because he's worried about you?"

*I think so. He's a gentle soul.* Nanae looked down; she seemed at a loss about what to do next. I began to understand why Kanako got so irritated with her. Nanae was dressed up; maybe she'd been to a party. She was wearing a thin layer of makeup and a pretty suit. Her hair was braided in back. It was a style that suited her.

*Naoya and I,* she wrote and then stopped. She didn't seem to know how to continue. I felt like she was telling me that the trust they had in each other wasn't something you could easily describe in words. She gripped the pen and thought hard.

If Shinji had been here and he'd been reading my thoughts, he would have told me I was jealous. I took the calendar out of her hands, set it down beside me, grasped her arm, and pulled her toward me. I pressed my lips against hers. The pen fell out of her hand and rolled on the floor.

I may have startled her, but she didn't try to push me away. Her lips had a faint taste of wine. I couldn't bring myself to let her go and held her tightly in my arms. Nanae settled her head against my neck, and she clung to me just as fiercely.

Just then there was a knock at the door, and Nanae pulled quickly away.

"Nanae? Your bed's all ready!"

I spent the night leaning against the door of Nanae's apartment. I smoked one cigarette after another as I gazed up at the sky until it got light.

That gray car. The man in the driver's seat. What did he want? I wasn't scared of him, but I couldn't leave knowing that someone might come and disturb Nanae again.

I imagined Shinji laughing. *You've got it bad*, he'd say.

# 5

"Your luck's been bad lately," the colleague who sat across from me said. "You missed another guest again today!"

"Who?" I asked.

"Last time it was a pretty girl, but this time it was just a cute little boy. He was sitting there," he pointed to my chair, "until about half an hour ago. Said his name was Shinji."

Just as I expected. "How did he seem?"

"Pretty depressed, actually."

Another magazine that had come out yesterday ran an article about Shunpei Kakita. The title was "Gone Too Soon: Sorrowful Prayers for a Young Friend." The article had outlined the story from the manhole incident to Satoshi Miyanaga's suicide; it was simply a summary of an interview with Kakita. There was, of course, nothing in it about Shinji or me, but it couldn't have been easy for the boy to read.

The magazine's intentions were not clear. In a sense the article seemed to ridicule the lack of common sense of the two youths. On the other hand, it glorified their friendship. Ikoma had read the article in the copy on my desk and had summed it up in a single word: "Trash!"

The most offensive part of the whole article was the lack of any sympathy or consideration for the parents of the little boy who had fallen down the manhole. There were even photos of several of Kakita's paintings. There were comments from a young art critic who praised him for his "sensitivity."

The magazine itself was not a magnet for major advertisers, and it didn't splash the title of the article on the cover, so I had hoped Shinji would miss it, but that's not the way it had worked out.

"I wasn't here the whole time, but he and Kanako were chatting, so she might be able to help you out." When I went to look for her, she was gone. She had taken the afternoon off.

"Then maybe she left with the boy," my colleague offered. "They seemed to have struck up a friendship."

I could just imagine. Kanako had been unusually quiet lately. She didn't look at me or try to start any conversations. It was uncomfortable, but I had decided to leave things as they were. Then, yesterday she had taken the day off. The reason she gave was that the taxi she had taken late the night before had been in a collision. She hadn't been injured, but she'd looked awfully pale. The editor in chief had called her over and sent her home.

I picked up the phone to call Shinji right at about the time I thought he'd probably be getting home, but his father said he was still out. His father confirmed that Shinji had been shaken up by the article.

"He was furious! I told him to forget about it, but . . ."

"He was angry?"

"He thought it was horrible."

"I heard that he was upset when he came out to the office today, too."

"Things have been hard, but I hear he's going to be meeting next week with the police officer you set him up with."

"That's right." When we had set the date he'd asked politely if I couldn't wait until after he finished up some tests at school. Then he could concentrate on the matter. I was relieved to hear that he was at least trying to lead a normal life for a boy his age.

"I'll have him call when he gets home," his father said. "I'm sure he's got things to talk over with you—I know you're busy."

"I don't mind. I'll be at work until late tonight. I'll call back if I don't hear from him." I was busy on a feature about a series of hit-and-run incidents that had taken place during the year. There were too many to blame on statistics. The editor in chief had decided we could no longer refer to them as accidents. We planned to run a series of nine articles before the end of the year.

Every evening we'd been following the same pattern: we'd start a discussion in the office and then move it to the conference room and finally to our favorite pub. There was a running debate between the editor in chief, who'd never had a driver's license, and a reporter who loved cars and had driven trucks for a transport company as a college student. The rest of us joined in on whichever side we tended toward that day. Over the hubbub in the bar, I heard someone calling my name. There was a phone call for me. It was Shinji.

"The man in the office told me to try this number," he started. His voice was low. I looked at my watch; it was after ten.

"Are you at home?" I asked.

"Yeah, I just walked in."

"Late, isn't it?"

"I guess so."

He really did sound depressed. "Try not to worry about that article about Kakita," I said. "It won't do you any good to get upset over it."

"I know, but it's just that I . . ."

"You've got tests coming up, don't you? You need to hit the books."

"Listen," he tried again. "Have you had any . . . unpleasant things happen to you lately?"

"What do you mean?"

"Unpleasant. Bad. Anything like that?"

I thought about the threatening letters. "What do you mean?"

"Oh, nothing. Forget it."

"What's the matter? What is it?"

"Nothing, really. I'll see you next week with that detective. Bye." It was if he was trying to escape.

After another hour passed, I was called to the phone again. It started with the same line Shinji had given me.

"I was kindly told to try this number." It was *that* voice.

"I'm listening."

The rest of the office staff were in the back room shooting off their mouths. I could hear the editor in chief over them all. They were all arguing; I was afraid they'd make it impossible to hear my caller.

"Sounds like you're having fun there," the voice said.

"What do you want?"

"You still don't know?"

"I only know that you've got a tail on me and you've painted up the hallway where I live!"

The voice laughed. "And not long ago, I made a big mistake. Got my picture taken. Well, enough of that. I don't have a face. Nobody's going to remember me until you do. Have you thought good and hard about what you did?"

"I hate to disappoint you, but I'm not going along with your threats."

"Well then, don't blame me for what happens."

I forced myself to stay calm. "I have no idea what you're talking about. But if it means so much to you, why don't you just tell me? Tell me what I did. I'm ready to take the time to listen to everything you've got to say."

From the back room, the editor in chief had got a look at my face and clapped the shoulder of the reporter spouting off next to him to shut him up.

"Why should I do you the favor?" the voice came back.

The editor in chief pushed some other guests out of his way as he came over to me. I indicated to him who was on the line, and he shoved his ear up to the receiver.

"Have you seen Saeko?" the voice asked. "I hear she's married and got a family of her own. Too bad for her she had dealings with you."

"There's nothing between the two of us anymore. Why pick on her?"

"Because I want to. I'll choose whoever I like."

*Choose whoever I like?*

"You goddam—"

"You've got a week. I'll give you that much time." The voice had gone flat. "Spend it going over your life carefully. If you don't figure it out by then, well, I'm sorry."

"Hey!"

The caller cut the line, and I banged the receiver back in place. The editor in chief looked at me through eyes shining with alcohol.

"Are you sure you don't know what he's talking about?" he asked me.

"If I did, I wouldn't be in this jam."

"You better not be lying."

"Cut it out."

"Your enemy is serious."

"I'm aware of that."

"He's reeling you in. There's no telling what he'll do. You'd better be ready.

If a week passes and nothing happens, you can laugh it off. Is that Saeko he's talking about the one you were engaged to? Have you contacted her?"

"Yes, she knows what's happening. I've asked her family to keep a close watch on her."

"Who else? Is there anyone else in range, other than your family?"

Nanae was the only person I could think of.

6

She was at home and still up. She opened the door with a puzzled look that relaxed into a smile when she saw me. She raised her hands questioningly, then quickly went back inside to get her whiteboard.

"I'm sorry to say I haven't found Naoya," I said when she got back. Her arms dropped to her sides. "I've got a favor to ask."

She cocked her head and gestured me inside. A cuckoo clock in the kitchen sounded off as I slipped out of my shoes. It was midnight. Her room was neat and tidy; she had put everything back in place. No one would guess the place had been ransacked. I had contacted her several times since then and talked to her neighbor. I'd learned that her window had been replaced with wire-reinforced glass; and that the outside door to the building had been fitted with a lock, and keys distributed to the residents; and that they were locking up at midnight. I'd arrived just in time.

"I want you to go away for a week. Go stay with a friend. Or move—I'll make the arrangements. Please."

She turned away and went to the sink to fill the teakettle and set it on the stove. I got the feeling she was thinking through what I had said. She came back to the table and began writing.

*I guess it doesn't have anything to do with the burglar who broke in last week, so I can't answer until you've explained yourself.*

"Can't you just do it without asking questions?"

*No.*

"I asked you to move after the burglary, too."

*I've told you it's hard for people like me to find a place to live.* She looked up at me accusingly, and then wrote some more. *Landlords object. The guy who owns this place is unusual.*

Why hadn't I thought of that? Here she was, a model tenant who kept her place clean and had a job that paid the rent. How could anyone be put out because she had a disability?

She wrote, *They just say they're sorry, but they can't make exceptions.* She nodded for emphasis.

I had no choice but to tell her the whole story. She listened to it from start to finish, only standing up once to turn off the burner beneath the teakettle. As she poured the hot water in a thermos, the words I was speaking seemed to lose their truth.

"And that's it," I said, spreading my arms out. "It's no joke."

Nanae smiled, and then wrote, *Who's laughing?*

"It's just for a week. Please go somewhere where you'll be safe. He knows you live here, and he's been here once. I'm worried about you."

*Didn't he come for the photographs?*

"I don't know that for sure."

She sat and thought, tapping the pen against the whiteboard as she did. *Aren't you in danger? That should be your main consideration.*

"I don't know. Based on what he said, he'll be going after someone close to me. And that's even more frightening. To tell the truth, I'd be happier thinking that I would take the brunt of whatever it was I did. You've got to understand that."

Nanae nodded. *Do you know why you're being threatened?*

"No idea. I feel like I've said those same words a million times. Either that or I've just plain forgotten."

*Are you going to think about it for a week?*

"As hard as I can."

She sat at the table with her chin in her hands for a while, just gazing at her whiteboard.

She finally wrote, *What about Naoya?*

"He's got nothing to do with this," I said so quickly that I surprised even myself.

Nanae shook her head and wrote, *He told me not to have anything to do with you.*

"He told you to pretend not to know anything about him."

*That wasn't all. He told me nothing good could come of a relationship with you.*

I read what she wrote twice, and then asked, "What did he mean?"

*I don't know.* Then she erased the previous sentence. I watched *Nothing good could come of a relationship with you* disappear.

"He warned you."

Nanae didn't answer. The room went silent. She finally pulled the board toward her and wrote, *I'm staying here.*

"But—"

*There's no telling if things will settle down in a week. Is this person telling the truth? We don't know. I'll be careful.*

"Aren't you scared? It might be worse next time."

*Aren't you scared?* She looked sad, as if she was sympathizing with me.

"Yes, I'm terrified," I admitted.

*I'll be fine. Why would someone who was threatening you come looking for me?*

I looked into her face. "You really don't know?"

She looked down and wrote some more. *Do you?* Then, once again, she turned her back to me and went to her cupboard and took out two teacups. I heard her footsteps.

I stood up and walked over to her, and she didn't stop what she was doing. I came up behind her and put my arms around her, and she finally lowered her arms. She had her hair in a braid that hung over her right shoulder. I saw the nape of her neck. Her hair smelled good.

Nanae turned around in my arms and lifted her face. She looked into my eyes as if she were searching for something.

"Did you find the answer?" I asked. "Feel free to search as long as you like."

The corners of her eyes went soft. She let her arms fall and leaned her forehead against my chest. She sighed as if relieved. I let my head down, and felt my cheek touch her cheek and ear.

Holding her, I turned out the light, and the room filled with darkness. There were no enemies or any danger in it; I didn't even need to think. I could leave it all to the night.

"Are there all fifty characters?"

Nanae nodded in response to the question.

Lying next to each other on the futon looking up at the ceiling like that, I had an unsettling feeling of peace. I could feel the warmth of her body, perfectly molded against me, my arm wrapped around her.

She had one hand peeking out from the covers, and it made a shadow on the wall. She was teaching me sign language.

"It's sort of like *Close Encounters of the Third Kind*." I raised my right hand and copied her.

"How do you say 'you'?"

She pointed to me.

"How about 'me'?"

She pointed to herself.

"Okay, those two are easy. How long do you think it'll take me to learn?"

Nanae lifted her head and gave me a look of disbelief.

"Of course I will!" I exclaimed.

She shook her head and raised a finger.

"One month?"

No, she shook her head again.

"A week?"

She gave me a gentle shove in the chest.

"A year? Do you think it'll take that long?"

She nodded this time.

It seemed like a long time. I'd have to really work at it if I wanted to be able to communicate freely with her. I didn't think I'd mind it much, though. I realized that it must not have been a problem for Naoya.

"If only I were psychic," I said.

Nanae turned over and propped herself up on her elbows. She was shaking her head again.

"No?"

She nodded deeply, as if it was definitely not a good idea. I propped myself up on my elbows. "Tell me what he showed you."

Nanae slipped out of bed, grabbed the blouse that had fallen on the floor, ran her arms through it and went to the kitchen for her whiteboard. I propped up a little stand for it that she had placed next to the futon. She brought the board in, got it in place and then squinted at it. Then she wrote.

*He told me he could understand everything I was thinking.*

"So you were able to have conversations without this board?"

*When we were in the same room.*

"What about other times? Shinji told me Naoya could move from place to place."

*Teleportation?*

"Yeah, that's it."

She shook her head to indicate she'd never seen him do it. She put one finger on her mouth and then moved it quickly to my temple.

"He talked straight into your head?"

She nodded.

"Shinji told me he could communicate with him like that."

She nodded and pointed to her own chest.

"You, too? You talked straight into *his* head?"

*I can do it,* she wrote.

I laughed. "You're a psychic too?"

Nanae gave me an "of course not" sort of laugh.

*But it's hard for a psychic to speak into the mind of a normal person. Naoya only did it once for me.*

"What do you mean 'it's hard'?"

*For both of us,* she wrote, and then added, *He only communicated a few sentences, but the next day my head hurt so badly I couldn't even move.*

I wondered if such a thing was possible. She could tell from my expression that I didn't believe her. She finally wrote some more. *If I were a psychic, I'd be a little more useful to you.*

"You're doing just fine," I said as I brushed a few stray hairs off her face. She moved her hand as if she were cutting the air in front of her.

"Thank you?" I asked.

She nodded. She lay there for a little longer with her cheek cupped in her hand like a child, before she gripped her pen and wrote some more.

*There was something Naoya often said.*

"What?"

*He promised to find someone just right for me.*

I fixed my gaze on the board and thought.

"He didn't think he'd be right for you himself?"

She looked off into the distance and thought before writing, *It was me. I don't think I was right for him.*

"I wonder."

*He made me feel safe, so I guess you could say he was useful. And he didn't mind me using him that way.*

They were sad words. "You must have been lonely. We all are, but we manage to hide it."

Nanae nodded in agreement. Naoya had been able to see inside her. And that's why—for some reason inappropriate to my present circumstances, the face of Asako from the gas station popped into my mind. That carefree young lady. She and Naoya had been close.

It might have been because Asako had been, for better or worse, so transparent. Some might even say she was flaky, but that lack of depth was probably a comfort to Naoya.

*I liked him,* Nanae wrote and looked into my face. I silently reached out and touched her hair.

*He scared me, but I also felt sorry for him.*

"Because he suffered?"

*No,* she said. *He could be terribly cruel. Since he could see inside people's heads, he had a hard time trusting anyone. He even picked on me.*

"Let me guess. He said bad things about your friends or people you trusted? He told you what they were really thinking?"

She nodded, and I felt a shiver run down my back as I thought about how far into my head Naoya must have seen. What had he seen that made him warn Nanae not to have anything to do with me?

The doubts I felt were reflected onto Nanae's face. I smiled to see if I could wipe them off. She grinned back as if playing along. Then she suddenly went serious and sat up. She pointed to me and then made a movement as if clawing at her chest with both hands.

"What's that?"

She repeated the gesture.

"You are—" I figured it out looking at her face. "Worried?"

*Yes,* she nodded.

"You don't have to worry about me. I'm fine."

This time she didn't smile even a little.

"It's hard to investigate yourself!" Ikoma said.

I knew that. It didn't work the same way when you were your own subject. It's a little like not being able to see the tip of your own nose.

Ikoma had been on my case like an examiner during the Spanish Inquisition. After three days of this, it was getting old.

"Out with it!" he commanded.

"I've already coughed up everything, including the lining of my stomach," I protested.

"You're like my wife when she's constipated. No matter how much she manages to get rid of, she knows when there's still something left. It's the same with you."

"Quit talking like that."

"I've got a dark past of my own. If it was me, I'd have plenty to draw on, that's all I can say."

"Like what?" I demanded.

He shook his head. "Aw, maybe there's not really that much. There's the kid who committed suicide during the ESP fad. But, you know—and I'm not just trying to defend myself here—that wasn't entirely my fault. When you're in this business, you get on people's nerves. But not all by yourself. We've got our magazines and newspapers pressuring and prodding us."

I had managed to think of a few potentially damaging sins I'd committed. One was a civil case I'd reported on four years ago. It was a common sort of property dispute, but it involved an inheritance, and it got nasty. It was just when land prices had taken an upward swing and we'd done a feature on problems related to real estate.

"I heard that when you were interviewing the plaintiff, the head of the defendant family came in to stir things up."

"That's right. He was drunk and swinging an aluminum bat."

"A nasty drunk, eh? Did it come to blows?"

"Some. He calmed down once I took his bat away, but he screamed at me as he left—*I won't forget this!*"

It didn't seem likely, but we looked him up anyway. The man had died. The case was ongoing, but both sides were tired of the whole process, and they were moving toward a settlement.

There had also been a woman with a touch of paranoia, and for a moment I thought she was the force behind this whole mess. We'd run an article about a fire at a Tokyo "love hotel." This woman claimed she'd been in one of the photos we took and as a result had lost her job when it was rumored she'd been at the hotel with her boss. She wanted something from me for her trouble.

A little research, though, showed that she'd quit on her own, and there was no evidence that she had been having an affair with anyone at work. It had all been a lie.

"So it was all made up?"

"Yes, but she convinced herself it was real. She showed up in tears and detailed everything that supposedly happened. She was certified as delusional."

"But why didn't she go after the photographer who took the shot?"

"I was the first person she talked with when she came to the office."

"You're not too sharp, are you?"

"Shut up! I didn't have much choice when she came storming in."

Ikoma couldn't stop laughing.

"You tell me how I could have politely avoided it when there were ten others standing there watching."

"Well, she *was* quick on her feet."

"In the end, it was all for the best. Her parents showed up to take her home, and the police never got involved."

"You've led an action-packed life, haven't you?" Ikoma smirked.

"I suppose her father might still have it out for me."

"I doubt it," Ikoma summed up.

And he turned out to be right. We called up the Hachioji office and learned that the woman had seen a professional and was now in the pink of mental health. And she'd gotten married. We also found out that she had even come in to apologize.

"And that was our last prospect," sighed Ikoma, leaning back in his chair and staring up at the ceiling. "Okay, this is your last chance. If you raped and murdered a woman and buried her in some forest, now's the time to come clean."

I kicked his chair.

I kept in touch with the Kawasaki family to make sure Saeko was all right. I only ever spoke to her husband or the secretary, but they always had their stories synchronized—nothing out of the ordinary had occurred.

Once Reiko, the secretary, had almost laughed. "You've got quite a problem on your hands!"

All I could do was make a noise in agreement.

"But," she added, "we're counting on you to make sure it ends up being something we can all laugh about later."

"Leave it to me," I said.

I knew I should mention the matter to Shinji since I'd been so involved with him. But, fearing I'd alarm him, I approached his father instead. Inamura was concerned when he heard the story.

"Are you all right?" he asked me.

"Yes, nothing has happened yet. There's a good chance this is nothing more than an empty threat. But I did want to let you know." I couldn't help remembering the words of the caller: *I'll choose whoever I like.*

"I'll keep an eye on Shinji," Mr. Inamura said. "The last few days he's been holed up at home studying for tests. He's home early every day."

"Quite the student these days?"

"I guess so. He hardly has anything to say at home—he's working too hard. He goes off for walks, but he's always home before dark. So you don't have to worry about us."

"You're the one we're worried about!" said Ikoma later.

"I'll be okay. It'll work out."

"You used to run marathons in college, didn't you? We can count on you to make a quick getaway, I guess."

"It was marathon relay racing."

"All the better. At least we'll know you'll have a destination in mind when you set out!"

We ended up laughing about it; there just didn't seem to be any urgency in the situation. I only had a week, but I couldn't dig up anything bad enough to feel guilty about.

"Unjustified resentment is the worst kind, you knuckleheads!" It was our editor in chief, and he remained the most concerned about my situation. He was also the one reminding me that I would be writing up a gripping article describing the whole ordeal when it was over.

I was seeing Nanae regularly—or rather, I was commuting to her place nightly. There was one night I called to cancel because of a pressing errand, but other than that I was as good as living with her.

"Don't even try to act shy," Ikoma instructed me. "You might as well be with her so that neither of you have to worry." By the fourth day, he was demanding to be introduced, and he followed me to her apartment.

Nanae fell over herself laughing atIkoma's stories. It was almost painful watching her laugh because she didn't have a voice; I was afraid she might hurt herself.

During a few moments when Nanae went to the kitchen, still laughing and wiping her eyes, Ikoma whispered, "She's a great girl! I think you've caught the brass ring with this one. Makes me wish I were ten years younger."

Later, Nanae complimented Ikoma in a similar way. *I like him*, she wrote. *Do the two of you always talk like that? What comedians!*

"Sometimes people toss coins at us!"

She didn't seem fearful when we were together, but she jumped when the phone rang, and I occasionally caught her looking out the window.

"Are you thinking about Naoya?" I asked, and she nodded. "Do you get the feeling he's trying to contact you?"

She shook her head sadly. She didn't know. And so the time passed as we waited for the week to be up. The afternoon of the sixth day was the day I had arranged for Shinji to meet the former policeman who had experience working with psychics.

# 8

Kaoru Murata had an appearance that reminded me of a character I'd seen in the movie *The Iron Man*. The retired policeman was tanned and had a cropped but full head of hair that was well on the way to becoming completely gray. He was tall for a man his age, and broad-shouldered. When we shook hands, a faint scent of mothballs came from his steel blue wool suit.

"It's been a while since I've been in the city," he said in a low, raspy voice. "But no matter how often I come, I still can't figure the place out."

"Did you get lost?" I asked.

"That's not what I mean," he said, shaking his head and smiling.

It was three p.m., and we were in the conference room. Murata sat in a chair with his back to the window. Kanako came in with tea, and he thanked her in a low voice.

Shinji was due in another half hour. The sun poured in, and with the window opened a crack, we could hear some of the noise from the street.

Other than a small tape recorder on the conference table, I hadn't prepared anything for our meeting. Murata, too, had shown up empty-handed. "I'm not a scientist," he had told me. "I just want to talk to the boy."

Murata sat with both hands on the table, watching me with his jet-black eyes and an expression that remained unchanged no matter what I said. I wondered how many criminals had confessed their crimes after a single look from him. I had always been of the opinion that there were three types of person who could look at another without revealing a thing about themselves—a brilliant detective, an evil-hearted criminal, and a madman.

"How are things going now?" he asked. "Have you decided to believe the young man, or rather the two young men?"

I looked down at the table.

"To tell you the truth, I still haven't made up my mind." I could feel the stress in my voice. I felt like I was being formally interviewed. "I'd *like* to believe what they say."

"That's no good," he answered without changing his expression or even moving his head. "It's the worst possible attitude to take."

"Why?" asked Ikoma.

"There's no problem with being undecided; just don't vacillate."

"Vacillate?"

"That's right. If someone wants to scam you, he'll wait for the chance to manipulate you. Like a puppeteer. If he's trying to pull something and succeeds, it'll be because you gave him the opportunity; you tried to be nice—it's almost condescending."

I opened my mouth to object, but Murata put up his hand to stop me and continued. "Saying you want to believe is meaningless. Either you believe or you don't. Or you become a machine for collecting data and throw away all of your deductive reasoning and your feelings of empathy."

I was at a loss. "Can you really do that? Even if the subject is standing right in front of you?"

"Nope, it's impossible," Murata admitted. "What I mean is, it's a process."

Ikoma burst out laughing. Murata went on. "If Shinji Inamura were a psychic, he'd be able to see your defensive emotions. The fact that he has asked you over and over to believe him means that, sentimentality apart, he really wants you to understand and accept his powers. But you don't. If he were a crafty scam artist, he'd still be able to understand your feelings. He'd use them to lead you around by the muzzle. Whichever way it works out, there's not much in it for you."

I wanted to argue, but I was speechless.

"I know how you feel," Ikoma said, consoling me.

Murata laughed. His face was much gentler when he smiled. "I've made so many mistakes. Don't worry. You're not the only one."

"How many do you know—psychics, I mean."

Murata cocked his head to the side and thought. "Well, I was on the force for thirty-five years. Maybe five or six. If you add the psychics who haven't figured themselves out yet, maybe ten."

"Is that possible—someone not knowing their own powers?"

"Sure," Murata said. "That's possible for people who don't have a lot of power, and whose power only works sporadically. Either of you might be one."

Ikoma and I looked at each other. "I don't know about me," said Ikoma, "but I'm pretty sure my wife is psychic. I don't seem to be able to hide anything from her."

"That's a different phenomenon altogether," laughed Murata. "Family members spend so much time with each other that they send and receive more information than they're aware of. Your wife knows the way you'll sit in this chair when you arrive home. She knows how long it'll take after your bath before you put your clothes on. And you know the same thing about her, even though neither of you have talked or thought about it. So if you come home one day and cross your legs in a way that's different from usual, she'll automatically get a sense that something is off and wonder if anything is wrong." Murata's voice was low but clear as a bell.

"It's easy to impress people like that because you've got so many topics to choose from. Just because you live with someone doesn't mean you know when you've been fooled. Look at simple magic tricks. A little sleight of hand, and cards and coins disappear right before your eyes. But you can't know how it's done unless you discover the trick. It's easier to fool someone close at hand than someone in an audience ten yards away. It's the same thing with families. Parents are the worst. They think they know everything there is to know about their children. There are endless opportunities to fool them."

Murata picked up his teacup and sipped at it slowly. He fixed his gaze on the table center and continued talking. "From what I've heard about Shinji, he doesn't read unopened letters or guess what's been written on the blackboard with a blindfold on. He's not pulling off remote tricks that can be done without information on witnesses, so it will be a simple matter to find out whether or not he's telling the truth."

I lifted my head to look at Murata.

"Ask him a question that even you don't know the answer to. Ask him what he can tell you about facts and events that even you don't have information about. Then go back and look them up. But don't let him see you doing it. Do it over and over. Not just once or twice. Don't stop even if he tells you he's not feeling well; patiently ask him over and over. Scam artists can't continue for very long.

Murata let out a long breath. "It's not easy, though, thinking of things that you don't know but that you could find out with some effort. Can you think of anything?"

Ikoma spoke before I could open my mouth. "Those letters!"

"I was thinking the same thing," I said, "but that would be too much for him." As a matter of fact, I'd kept the idea to myself, but I had considered asking Shinji to help me out. I was worried, though, that he'd end up hurt, the way he had with the manhole cover business. I didn't want to use him.

"Why not?" Ikoma was adamant. "It would be a lot easier to check out than the history of who'd been sitting in these chairs. Not to mention it'd be two birds with one stone. It's worth a try. We wouldn't be putting him in any danger."

"I really don't want to. There must be something else."

Ikoma was persistent. "The worst thing you can do is give the boy a break from something too difficult."

Murata quietly broke in. "So you've got something to ask him?"

"Yes," said Ikoma with confidence.

"Fine. Don't tell me what it is. I'll talk to him and ask him about it when the time is right. Then you can let me know what happened."

He sounded so stern, I hoped he wouldn't frighten Shinji.

"You used a psychic to solve a case about missing women, as I recall," said Ikoma.

"That's right," answered Murata. "It was almost twenty years ago."

At the time, there was a series of cases in the Kanagawa area. Four women aged eighteen to twenty-five suddenly went missing. The Kanagawa police threw out a huge net but came up with nothing. There were few clues, and they began to lose hope of ever solving the cases.

"I had been taken off active investigation," Murata explained. "But one of the missing women had a colorful past, and I was sent to check on it. We assumed that there was almost no possibility of the perp being someone the women knew. It didn't make sense, but we had to investigate all the leads we could find."

"So tell me about the psychic."

"All right, let's say her name was Akiko. Akiko was a friend of one of the victims. I met her during the course of our investigation. She came right out and said that she might be able to help us. Of course I didn't believe her. But she wouldn't let up. I was intrigued, and I couldn't see any harm in it."

"Why did she speak to you first?"

He almost laughed. "She said she knew she could trust me. While talking together, she said she had discovered inside my head a carefully controlled scrapbook. She said she decided I wouldn't blab everything she told me to the others. She also said she didn't find me intimidating!"

Ikoma looked over at me as if he wanted to speak, but Murata went on. "I took Akiko to the last place her friend was seen—a bowling alley parking lot. She'd been bowling with her boyfriend. On their way home, he realized he'd forgotten something inside, and he left her alone for five minutes. She was gone by the time he returned."

The other disappearances had happened in similar circumstances, and there had been little in the way of evidence. "Akiko told me that she could 'see' a truck with a long hood." Murata seemed to be pulling the story from the depths of his memory, and he frowned slightly. "She said the hood was green, and it had yellow paint splashed on it. I was disappointed because I was sure she was playing with me. I demanded to know why she couldn't 'see' the license number. Akiko was silent, but then she asked to be taken to the places the other women had disappeared from."

"Of the other three places, Akiko 'saw' the same truck in two. In the other place she 'saw' the back of a large man walking away with long strides. On his back was a large patch in the shape of a bird spreading its wings. She also said there was a strange smell like something rotting. And dark, muddy water. She thought maybe it was a pond. It was surrounded by garbage, old tires, and so on. I thought it might be a junkyard—one near a pond. Workers at such a place might wear uniforms with a bird-shaped logo. I began to look around."

"Did you find it?"

"It took two months. It was somewhere on Karasuyama—a small transport company that had gone out of business. The only thing left standing was the men's dorm. There was one guy left in it. He'd refused to leave.

"Behind the dorm was a small, dirty pond—more like a puddle, really. The place didn't look fit for habitation. It was more like a shanty than a building.

We looked inside, and hanging in one of the rooms was a jacket with a bird on the back of it. My legs almost gave out from under me!"

After a pause, I asked, "So was he the guy?"

Murata nodded. "We found the bodies of the four women in the pond in back."

Ikoma had crossed his arms over his chest. He nodded deeply as he listened.

"Of course, we found the bodies later. I had to have a pretense to investigate further. Fortunately, one of investigating officers had found a track from the same tire at each of the crime scenes. We had been going through every possible model we could find—we would have found the guy eventually, so I decided to pay him a visit and check out the tires. That's when I saw the truck with the green hood—and splashes of yellow paint. It was a truck from the bankrupt company. He had covered the name and was using it himself.

"I lied to him and told him we'd found some woman's hairs in the truck bed. I asked if they came from his girlfriend. The color drained from his face, and he began to run. That's when I arrested him."

Murata shrugged his shoulders. "Another detective asked me how I'd figured it out. The guy in the dorm was a bit strange, but no one considered him capable of murder. But I couldn't tell any of the others about Akiko because I had promised her I wouldn't. She didn't want public attention. She only wanted justice for her friend."

"But afterward—"

"Yes, I used her again. With her help we were able to solve other cases, but not all of the ones she assisted with. I couldn't keep her a secret forever, and eventually I introduced her to my section chief. We always treated her assistance with as much confidentiality as possible."

"What's she doing now?"

"She's married and has children. But it took a while for her to get that far. She told me the more you knew about people, the harder it was to fall in love. And she almost committed suicide when she was about thirty. It was then that I decided not to ask for her help any longer. I realized what a burden it was for her."

"Yeah, that makes sense."

Murata's expression finally dissolved into a soft smile. I saw the strong line of his jaw give way like the hard edges of a piece of ice as it melts.

"Akiko once said to me that I was just a person, and so was she. She said there was a limit to what we were capable of. She'd always had that power. In line at the supermarket cash register, she could hear the woman behind her trying to figure out how to murder her mother-in-law without anyone figuring it out. When a car passed her at night, she could tell the driver was trolling for a cheap girl, and on and on."

Ikoma winced as he listened, rubbing his forehead.

"She could hear it all, and she knew the individuals would put their plans into effect unless she did something. Fortunately, she'd given up on trying to deal with it all. She said she knew it wouldn't make any difference if she followed them around and told them to stop it, but still it was agonizing to stay silent."

I remembered what Shinji had told me. He said that Naoya had told him to stay out of other people's business unless he was prepared to take sole responsibility for them.

Murata went on. "I made things even worse by asking her to reenact the tragedies that had taken place. I'm sure she'd died a little each time she had to experience the murder of a victim. I led her down a destructive path. It was so hard for her, and her powers began to diminish. Either that or she got better at controlling what came into her head. Anyway, we broke off our professional relationship when she was thirty-two. We still send each other New Year's cards, but that's about it, and I think that's the way it should be."

He stopped and nodded as if agreeing with himself. "The problem was that she and I became famous among some of my colleagues. It was because of that ESP fad—there were articles about her in the papers. But it was thanks to them that I met a few more psychics. None of them were as powerful as Akiko. If this young man is as strong as you say, it will be the first time in a while I've met anyone like him."

We fell silent, but we could hear telephones ringing and beepers going off in the office. The atmosphere in the conference room was so different—it was hard to believe we were even in the same building.

"Shall I show you my good-luck charm?" Murata offered in a brighter tone. He pulled something small and white out of his pocket.

It had a string attached so he could put it around his neck. It was a horn-shaped object made out of either ivory or plastic.

"What do you think it is?" he asked us.

Ikoma thought and finally gave up, "I don't have a clue."

"It's the sort of button used on duffle coats!" I said.

"That's right! I mean, that's what I think it was. I guess someone dropped it." Murata laughed. "Four years ago, when I was still on the force, my six-year-old grandson picked it up on the grounds of a neighborhood shrine where he'd gone to play. The shrine supposedly housed the spirit of a dragon that used to live in a pond on the premises. He asked me what I thought it was, so I said it must be a dragon's tooth. He was in awe, and asked me what a dragon was and whether it was scary. I told him it wasn't scary. I said the tooth would protect him from harm. Then my grandson said I should carry it with me so that bad guy, would never hurt me. I've had it with me ever since."

He folded his hand around it and continued speaking. "You know, I often get the feeling that we all have a dragon inside of us, with strange and unlimited powers. Sometimes the dragon is asleep, and other times it's awake; sometimes it wreaks havoc, and at other times it's under the weather."

Ikoma and I both studied Murata's face as he went on. "All we can do is believe in the dragon's powers, and pray that it will protect us from harm and help us grow in the right direction. Once the dragon wakes up and moves into action, we just have to hold on for dear life and hope for the best—it's not likely we'll ever tame it."

Murata looked down at his own hands, almost as if he could see all of the experiences he had had during his career passing over them. "If this Shinji Inamura is truly a psychic, then he's probably one of the few who has woken up his dragon. He's trying to master it, or at least get it moving in a certain direction. No one can save him but himself, but I may be able to lend a hand." Murata's smile was gentle. "I wish he'd hurry up and get here!" But there was no sign of Shinji.

Thirty minutes later we got word that he'd been taken off to a hospital three hours earlier.

# 9

Shinji was in the Sakura City Hospital. Ikoma and I went right out to see him, but I couldn't figure out what had happened. His parents were equally confused.

"We got a call from the police—"

"The police in your area?"

"Yes, at about five p.m. Somebody had found him unconscious behind a warehouse in the Sakura industrial district. They got his name from his student ID card and called us."

Five o'clock on a mid-November evening meant that it was already dark when he was found.

"What was he doing there?"

"I have no idea." Shinji's father was trembling as he wiped the perspiration from his brow. "We don't have a clue. The school said he was absent today. But he left home this morning as usual."

The first thing that came to mind was that the Sakura industrial district was close to the scene of the manhole crime scene. I felt a rush of fear to think that that incident still had all of us in its grip. Next I thought of the threats I'd received. Had the perpetrator decided on Shinji as his victim? I muttered something along those lines to Ikoma.

"Hold on there," he said, clapping me on the shoulder. "It's only the sixth day."

"Well, but what's to say we're dealing with a fair-minded criminal?"

"What reason would he have for going after the kid?"

"I don't know. What reason would he need?"

"Cool down a second. Let's go outside and take a few deep breaths."

The first word we got on Shinji's condition was that it was serious. As the situation became clearer, things looked even worse. According to the doctor, the boy had been severely beaten.

"He's got a concussion, and there are bruises all over his body," the physician reported. "They found him at the foot of a steep slope. There was a narrow stairway down the slope, and it looks like he might have fallen down it. I believe that's when he broke his left femur."

"Will he make it?" his father asked quietly.

"He's young," the doctor assured us. "His muscles absorbed must of the shock, and he has a strong heart. He'll be fine. I'm a little worried about the concussion. We'll run some more tests when he's stronger. Have you spoken to the police yet?"

"Yes. But it still doesn't make sense," Shinji's father said.

"They tell me he was mumbling something in the ambulance."

"What was it?"

"Something about someone being murdered. He must have had a terrifying experience."

The operating room and the ICU were at the end of a long linoleum hallway. We were only allowed as far as a bench several yards from it, and we sat there, waiting.

The police said he didn't seem to have been robbed. There had been no witnesses. The kind soul who reported him thought he was a drunk who had passed out. It was a fairly deserted spot, and we were lucky that someone had happened along and spotted him.

The doctor came out of the operating room at about ten and approached Shinji's parents.

"We've moved him into the ICU, but he can't have visitors yet. Why don't you go home for a few hours?"

Just then I heard some irregular footsteps coming down the hall. Ikoma and I looked at each other. Coming down the brightly lit corridor were Nanae, and—

"Who is it?" Ikoma asked, squinting his eyes to get a better look.

"It's Naoya Oda," I replied.

Just like the first time I'd met him, he was dressed in a shirt and faded jeans. Nanae was supporting him as he walked. He dragged his left leg and his face was set in a grimace. He had head injuries as well. I could see that he was suffering exactly the same injuries as Shinji.

A mirror image. Or twins. If one got hurt, the other one bled.

We stood staring at the two as they made their way forward. Naoya was much taller than Nanae, and it was all she could do to keep him on his feet. Finally coming to my senses, I ran over and lent an arm. Naoya seemed to notice us for the first time. Until then he'd had his eyes focused on the door to the operating room.

"Yo!" he called out to me in a hoarse voice.

"I'm okay now," he told Nanae. "You can let go." But she seemed to need to hold onto him as much as he needed support. "It's all right," Naoya repeated, trying to smile. He gently pulled Nanae's hand from his, then leaned against the wall to support himself. I put my arms out, but he shook his head. "Don't touch me, I'm fine."

"Let's get you in to see a doctor," Ikoma said.

"No," he said without hesitation. "I'm not really hurt." He lifted his other hand and indicated the end of the hallway. "Shinji's in there, isn't he?"

I nodded. "But you can't see him. He's in critical condition."

"I know. I just want to be close to him." Naoya took a shaky step forward. "I've got to talk to him."

Nanae held out her hands; there were tears in her eyes. Naoya weakly waved her away. With one arm against the wall, he made his way down the hall until he reached the operating room. He put his head against the wall and stood there.

He didn't move a muscle. The Inamuras leaned against one another and watched him.

"What happened?" I whispered to Nanae. She began to trace characters on the wall with her hand. *He showed up this evening.*

"Was he like this when he got there?"

Nanae nodded. *He could hardly move.*

She explained with a combination of tracing words on the wall and the little bit of sign language I'd been able to pick up.

*Then he told me about this hospital and asked me to bring him here. He couldn't walk by himself.*

"How did he know to come here?" Ikoma asked.

"He just knows."

Naoya sat on the bench, bent over. I could only see his bony back. He was so concentrated within himself that he didn't even seem to notice us standing there next to him. Nanae edged over and gently put her hand on his back, but he didn't look up.

The air in the hallway grew heavier. At first I thought I was imagining it, but soon I could feel the air pressing on my arms and shoulders. It was as if the laws of gravity no longer applied in our small corner of the hospital.

I couldn't even respond to Ikoma, who loosened his tie and asked, "Is anyone else finding it hard to breathe here?" Something large but invisible was going back and forth through the air. Naoya's painfully thin back was bearing it—and then tossing it back. I recalled Shinji telling me how it was like he always had an antenna up.

There was a sound in the air; it went right past me.

*I can't bear it anymore.*

This time everyone heard—or, rather, felt—the words. The Inamuras stood staring at Naoya. Nanae pulled her hand back and moved away from him. She walked backward until she bumped right into me. She jumped in surprise, but I pulled her toward me.

"What's going on?" I asked.

Ikoma's face was frozen. We all stayed rooted to the spot for more than ten minutes before Naoya slowly sat up. At just the same moment a doctor came through the operating room door.

"Shinji's parents can come in. I'm sure you'd like to see your son. I can only let you look through the glass because he's still in a coma, although he is out of danger."

The Inamuras leaped up. The rest of us all walked over to the door. Naoya tried to stand.

"Where do you think you're going?" Ikoma said to him.

Naoya managed to whisper, "Home. He's . . . Shinji's all right now." Naoya was still shaky. He dragged one foot and kept one hand on the wall as he walked, to support himself.

"You won't make it alone. Stay here a little longer."

"I'm fine." Naoya turned toward me and said, "It's not your fault."

"What do you mean?" I asked.

"Shinji. It's not your fault. It doesn't have anything to do with you. Shinji . . . made a mistake. That's all." Then he mumbled something to himself. "I don't know how many times I said . . . but . . . he always had to do the right thing."

Nanae uncrossed her arms and moved toward Naoya. He smiled.

"Don't worry. I'm all right. Thanks for everything." He reached out his hand and touched her arm. "Don't look so sad, okay?"

I looked up and saw him looking at me. His eyes were clear; it would be impossible to hide anything from them. He turned back to Nanae and rubbed her arm softly, then turned around to leave. She tried to follow him, but he turned and spoke sharply. "Don't come after me!"

Nanae put both hands up to her mouth, and he gazed at her.

"Goodbye." He started to walk, taking one painful step after another. Neither Ikoma nor I moved a muscle until the hallway door closed soundlessly.

"Hey!" Ikoma mumbled as if suddenly waking from a dream. I began to run. Pushing open the door we found ourselves outside in the ambulance parking area. Ikoma followed and our feet pounded against the concrete.

We could see Naoya walking ahead of us, along the plain gray wall of the building, his haggard back washed in the light of the emergency entrance. His steps were shaky and his shoulders slumped. He stopped just as I was about to call out to him—then he disappeared.

There was no other way to describe it. It took no more than a second— just long enough for my pulse to beat once.

As I watched him go, I realized I was holding my breath. There was a blinking red traffic signal off in the distance—his body had blocked it from my vision moments earlier.

Naoya was gone. There was no trace of him. The hospital parking lot was brightly lit, with no shadows to hide in. I looked toward the sign of the ambulance entrance. Nothing.

"What happened?" Ikoma gasped for air and looked all around.

"He's gone."

"What do you mean?"

"You saw it. He can disappear if he wants to." *And go wherever he wants,* I thought. Ikoma's face was ashen.

"Are you out of your mind?" he said.

"Yeah," I replied, looking off in the same direction he was.

PART 6
# The Incident

I had a dream. I was in a town I didn't recognize, and a breeze was blowing. The sky was cloudy, but everything was oddly bright. I stood on a corner, aware that I was dreaming.

Next to a low concrete wall was a steel fence that I was standing alongside. Beyond it was a small park where a group of children in faded blue smocks stood in a circle holding hands. I saw Nanae in the middle of the circle, wearing the same colored smock. She clapped her hands and sang, making the children laugh.

She was singing.

I realized I was hearing her voice for the first time. There was nothing special about it—it seemed simply natural. As long as she was in my dream she was able to sing. And talk and laugh.

I didn't recognize the song. It was like a combination of a nursery rhyme and a hymn—though I had never really paid much attention to hymns before. Nanae didn't realize that I was watching. I didn't think she'd hear even if I called out to her. That's another reason I knew I was in a dream—she ought to be able to hear me from that distance. So I tried to call her, hoping I could wake myself up, too.

It was just then that I noticed that she wasn't singing; someone else was. Naoya Oda was there, wearing a white shirt, standing just outside the circle. He stood there singing and staring at Nanae and the children.

It was his voice.

Naoya didn't notice me either. It was as if I wasn't there at all. Naoya continued to sing, with the hint of a smile on his lips. The children jumped and danced and Nanae laughed.

Next I tried calling Naoya.

He lifted his head and saw me, but he didn't stop singing or smiling. All he did was slowly turn his back to me—as if he was standing on some kind of rotating disk. Then he began simply to get further and further away. He was moving somehow, although I couldn't see his feet.

I tried to follow after. I tried to climb over the fence, but it just kept getting higher. Beyond it Naoya was already far away. I saw something red flowing down his back, leaving a trail on the road as he disappeared.

When I woke up, Nanae was looking into my face. She was wide awake. She'd been trying to shake me. The first thing I felt was the warmth of her hand. It was so hot I thought she might have a fever. I finally pulled myself out of my dream and saw the ceiling in her apartment. What a dream!

There was light from a small lamp that Nanae must have moved away so it wouldn't blind me. She seemed to have been awake for a while.

"Did I wake you up?" I asked.

She shook her head. She lightly touched my forehead with a fingertip. I was sweating.

"Was I groaning?"

She nodded.

"I was having a dream."

She tipped her head to the side as if asking what the dream was about. Her expression was that of a mother at the bedside of a feverish child.

"What time is it?" I stretched my neck to see the alarm clock. It was two a.m. That meant the date had changed, and it was now the second day since my week was up. Aside from Shinji's injury, nothing of import had happened.

Shinji was out of danger and conscious again. The hospital had only allowed his parents and the police officer in charge of his case to talk to him. According to his father, though, Shinji couldn't talk and didn't seem to be aware of what was going on around him.

At any rate, we couldn't dismiss the possibility that he had been attacked by whoever was threatening me. Ikoma was sure the two incidents were unconnected and that the threat was a bluff.

"Think about it," he said. "Whoever it was has managed to achieve his goals without lifting a finger. He managed to get us all upset by setting a time limit. It was probably what he wanted all along. Just to have some fun with us. You could really wear a person out like this."

It made sense, but I couldn't believe it. I had to wonder if we'd seen the end of it.

Nanae looked worried, so I tried to smile for her. "This is the worst time of night for dreams," I said. She lifted her right hand and knocked her chin twice with the side of her pointer finger. It was the sign for "Really?"

"Sure," I answered. "That's because your blood is circulating so slowly while you sleep."

She didn't seem convinced. I pulled the covers up over her shoulders and she fell right back onto her pillow. She hadn't been sleeping well lately herself. Sometimes I'd think she was asleep and look over to see her eyes open. And she wouldn't answer me when I asked what the problem was.

"There was a friend of mine from college," I began, and she turned to look at me. "No matter how soundly he was sleeping, he'd always wake up right before an earthquake hit. If he didn't have to pee and he was awake, we knew for certain that there'd be an earthquake."

I finally got a giggle out of her.

"Funny, huh? But he was dead serious. When you sleep, you use parts of your brain that you usually don't. He said it was a kind of intuition that he didn't have when he was awake. So who knows, it might happen now. There could be an earthquake any minute . . ."

I shook my head for emphasis, and the phone rang. I leaped out of bed to grab the receiver. Ikoma started speaking before I could say anything.

"Were you up?"

"Yeah."

"You've got good instincts," his voice was low. "You sitting down? You should be." Ikoma sounded wide awake. I pictured him dressed and ready to head out the door.

"What happened?"

Ikoma dropped his voice again. "Look, I'll explain, but you've got to act in a way that doesn't frighten your girlfriend."

Nanae got out of bed and watched me.

"Listen carefully. The police are looking for you."

I was so shocked that my expression froze.

"They didn't find you at home, so they've been looking everywhere. They called me. I told them where you were, so you're about to get a visit."

"But why are they looking for me?"

Ikoma took a deep breath. "Saeko Kawasaki was kidnapped late last night."

There was no hiding my shock at this news, and no hiding it from Nanae.

"That's all I know. She's been abducted, and the police are looking for you. Just wanted to give you a heads-up, so you'd be ready for them when they get there."

The knock at the door came just as he finished speaking.

The two detectives were both dressed in gray, as if they'd consulted on their outfits beforehand. One spoke, one observed, and both blocked the exit.

The explanation they gave was simple. Saeko had been kidnapped in an alley near her home at about eleven-thirty the night before and had not been seen since. Someone claiming to have done the deed had made a call, and Saeko's husband, Kawasaki, had called the police at 1:35 a.m.

"We're here to escort you," said one of the detectives. "We want you to go with us to the Kawasaki home. You'll get instructions from the men there."

"But why me?"

"The kidnapper wants to negotiate with you."

There was no reason to ask why that might be. The detectives already knew the whole story. I remembered the voice on the phone: *I'll choose whoever I like.*

"We've heard about the threats you received. Kawasaki told us all about them. It looks like they're no longer just threats."

Nanae and I stood awkwardly in the kitchen with the two detectives. The cold of the floor seeped through my feet and into my legs.

"We'll do our best to protect both you and the victim," the detective went on.

"Although," the other detective said, speaking for the first time, "there's a good chance that you might be involved in this whole thing."

It was beginning to sound like the old game of good cop, bad cop.

"I understand," I said, but Nanae's eyes were full of disbelief.

The detective looked at her. "It's our job to doubt people. Are you the girlfriend?"

Nanae nodded defiantly. The detective lifted an eyebrow in surprise, so I spoke up.

"If you have any questions for her, you'll need to have a sign language interpreter. That is, of course, if you've got someone who can do that."

"Meantime, we'll get a female officer over here," the detective said.

He turned back to me. "I'm sorry to have to do this, but I need to have you raise your arms and spread your legs."

I did as instructed, and the detective made a quick body search. Then he pointed to the door. "Go outside. There's a car to take you. We'll keep a watch here, so you won't have to worry."

"I'll be counting on that."

The silent detective came over and grabbed my elbow with one hand while opening the door with the other. I wanted to say something to Nanae on my way out, but I couldn't think of anything. She signed a couple of words to me, and I understood them immediately: it was the traditional phrase Japanese use to see people off—with the understanding that they'll be back home later.

The stars were still out and the night sky was clear. The moon was slightly past full, and it hung in the sky at an odd angle—as if someone had flipped it up there and it had stuck like that.

As the two detectives and I hurried toward the main street, a taxi passed us up and then stopped about two yards ahead. The detective pushed my head down as I got in.

"There'll be another taxi following, but don't pay any attention to it." Another detective was playing the role of taxi driver. After we pulled out he spoke to me. "When you get out, try to look as if everything is normal. We don't know if the kidnapper is watching, so pretend that you're planning to pay the ransom. Just try to stay calm. Do you understand?"

"The meter . . ."

"What?"

"The meter isn't running."

The detective smiled. "That's right," he said. "Very good."

# 2

The lights shone from the first floor of the Kawasaki home. Akio Kawasaki was the first one to greet me. He was still wearing a tie, and he looked as if he had just got home from work and only removed his suit jacket. He didn't say a word, but glared at me. His face was pale and his arms shook at his sides. He folded his arms in an attempt to stop the shaking.

"Look what you've done—" he began.

"I'm so sorry." I could only apologize.

His head hung down, and he rubbed his temples. "No, no, I'm sorry. There's no reason to blame you. I know that, but . . ."

I was led into the house and met by a pudgy-looking man. He wore a gray suit with the jacket open.

"You must be Shogo Kosaka," his baritone voice boomed out. "Come this way."

There were four other men sitting in the living room. The curtains were tightly shut. The pudgy one led me over to a shorter fellow sitting on the couch. When he stood up, he only came up to my shoulders.

"I'm Captain Ito from the Special Investigations Division," he said. His manner was very relaxed. He quickly introduced the others and explained that they were the squad assigned to the case. "I'm sorry to have to drag you out here like this, but I need to ask you to follow my directions exactly. Are we clear about that?"

"Yes, I understand," I said.

The pudgy baritone motioned for me to sit down. He was Sergeant Naka-giri. He and Ito were the only ones whose names I remembered. They both looked to be in their fifties, although the lower-ranking Nakagiri seemed to be the older of the two.

There was a white telephone on the coffee table. A tape recorder was attached to it, and a set of headphones. A large map was spread out, and two locations on it were circled in red. One was the Kawasaki home, and the other was the spot where Saeko was kidnapped. A circle with a two-inch radius had been drawn around the house.

The decorative atmosphere that had pervaded this room the last time I was here was completely gone, and it was now a dedicated command center. The plants that I imagined Saeko had carefully nurtured had been shoved to the side. The doors that divided this room from the next were standing open. Two detectives were setting up a radio.

"Let me explain what we've got so far," began Captain Ito. The hand he set on the table seemed unusually large compared to the rest of his body. "We still don't know how Mrs. Kawasaki was kidnapped. All we know is that she left the house on an errand, and that was when—" Ito pointed to the red mark at the top of the map "—she was kidnapped here. It was at an intersection of this narrow road. There wasn't anyone else around; at least we haven't found any witnesses yet. There've been no reports of cries for help or sounds of a struggle. We have located one of her shoes."

Ito looked directly into my eyes as he spoke. I knew he wanted to see what my reaction would be to all this. Kawasaki wandered into the room and fell heavily onto the sofa. I glanced at him.

"You were out, right?" I asked him

"You don't have any right to question me," he spat out. Then he rested his head dejectedly on one hand. "I had an important meeting to attend."

"But your week was up," added Ito.

"That would have been the last day."

"Yes, but it still wasn't safe," Sergeant Nakagiri spoke up. "It's amazing how human beings will stick to a schedule no matter what."

"I didn't take any of this seriously enough from the start," moaned Kawasaki, his head still down. As he let out a deep breath, I could smell the alcohol on his breath.

"After all these years, why did my wife have to get mixed up with you again? Why did all this have to happen? Were the threats made by someone who thought you two were still together?"

After a few moments of silence, Ito looked at me. "I'd like you to answer that question honestly. Were you still seeing Saeko Kawasaki?"

"We haven't spoken in over three years," I said. "I only contacted her because of the threats. I didn't know where she lived or even that she had married."

Captain Ito answered in a voice that seemed, if possible, jollier than before. "It may work with others, but you know you can't get away with lying to us. You'll just make things more difficult for yourself."

"I'm not lying."

"I don't believe you," Kawasaki grumbled. His cloudy eyes were focused somewhere in the vicinity of my left ear. "You're a liar."

"You're free to believe whatever you like!" I said, and the two detectives exchanged glances. It looked as though they were trying to size the two of us up. "No matter what you think, I have had absolutely nothing to do with your wife. That's all there is to say."

Kawasaki's voice rose a couple of decibels. "Then why was she kidnapped? Huh? Why? If you weren't having an affair, why would someone think they could get back at you by kidnapping her?"

Sergeant Nakagiri put a hand on his shoulder to hold him back. "Take it easy, now. I'll let you know if we get a call."

Kawasaki continued to glare at me, but when he looked over at the detective, his expression was like a balloon that had lost its air. He stood up, clearly exhausted, and said, "I'm going to wash my face."

It was then that Reiko Miyake, his secretary, appeared. I heard the front door open and close in quick succession, and when I looked up, she was already standing in the room. Her face was pale, devoid of makeup, and her lips made a flat line across her face. She wore a drab-looking dress, and her feet were bare. It was clear that she'd thrown on the piece of clothing closest at hand and come running over. And she still managed to look beautiful.

Kawasaki came back from the bathroom. Nakagiri quickly stood up, put one arm around Reiko and another around Kawasaki, and led them into the kitchen. He was talking in a low voice, and I couldn't catch what he was saying. I also heard Reiko address her boss, but that was after Nakagiri shut the door behind them.

Captain Ito turned once more in my direction. "Now then, I'd like the full story of how all this began. Start at the beginning, and don't leave anything out."

I did as I was told, and Ito only interrupted me twice. Once was when I was telling him about the blank letters.

"Where are the letters now? Did you throw them out?"

"They're in my desk at the office. There were eight in all."

Ito sent a man out to retrieve them. The next time he stopped me was when I got to Shinji's injury.

"And the boy was a personal acquaintance of yours?"

"That's right."

"Have you known him long?"

"No, I only met him recently."

"Can we talk to him?"

"Yesterday he was still in a coma and unable to speak."

Ito flipped through his notes. "How about Nanae Mimura? You're close to her, aren't you? Tell me about her."

"I've been seeing her for the past month."

"I see," Ito put the notes in his pocket. "It's strange, isn't it? Someone threatens you, but they target a woman from your past rather than your present."

"Yes, it seemed odd to me, too. Why would someone bring up Saeko's name after all this time? I don't have a clue."

Ito tapped his chin with his finger and thought for a while. "Who do you imagine would be angry at you for your relationship with her?"

"No one," I said.

Ito looked surprised. "Are you sure?"

"I've been thinking about it ever since this whole mess began. I can't come up with a thing. It would make more sense if someone was out to get *Arrow*, the magazine I work for, and used me as the target."

Ito nodded, considering the idea.

I went on. "I just can't figure it out. Why me? And why would Saeko be involved? I've received only two calls from whoever is making the threats. I told him I was ready to listen to his complaint, whatever it was. But he refused to tell me anything. He didn't give me a thing to go on."

"Would you be able to recognize the voice if you heard it again?"

"I would."

"Which means," Ito put his fingertips together, "we'll just have to ask the kidnapper about it."

I looked over at the phone, but it hadn't rung since I'd been there. A detective in the next room called for Ito. He hopped up and went over. He came back in a few minutes, but his expression was exactly the same as when he'd left. Even his voice was unchanged.

"They were gone," he said, sitting back down.

"What were?"

"The eight letters. They weren't in your desk."

# 3

The phone finally rang at 3:20 a.m. The deepest part of the night was past, and I was just starting to get sleepy when the ringing began. It seemed abnormally loud and shrill. Kawasaki looked at Ito as he picked up the receiver. Nakagiri, wearing the headphones, turned on the recorder and nodded at Ito.

"Kawasaki here." His voice was raspy, and I saw his right eyebrow twitch. He answered "Yes, yes," to the caller, trying to get him to move on. "Do you have Saeko? Is she all right?"

Apparently, he didn't receive an answer to his question. Kawasaki's face was bathed in sweat as he turned to me and held out the receiver.

"He wants to talk to you!"

I put the phone to my ear and got a husky voice that barely sounded human.

"Good evening, or should I say good morning?"

It wasn't the same voice that had called me twice before. I was taken aback and couldn't respond immediately. Ito was watching me intently, and he raised a questioning eyebrow.

"Hello?" the voice persisted. "Kosaka? It's me, your old pal."

"Your voice is different."

"Is that so? There's no need for surprise. Everything has happened just as I told you it would."

I nodded toward Ito and said, "The week was up a couple of days ago."

"Well, I've got other business to worry about, too."

"Is Saeko safe?"

The caller gave a gravelly laugh. "Are you worried about her?"

"Of course I am. Why did you involve her in this?"

"You still can't figure it out? You should be pleased. This is your chance to make amends for your past mistakes. Why can't you remember?"

"I don't know what you're talking about. I'm afraid you're the one who's mistaken."

I thought that if I challenged him a little he'd react, but he just kept up that obnoxious chuckle. Although I noticed something else too—he sounded out of breath.

"Hello?"

"I'm sure you'd like this conversation to go on longer, but I can't let that happen," he said, suddenly speaking more quickly. "I've got Saeko Kawasaki here with me, and I'll give you proof. I'm only going to say this once, so listen carefully. Go over the Tsukuda Bridge, and turn onto Kiyosumi Road. When you pass Shosen College, just before you reach the intersection with Eidai Boulevard, you'll find a restaurant called Iris. Pop into the men's room. But you've got to go alone. There better not be anybody with you. I'll know if you don't follow my instructions and fulfill my demands."

"What demands?"

The caller didn't even listen to my question but hurriedly hung up. Just before he did, though, I heard that hard breathing again.

"Did you get anything?" Ito called out to the men in the adjoining room. A young detective peeked out, scowling. Behind him I could hear someone else jabbering into a radio set.

"We got it! The call came from a public phone at the Wangan landfill. A squad car is on its way."

Diagonally across from me, Kawasaki grabbed the arms of the chair he was sitting in. "Can you really figure it out so quickly?" he asked.

"That's the way it works," the detective answered. "Call tracing technology has improved. It only takes one minute now."

Captain Ito stood up and moved into the next room. Sergeant Nakagiri stayed with Kawasaki and me in the living room, but now I knew what we were waiting for. Kawasaki kept wiping the sweat from his forehead as Nakagiri rewound the tape to listen again.

I imagined the speeding patrol car and police officers running. Law enforcement doesn't quit work for the evening and go home, I realized anew. Voices flew in over the radio. I imagined the advance on the public phone. If the police were faster than the kidnapper, it could be over in a matter of minutes now.

I thought about my colleagues on the other side of the wall of the media ban—waiting, I was sure, just as we were doing. I had never reported on a kidnapping myself, but I'd heard stories. Media outlets rented out news vendors' stalls and coffee shops on the front lines to wait for the police to lift the ban so they could begin coverage. The reporters were like sprinters at the starting blocks.

I waited ten or fifteen minutes, but it seemed longer. When the captain returned and took his seat, we all raised our heads as if on command.

"We were close," he said in a perfectly normal tone of voice.

Kawasaki let out a deep sigh and curled up into himself, his head in his hands. His secretary, Reiko, stood next to him and gave him a reassuring pat on the back. It was the first time I'd seen any sign of intimacy between the two.

Nakagiri casually rewound the tape and replayed it. Ito pulled out a map of Tokyo to try to locate the restaurant the kidnapper had named.

"Let's wait for our next opportunity. There's still plenty of hope," he said to Kawasaki, who nodded but kept his eyes closed.

After a while he opened his eyes and spoke. "Are you sure we haven't made things worse?"

"Don't worry, we're taking every precaution," Nakagiri said. Then he turned to me. "You sure it was a different caller this time?"

"I'm certain."

"He used a voice modifier, we know that," commented Nakagiri. "But it was strange."

"What was?" I asked.

"The caller. He was out of breath. Did you notice?"

I nodded. "Yes, it was almost as if he were gasping for air."

"Did you notice that in the other calls?"

"No, not at all."

Kawasaki suddenly banged his fist on the table. "So, are you worried about the kidnapper's health?" Reiko took his arm to calm him.

"You will go, won't you?" Ito asked me.

"Of course."

"It might be dangerous."

"He knows what I look like. You can't send somebody else in my place."

Ito stood up. "Fine then. I'll arrange for a car and a surveillance detail. We'll outfit you with a microphone. If you sense any danger at all, get out of there right away. You got it?"

"Now you're watching out for *his* safety?" Kawasaki's voice turned nasty. "This is all your fault," he sneered at me. "No matter what happens, bring Saeko back with you."

"That's what I plan to do," I said, "but not because you asked me to!"

Kawasaki drew back. Reiko was much calmer than he was and gave me a look of apology.

The detectives finished their preparations and Ito gave us all strict instructions. While we waited for word that the backup squads were in place, I went over to Nakagiri and leaned in to say quietly, "There was something else that bothered me."

"What was that?"

"He didn't say anything about not contacting the police."

Nakagiri nodded.

"Is that usual?" I asked.

He shook his head. "It's a first for me." It was obvious that he shared my concerns. His knit eyebrows gave it away.

I found the restaurant right away. It had a revolving sign on the side of the road. The walls were made of glass and covered with cartoon characters and pop art.

I drove up in my false taxi, and the driver deliberately went around to the back after circling the parking lot in which three cars were parked. One of them had been obviously modified to suit the taste of its car-buff owner.

"Get out slowly," the detective-driver instructed me, checking in front of and behind the car. "Don't look back. Three officers are already inside. Don't look for them. Follow the kidnapper's directions."

The place had several customers, even at this time of night. I walked in and glanced around as if looking for a place to sit. One table was occupied by a group of rowdy teenagers that I assumed came in the modified car. A couple was sitting at a table in the center of the room. A middle-aged man occupied another, with newspaper spread. There were two unhappy-looking young men at the counter slurping coffee. I could see that one of them had a earphone, like mine, in his left ear. He sat with his elbow on the counter, his hand supporting his head in an attempt to hide it. No one would notice if they weren't looking for it.

My instructions from the police were not to go straight into the men's room, but to draw out the encounter as long as possible. The kidnapper might be observing the situation.

A waiter came over to me and indicated a table by the window. As I passed the teenagers, the smell of cigarettes and sweaty bodies wafted over me.

As I sat down and ordered coffee, I heard a voice in the earphone. "Is there anyone here you recognize?"

I'd been told to use as few words as possible, so I simply said, "No."

"Fine. Please go to the men's room now."

As I stood up and walked down the aisle, the restaurant door opened and another customer came in. It was a detective. Exactly five minutes had passed since I walked in.

The men's room was tiny. There was a stall and a urinal, a sink and a window with frosted glass. A paper towel dispenser. There was nothing over the sink or on the tiled floor. I shoved my hand in the wastebasket but found nothing but used paper towels.

I opened the door of the stall. It hadn't been cleaned recently, and it had trapped the leftover stink of customers past. The toilet paper holder was empty, and a partially used roll was perched on a triangular shelf in the corner. I opened the tank of the toilet—nothing but water.

"I can't find it," I spoke into the wireless microphone under my shirt collar.

"Did you check everywhere?"

"Yes, but there's not really anywhere to check."

"Stay calm, and take another look."

I rechecked each item, moving them around. Nothing looked out of place. When I bent down to look behind the toilet, the wireless mike swung down and hit my ribs, making a loud sound. I stood up and turned around to find the middle-aged man who'd been reading the newspaper. His steps faltered— he was drunk. When he hit the switch by the door, the vent fan turned on.

The man looked at me with heavy eyes and stood there for a few seconds before speaking. "Do I have to pay you to take a dump?"

I stood to the side and let him in. He lumbered into the stall and slammed the door shut.

"What's going on?" asked the voice in my earphone.

"Someone came in," I whispered. "I don't think he has anything to do with me."

"Then come on out. One of our female officers checked the ladies' room and found nothing. This might have been a diversion."

By the time I was back in the restaurant, the teenagers were paying their bill at the cash register. I thought for a few minutes as I waited for them to finish. I stopped a waiter passing by and asked, "Was anything left in the men's room during the past hour or so?"

"Oh, you mean the wallet?" he quickly responded. He looked under the counter and pulled it out. "It sure looks like it belongs to a woman, though."

The wallet was red leather—it must have been new, it was still shiny.

"Do you mind if I look inside? I think my girlfriend forgot it."

"Go ahead, but there's no money, no cards, nothing." The waiter smirked. "It was in the wastebasket in the men's room."

I opened it, and as the waiter said, there were no bills. Nothing but a plastic card. It was the type used in doctors' offices and had the name of an obstetrics clinic along with the name "Saeko Kawasaki."


"Did you find it?" The voice on the other end of the phone got right down to business. It was just about five a.m. "I keep my promises. So now you have proof that I've got her."

"Let me talk to her. I want to make sure she's all right."

"Sorry, but she's asleep. Keeping her up all night would be bad for the baby, right?"

I tried to think of something else to say to keep him on the line. I decided to try entertainment. "Say, how about a trade?"

"A trade?"

"That's right. Your beef is with me, right? How about exchanging me for Saeko? I'll meet you anywhere you like if you promise to let her go."

The man at the other end wasn't breathing as heavily as he had been during the first call, but he still sounded worn out. Nakagiri frowned as he listened. I could tell he was wondering about it too.

"Sorry," he said.

"Why?"

"Nobody would pay for *you*."

Captain Ito leaned forward.

"Money? Is that what you're after?"

"Of course. You ruined my life, and someone's going to pay for it. It has to be someone who's worth something, so that's why I chose Mrs. Kawasaki."

I was bothered more by the words this man was choosing than by what he had to say. He definitely wasn't the one who had called me before. The voice was younger.

"How exactly did I ruin your life, young man?" The reaction was swift.

"What do you mean, 'young man'?"

"Am I wrong?"

"You smug bastard!"

"Sorry, I didn't mean to hurt your feelings. How much was it you wanted? How much will it take to put that life of yours back together?" I spoke with one eye on the second hand of the clock. I'd kept him talking for a minute. Kawasaki walked over with a malicious look on his face. Once again I heard the caller gasp as he took a breath.

"One hundred million yen," the voice said. "I'll call back. The police get in the way."

"Police? What are you talking about?"

"I know you called them." I heard a crashing sound as if the receiver on the other end had been thrown across a room. A minute and twenty seconds had passed. There was a burst of static, and then I heard another man's voice. It was a detective from the other room. I passed the phone to Ito, who grabbed it immediately.

"That was a long call. Our men must have got him this time!" Suddenly the captain's expression turned grim. "What do you mean he's not there anymore?"

When he put the phone down, Kawasaki spoke, his face dripping with sweat. "Where was he this time?"

"Adachi Ward. A public phone in front of Akabane Station."

Nakagiri rewound the tape again and muttered, "Maybe he's got wings."

"But we know he's human," Ito said, looking at Kawasaki and me. "We found the phone booth, all right. There was a drop of blood on the floor. The kidnapper is injured."

That morning, Kawasaki began making arrangements for the ransom money.

"Do you plan on coming up with a hundred million?" Ito asked.

Kawasaki's face lost its color as he responded. "Of course! I've got to find a way to come up with it before the next call!"

"I'll go take care of it," said his secretary. "You should stay here."

Kawasaki glared at me and turned back to Ito. "There's nothing for me to do here. You'll call me if you hear anything, won't you?"

"Of course I will. I'll send a man with you. You've got to be careful."

Once Kawasaki was gone, Reiko spoke hesitatingly to Ito. "Shall I find something for you to eat?"

"Thanks, we'd appreciate it."

Now that the sun was up, the neighborhood was coming alive. No one passing by could have imagined that this house was full of police and their equipment, all tasked with saving a life.

I heard the newspaper being delivered at about seven. Nakagiri mumbled something about how late that was. "Our paper comes earlier," he said.

We had breakfast, and then there was nothing to do but wait. The detectives sent and received messages using their radio, and I occasionally heard quiet footsteps coming and going. The detectives must have had to report on the two calls from pay phones during the night, but there was nothing new to work on.

"You must be tired," Sergeant Nakagiri said to Reiko. He seemed to be crooning to her gently with his beautiful baritone voice. "Why don't you go home? I'll have one of my men take you."

Reiko refused just as gently. "I'll stay here in case I'm needed. I'm worried about Mrs. Kawasaki, and I'd be at loose ends at home."

"What about your work at the school?"

"My boss will be back here."

"And you?" he turned to me.

"My office knows where I am. And I've got to stay too."

"That's right. We'd be lost without you," the detective said with an air of embarrassment. Once more he addressed Reiko. "Miss Miyake, how about getting some sleep? I think that might be best."

Reiko hesitated, but the detective insisted, so she made her way upstairs. As soon as she was gone, Nakagiri came over to me. Ito headed toward me, too.

"We've got a question for you."

I was sure they must. "What is it?"

"Is Reiko Miyake really just a secretary?"

Looking at him up close, I saw that Nakagiri was pudgy all over. His cheeks, his nose, everything but his eyes; his gaze was piercing.

"Why are you asking me?"

He grinned. "My men have the information. They told me everyone knows, and I figured your occupation would make you privy to this sort of gossip."

I let out a sigh, "Yes, I know about it."

"So Kawasaki and Reiko are lovers. She's four years older than he is."

"See? You know more about it than I do."

Just then Ito broke in. "What's on your mind, Nakagiri?"

Nakagiri said, "Nothing. I just like to share gossip."

When I glanced at Captain Ito, he was as expressionless as ever, but I could see a glimmer of interest. He looked like a fisherman who had felt the slightest of tugs at his line.

"The caller told you you'd ruined his life, right?" His voice had a warmth that seemed at odds with what he was saying.

"That's right."

"Have you come up with any new ideas about what he's after?"

"None at all. I've gone over all my work from the time I met Saeko but found nothing."

The detective nodded in agreement. "I understand what you're saying. I'm in a line of work that seems geared to ruining people's lives if I slip up, but if I had to come up with any specific cases where I've done it, I wouldn't be able to."

Ikoma had said the same thing.

"What seems unnatural to me . . . ," I began.

"Yes?" Ito and Nakagiri spoke at the same time, leaning forward.

"I mean, he kidnapped a woman—that's no small crime. But no matter how often I ask what I did to deserve this, he won't give me a clue. Not even a whiff of an idea of what he's talking about. 'You ruined my life!' he claims. It's a pretty clichéd line. Anybody could use it."

The two detectives looked at each other, and Ito said, "Meaning?"

"I get the feeling I'm being used."

"You do?"

"Right. The kidnapper doesn't want us to catch on to the real reason Saeko was abducted, so he's trying to pin the blame on me. When I think of it that way, it explains all those half-baked threats and the refusal to give me any reasons for it all."

Ito glared at the phone. Nakagiri stared up at the ceiling.

I said, "I'm a journalist. I've had people yell at me before, and there have been plenty of complaints about stories. I know when someone is serious— no matter how absurd the situation seems to me."

"So this guy hasn't convinced you?"

"Exactly! The man who's been calling since yesterday doesn't have any urgency. It's just a feeling I got from talking to him. You can take it any way you like."

"That makes sense," Ito said. "You're like us. It's part of your job to figure out what people really mean when they talk to you."

I was afraid Reiko would come downstairs at any moment, so I lowered my voice. "I'm trying to be hopeful—but it has to do with responsibility. I couldn't say this in front of Kawasaki or his secretary, but . . ."

"I understand," Ito said, cutting me off. "I've considered the same possibility. The kidnapper might not have a reason to hold a grudge against you. If he tried to lie, he could be caught in it."

Nakagiri was still staring at the ceiling. "Or this guy really does have a grudge against you, and he wants you to suffer for it for the rest of your life."

My head drooped. "There's always that, I guess."

"But if that were the case," Ito said, "it wouldn't make any sense to kidnap

Mrs. Kawasaki, someone Kosaka hasn't had contact with in years. That's what I don't understand."

Nakagiri smirked, "Captain, how many years have you been married?"

"What does that have to with—?"

"Thirty-five years, right?"

Ito looked self-conscious. "Something like that."

"I'm in year thirty-three," Nakagiri said, rolling his eyes. "We've done well to keep it together this long, but just hear me out." He turned to me. "When people have relatives in the police, mass media, in the medical field, or the law, they get used to it. They know something might happen and, unconsciously, they're ready for whatever it might be. Kosaka, if I were in the same position as you, if my wife or son were put in the way of danger, I'd be cool about it."

I thought a moment and then nodded. I remembered when my landlord said he wouldn't mind having me as a tenant, insisting that he was a "champion of justice" who would defend the right to free speech to his dying day.

Nakagiri went on. "You see what I mean? My wife understands because she chose to marry me, and she knew about the work I did when she made her choice. That's what she tells me anyway. Of course, it would be hard—really hard—for me if anything happened to my family, but it would be easier to deal with than if someone I didn't know had to suffer on my account. Do you see what I'm saying?"

"Yes, I do."

"It's the same with you. It's got to be harder for you now than if a member of your family or a friend or girlfriend were kidnapped. The culprit has hit you in a spot you weren't prepared for—you don't know how to deal with the abduction of Saeko Kawasaki, a woman who no longer has a connection to you, someone with her own life to live. It's got to be hard for you in a different way."

He was right.

"So that was the idea," said Ito in a low voice.

"And this family . . . ," Nakagiri began.

". . . will come up with the ransom money," I finished.

"That's it," he said. Then he mumbled, as if to himself, "People can be pretty clever."

There was a heavy silence. After a moment I broke into it, saying, "I've heard that adult hostages are rarely returned alive. Is that true?"

"It's true," said Nakagiri quietly.

I closed my eyes and watched the geometrical patterns move in my head.

"But it's less so nowadays," the detective continued, as if trying to undo the damage of his previous remark. "It happens to children, too. Anyway, it's better not to jump to conclusions."

Ito spoke up next. "You said the voice of the caller was different this time?"

"Yes," I was still sure of that. "Not just the voice, but the way he talked." I explained to the two of them what I meant, and they took it in a completely different direction.

"He's injured, of course," Ito mumbled. Nakagiri was once more staring at the ceiling.

"He might not call us during the day," I said, and Ito looked at me questioningly. "He'd be easy to notice in a pay phone if he was injured, right? He'll need to rest and see to his wounds."

"We've notified hospitals," Ito said. "But you're right, he might not be able to move."

We had been waiting ever since the sun came up. The kidnapper had not called.

There were no calls that evening, and soon it was night. The atmosphere was thick with frustration at the lack of leads, and Ito's expression became darker. He'd begun to make arrangements with police headquarters about what to do if we lost all contact. We didn't know how badly wounded the culprit was; there'd been no reports of a suspicious character visiting a doctor for treatment.

The police had been around to the homes in the vicinity making discreet inquiries, but they had no leads.

"Some of the neighbors mentioned seeing a boy they didn't recognize," one of the lower-ranking detectives reported. "They said he was looking up at the second-floor windows of this house. He was pale and seemed ill."

Ito shook his head. I suddenly had images of Shinji, but I quickly put them aside. Certainly he hadn't had "known" this was going to happen. He couldn't have.

Kawasaki came home after getting the ransom money together. He sat looking at the wall, exhausted and with a silver-colored trunk full of money at his side. Reiko looked dazed.

All I was able to do was watch the hands of the clock go around and around, and think about the same thing over and over. It was torture. I prayed for the kidnapper to make some kind—any kind—of contact. I swore to myself I'd do anything he asked. I just wanted him to hurry up.

I stood up to look out the window from between the curtains for the umpteenth time, when I felt a tap on my shoulder. It was Nakagiri.

"Someone to see you."

At the back door, there was a patrol car stopped next to the fence. A detective sat in the driver's seat, and in the back were—Ikoma and Kanako, our receptionist.

The driver got out, and Nakagiri and I got in. Before I could say a word, Ikoma began. "Kanako's got something to say to you."

I could tell she'd been crying. Her eyes were red and swollen. Her makeup streaked down her tear-stained cheeks.

"What happened, Miss?" asked Nakagiri. Kanako opened her purse, which she had set on her knees, and took out the eight letters I'd received from the kidnapper.

"I took these out of the office without telling anyone," she sobbed. "I'm so sorry!" She put her hands over her face and wept.

I looked at Ikoma, and he glared back at me. "Remember all those books you bought? Was there one, *Fortunetellers with Good Track Records*?"

Nakagiri looked puzzled.

"Yeah," I answered. "Something like that."

"She said she got the idea after reading it. She wanted to show them to a fortuneteller who might be able to read something from these letters."

I remembered noticing that the book had been moved. While I thought about it all, Ikoma clapped Kanako on the shoulder. "So don't get mad at her, all right? She was just trying to help you out."

"Don't worry," Nakagiri said gently. "Those letters didn't have much to tell us anyway."

That just made her cry harder. She tried to talk between sobs. "I just wanted—to—be—helpful . . ."

"I know, I know." I turned around and patted her on the head. I could feel her shaking. "You've had them all along?"

She shook her head. "No . . . I lost them!"

"What?"

"She went to meet the fortuneteller, and on the way back, the taxi was in an accident. Remember?" Ikoma said. "In the midst of it all, she lost track of the letters. She was sick about it."

Kanako sat up, wiped her face, and began to explain. "I was so worried I didn't know what to do. It was too late to tell you, and then that boy came. That—remember?"

"Shinji," I said, and I remembered how worried he had been.

"He—as soon as he came, he knew—he knew something was wrong. He promised—he said he'd find the letters."

Now I remembered that I'd seen the two of them talking.

"I don't know how he did it. But he found them! He held my hand, and we went everywhere I'd been. He said, he knew—he could tell where I'd been."

Ikoma put his arm around her to try and console her. "There was a clerk in a cigarette shop that picked them up. He had them. He didn't know if he should take them to you or not."

"What happened?" asked Nakagiri. "Was there some kind of problem?"

Of course there was!

"What did Shinji do when he found the letters?"

Kanako took a few breaths and explained. "He, he—was paler than me. He asked me—he asked me to lend—let him borrow them."

"So he took them?"

"Yes. I—I was terrified. But, but after—two days, he brought them back. But, but I never got the chance to put them back in your desk. They got— d-dirty. I knew you'd notice."

I could see now that they were dirty. There was even a footprint on one of them.

"I'm so sorry. The, the police came today, and, and I didn't know what to do. I spent all day worrying, and then Ikoma said . . ."

"She looked awful," said Ikoma. "That's why I asked."

"I'm so, so sorry."

"That's enough," I said. "You can stop worrying about it now." I was barely conscious of what I was saying. The letters felt so heavy in my hand. Shinji had seen them.

I remembered that he'd asked me if anything unpleasant had been happening to me lately. The neighbors said they'd been seeing an unfamiliar boy around. He knew. He must have figured out what the person who had sent them had in mind. And now he was in the hospital. The abductor had made good on his threats.

The ambulance attendant had mentioned that he'd been mumbling something about getting killed. I remembered Naoya showing up at the hospital. What he'd said. What he'd done. He'd said he had to talk to Shinji.

So he knew, too. During those few moments when the air had seemed so thick, had Naoya been communicating with Shinji? What if he'd called Naoya to him for help? What if Naoya had come to help him?

What would he have done?

*Stay out of other people's business unless you're prepared to take sole responsibility for them.* Shinji had told me that that was what Naoya had instructed him.

The voice of the abductor was different this time. It was younger. And he was wounded . . .

The caller was Naoya!

Just then another detective tapped on the window.

"There's another call from the kidnapper!"

It was 8:45 p.m.

# 5

At exactly 11 p.m., I stood in the spot the kidnapper had specified—next to a yellow public phone in a small aquatic park in Edogawa Ward. It was called an aquatic park, but in fact it was located in what used to be a tributary of the Edogawa River. It was now landfill, with the formerly straight river now curving through a concrete riverbed. Greenery had been planted on the landfill for a pastoral effect, a recent result of urban planning, no doubt. The park itself was three yards below the concrete riverbanks that were gently sloped on both sides.

I had come in one of Kawasaki's cars, parked it in a nearby used-car lot, and, as instructed, left the money in the back seat before walking to the park. As I looked over in that direction from the park, I could see the bunting that decorated the dealership fluttering in the breeze even in the dark.

The park was quiet and had already been securely closed up for the night. And in any case, this was not a part of town people would visit at night, what with the used-car lot on one side and a food company distribution center on the other. There was one small restaurant at the end of the bridge that crossed overhead, but I doubted that anyone could see down to the park from there.

I could hear trucks speeding down a four-lane highway in front of the distribution center, and when I turned to look off in the distance behind me, I could see warning lights blinking at the top of a high-rise apartment building and the emergency night lights of a high school.

It was the perfect spot for the perfect night. I had been assured that the car lot and restaurant were full of detectives and SWAT teams. The closest surveillance team was in a van parked just below the bridge. The wire under my coat linked me to them.

At first the police told me they couldn't risk sending me alone. They said they could send a substitute; it was so dark the kidnapper wouldn't know the difference.

Ito had said he didn't like the idea of separating me from the money—they had no idea which one the culprit would be more interested in. There was a chance he'd rather harm me than take the money—or *before* taking the money.

I had no intention of backing out now, and ironically, Kawasaki eagerly agreed that I should be the one to go. He didn't want to endanger Saeko if the kidnapper figured out he'd been duped. I was sure that he didn't care whether I lived or died.

At any rate, I fully planned to go alone. I had to do what had to be done. I wanted to reassure the agitated detectives that there wouldn't be any danger involved.

All I had was my intuition, but I was confident that the "kidnapper" was Naoya Oda. Right now he was in charge of the entire situation. The question was why he'd gone to the trouble, and I was worried about his wounds.

What had Shinji "read" from those eight letters? What had he asked Naoya to do for him? What had he himself tried to do? I wanted answers.

11:15 p.m. The telephone began to ring.

"You're right on time," the familiar voice said at the other end of the line. But it sounded hoarse, and the breathing was labored.

"What should I do next?"

"Let me see . . ."

I had to control an impulse to urge him on before his location would be given away and he'd have to move again. *Hurry!* I bit my lip to keep from saying it.

"Take off your jacket and all those devices you've got connected to it. Then walk upstream from where you are now. There's a pond—walk over to it."

He hung up. I did as I was told, and I could hear a voice chattering into my earpiece.

"What do you think you're doing?"

"I'm following instructions. I don't have a choice!"

I followed a path down to a body of water that was more like a large puddle than a small pond. The surface was black and I could hear the grass around it rustling in the breeze. In just my shirtsleeves, I could feel the cool of the night.

It was dark and quiet. There was no one there. I knew I shouldn't say a word but just think it. In the dark I could see a single white flower blooming. I had no idea what it was. I focused on it so I could concentrate my energy, and I took a deep breath.

*Are you close by?*

There was no response.

*Where are you?*

I knew I was taking a gamble, but then I got a response. It was surprisingly clear.

*I'm too far away to be caught.* It was Naoya's voice.

I unconsciously lifted my head to look around. I could see beyond the recently planted trees to the lights of town. The moon was out. This was the only dark place around.

The breeze made ripples on the surface of the water.

*You figured it out*, Naoya's voice told me. *I was surprised to have you call me first.*

*I know you're hurt. How bad is it?*

*I'm fine.*

*Why are you doing this?*

There was no response.

*Why are you doing this? What can I do to help you?*

I felt the back of my head go numb.

*Just come with me now. That's all I need. Act like nothing's going on.*

*Are you sure that's all?*

The numbness spread out.

*I'm sure. Do everything exactly as I tell you. Please don't think about anything else. Otherwise everything will be ruined.*

*Okay, I'll do as you say.*

There was a pause, and then I heard a voice that sounded exhausted. *Saeko is safe. Just relax and do as I say.*

I had to focus hard to hear the end of the sentence. I wanted to tell him to stop. In my head, I said, *Stop all of this, and leave the rest to the police. You'll kill yourself.*

*Run,* said Naoya, *as fast as you can. You're going to feel dizzy when I pull away from you, so be careful not to fall.*

At just that instant, I felt my body float. It was like a hand supporting me was suddenly pulled away. Everything went black for a couple of seconds, and I reeled backwards.

My pulse raced and I broke out in a cold sweat. I lifted my hand to feel the back of my head, and it was still slightly numb.

Suddenly, a siren coming from the direction of the bridge broke the quiet. As I watched, I saw three fire trucks, including a ladder truck, pull into the used-car lot. I could see the red emergency lamps spinning around. I ran for the park exit, and I saw a troop of firefighters heading down the bank. Curious onlookers raced over from the restaurant. Before I knew it, there was a crowd of people who had nothing to do with the incident.

Confused detectives got out of the surveillance van. There were people everywhere—on the bridge, in the road.

"What's going on?" someone yelled.

"Someone reported a fire!" was the response. The only sparks, though, came from the unfortunate meeting of the police and firefighters.

One of the young detectives made his way over to me. "Are you all right? Were you hurt?"

"I'm fine," I replied. "What about the money and the car?"

"Return to the van!" came a stern command and the detectives disappeared back inside.

I ran over to pick up my jacket and the earpiece, and heard even more confusion over the wire.

"There's no problem here. What happened?"

"I don't know. Someone called the fire department—"

I was almost out of the park when I saw a familiar face in the sea of onlookers—I stopped listening to the chatter in the earpiece. There was Shunpei Kakita, the other would-be artist, among the crowd in the park. There was no mistaking him. There were too many people for me to run over to him, but I did my best not to lose sight of his long, thin shadow. I'd managed to cross the bridge when someone clapped onto my wrist.

"Where do you think you're going? Come back! Back over here!" It was one of the detectives. He was red in the face, and as I looked over at him, I lost sight of Kakita.

Around midnight, the phone began to ring.

"I wanted to check something out." Naoya's voice was even weaker than before. "I knew that if I called the fire department, any police in the area would come out of the woodwork. Even the stupidest criminal would never come for the money in a place like that." He hung up before the police could figure out where he was calling from.

"Where is he?"

"We could only tell that he was in Edogawa Ward."

He might be unable to go any further, I thought.

"He's a thorough son of a bitch," hissed Kawasaki.

"He's making fools of the police." The money was untouched, and so was the car. The kidnapper had not appeared.

I knew I couldn't reach him, but I tried. *Why, why are you going to all this trouble? What do you need to do? End it all now before it kills you!*

I got my answer about thirty minutes later. The phone rang again. "You better not have the police with you next time!" said a harsh, gasping voice. "This will be your last chance!"

# 6

Kawasaki declared that he would go this time.

"He's completely unpredictable. How can I sit here a second longer? I don't need police protection either—I'm going!"

"But he's not asking for you," I said calmly, after considering the time and place I'd been instructed to show up.

Kawasaki came at me with clenched fists. He clipped me on the jaw before a detective could pull him away, but it didn't really hurt. In fact, I was surprised that that was all he was capable of. It wasn't the punch of an enraged man.

"Cut it out!" Nakagiri sounded more annoyed than alarmed.

"It's your fault!" Kawasaki seethed, almost foaming at the mouth. "Do you understand? You caused all this!"

Well, that takes care of the niceties, I thought. "I'm sorry, and I can apologize until I'm blue in the face if that'll help, but you need to a grip on yourself!"

Kawasaki, still shaking, took a chair. Reiko put her hand on his arm, softly comforting him. She hadn't budged from the house, and she remained calm the entire time.

"I don't need protection," I said as I looked up the location on the map. The beach I'd been directed to was about an hour's drive.

"That's not your call," Ito said.

"He's bound to see you. There's nothing but sea and sand. What are you going to do if he refuses to show up again?" I was determined to follow Naoya's orders, and he'd specifically said police would not be tolerated.

He'd asked me to follow him without question. Even though he'd used a voice changer over the phone, I could tell he'd reached his limit and was losing strength fast.

"You leave that to us," Ito huffed. "It's not something for you to decide." He was fussing with that wire again. He tapped me on the shoulder and turned his pudgy face up to me. "Take this!" It was a bulletproof vest.

"I won't need it," I said. "There won't be any bullets flying."

"How can you say that?" Nakagiri asked with a smirk. "Just take it—do me a favor."

His eyes were tiny, but deep inside I could see that he wasn't fooled. He was laughing at me in a way only I could see.

"Nakagiri," I asked in a whisper. "Are you onto something?"

"And what do you mean by that?"

A wave of uncertainty passed over me. What did he know? He couldn't know about Naoya.

"Listen carefully," he whispered back as he fixed me up with the vest, "Nobody pulls the wool over the eyes of the police!"

"What's that supposed to mean?"

"You'll find out," he said, cinching the belt so tightly I could hardly breathe. "Oh, sorry about that," he apologized. "Kosaka, you look pale. Are you feeling okay?"

I began to get a headache; it came over me as strongly as the numbness to the back of my head when Naoya had communicated with me. My head felt like it was in a vise. It was stronger than any other power I'd experienced. I began to feel sick from the pain.

I couldn't imagine how much power Naoya was using when it was now that he needed to keep it under control. A chill ran up my spine. Fearing that I might not get there on time, I felt even worse.

"You'll be taking Kawasaki's car, and you'll have a detective in the back. He'll stay hidden, don't worry."

As Nakagiri spoke, he attached the wire to my clothing and tested it. His blasé expression was hiding something, I was sure.

"Nakagiri?"

"Hmm?" His expression began to change as I stared at him. He blinked his eyes and glanced around. Kawasaki was hollering at Ito, still demanding that he go along. Nakagiri motioned me closer and whispered in my ear.

"Just do whatever the kidnapper tells you to. I don't believe you're in any danger—except maybe emotionally!"

"So I'm just being used?"

Nakagiri nodded, "And there's something else. We're afraid that Mrs. Kawasaki might already be dead. Probably killed right after she was abducted."

He said they were pretty sure that killing her had been the point of this entire ruse. "But we've got to find something conclusive. Just stick with us a little longer."

Nakagiri's expression returned to its usual nonchalance, and he clapped me on the shoulder. "Let's get going!"


I turned off the engine and heard the wind from the sea blowing across the beach. It was 1:20 a.m. I was blasted by the moist wind when I got out of the car. I could see clouds whipping across the sky from east to west. There was the smell of the tide and a hint of rain in the air.

I left the car in the beach parking lot as instructed. *Come alone!*

Once again I left the money in the car. Captain Ito saw it as an attempt to separate me from the money, but I knew better. The abductor was not going to get rich off this scheme. Nor did he have any business with me. The whole thing was a farce.

I followed the signs to the beach. I felt sand under my feet as soon as I left the paved road. There was no one on this vast stretch of beach. I kept walking, occasionally wiping off the grains that blew onto my face. And with every step, my head pounded in pain.

Far off, I could see what looked like a flimsy-looking building with a light on. The structure was still under construction, and in the night, its naked steel girders looked like a huge dinosaur fossil. Next to it was a crane stretched out toward the sky. At the top of it was a red light.

It was a place where no one could hide.

I walked up a small slope, and from the top I could see the gray of Tokyo Harbor.

Lights were blinking even farther off. I looked around me. The lights were from expressways and buildings and towns, where huge numbers of people were asleep. All I had here was dirt, sand, stone, and a faint hint of ocean spray. The odor was a mixture of seawater and oil. The wind was fierce.

I stopped at the top of the hill, put my hands in my pocket and waited.

"Can you see anyone?" the voice coming through my earphone asked.

"Nobody," I answered. There was no way I could.

*It was all a farce.*

The day before, I'd come pretty close to what the detectives had been thinking as I discussed the case with them. All those claims of a need for revenge had been lies. It was no more than a cover.

The idea had been to make it look like someone was after me, when the real goal was to kidnap and murder Saeko. The old bait-and-switch—someone had gone to a lot of trouble to pull it off. Revenge, ransom—there would be a series of demands and hours of waiting, but the culprit would never show up.

It was all a plan to mask the real reason why Saeko had to go. Unfortunately, the ones who planned it made a few miscalculations.

The first was to choose me as the target. Just because I worked in mass media, they were sure I'd had stories or covered cases where I'd made enemies.

The second was underestimating the police. At least they underestimated Nakagiri, who was sure Saeko was long gone.

It turned out, though, that Saeko was safe—because Naoya got involved, and that was the third and fatal miscalculation.

*Where are you?* I lifted my face to the wind and called out in my mind. *It's safe to come out. The police have figured it out.*

*Come on out!* I tried it once more, and a weak voice resounded in my head.

*Head toward the sea . . .* Once again something gripped my head, and it began to ache even worse. *Go a little bit further . . . over to that fallen tree.*

Over to the left was a twisted tree that had fallen on its side. Waves lapped against it. As I drew closer, I saw that the tree was artificial; it was a part of a seaside landscape, and there were a number of other pieces like it.

Lying in the shadow of the tree, washed by the waves, was a man.

I bent over to lift him and saw that the unfocused eyes in the leaden face were open, as if staring back at me. It was the man who'd been following me in the gray sedan. I remembered the face from the photo Nanae had taken from her apartment. He'd been stabbed to death.

I spoke into the wireless mike. "I've found a dead body."

"You've found what?" the voice at the other end responded.

"It's the kidnapper. He's probably been dead a day or two. Come have a look for yourselves."

The voice stopped, but I could hear movement on the other end. I stood up and closed my eyes for an instant against the wind. When I opened them, Naoya was standing before me.

I still remember what he looked like. White as a sheet, his arms dangling at his sides. The wind blew his hair in all directions. He fell toward me in slow motion. I caught him in my arms and felt the full weight of his body. His head dangled back, and his eyes opened skyward. His skin was clammy, almost as if he'd been wrapped in a damp blanket.

"We did it," he muttered in a voice I could barely hear. He had used the last of his energy for this final transportation.

"Don't try to talk," I pleaded. I knelt down with him still in my arms, laid him on the sand, and spread my jacket over him. He blinked. He had been stabbed in the lower abdomen, and blood poured from the wound.

I could hear the detectives running toward me, and I yelled in their direction, asking for an ambulance.

"I made a mistake . . . and this . . ."

"Stop talking!" I waved my arm to the detectives, and Naoya pulled at my sleeve.

"I left . . . the knife." He tried to say something else. His lips were moving, but nothing came out. I felt something for an instant in my head, but there were no words.

His hands and cheeks were cold. I felt the slightest of tremors running through his body.

The detectives surrounded us. One sank to his knees. His jaw trembling, he asked, "What—what happened here?"

"Shh! Keep your voice down!"

"But where did this guy come from? How'd he get here?"

The rest of the group was abuzz with the same questions.

His head in my arms, Naoya smiled faintly and tried to shake his head at me.

"I understand," I said, my own voice beginning to shake. "You don't have to worry. Relax."

Naoya closed his eyes, and his head tilted to one side.

Akio Kawasaki was in the group. He almost fainted when he saw the dead body in the shadow of the tree.

"Where is she? Where's Saeko?"

"That's a good question," I said quietly. "She's got to be here somewhere."

"Are these the kidnappers?"

I heard the siren of an ambulance approaching. The news picked its way through the mob of detectives.

As the medics put Naoya on the stretcher, he squeezed my hand once more, and at the same time I heard a voice.

*Take good care of* . . . I knew what he meant, and I squeezed his hand back to assure him I'd look after the others. Then I let go, and the door of the ambulance closed.

The leader of the backup squad came over to me; I could almost see the thoughts racing through his head.

"Did he say anything when you found him? What did you hear?"

I ignored him, and addressed myself to Kawasaki. "He told me your wife was safe."

"Did he say where she was?"

I shook my head. "But she's alone. Now all we have to do is find her."

Kawasaki looked up at me and then shifted his gaze out to the water. He dragged himself to his feet, and, supported by one of the detectives, headed back the way he'd come.

My eyes blurred from the wind and the pain in my head. But I knew who could tell me where Saeko was.

# 7

When I reached the hospital entrance, there was someone sitting on the bench near the door, his head in his hands. It was Shunpei Kakita. I looked down at him, and he peered up in my direction. He looked haggard and seemed to be in great pain.

That's when I knew.

"Your head hurt?" I asked.

He nodded, obviously in agony. "I'm hearing voices!"

Naoya had used him. He'd had Kakita handle the parts he couldn't do himself.

"What are you doing here?" he asked me.

"Good question," I replied. "Did you go to that restaurant, Iris? Did you put the red wallet in the wastebasket in the men's room? Did you make that call to the fire department and send them to that park in Edogawa Ward?"

He looked up at me as if he couldn't believe what he was hearing—then nodded.

"Forget about it all."

"Huh?"

"It's all over. Forget it ever happened."

"But—I . . ."

"Let me guess why you followed the directions you heard in your head." I looked up and over toward the ICU, where Shinji was still in critical condition. "You felt guilty about what you did to that boy. Am I right?" Kakita looked awfully small.

"I—that boy in there *told* me."

"*What?*"

"He came to see me again. He said he knew my friend had wanted to confess. He said he knew everything. He said I should never forget that he knew everything I'd done."

Shinji had known . . . and he hadn't been able to keep it to himself.

I remembered Naoya calling him a champion of justice.

Kakita went on. "He told me that I shouldn't feel relieved because Miyanaga killed himself. I—I . . ."

It turned out Kakita was the one who had beaten Shinji to within an inch of his life.

He was crying. "My head, it hurts so bad! That voice told me that if I wanted to make up for what I'd done to the boy, I'd better do as I was told. I'm scared. Should I apologize? I can't bear the pain!"

"You'll feel better before long," I said, walking off. "Go home now. It's all over."

Kakita's voice followed me down the corridor. "Don't leave! What happened? Whose voice was that?"

"Just a guy," I said and climbed the stairs.

I managed to avoid the nurses' station and found myself alone in a hallway. The lights were turned down. I heard voices around the corner, so I pressed up against the wall until they had passed. Then I looked through the glass to the ICU.

Shinji was sleeping. A thin green line raced across the monitor next to him. His IV bag was more than half full. It dripped into his arm at a pace so slow watching it could put you to sleep.

He looked very small under the bedding, but inside that thin little body was an enormous energy force.

I wondered if he'd wake up if I called or whether he was still "talking" to Naoya. I pressed my forehead against the glass and forced my mind into the deepest spot inside myself I could find. I hoped Shinji could grab onto me if I stayed still.

Brain waves. I wondered what the doctors had found when they checked his brain activity.

Then I heard him.

*Kosaka?*

*Yes, it's me.*

*Do you know who this is?*

*Yes, I can hear you, Shinji.* My head felt like it was going to split open, but I was glad. I laughed out loud! Shinji's eyes were still closed; he was still in a coma.

*I know it hurts,* Shinji said to me, *so I'm only going to say this once and then leave you alone.*

He told me. The place and what I should look for.

*You knew all along,* I asked.

*Yeah.*

*Thanks.*

I felt his hand on my shoulder, and then he left me. I couldn't move right away. I put my hand against the glass and waited until I regained my stamina. Then I walked off.

As I headed down the hallway the way I'd come, I heard a soft moan. It was in my head. Shinji and I must still be connected; it was like starting to put down the receiver and hearing the voice say something at the other end; I almost missed it.

*Naoya just died.*


Shinji had sent me to a small abandoned warehouse near the landfill park. The first floor was full of waste materials, and a stairway led to the second floor. The lights were off, but I could see light coming from one of the upper floors. That must be where they were keeping Saeko.

The second floor was empty, but there was a single door that was partly off its hinges. All I had to do was sit down in its shadow and wait.


I didn't hear the footsteps right away. Security lights from the building next door came through the tiny window in the hall, and I used the illumination to look at my watch. It was 2:45 a.m. That didn't take long, I thought to myself.

I leaned against the wall and held my breath as someone came up the stairs. The footsteps were so soft, I wondered if the person was wearing shoes. They went past the second floor and on up to the third. I waited a few moments, then stood up and followed.

Yellow light leaked from a room at the far end of the third floor. The door to the room was open. I didn't peek in, but I snuck behind the door and put my ear against it.

"Who is it?" I heard a voice say. If I wasn't mistaken, it was Saeko. Her voice was hoarse and she sounded frightened. "Who's there?" Then she said, "Reiko! You found me! Thank goodness!" She begged Reiko Miyake to hurry and untie her and went on about how scared she'd been. She asked her to call the police. There was a pause, and Saeko spoke again. "What is that?"

"I'm so sorry," Reiko finally spoke, cool and calm as ever. "This really should have been taken care of days ago."

"What do you mean? What are you doing with that?"

"You're supposed to be dead!" Reiko's voice was even; there wasn't a hint of emotion. She was clever, and I knew now that she'd been in charge the whole time.

"Our plans may not have worked out, but you still need to die, Saeko." Reiko mumbled something about how they should have done it this way to begin with.

"Akio's idea to kidnap you was ridiculous. We could have avoided all these problems if we'd been more decisive from the start."

"What are you saying?" Saeko's voice wavered. "Why do you—you have to—what plans? What does Akio have to do with this? Does he know the man who brought me here?"

"He knows him, all right. He paid him to do it," Reiko said, still calm. "Akio hired him so it'd look like you'd been kidnapped and murdered."

I wondered how much they'd promised him. It was ironic now. Reiko and Kawasaki had probably miscalculated how quickly the police would be able to trace their phone calls. That was why Kawasaki went pale every time the kidnapper-for-hire made a call.

"Akio spent so much time with that man. They had it all worked out; they said it would be fine. They swore the police would never figure it out."

Saeko began wailing again. "Why would you and Akio want to kill me?"

Because even photos in an album can be ruined, I thought to myself.

"You're in the way," Reiko said simply. "We're sick and tired of you, and we certainly don't want your baby. Akio is ready to break away and set out on his own. He doesn't need you; he's got everything he needs."

She sounded as if she was explaining things to a child.

"If you die now, no one will know what happened. They'll believe the kidnapper did it." Then she dropped her voice and asked, "Why did you laugh off the idea of a divorce?"

Now Saeko was angry. "And why should I have taken it seriously?" she demanded.

"Because it was serious."

I moved out from the shadow of the door and looked inside the room. Reiko had her back to me, and I calculated that I could reach her in four steps. I took a deep breath and made my move just as she raised the knife.

She wasn't expecting anyone to come from behind, and to make things easier, she had on gloves. I grabbed her arm and twisted it behind her back, and the knife instantly fell to the floor. I kicked it into a corner and grabbed Reiko with both arms.

She struggled with every ounce of strength she had.

"It's over!" I yelled, and my head began pounding again. "The police know it was all a fraud."

Reiko stopped fighting. I loosened my grip and her knees began to buckle. "But how? How did you know?"

"Because," a new voice said, "we've been following you!" I turned around to see Sergeant Nakagiri standing in the doorway. "But I couldn't tell you how Kosaka knew," he laughed. "It's all over now."

Several other detectives appeared at his side and led Reiko out, one detective on each arm.

Nakagiri bent over Saeko. Her arms and legs were tied up, and bruises remained after he finished undoing the ropes.

"Are you hurt?" he asked. "An ambulance will be here any minute."

Present circumstances aside, Saeko hadn't changed at all.

"I've been here . . . the whole time," she mumbled, her eyes moving back and forth between Nakagiri and me. "Nobody heard when I yelled for help."

"Well, you're safe now," Nakagiri consoled her. Then he looked up at me. "How did you know she was here?"

I was suddenly too exhausted to explain. "I asked the young man at the beach."

"Why didn't you tell us sooner?"

"I'm a reporter, remember? I needed to find out for myself."

"What young man?" Saeko asked, gripping Nakagiri's arm. "The one waiting when I was brought here? He fought with the man who kidnapped me and killed him . . ."

So it was just as I thought. When Naoya overheard Kawasaki, Reiko, and the hired kidnapper making their plans, he'd arrived ahead of them and waited. He must have intended to overpower the man and take Saeko straight to the police. But it didn't work out that way.

In the struggle, Naoya had ended up killing the kidnapper and getting stabbed. With him out of the picture, there was no one left to prove who had been in on the abduction and what they planned to do with Saeko. If he let Saeko go, Kawasaki and Reiko would be free to make another attempt on her life.

Even if he had tried to convince Saeko who was behind it all, she never would have believed it. It definitely wasn't one of the pictures in the album of her ideal life. Naoya had read her mind and knew this. That was why he decided to stick with the plan a little longer. He wanted Kawasaki and Reiko to think they were in the clear—so he could turn it all upside down on them in the end.

If Naoya had had the energy, he probably would have been here when Reiko or Kawasaki—or both—arrived to finish off Saeko. It would have been the only way to convince her of the facts. But Naoya's strength had given out before he had the chance.

"That young man . . . ," Nakagiri repeated as the sound of sirens approached the warehouse. "How did he learn what Kawasaki was planning?"

"No idea," I said. "I guess we'll never know."

All of a sudden Saeko seemed to snap back to the reality of what was happening. "What are *you* doing here?" she demanded of me.

By the time we were out of the building I was too dizzy to stand. I had lost all sense of time, and I sat down on the shoulder of the road. I watched in a daze as the patrol cars came speeding up and the police officers stormed into the warehouse.

Finally I heard the drone of approaching helicopters. The media ban must have been lifted, I thought. I felt an arm around my shoulder. It was Ikoma.

"You look awful," he said, and helped me to my feet. "But the editor in chief is in raptures."

"About what?"

"The firsthand account he's going to get."

"And who does he think is going to write it?"

Ikoma had parked his car on a bridge a short distance from the warehouse. He leaned me up against it and pulled a pack of cigarettes out of his pocket. I took one but could hardly taste it.

"Naoya Oda is dead," I said.

"I know."

"Have you heard what he did?"

"Not yet."

"I'll tell you all about it when I'm feeling better." I closed my eyes. My head was pounding, and I was still dizzy. I suddenly realized the painful burden that Naoya and Shinji had had to bear.

"But there's one thing I do know." I could hardly hear the sound of my own voice.

"What's that?" Ikoma blew out a puff of smoke.

"You remember that crazy bet we made? The one where you didn't believe I'd ever find proof that psychics are real . . ."

Ikoma stared at me for a while, dropped his cigarette on the ground, and stamped it out.

"This should add ten years to my life," he said as he drew back the pack of cigarettes and flung it into the river below. "You win."

*Of course I do*, was what I planned to say as everything went black.

# EPILOGUE

Out-of-season flowers bloomed in the hospital courtyard. I was pretty sure they were azaleas. They had a lovely scent. It was mid-December. The incident involving Saeko's kidnapping had seen its day, and society had moved on to the next topic.

"I was determined not to make the same mistake twice," said Shinji, leaning back in his wheelchair and looking off into the distance. Kaoru Murata, the retired detective, had just been leaving when I arrived. Shinji had apparently shed a few tears, and it had helped unload the burden he still carried.

"I didn't want to do the same thing I had with the manhole cover business. I knew it would be wrong to use my power and get someone outside it involved. It always makes things more complicated. Mr. Murata agreed with me. But he said it was foolish to try to take care of matters on my own. It was all I could think of at the time."

I understood what Shinji was trying to say. When he and Kanako had found the eight letters I'd received, he'd been able to sense that they were sent by Reiko Miyake. He had soon figured out what she and Kawasaki were planning, but even now he still wondered if things would have turned out better if he'd told the police or me.

The police probably wouldn't have believed him. They might have questioned Kawasaki, but they wouldn't have discovered anything concrete. The two lovers might have postponed the project and waited for another opportunity to carry it out.

But what if I had known? I figured that, in the end, I would have believed Shinji. But what good would it have done? If I'd informed Saeko that her husband and his lover planned to murder her, she never would have believed me.

"We had to catch them in the act," Shinji mumbled. "And when I figured that out, I. . ." I sat down on a bench and listened. It was perfectly blue and peaceful. "If that punk hadn't beat me up, Naoya wouldn't have got involved." He looked down at his wheelchair. "You told me to leave well enough alone, but I had to try to force Kakita to take the blame for the manhole cover incident. What did I think I was doing?"

"Stop blaming yourself."

"But . . ."

I knew I would have to talk to him about this eventually, so I sat up straight and turned to look at him. "Thank you," I said, "for all you've done."

Shinji was silent.

"And I apologize from the bottom of my heart. You and Naoya tried your best to help me, and both of you suffered for it. I'll never be able to make it up to either of you."

"Now you stop!" Shinji said gently. "It's not your fault. You don't have the same powers I do."

"But Naoya died because of it."

Shinji bit his lip and shook his head. "It was my fault; I called to him for help. I couldn't take care of it myself, so I thought he was the only one I could depend on. After that, I followed him around as well as I could with my own power."

When the ambulance had picked Shinji up and he'd been muttering something about a murder, he had meant Saeko. He must have been calling to Naoya to save her.

"Saeko was expecting a baby, wasn't she?" I nodded, and Shinji smiled. "Naoya loved babies. That's why he tried so hard to save her. And you know what? When Naoya died, as I felt him leaving my head, he was chuckling."

"Really?"

"Yeah, it was like he was satisfied with a job well done. He was proud of himself for it." Shinji seemed almost jealous, but I sincerely hoped he was right about that.

I remembered a conversation I'd had with Sergeant Nakagiri after it was all over:

"That Naoya Oda pretty much sacrificed his life for Saeko Kawasaki."

When I agreed with him, he added, "But we saw through the ruse of the kidnapping without him. I guess he just didn't have faith in the police."

"Aren't you forgetting something?" I asked. "Even if the police had been able to arrest Kawasaki and his mistress, you wouldn't have been able to prevent the murder. Naoya was the only one who could do that."

"I miss him," said Shinji, batting his eyes to hold back the tears. "I miss him, but that's my punishment; something to remind me never to forget about him. The next time something like this happens, I'll be the one to take care of things. Otherwise, life won't be worth living."

It had been a while since I'd thought about the value of life.

"I'm sure there's a job for me to do," he went on. "There's got to be one for everybody, a job we were born to do. It may sound weird, but you know, it might not be a bad idea to spend one lonely night a year thinking about that sort of thing."

There was only one person I told the entire story to, from start to finish, and that was Nanae. Before I began, she showed me a mobile she had. It was made of different metal shapes hanging from string. Once the mobile was hung, it would move irregularly and the pieces of metal would rub up against each other. It was the sound I'd heard in the background those first times I'd called her.

*Naoya made it for me*, she wrote. *I laughed and told him it was too noisy to hang up, but now that he's gone, I put it up when I feel like calling him.*

She listened to my entire story, her head in her hands, looking up at the sky from time to time. When I was done, neither of us had anything more to say. It was Naoya who had brought us together, and I had no claim on her now that he was gone.

I didn't have the courage to ask her what she wanted to do next. I was afraid that if I told her I didn't want to let go, I'd be forcing her to put up with my irregular and unpredictable lifestyle.

Nanae stood up and went to get her whiteboard. She wrote something and showed it to me.

*I knew.*

"What did you know?"

She wrote without hesitation. *The reason why you and Saeko broke up.*

I had to stop myself from gasping. "Did Naoya tell you?"

She nodded. *I think he said you had been badly hurt, and that you tended to keep people at arm's length. He said you were too much trouble to deal with and that I should stay away from you.*

She laughed as she watched me read.

Too much trouble to deal with, eh? I definitely wasn't the man for Nanae. And was that all he had said? There might have been more, I thought. There must have been things he knew about without having to hear them from Shinji. He had read the mind of the man tailing me. He knew what the man hired by Kawasaki to kill Saeko had been thinking. He must have known I'd be involved in the incident.

But he hadn't been able to say anything. That's why he had warned Nanae away from me.

If Kawasaki's plan had succeeded, I might have spent the rest of my life in shackles—the shackles of knowing that someone had died because of a grudge held against me. And I would never have known what it was.

Nanae never would have been happy with a man like that. But, it hadn't turned out that way.

At the hospital, when we'd all gathered to find out about Shinji, Naoya might have realized what was coming, that things would work out. Maybe *that* was why he had given his life to stop Kawasaki and Reiko from murdering Saeko. It hadn't been for my sake, nor for Shinji's. It was all for Nanae.

Chuckling in his last moments, he had realized that he had done for Nanae something I never would have been able to.

"So, where do you want to go from here?" I finally got up the courage to ask.

Nanae thought, and Naoya's mobile clinked softly over our heads.

Ikoma was quick on the draw. "Who do you plan to ask to stand up with you at the wedding?" We were out on a story, but it was all he could talk about.

I laughed. "We haven't got that far yet!"

"Don't ask me to do it. My wife might ask for a new kimono for the occasion."

There was only a week left in the year, and life was as busy as ever. There had been a big fire in the downtown area, and we'd been prowling the site since early morning.

"It's lunchtime," Ikoma announced. "Nanae's nursery school is around here, isn't it? Go get her, and I'll treat you both to lunch. You can call it a pre-wedding celebration."

The children had just been let out to play. Tiny figures in navy blue smocks jumped and ran around the grounds. Nanae wore a smock of the same color and was standing next to the slide. It was almost the same scene I'd seen in my dream.

Naoya must be somewhere around here, too, I thought.

"Quit standing there like an idiot," Ikoma prodded me and waved his own hand. Nanae saw us and smiled, nodding in our direction.

I used my beginner's sign language. *Can you go out with us for lunch?*

Nanae laughed and nodded. *Wait a minute*, she signed back.

"Now that is convenient," laughed Ikoma.

I watched the children playing. I wondered about the various lives they were destined to lead. Then I wondered if Naoya might be reborn—I hoped things would be different for him the next time around.

I was probably being too optimistic, but I wanted to believe it was true. If he ever walked on the Earth again, I prayed he would have an easier and more comfortable time of it. I hoped he'd manage to live devoid of pain. The next time, I prayed he'd find happiness not only in helping others but from letting others be of use to him.

Inside all of us, we have a dragon, a sleeping dragon with infinite power of an amazing form. Once that dragon wakes and rears its head, you can only pray for what might happen next:

Please let me live a long and righteous life. Save me from disaster.

And please, let the dragon protect me . . .

It's the only thing we can do.